I0712694

GIRL GAME

Balls Out

Alexandra Elinsky, PhD

PENGUIN
PUBLISHERS

GIRL GAME

Balls Out

Alexandra Elinsky, PhD

Author Bio:.. i

Introduction: The Ant in All of Us ix

Chapter 1 Balls Out 1

Chapter 2 Lottery or Luck 16

Chapter 3 Throne of Authority 38

Chapter 4 Your Magic Zone 61

Chapter 5 Slow Ya Roll – The Power of Patience................ 68

Chapter 6 The Fight of Your Life.. 80

Chapter 7 Orbit of Love... 96

Chapter 8 Your Allstar Players – Emotion and Logic 114

Chapter 9 Romance is an Illusion 125

Chapter 10 The Three-Course Meal: Exploring a Woman's Sexual Needs . 136

Chapter 11 You're Still Expected to Live 145

Chapter 12 Becoming a Man: Women Have no Power in a Relationship .. 162

Chapter 13 MVP – Most Valuable Player............................ 173

Chapter 14 Emotional Infantilism....................................... 187

Chapter 15 Wanted 196

Chapter 16 Exposed: Decoding the Dating Game 216

Chapter 17 Alaska 239

Chapter 18 Endlessly Intriguing – The Everything Girl 266

GIRL GAME: BALLS OUT *has been copyrighted in 2024.*

Author Bio:

Dr. Alexandra Elinsky

2X Best Selling Author | Renown Entrepreneur | Celebrity Keynote Speaker

21X Award-Winning Author and Entrepreneur with first book, **_GIRL GRIT: SAVAGE NOT AVERAGE_** receiving six literary awards within the first six months of publication:

- LitPick – 5 Star Book Award
- Infinite Generations / Positive Impact Book Awards – 5 Star Gold Book Award
- International Impact Book Awards – Won in 3 categories: 1) Female Empowerment
  2) Feminist Advocacy and 3) Social Change
- BookFest 2025 – First Place Winner, Relationships and Communication
- BookFest 2025 – First Place Winner, Transformation
- BookFest 2025 – Third Place Winner, Inspiration

GIRL GRIT: SAVAGE NOT AVERAGE, is available internationally for purchase at retailers including Amazon, Barnes and Noble, Walmart, Books-A-Million and more!

Dr. Elinsky social handles –

https://www.linkedin.com/in/alexandraelinsky/

https://www.instagram.com/bossdivalibra/

Dr. Alexandra Elinsky: (2X) #1 Best Selling Author, Celebrity Keynote Speaker, Entrepreneur, Leadership / Empowerment / Ascension Coach, Mother, and 21X Business and Literary Award Winner with 15+ years' experience coaching and training professionals globally. With clients in 20+ countries around the world, Dr. Elinsky has helped individuals achieve personal and professional excellence. Recognized time and again for business mastery and meritorious performance, she has been awarded Top International Empowerment Coach of the Decade by IAOTP, Top International Empowerment Coach of the Year by IAOTP, Empowered Woman of the Year 2025 by IAOTP, Best Coaching Services in the USA by Stellar Business, Top 5 Coaches of the Year by Female Voice Awards, 5 Star Gold Book Review (Highest Accolade) by Infinite Generations / Positive Impact Book Review, Female Empowerment, Feminist Advocacy and Social Change Book Award by International Impact Book Awards, Top 5 Most Aspiring Businesswomen by CIO Today, Global Recognition for Leadership Excellence by Global Awards, University of Akron Leadership Excellence Award, The Chicago School of Professional Psychology Distinguished Alumni Award, Empowered Woman 2024 by Empowered Magazine, 5-Star Award by LitPick Reviews, Three awards from BookFest 2025 (2 in First Place), Visionary Voice in Leadership Coaching – Human Resource, USA by Fluxx Events 2025, and Woman of the Year 2025 by the CIO Times. Gracing the front covers of business magazines CIO Today, Passionate Magazine, Conglomerate Magazine, and The Business Fame with additional recognition in ABC, NBC, and Fox news outlets, Dr. Elinsky's message of grit and transformation continues to expand globally. She was selected as part of World Magazine's 40 under 40 Emerging Leaders to Watch in 2023. Her first book, **GIRL GRIT: SAVAGE NOT AVERAGE,** *was released on November 8th, 2024. Dr. Elinsky is determined to spread her message of human empowerment and self-esteem globally, spreading her fire everywhere she goes.*

Failure: most people's worst fear. As I reflect on my topics for **GIRL GAME: BALLS OUT**, I authored this book because I felt like something was inherently wrong with me. Why did every guy I like eventually dump me? Why did I have so much self-hatred, and why was I so hard on myself? Why wasn't I able to grow my business fast enough? Why was I struggling with massive insecurities? Why did I care about what other people thought of me? Why is my primary objective to please other people? As I wrestled with these issues, I began a healing journey that catapulted me into nearly 100 years of research on **human psychology, human behavior, success, healing, and growth.** Through this **transformational healing journey** and becoming a **SECURE HUMAN BEING** not only have I overcome all my own limitations and fears, but I have also gotten whatever I want by understanding the **psychological strategies** needed to win in life, love, and business.

GIRL GAME: BALLS OUT is a **non-fiction self-help psychological deep dive** challenging the beliefs we hold about ourselves, including the myriads of ways we self-sabotage as women, especially when it comes to being a people pleaser or **glutton for punishment. <u>We were not put on this earth to suffer; we were put on this earth to ascend.</u> GIRL GAME: BALLS OUT** is a **self-discovery journey** challenging you to think in ways you have not before. It is an unveiling of your **subconscious mind** and how you can harness its power to **achieve massive success, happiness, and healing. GIRL GAME: BALLS OUT** discusses such topics as **human emotion, Attachment Theory, healing, relationship dynamics in sustaining attraction, and becoming the woman you want. GIRL GAME: BALLS OUT** explores gender disparities as many of us were raised as a gender and not human beings. **GIRL GAME: BALLS OUT** is a **roller coaster of insight and emotion.** You will learn how to suffer well, and that suffering is the fuel you need to get anything you want in life. **What is ascension?** How do we ascend? **Why do we ascend?**

<u>**Ascension is the antithesis of suffering.**</u> The only choice we have is not to fall into the **Abyss of Misery**, forever stuck in feelings of defeat, loneliness, unworthiness, and self-sabotage.

GIRL GAME: BALLS OUT inspires, empowers, and builds a confident, self-assured, bullshit-free woman who is <u>**no longer a victim of circumstance but rather a champion of transformation**</u>. I will teach you how to take the most catastrophic and traumatic events of your life and transform them becoming a powerful and magnetic woman who has kissed fear, doubt, Depression, and unworthiness goodbye for good.

My purpose as an author is to teach readers how to become more human by expressing their own humanity in an authentic, productive, and purposeful manner filled with all the blessings life has to offer.

Stop doubting and shrinking your greatness. You stop the need to be liked and accepted by others, which is absolutely crippling to your worth. You've got to brave up. You got to dig deep inside and rescue the person lost inside of there... ***confidence is the most attractive quality in any person.***

Abandoning the self is the worst type of abandonment.

Further Considerations

I consider myself a **Social Justice Warrior.** This means the topics I write about are truthful and sometimes not pretty. I am not afraid to call out reality. In this book, I discuss a certain type of man and a certain type of woman. In no manner is this text intended to generalize suggesting that *all men are like this,* and *all women are like that.* <u>**This book makes no generalizations.**</u> However, it does address *specific and common behaviors* in many men and *specific and common behaviors* in many women, which is often part of our *gender social conditioning.* I discuss *specific realities and situations* many can relate to as these are often understood and experienced by many (but not all) in society. I address such as men and as women. Be advised once more that the context is *not intended* to generalize but rather *illuminate common frustrations* experienced in everyday life. <u>***We cannot say all men are like this and all women are like that, but we can address social problems head on.***</u> If we don't proactively solve problems, they will never go away. **Problems cannot solve themselves.** <u>***Only by intention and understanding can we have a more fulfilling existence.***</u>

To the reader – heed with intentionality every point in this book. I am living proof these concepts work. Since stepping into my own **GIRL GAME,** *two years after writing this book, my heart has never been broken again. Men literally worship the ground I walk on incessantly chasing me months and years after I diplomatically ended things. I have more love and attention now than ever in my entire life. Similarly, opportunities will begin to fall out of the sky for you. You won't even see them coming. Everyone will want you. You will make more money than ever before, have more friends, more love, more attention, you will be treated like a celebrity and revered if you heed my words, embrace your* **GIRL GAME,** *and BECOME* **FIREWOMAN.**

These are only psychological principles that stand the test of time.

Dr. Alexandra Elinsky

World Renown Coach & Multi-Award-Winning Author

GIRL GAME: BALLS OUT

A message from Dr. Elinsky

Dear sister,

My name is Dr. Alexandra Elinsky. Thank you for embarking on this journey with me through the work and advice of **GIRL GAME: BALLS OUT.** This is **your journey** dedicated exclusively to you. My intention as a writer of the **female experience** is simple: **help women evolve into full human beings.** I pray that your eyes, ears, and hearts will open and understand. The journey is long and painful but also satisfying and inspiring. My job as a writer and coach is to support you on your journey through **the power of understanding**. Accept the material you are about to read, as my purpose is to challenge your perspectives and early childhood teachings. The path to becoming a full, whole human being is an **ever-evolving growth process.** Take my hand now. I am with you.

Dedication

This book is dedicated to the scapegoat.

Do you ever wonder what kind of world we might live in if women spent their precious time chasing their dreams instead of trying to fix an unfixable relationship? ***Relationships should not be the acme of existence for women... <u>their potential should be.</u>*** Being too hasty is never going to help you win the game. To be successful in life, love, and business, we must ***slither like a snake*** (deploy a keen strategy) winning all the rewards we want for ourselves. Anything is attainable. ***You can have anything you want. This book will teach you how.***

Everything happens in due course.

Introduction:
The Ant in All of Us

Before you begin reading, understand what kind of person I am so that my words and teachings will resonate with you. I am the type of person who will not and cannot step on an ant. It might sound silly, but I cannot and will not step on an ant. I am HIGHLY AGAINST killing anything or anyone, no matter how small or insignificant they may seem. Why am I like this? Maybe it is because I have a heart, and I care deeply about all creation. We all serve a purpose on this earth no matter who we are, what we've done, how insignificant we might seem to ourselves or others, what crimes or sins we have committed, or what we become. I love all people – no matter who they are or what they've done. **We are commanded to love.** I am a **heart writer**, which means I write only from my heart with an outpouring of love for you.

There are days when you feel like an ant. You feel small and insignificant like you don't really matter, and your life doesn't mean anything. You try so hard just to get nowhere, or you love so much just to get your heart ripped right out of your chest. You work so hard for only minimum wage, or you bend over backward for your kids and family just to beat yourself up every day because you think you aren't doing enough. Others have treated you like you are nothing to them, so you feel not good enough, you feel low, irrelevant, unwanted. **You feel the way you do about yourself because of how others have projected their own ugliness and insensitivity onto you.** You then internalize those messages about yourself, and they become your reality, giving others the power and control over you.

Women are **naturally oppressed**. If you want to be exploited and persecuted, all you need to do is be born a woman. It is that simple and **fundamentally unfair**. We might have been born disadvantaged, but that does not mean we are broken. **_Defeat is a choice._** A choice only we can make. Because women are still largely regarded as the second sex, we experience **_perceived unworthiness. Unworthiness only because of body parts._** Less than only because of body parts. Ant-like only because of body parts. Those words remind me of my own womanly handicap because I did not win the lottery of being born male.

It is easy to understand why we hate ourselves so much. Why many of us lie in psychiatrists' offices taking pills every day. Why some of us turn to the bottle, overeating, or have excessive shopping habits. We can never be happy, and we certainly don't feel complete. We live our lives as we watch more of our essential humanity removed until we look at ourselves in the mirror no longer recognizing the person staring back at us. Why we feel never good enough, less than, rejected, failures, and victims. **_We subscribe to ideas of marriage and motherhood because we are told that is where our worth lies._** We become obsessed with getting married and motherhood because if we don't, well then, we aren't worthy women and have disappointed our families and failed society.

I assumed that the more I humbled myself, the more I let people walk all over me, the more they would love and respect me, **_but the opposite is true._** This is why I can't kill an ant because I see myself inside of it. **_I see myself as a little creature just wanting to live her life without anyone stepping on her. We do not become powerful by stepping on others. We become powerful by ascending ourselves._**

I am an **Ascension Coach**, which means I empower people forward in life toward self-actualization. **_Many people never achieve self-actualization because they allow others to step on them._** They never perceive themselves as more than ants (Imposter Syndrome). They remain stuck, self-defeated, and depressed most of their lives. They walk around with negative attitudes and grumpy chipmunk faces because life never goes their way. They are constantly in a state of one step forward and two steps backward.

Sisters – this is the kind of person I am. This is my character. This is what makes me me, and I am your friend. Hello! I authored this book for YOU. With YOU in mind. ***I want you to heal…for good.*** Ascend with me, leaving all the bullshittery of life behind.

Another thing you should know about me… I cannot judge others. I do not judge others, and I refuse to gossip. ***Judging others and gossiping are entirely unproductive hobbies and do nothing to advance you.*** When you judge and gossip about others, you are taking focus off yourself and putting focus on those you are judging or gossiping about. Everyone loses in this scenario. ***It is a self-sabotaging hobby fueled by self-hatred.*** If you are judging others and or gossiping, then reflect on why. ***What inside of you do you need to pluck out? What ugly exists inside of you making you feel the need to devalue and discount the worthiness of other people?*** Ruminate on this.

Moreover, I am not a candy cane and gum drop writer, which means I express the truth based on observations and research. The truth is painful, but I would rather you have the truth than the lie. People lie all the time; I do not want to be one of those common liars. If you cannot handle the truth, then that is your own problem. I suggest you ***self-reflect***. Those who search for answers find them. This book answers life's toughest and most heart-wrenching questions. Understand who I am as a person so that as you read, we have already built rapport together.

The Defender

My name, Alexandra, means **the defender** or **to defend others**. That is exactly who I am. I defend others and in this book series, ***I am defending women.*** Many of the topics in this book consider childhood abuse and ***emotional neglect*** because my research is focused on that topic. I am against all forms of childhood abuse and neglect. I wish I could save and defend every child from the childhood abuse and neglect they experienced. **When I mention the word neglect throughout this text, I am referring primarily to _emotional neglect_ and not physical neglect. _Emotional neglect_ is far more common as most children do have a roof over their heads and food in their bellies.**

I defend the little girl (now an adult woman reading this book) who was abused and emotionally neglected as a child. I know not everyone reading this book was abused and or emotionally neglected, so you may or may not relate. However, please be open-minded to learn about this topic as it is important to discuss and understand. To those who were abused and or neglected to a greater or lesser degree, I am defending you now in this book. I am going to illuminate **sensitive subjects.** I will guide you on your **healing journey**. I couldn't protect you as a little girl, but I can come alongside you now with a shield of armor and help you realize that **no weapon formed against you shall prosper (Isaiah 54:17).**

The Murderer

I perceive every human being as a human being. I could look a murderer in the eyes and tell that person that they are deeply loved and forgiven. That person started their life as a baby, and all babies need love. Some babies do not get love, which is tormentingly sad. I am convinced that every person who has ever hurt another person, be it murder or something more trivial in comparison, does so because they do not have enough love in their life. If a person had sufficient love in their life, they would never have committed that murder or offense against another.

All crime is an act of insufficient love. Love is the foundation of life and without it, all hell breaks loose. Too many of us have not had sufficient love in our lives beginning in childhood.

Emotional neglect of children is more common than what is known and realized. Keep in mind there are levels of neglect. As with anything else, ***emotional neglect*** is placed on a spectrum from extremely mild and almost unnoticeable to extremely severe. ***It is impossible to commit a crime unless there is barbarous internal conflict within oneself.***

Whole, healthy, and happy people do not commit crimes. ***The murderer has been murdered by someone else first.*** The murderer hasn't lost their life, ***but they certainly have lost parts of themselves.*** A precious part was psychologically murdered by another. It was no surprise to learn that some of the most famous serial killers and mass murderers were severely neglected and abused as tiny children, some as young as babies, which is entirely disturbing.

All our adult problems stem from childhood in one respect or the other and are compounded with age. If we were not neglected or abused, then sometimes our childhood teaching and conditioning impacted us in such a way that we become toxic adults. The teaching of our early days damages us. An example I can give is religious harming such as guilting and shaming your children. ***I want children raised as human beings and not perfectionists.*** Murderers were lied to because they had not yet found the truth of love. ***They take whatever love within them, morphing it into hate destroying others.*** Their hearts have turned cold because the lack of attention and love was cold in childhood. ***<u>All they know is coldness, so that is all they can give. They have not experienced love, so they cannot give it.</u>***

The Bigger Picture

Some babies become celebrities, some become commonfolk, some become scholars and writers, some become professionals, some become criminals, some become parents, some become alcoholics, drug addicts, or other kinds of addicts, some become influencers, and so on. ***All babies need*** *love.* All babies need **emotional nurturance**. What will you become? What are you becoming? Life is difficult for all. The difficulty of life is a fundamental Buddhist principle. You cannot escape suffering. Although circumstances differ significantly, the suffering is all the same. ***What matters is what you do with the suffering; what will you turn it into? Will you turn your suffering into love and bless the world? Or will you turn your suffering into hate and destroy it instead?***

I took all my suffering and decided to write my **GIRL GRIT** series. I knew that my words would resonate with women and inspire them globally. I knew my pain was relatable and real, and I love real. I am an advocate for reality, for truth, and for knowledge. This is how I demonstrate my love, through my words and teachings. I pray you experience the gift of healing and ascension that I have.

Next time you see an ant (someone you wish to judge or gossip about), instead of stepping on that person, think, how can I inspire this person? How can I show this person love?

On that note, beautiful sister, enjoy **GIRL GAME: BALLS OUT!**

Balls out, baby!

Love,

Dr. Elinsky

Chapter 1
Balls Out

"The word courage is found in the word encourage because it takes courage to encourage someone. May all sentences weaved together throughout the pages of this book provide generous encouragement for you because of my courage."

A personal note to take with you from Dr. Elinsky as you read...

As you read my words in this book hold fast to the knowing of Luke 17: 21

*"Nor will they say, 'See here!' or 'See there!' For indeed, **the kingdom of God is within you**."*

Because the kingdom of God already exists inside of you, you have ALL POWER to heal for good, make all your dreams come true, and ascend always. I pray this journey will deepen your love, broaden your understanding, and show up for you in totally unexpected ways. Stay blessed, dear sister.

Hiding From the World

Virgil Publius Vergilius Maro, a famous poet, expressed, **"fortune favors the bold."** My way of saying this is, **"if everyone were bold, success would not be coveted."** Failure is not real and does not exist, because the ONLY answer in the world is **YES**! There are **three components** determining those who succeed versus those who fail, and they are:

1) **Bravery / Risk Level**
2) **Effort**
3) **Perseverance**

You need these and only these three components to succeed in whatever it is you set out to do in life. Bravery and risk are synonymous. Being brave is a risk, which is why most people live in fear. They are afraid of risk, so they would rather not try and so they don't. Therefore, they never even give themselves a chance. ***Effort is action.*** You cannot sit on your ass and expect results. That is not how life works. Nothing is given freely. ***Make the effort necessary, and the rest will become effortless for you.*** Perseverance is the antithesis of failure. ***The only way to fail is to give up.*** Failure is not real. It is something you made up. Failure can only survive if you feed it. Starve failure. ***<u>Success is the only option.</u>***

Say to yourself now: ***<u>I AM ALWAYS THE RIGHT CHOICE.</u>***

Every single one of us has something useful to say. A message to teach or an idea to share. Yet so many of us choose to silence ourselves because we live in this perpetual cycle of ***caring about what everyone else thinks of us***. What would happen to you if you stopped caring about what others thought of you? What would your life look like? What could you achieve? What could you overcome? ***Stop silencing yourself.*** You must. No one is putting a muzzle on you. ***Only you put one on yourself.*** You have something to say. You have a message for the world. So, say it. Share it. Express it.

Are you hiding from the world? Have you faded into the ***unrecognition of the self***? When I look around me, I notice girls (and women) hiding. I see women hiding themselves. I notice men hiding their women. ***People are afraid to be seen.*** It is safe and comfortable (to a degree) to hide away from the world. ***You hide because you think it is the right thing to do.*** You were trained and conditioned to hide. ***<u>To be seen, not heard.</u> To be as invisible as possible, but only around to serve and care for others.*** To not make too much noise, not be too ambitious, not be too educated, not be too well-spoken, not be too much fun, and not dress over the top. Just to cooperate and conform to other people's standards and expectations of you. *Forever fading...forever less human...forever hiding away from the world.*

I remember the *vivacious, effervescent woman* I used to be before I allowed others to dismantle my self-esteem. Before I stuffed myself into a box fitting neatly and tightly into someone else's idea of a good and godly person. *The more I did that, the less human I became. The more I conformed, the less I transformed.* To be alive, fully alive. Not restricted, not held back, not obedient, not submissive, not a house slave, not a caretaker, not everybody's everything, not a sex object...

Are you hiding from the world? Do you not recognize yourself anymore? Have you metamorphosed into someone you hardly know? Do others limit and restrict you? Are you damned if you do and damned if you don't? Do you live in an ocean of feminine guilt and shame? As an author and friend of yours, I want you to understand something before you read any more of this book. *Understand that reading this book is time spent exclusively for you—* for your journey, growth, and transformation. As an author, I am a healer as it was other books and other authors who have healed me. They have given me a great gift of understanding and healing, and that gift I want to give now to you. As you continue your journey of reading my words, reflect on the myriads of ways you might be or might have been *hiding from the world.*

As an author, coach, and practitioner, I encourage all clients, readers, and friends to always become more human. *We become more human when we pause to recognize and appreciate our own humanity for what it is and what we wish it to be.* We are so fixated on other people: their problems and issues, pleasing them, making them like us, comparisons, competitions, fixing and changing people that we take the focus off ourselves. ***We need to stop fixating on others and start fixating on ourselves.*** We must stop killing ourselves with people pleasing and start people pleasing ourselves. ***We must stop hiding from the world!***

Becoming a Human

You become more human when you invest the same time and energy you freely give to others and instead give it to yourself. ***Stop revolving your entire life around a man who is, whether directly or indirectly, trying to hide you from the world.*** You become less human when you allow others to control and manipulate you. It's called ***duping,*** and I will discuss this topic extensively later in this book. ***I wish to make abundantly clear that I am not an advocate for manipulation or "game playing," but this book delineates how to play the game and win strategically and intelligently with an armor of self-awareness and protection.***

I refuse to allow women to be duped again! Duped = manipulated. This manipulation most often comes from men, your friends, your family or often all the above.

When you grow, learn, and continuously educate yourself, you become more human. My wish is that this book will support you on your journey toward spiritual growth, healing, and becoming more human. ***Stop hiding from the world.*** Stop allowing others to hide you from the world. ***The only way to stop hiding from the world is to STOP.*** You perpetuate a significant portion of your own sorrow through self-flagellation and what I love to call ***being a glutton for punishment.*** Women are notoriously gluttons for punishment. We do too much and take on too much. We pick up the slack and kill ourselves in ***perfectionism*** and ***impression management. STOP IT.*** We work 18+ hour days managing everyone's lives, even other grown-ass adults! We often carry the burden and the sorrow for all (***emotional labor***).

We care when others give not a single shit! We cook three meals a day! We pick up after others. We solve problems that never actually get solved because other people refuse to take *personal responsibility* for themselves. *We are gluttons for punishment. And then we inevitably divorce or end up in a mental institution when we cannot stand punishing ourselves any longer, once we've hit our absolute breaking point, and we are strong AF leading up to that point in time!*

Surround yourself with positivity and progression, mastering peace and emotional control. Pluck out all toxicity within you, including negativity, shame, guilt, self-flagellation, insecurities, limiting beliefs, excuses, and any other *emotional diseases.* Replace all with peace and tranquility. Find joy and experience life to the absolute fullest. Embrace all sorrows and all joys, all heavens, and all hells.

I discuss some of my own journey and stories throughout the series, as I never miss an opportunity to experience all of life's heavens and hells. *This book is full of mystery, excitement, romance, healing, living, heartbreak, and pure hell.* To become a well-rounded woman, you must embrace ALL life gives to you and not just the pleasurable, joyful moments. *Pain is necessary to become a full human being. <u>You cannot ascend without pain.</u>* You cannot gain without pain. Accept life as it is handed to you but take the necessary responsibility for transforming your life.

In this book, you will learn all the strategies to become a full human being, ascend into your seraphic badassery, and kiss all the bullshittery goodbye for good. Walk toward the sun, have fun, and please stop *hiding from the world.* You were born to live, you were born to be alive, and you were born to shine. Let's show them what you are made of! I am, you are, we are WOMEN! I am, you are, we are FULL HUMAN BEINGS.

Why You Should Never Listen to What Other People Say About You

Never listen to what other people say about you. *It is a strategy of theirs to pull you down to their level, which is rock bottom.* People who are ascending in life do not have time to gossip about or judge other people. They do not have time to bully, pick on, harass, upset, or belittle others because ascending people are far too busy and focused. I have had TWO female friends tell me that it is WRONG of me to empower other women. A year after that, I won the award *Top International Empowerment Coach of the Year 2024*! What if I had listened to them? What if I had agreed? "Yeah, you're right, Caroline and Ashley, it is wrong of me to empower other women. I suppose I should stop now and return to my old mundane and miserable life." If I had done that, I would never have won that major award! *When people say shit like that, it is because they are threatened and jealous of the power you hold in the world.* So, sister, say "f*ck you" and keep doing it anyway. Trust your knowing. *You might just win an award for the very thing someone tried to dismantle in you.*

The American Dream – Supposed To's & Expectations

Imagine you are playing a game of chess. Chess is a game of strategy. Each move carefully planned and played. You must watch your opponent's moves closely paying attention to all actions within the game. If you want to win the game of chess, then you must think strategically. The same goes for winning the many games of life. Remember the game Candy Land where you started from Point A and had to play the board until you reached the finish line? That is your life. Point A is when you enter this world, and the finish line is your death. Everything between is your life, and it will play out exactly as it is meant to, with all the good, the bad, and the ugly.

Life will give you plenty of gifts and surprises if you are open to receiving them, but similarly, life will also shit in your face and stab you in the back. **No one is immune from disaster.** Everyone puts their best lives and selves on social media, but much of that is fake, creating the illusion of happiness and success. Social media is simply an instrument feeding our fragile egos. We need to feel special, important, and worthy. We construct our story exactly as we like it to be and showcase it out into the world via social media. We hide our pain, our failures, our traumas, our tragedies, our misfortunes, our heartbreaks, and our problems from the world, shielding them as if they do not exist at all. **We take all our problems and sweep them under the rug instead of tackling them head-on.**

Do not focus on the shit life throws your way but rather on all the gifts, surprises, and blessings it bestows upon you. Focusing on negativity perpetuates negativity and serves no productive purpose in your life. In the game Candy Land, you always move forward progressing to the end. That is life. **Life is onward. Always progress forward.** Many of you remain stuck in nothing, neither forward nor backward. You accept your life as is and never venture out to change and make it better. **You remain stuck in self-sabotage.** You feel comfortable and complacent there. You are missing the point of the game here. The idea is always to move forward and never backward (nor remain stuck). Push forward. To win massively in life (which you are entirely capable of doing) requires **grit and patience**. It requires thick skin and a **bullshit-free attitude. Furthermore, and most importantly, it requires <u>using your brain, the greatest asset you own.</u>**

Life is all about skill, and games are all about strategy. Plan every move carefully and strategically, leveraging patience and intellect to their maximum capacities. You cannot win if you do not deploy carefully planned strategies getting from Point A to the finish line. Journey before destination: it is not the destination that you should look forward to but rather your journey. Your journey will bring sorrows, joys, miracles, pain and suffering, heartache, surprises, fortunes, misfortunes, illnesses, diseases, good times, bad times, friends, enemies, opportunities, gains, and losses. That is life, and it is all beautiful. Even your pain and suffering are beautiful because you learn the most powerful lessons from them.

I built my businesses from the ground up with nothing except for the brain in my head. I had no starting capital, no handholding, no mentors, no guidance, no opportunities, no privilege, and no resources. But I had the most potent resource of all, my brain, and I wasn't afraid to use it. My brain (given to me by God) is what has manifested all that which I am fervently blessed with. In this book, I am going to pour out my blessings onto you so that you can live the abundantly blessed and powerful life that I know well. Turn on your brain right now. Absorb and digest this material deeply within your soul, allowing it to penetrate your mind, body, and spirit. *Feel all your emotions intensely so that you can heal and understand your journey better.* By deploying my methods and strategies, you will win in all aspects of your life, be it love, business, mental wellness, family life, hobbies, interests, and purpose.

Life is weird, hard, challenging, happy, sad, joyful, miserable, and wonderful happenstance. *You get the life you get, but you create the life you want.* For many of us, we have a certain mental image of how our lives will or should play out. As girls, we are forced to go to school, we may or may not attend college, and we acquire some sort of job or career. We are told to get a job and establish a career. We are told to become wives and mothers, our supposed highest calling. Many of us believe, hope, and pray we will get married someday. Many of us want children. And then we die. And that's life, plain and simple.

Born, Live, Die

You are born, you go to school, you make something of yourself, or you don't; you get married, or you don't; you raise children, or you don't; you live your mundane life. Most of us just simply managing day by day on anti-depressants, wondering what is wrong with us but can't quite figure it out. We are told how we should live our lives. We are told what we want. We are told what to do or what not to do with our lives. Many times, we adopt the lives and hobbies/interests our parents had. We are controlled by everyone and everything until we say "f*ck it" and then stop allowing everyone and everything to control us. We allow others to control us because, as women, we believe that is the right thing to do. As women, we are supposed to agree, we are supposed to be amicable, content, gentle, sweet, passive, non-confrontational, keeping our opinions to ourselves, not talking back, and basically, yeah, taking care of everyone and everything, because we are the designated caregivers *just because of our gender.*

You know what I have to say about all of that? F*ck it! That's what I have to say. I did everything I was supposed to do. I was born. I went to school. I graduated. I went to college. I made something of myself. I got married. I had a baby. I served everyone. I was nice, kind, and pleasant to be around. I did not cause any problems. But, despite being "as perfect as I was" and doing everything "the right way," life still punched me in the face and stabbed me in the back, so now I say, "f*ck it," and that's all there is to it.

The only thing you are "supposed to" do is live your life, your one and only life. That's it. To do all the things that bring you joy, make you smile, make you laugh, make you feel powerful and accomplished, and make you feel purposeful and satisfied. That's it. But you stuff yourself in a box. We all put ourselves into a box because everyone else puts us into a box due to the ways we are raised. Oftentimes by people who mistreated us.

Balls Out, Baby!

If there is one thing that men have and women lack, it's balls, literally and figuratively. **Women should grow a pair of balls.** For centuries, women have been made to feel less than by their partners, friends and family, society, and mostly and sadly, by themselves. It is time, ladies, that we rise from the ashes in the flames that have burned our personhood and balls out return to our true selves, our core selves, our inner person longing, screaming, crying, begging, needing, and hoping to be seen, heard, listened to, and always treated as an equal. **This is a battle for your personhood.** This, my dear sisters, is called the **game of life**, and if you are not properly prepared to play the game, you will lose. You will lose so much… your mind, your joy, your peace, your patience, your zest, your spunk, your confidence, and your personhood. **This is a book that will teach you how to win the games of love, business, and life.**

Limited or Limitless?

I have worked with many women over the years in my practice, and there is one thing we all seem to have in common to a greater or lesser degree and that is an **easily accessible diminished version of ourselves**. A lowering of our confidence and ability to satisfy the undeserving other. I have practiced this reality. I refuse to tell anyone, especially men, that I have an MBA, PhD, and two profitable businesses unless it comes up in conversation. I have balls, but in the presence of men, I hide them. I still act like I need recusing when clearly, I don't, but this is the conditioning of women- that we are weaker, lesser, subservient, helpers, docile, nurturing, the supporting role, and never the **star of the show. The man has been for centuries the star of the show.** The man is the main attraction, and we are the popcorn and cotton candy stand that fill out the remainder of the amusement park.

Since society has pushed us down to ground level, we, too, push ourselves down to ground level, most of us staying there for an eternity, living in anxiety, Depression, and perpetual sorrow with a black cloud looming over our heads in every situation we encounter. Humility and limitlessness are two different things. ***To be masterfully humble, we must first understand and acknowledge our own humanity, but often, we don't because we live to serve and give to others forever sentencing ourselves to a lifetime of servanthood instead of opportunity.***

I Hate the Kitchen

Were you really born to spend a significant percentage of your life in the kitchen, being everyone's source of life, cooking, cleaning, picking up after, and arranging everyone else's life except your own? If you do this and you do this joyfully and with purpose, then I applaud you for doing what works and what is best for you. For the rest of us hungry for something the crockpot and oven cannot produce, I urge you to listen carefully to my words. Consume and digest them. Allow them to permeate your soul and sharpen your mind. THIS IS YOUR LIFE, sis. If you live it with purpose and power, then you have won the game of life, and if you live it with regret, sorrow, and upset, then you have lost the game of life.

In this book, I will provide a blueprint concerning how to strategically win in love, business, and life. It will serve as a guide challenging and steering you in the right direction, providing understanding and opportunity broadening your scope of existence within the vastness of the universe. Much of your childhood has been chosen for you, and there was nothing you could do to change it; however, the opportunity lies here in adult life. ***<u>You control your adult life, or it will control you.</u>***

The Greatest Lack

Most of us lack nothing of necessity. Most of us have housing, clean water to drink, a bed to sleep in, food in our fridge, and family and friends in our social circles. **There is one significant construct we all lack to a greater or lesser degree and that is <u>confidence</u>.** Confidence is an innate trust in the powers and abilities of the self. Confidence is only built internally and not externally. External forces can crush confidence, but only internal forces can rebuild it. **Confidence is a gift, your most powerful gift.** Confidence will singlehandedly gift you with whatever it is you truly want out of your life, and without it you cannot access the power in your personhood. This is why our society (other women and men, media, circumstances, etc.) tries to crush your confidence. **They do not want you to be motivated and powerful. They need you in the kitchen, away from the real world.** They need you to serve everyone and everything so that you will make no significant impact on the world outside of your home.

All women I have worked with lack at least some confidence. When you are born, you are born with everything you need internally to stand a fighting chance in this life. You truly have it all at birth. Through our upbringing, our environment, our social, political, and religious influences, our circumstances, and our education, slowly but surely, we negate our real potential until we are convinced, we have nothing of value to offer the external world. Keeping to ourselves, moping about in our busy lives, distracted by all the bullshittery placed in our life on the **Negativity Train** riding into the black abyss of pain and suffering because that's life! Right?

The Star of the Show

Listen to me, what the f*ck is stopping you? What is holding you back? Who is holding you hostage? You know what is stopping you? You. That's it. Because that power IS still inside you. It just has been put to sleep by the little anesthesiologists in your life. That is your subconscious because deep down, you know damn well you have potential and power. ***You know what divides and separates? Gender!*** We are assigned certain roles, conditions, and expectations only because of our gender and not because of actual ability. We have extraordinarily gifted women who would have been exceptional writers, experts, politicians, leaders, artists, visionaries, creatrixes, CEOs, and entrepreneurs locked up in the damn kitchen for hundreds of years!

Picture this, let's turn the tables for a second and imagine that women for all eternities past have been the breadwinners. Let's pretend the men stayed at home and the women were out in the world balls out. Can you imagine what could have been achieved by them? We all know women are the more productive gender (sorry, I said what I said, and you know it's true).

Stop mitigating, self-defeating, self-sabotaging, and self-loathing. Grow a pair of balls and take on this wicked, wonderful world balls out. You stop being afraid. ***You stop doubting and shrinking your greatness. You stop the need to be liked and accepted by others, which is absolutely crippling to a woman's worth.*** You've got to brave up. ***You must dig deep inside and rescue the person lost inside of there.*** Dr. Penelope Russianoff declares in *When Am I Going to Be Happy*, "a column of confidence communicates itself to other people. We are all attracted to assured behavior. We all respect calm speech, carefully reasoned thinking, and cool judgment... the confident personality has the self-control to walk into good situations- and walk away from bad ones. The person revolving around a spinal column of confidence does not slink or flee from a rebuff but walks away with dignity and pride intact." ***<u>Confidence is the most attractive quality in any person.</u>***

Strength Training for Your Mind

The whole point of this entire book series is building a confident, self-assured woman. I call this woman **FIRE WOMAN.** You are **FIRE WOMAN.** She is within all of us. This book is **Strength Training for Your Mind.** It will teach you how to become mentally strong. It will educate, inspire, and empower you beyond your wildest imagination. ***It will turn your world upside down because most of what you have been taught your whole life is a lie and has created a shit ton of unproductive limiting beliefs inside of you.*** Mentally prepare yourself for what's ahead. Learn as much as you can. Read this book two or three times absorbing the information. Years worth of research from the world's most profound authorities, experts, and psychologists were studied by me to produce this work, and now I am contributing my own knowledge and insight to already established conversations on these topics with my own aphorisms, philosophies, and stories. Just as you work out and eat well, strengthening your physical body, you must also consume knowledge exercising and strengthening your mind. Your mind becomes strong when you learn. **Your mind loves knowledge because knowledge is mental food.** Use your mind; otherwise, you will lose your mind. All the answers you are searching for are found here in this book. Open your mind to learn all the wisdom I have spent hours collecting. I bring a powerful and life-changing message for you.

Sister – Get ready to embark on an adventure.

Chapter 1 Takeaways

> - Most of us are taught to hide from the world in a conforming manner.
> - Women need to become braver, "to grow a pair of balls."
> - Walk into the sun or fall into the **Abyss of Misery**.
> - You lack nothing. You are limitless.
> - ***Stop caring about what others think of you.***
> - You are the **Star of the Show** in your life – not your man or kids.
> - Always learn and grow. Knowledge is food for your brain. Nourish it daily.

Share Your Story:

In the space provided, it is time to share your story. How have you hidden from the world, and how has that impacted who you are today?

Chapter 2
Lottery or Luck

"Many women spend their whole lives wiping everyone else's ass that they don't realize their own ass needs wiping."

Significant and Important

There are two needs that everyone has: the need to be significant, and the need to be important. These needs reflect each person based on her or his unique circumstances, beliefs, and experiences, but the principle is **universally true.** Understand that you **ARE SIGNIFICANT**, and you **ARE IMPORTANT**. If you do not feel significant or important right now, then pause for a moment and think about **WHY** because this need lives deep within you. It is a human need. ***We all just want to F*CKING MATTER in the world.*** This is why we exist. You wouldn't be here if there wasn't a place and purpose for you in this world. ***Children are encouraged to believe everything they are taught at FACE VALUE. If someone directly or indirectly tells a child that she is insignificant and unimportant, then she will believe it.*** She does not know any difference. She does not know that she doesn't **HAVE TO** accept those statements as truths. Because she is a child, she does, and thus, her self-esteem is dismantled because she is not allowed a self at all. ***These early beliefs mutate themselves transforming into Depression in adolescence and adulthood.***

In many cases, it is the primary caregivers (mother and father), but it can be others who speak these negative and false beliefs of unworthiness into a little girl's head. ***Some examples include the following:***

1. Why can't you be more like your sibling?
2. We wanted to have a boy first.

3. You will never make it.
4. You are too short/tall, fat/thin, pretty/ugly.
5. I should have had an abortion / I wish you were never born.
6. You ruined my life / took away my freedom.
7. I wish it were you who died instead of __________.
8. You were an accident/mistake.
9. Get out of my hair / stop bothering me.
10. Shut up / stop talking.
11. Do us all a favor and go kill yourself.
12. You'll never be good enough.
13. You're dumb/stupid.
14. What can a child possibly be depressed about?
15. Stop crying like a baby.
16. You are dead to me.
17. You're a failure/disappointment.
18. What's your problem?

These statements are emotionally abusive. They are damaging. Your subconscious mind is both powerful and precious. ***It believes everything said at face value.*** As a little girl you internalize these statements to be true of you. Your subconscious mind has no other choice. What happens is you may become these things that are said about you. If you were told you are a failure, you may become a failure. If you were told you are dumb then your grades may reflect that, and you perform poorly in school. Dr. Joseph Murphy, in *The Power of Your Subconscious Mind,* has much to say about harnessing these powers that exist within you, "once you learn to contact and release the hidden power of your subconscious mind, you can bring into your life more power, more wealth, more health, more happiness, and more joy. You do not need to acquire this power. You already possess it. But you will have to learn how to use it. You must understand it so that you can apply it in all departments of your life." Another quote from this book, "the law of life is the law of belief. A belief is a thought in your mind.

Do not believe in things that will harm or hurt you. Believe in the power of your subconscious to heal, inspire, strengthen, and prosper you. According to your belief, is it done unto you."

Here is where the subconscious gets even more interesting. Dr. Joseph Murphy goes on to say, "your subconscious mind does not have the ability to argue or dispute what it is told. If you give it wrong information, it will accept it as true. It will then work to make that information correct. It will bring your suggestions, even those that were false, to pass as conditions, experiences, and events." This is why it is especially devastating to criticize, abuse, emotionally neglect, reject, insult, manipulate, or belittle a child because they will ACCEPT all of that as true and deem themselves **UNWORTHY** and **UNLOVABLE** human beings. This is why many people lack **CONFIDENCE** and *DO NOT LOVE THEMSELVES*. *How can they when the first messages they received as children were messages of unworthiness and rejection?*

The messages you heard were:

YOU ARE NOT GOOD ENOUGH

YOU ARE LESS THAN

YOU ARE UNWORTHY

YOU ARE NOTHING / YOU DON'T REALLY EXIST

YOU DO NOT MATTER

YOU ARE NOT LOVABLE

These manifest themselves into **LIMITING BELIEFS** crippling us our entire lives. It is likely that you were told these things because your parents, too, as little girls and boys, were also told these things, so instead of breaking the cycle, they preserve it.

Before you read any further, we will change our beliefs here.

YOU ARE GOOD ENOUGH

YOU ARE MORE THAN

YOU ARE WORTHY

YOU ARE SOMETHING / YOU DO REALLY EXIST

YOU DO MATTER

YOU ARE LOVABLE

Whatever we tell ourselves about ourselves and believe it, <u>it becomes the truth.</u> Your subconscious mind accepts it as truth (takes everything at face value) and thus manifests it. We are going to change your early belief systems as they directly impact every area and aspect of your life from your career, life as a parent, relationships, hobbies/interests, health (mental and physical), and finances. Those old beliefs I declare hereby are BULLSHIT. They are unproductive, meaningless, and harmful. Get rid of them. ***<u>It took me 34 years to finally learn and accept that I am worthy of love.</u>***

Sunshine in Your Mind – The Happiest Depressed Person Ever

Seven was my number. At seven years old, I had my first thoughts of suicide. At 16 years old, I had seven failed suicide attempts. I remember searching online for "quick, painless ways to kill yourself," ***and out of nowhere, a Bible verse emerged that saved my life. It read:***

Jeremiah 29: 11, "For I know the plans I have for you, says the Lord, plans to prosper you and not to harm you, plans to give you hope and a future."

At that moment, I emotionally lost it. Plans for me? Hope? A future? For me? This unworthy, less than, stupid, unlovable, low life who is just better off dead? It was as if the voice of God himself, in a voice as loud as a roaring lion, said, "Oh no, you don't, not this one. I formed you in your mother's womb, I called you by name, you are mine!"

If any of those seven attempts had been successful, you would not be reading this book right now. Shortly after the attempts I was hospitalized for a week. I remember the first time the Psychiatrist approached me in the hospital. He took one look at me, saw the smile on my face, and told me, **_"You are the happiest depressed patient I have ever seen."_**

It was a paradox. I was suffering and diagnosed with Depression yet still smiling. **_Somewhere inside the dark, stormy terrain of my mind lies sunshine beyond the horizon._** It wasn't hopeless. **_A baby is born with Sunshine in its mind._** We are not born depressed; our environments make us based on the beliefs we internalize. Every human being is born to love and be loved, to thrive, to be alive, to give, to receive, to grow, to learn, to explore, and to become a whole person. We are born with Sunshine, but people, situations, circumstances, beliefs, and abuse bring storms into our lives. This is why the world is so negative. **_Negativity breeds more negativity._**

Past all the Depression and unworthiness, there it stood buried behind not-enoughness was, **_A Shining Light._** We are all born with the light; some of yours are burnt out, and some are dimly lit. **_Set ablaze that light for all the world to see. Shine that light everywhere you go. It was not the hospital that healed me, the doctors, or the medications, but rather faith itself. Purpose. Purpose healed me. "I have a plan for you," sayeth the Lord, "I have called you by name. You are mine."_**

I hit rock bottom and paid a visit to a **_Spiritual Faith Healer_** who performed a miraculous healing on me. **_She filled my head with_** *positivity and thoughts of love and worthiness.* She told me I would have a beautiful life someday. She told me I would bless and inspire millions of people. She told me God was going to take me to the top. She told me not to listen to any negativity or gossip people spoke about me. She told me I would marry a wonderful man, and my influence would spread everywhere. ***She spoke light into my life.*** She spoke meaning and purpose into my life. She spoke the plan, and future God has for me found in Jeremiah 29:11. ***And the best part? <u>My subconscious mind believed her. Those early beliefs of unworthiness dissipated just like that.</u>***

I believed her, and I was ***instantly cured,*** and never again have I suffered Depression at any point in my life. ***My subconscious mind accepted those <u>new beliefs</u> at face value and so it was, so it was manifested just like that, and I was healed/cured instantly. It was a miracle, just like the miracles Jesus performed in the Bible. <u>It is faith that healed the sick.</u>*** If you are sick and crippled in your mind, then your faith can heal you if you believe it. Command your subconscious mind that you are healed, and so it is. My life was never the same after I saw the Faith Healer that day. ***I manifested everything she said I would.*** She even spoke of me publishing books 18 years before I started writing my first book! ***You speak it into existence, and so it is.*** This is why doubt and fear don't work. You must fully believe having total faith holding nothing back.

Fill your mind with Sunshine and not hurricanes, tornados, and tsunamis. You are your own worst enemy because of the lies and cognitive distortions that you believe about yourself. Because you believe them, they come true, and they create a multitude of storms in your mind absolutely annihilating everything in their path. This is why happy people get happier; depressed people become more depressed, smart people get smarter, rich people get richer, poor people get poorer, and negative people become more negative because they attract those things in their lives based on their **belief systems aka internal programming**. The bullshit ends now. ***Choose to fill your mind with Sunshine and watch as your whole life becomes brighter.***

The Lottery of Life

We are all born into the ***Lottery of Life***. Day one you just arrived here on earth. Poof! Now here you are on planet earth. This is your life; welcome to it! You only get one life; live it to the best of your ability. Understand there are some things about your existence you had no control over.

Let's look:

1. Which family you were born into
2. How many siblings you have
3. Was mom or dad married or not
4. Are mom and dad together or not
5. Were you born into a blended family
6. Did your mom use substances during pregnancy
7. Were you born with any birth defects or diseases
8. What types of foods did your mother consume while pregnant
9. The color of your skin
10. Your birth weight and height
11. Your first, middle, and last name
12. Your physical place of birth (hospital, home, outside, etc.)
13. The city/state/country you were born in
14. The type of love and treatment you did or didn't receive
15. Your assigned birth sex (female or male)

All these things you had zero control over; hence I call this the ***Lottery of Life***. Fate determined all of this for you. Fate sets you up to be discriminated against, privileged, loved, abused, advantaged, disadvantaged, healthy, unhealthy, immediate environment, and a host of other criteria. All chosen for you outside of your control. Therefore, we don't all enter the world the same as all our circumstances and genetics are entirely different from one person to the next. However, there is good news. Although in your earliest existence of experience you had no control over it, you do have control over your life now as an adult. You get to decide what kind of life you will have from this day forward. **You control your own fate now.**

Some of us begin this life advantaged or disadvantaged, loved and wanted or unloved and unwanted, the sex our parents wanted, or the sex they didn't want. Some of us have access to clean water, food, and a roof over our heads and others do not. Some babies are deeply held and cared for, and others are not. **There is something you must be aware of. <u>You have been strategically placed.</u>**

The One Thing You Can't Escape

Pain is the one thing none of us can escape. Whether physical or emotional pain is the universal constant. The purpose of pain is whether you leverage it. You have been strategically placed in your earliest existence, and that is who you are, so you must embrace it no matter how painful your upbringing may have been. No one's life is a big bowl of cherries. **No matter what people portray on social media, we all suffer the same.** You cannot escape this suffering of human existence because suffering is what makes you human. Each of our sufferings is unique to us and our experiences. This is why it is very wrong to judge other people. **Judgment and gossip should be replaced with empathy.**

Some of you have traumatic pasts. My heart breaks for you. I feel your pain deep within my soul. The pain of girlhood and of womanhood. You cannot change the past. You cannot change whatever happened to you. But listen, hey, you are still here, right? You are still alive, right? You are breathing, right? And you are still smiling? *You are a whole, wonderful, amazing, splendid, intelligent, beautiful, and creative person of significant potential and influence.*

Childhood emotional neglect and abuse are very real. Please stop pretending they don't exist. If you judge others, you have no idea the types of hell your fellow sisters have been put through, no idea. *STOP JUDGING!* Here is your opportunity, my sister, to turn that wretched pain into power. Turn it into passion! Turn it into potential! Turn it into possibility! Use your pain. *Make pain your friend.* Your pain empathizes with you. Your pain recognizes your humanity. *Your pain is asking you to heal.* Your pain wants you to maximize your worth. Stop sweeping your pain under the rug acting like it doesn't exist when it does.

Blessed are the disadvantaged, the unprivileged, the abused, and the neglected.

Blessed are you who have known more sorrow than joy. Blessed are you who grew up too soon. *Your pain has been strategically placed in your life.* I know this is difficult to hear, but you have a powerful story to tell. You have a certain gift that others who have not been abused or neglected do not have. That's the little secret of life. Life says, *"Hey, sorry I have to punch you in the face and stab you in the back, but rest assured I will give you something so f*cking mind-blowing that will not only heal you from this but also give you this incredible life full of purpose, passion, excitement, and meaning, it's going to hurt but not forever because I will give you the ability to heal."*

What Makes You Great

What makes a person great at whatever it is they do in life is pain. Pain inflicted onto a person by another person be it a parent, friend, partner, or someone they hardly know. We don't inflict pain on ourselves. In most circumstances, pain is either directed or projected onto us by another person. Usually, that person is someone we know well, like a parent or partner. Pain causes people to commit crimes and heinous actions. Let's take a serial killer, for example: to murder a lot of innocent people, you must feel pretty shitty about yourself inside. The emotional trauma you carry inside of you makes you feel awful, and because you have not learned to properly feel and regulate your emotions, you project that awfulness you feel onto innocent victim(s). *The severity of the murder reflects the severity of the murderer's feelings about themselves and the pain that it has caused them.*

Three years old. He was only three years old when the frequent beatings started. He, too, was a human being. He, too, was once a little baby who wanted nothing more than his mother and father's love and attention. But the baby was only three years old, and his father took out all his repressed fury on the little boy. <u>The little boy didn't even cry or scream.</u> He became so numb to the pain. His dad whistled at him like a dog to come over when he wanted to beat him. <u>The boy had not one person in his corner to protect him.</u> When he was a bit older, he tried to escape and got beaten so badly that it almost took his life. His name is Adolf Hitler, and he too, was a human being.

In no manner am I excusing Hitler's heinous behavior. But one does ask oneself, what in the hell makes someone kill millions of innocent children and adults? You'd have to not have one ounce of empathy or love in your soul because it was literally beaten out of you. *Three years old. The boy was only three years old. Nobody is born a murderer. They become one. Nobody is born evil. They become evil.* When all you have known is absolute fear and horror during your most formative years, how can you overcome it? You don't…you just pass on the suffering to innocent scapegoats. It does, however, help us understand criminal behavior, and the first step to change is recognizing that *1) childhood abuse and emotional neglect are far more common than anyone wants to believe or admit, 2) all criminals are human beings with feelings who need love and attention, 3) more education and awareness in society 4) learn to become more human understanding that people are not evil, but their behaviors are.* Have you ever studied abuse and neglect before? Maybe not. If you haven't, it is important to become educated on topics that impact the lives of so many people. Many people are negative and miserable. Many people have mental health issues. If we can get to the root cause of the problem, which does have something to do with childhood abuse and emotional neglect, we can begin to heal ourselves and everyone else around us.

I learned about the unspeakable upbringing of Hitler from Alice Miller in *For Your Own Good* and some of her other books. In *For Your Own Good,* she addresses, "if we do not do everything we can to understand the roots of this hatred, even the most elaborate strategic agreements will not save us. The stockpiling of nuclear weapons is only a symbol of bottled-up feelings of hatred and of the accompanying inability to perceive and articulate genuine human needs." She further expounds, "for many people, it is very difficult to accept the sad truth that cruelty is usually inflicted upon the innocent. Don't we learn as small children that all the cruelty shown us in our upbringing is a punishment for our wrongdoing?"

Miller posits quite a compelling argument in this book regarding how damaging child abuse is and how it can manifest in the life of the individual. She goes on to elaborate, "every great artist draws on the unconscious contents of childhood, and Hitler's energies could have gone into creating works of art instead of destroying the lives of millions of people, who would then not have had to bear the brunt of this unresolved suffering, which he warded off in grandiosity." And most disturbingly, "a child whose father does not call to him by name but by whistling to him as though the child were a dog has the same disenfranchised and nameless status in the family as did "the Jew" in the Third Reich. Through the agency of his unconscious repetition compulsion, Hitler succeeded in transferring the trauma of his family life onto the entire German nation." And the final point, "little Adolf could be certain of receiving constant beatings; he knew that nothing he did would have any effect on the daily thrashings he was given. All he could do was deny the pain, in other words, deny himself and identify with the aggressor."

Stop for a second and have a moment of silence for all battered children across the world, past, present, and future. I cannot understand a three-year-old boy beaten daily for doing nothing wrong until probably his teen years. Can you imagine the sheer horror of not having a mother, aunt, sibling, teacher, friend, or anyone wrap their arms around you and comfort you? Can you even fathom it? I cannot comprehend this magnitude of suffering. If you were a battered child, put your arms around yourself right now and hug her tightly. **You are the hero you need.** May we all become a beacon of light and hope and end child abuse now and indefinitely. **When adults heal, truly heal, they cannot abuse children. It is impossible.**

Pain makes you either great or abominable, but not both. The question you might ask yourself is why some people lean towards greatness, and others lean towards vileness. This is a tricky question, but it can be understood and explained. **Nurturance is a critical component.** Understand that child abuse and emotional neglect are common. I often wonder if neglect is more common insofar as I discern that many of us were not loved enough or were not loved in the way we needed. Your parents had their own lives and drama to deal with all the time, so it might have been difficult for them to fully give you the love and attention you deserve. **I am not saying your parents didn't love you, but they may not have loved you effectively.**

Alice Miller has authored several books on child abuse and neglect, and we can begin to understand that abuse and neglect exist because they are learned behaviors. In her book *The Untouched Key*, she states, "If these people become parents, they will often direct acts of revenge for their mistreatment in childhood against their own children, whom they use as scapegoats. Child abuse is still sanctioned-indeed, held in high regard- in our society if it is defined as childrearing. It is a tragic fact that parents beat their children to escape the emotions stemming from how they were treated by their own parents." She continues with, "till now, society has protected the adult and blamed the victim. It has been abetted in its blindness by theories, still in keeping with the pedagogical principles of our great-grandparents, according to which children are viewed as crafty creatures dominated by wicked drives who invent stories and attack their innocent parents or desire them sexually. Children tend to blame themselves for their parents' cruelty and to absolve the parents, whom they invariably love, of all responsibility." Most often, children are "punished" for being children, which is most disturbing. *Individuals tend to have their moments of revelation when they finally realize that, indeed, they didn't deserve it because, in all actuality, they never did anything wrong. They were never actually bad but still got beaten – that is when they finally understand that what they experienced was child abuse, no matter how frequent the beatings were.* No child should ever have to run away from their parent and live in fear while the parent is chasing them around the house. That is absolutely traumatizing. *Children must have the opportunity to live in love and not fear.*

Emotional Nurturance

Nurturance being the key ingredient means that those who were nurtured in some capacity, be it by good teachers, friends, extended family, neighbors, or some other influential person in their life then they will direct their efforts towards pursuing greatness, whereas the vile members of society were given none to minimal love. Their earliest interactions were callous and cold from a young age. The younger you were abused and or neglected, the more profound your behaviors will be. In other words, the great will be extra great if their abuse and neglect began before age five, and the vile will be extra vile if their abuse and neglect began before age five because, in either case, *both parties are compensating for what was lost to them as little children.*

Pain is fuel. Pain is energy. You are like a vehicle needing gas to run. All the pain you have experienced in life is the fuel you need to keep pushing forward, becoming your greatest self. *If you do not struggle, you will not have the motivation to be great.* If you do not have pain, you will not have the power for greatness. *Pain is what makes you powerful either in a productive or destructive manner.*

Self-Soothing

Pain is all around us. Pain is unavoidable. You experience all types of pain in your everyday life, some of it worse than others. Many children are taught to repress feelings. No one likes it when a child cries or screams. When a child is crying or screaming because something is upsetting her, the adult in her life will do everything she can, getting the child to calm down as quickly as possible causing no further upset and noise. However, in that process, adults are teaching children that it is not okay to feel. That it is not okay to express sadness or anger. Sadness and anger must be expressed. Repression is damaging and will put you in therapy as an adult, and you will have no idea why you feel as awful as you do. If a child is crying or screaming, the best thing to do is *let it run its course* and encourage that child to cry and scream it all out.

I knew a child who threw tantrums all the time. If he didn't get his way, he threw a massive tantrum. To stop the tantrum, his mother gave him whatever he wanted, so he learned to get what he wanted. All he needed to do was throw a tantrum, and it worked like magic. ***This mother did not solve the problem. She perpetuated it.*** What she should have done was to let him have a full-blown tantrum even if the tantrum lasted a full 24 hours. Those 24 hours of hell and the threat of burning the house down would have saved time and effort in the future. It also would have put a stop to both of their pain. ***Allow yourself to feel productive emotions. <u>Even bad emotions are productive emotions.</u>***

Self-soothing ***is a person's ability to calm herself down in circumstances of emotional distress.*** Self-soothing is allowing yourself to feel in those moments with positive self-talk, listening to music, taking a walk, sitting by yourself in complete quietness with self-love. ***Learn ways to self-soothe when you experience times of great difficulty.*** Self-soothing is part of emotional regulation. ***When you experience negative emotions such as anger, sadness, or frustration, for example, tell yourself that it is <u>okay to feel.</u>*** It is okay to be angry, sad, frustrated, etc. Emotions are what make you human, and without them, you would not be human. Dr. Penelope Russianoff, in *When Am I Going to Be Happy*, teaches us to "talk tenderly to yourself. Simple as it sounds, it is one of the most effective techniques you can use for breaking negative habits."

Hitler was robbed of his ability to feel as a child. He had feelings, and they were removed, locked away, and buried; therefore, he didn't feel. He became numb, and that is how he was able to kill thousands of people without empathy. You would have to be entirely depleted of any emotion to kill an entire race of people. If he were able to feel as a child, he could have been a great leader and not a mass murderer, but he experienced no warmth and no love. ***He was not given the tools to self-soothe.***

Emotional regulation is critical in your ability to feel and heal. Feeling is fundamental to human existence. We all have feelings of varying kinds. Every day and every situation bring with it new emotions. When you have any type of emotion, allow yourself to feel it even if it hurts, even if it makes you uncomfortable. Numbing your pain is not the solution. Repressing emotion is not the solution. ***Feel every ounce of pain and disharmony any single emotion is causing you. Allow yourself to become fully human.***

Learn **emotional regulation** as it is critical to your mental health. There is a formula for emotional recovery:

1. Fully Feel - (this is where you let it all out – hold no emotion back and suppress nothing).

2.Go back to your **Resilience Zone**. Once you have cleansed your body of the emotion it was feeling then return to your **Zone of Resilience**, your **Zone of Strength**.

Feeling and healing are essential to your growth and journey of becoming more human. If you do not heal, you will remain stagnant forever. There will be no true growth, no true personal transcendence. ***We cannot control what kind of pain comes our way, but we can choose how we respond to it.*** The ***power of choice*** is the greatest power of all time. You choose how to respond. You choose to overcome. You choose to rise above. You choose to ascend. ***You choose to make a better life for yourself, <u>but it all comes down to choice.</u>***

Life is Fundamentally Unfair

Based on everything you've learned so far in this chapter, it is plain to see that life is ***fundamentally unfair.*** This means that life itself does not owe you anything at all. You were born into the family you were born into, and there is nothing you can do to change that fact or the subsequent upbringing and early training you had. It is what it is, whether it was advantageous for you or not. Accept the facts through *awareness.* Awareness is the first stage in healing, and healing is the first stage in growth. I am sure you have received a taste of something in your life being *fundamentally unfair.* One common theme that many of us can resonate with is the fact that romantically speaking, the people we like/love tend to not love us, and the people we don't like/love tend to love and want us. I am aware that two individuals can be equally in love. However, unrequited love is common. Why is this a *fundamentally unfair* reality? Why did he choose her over you? Looks wise; she isn't all that and a bag of chips in your opinion. I am about to explain all of this in a psychological deep dive, so continue reading.

Do not expect life to be fair for you; that is unrealistic. But DO EXPECT life to bless you and gift you. Later, I will discuss the joy of receiving gifts, what those are, and when to identify them. Understand before you read any further that you are the authoress and creatrix of your life. You have heard me say this before, and I will say it again because it is an important concept. *You are the magician of your own life, carefully controlling and constructing your reality according to your <u>highest self</u>.* Some people sit around their whole lives and wait for things to happen to them, and others go out there and make shit happen. Which person are you? A good example of this is when people say something like "when I win the lottery," – how about you stop declaring, "when I win the lottery," *and create a hobby or business opportunity that will generate a steady stream of revenue for you. Just an idea.*

Change your thinking and thought processes. Instead of moping around thinking about how unfair life is (because let's admit AND accept that right now) that life is *fundamentally unfair*. Start taking advantage of the opportunities available to you with the resources you possess. Don't worry about the resources you don't possess, such as money for example, and start worrying about the resources you do possess such as your unique and innate talents and skills. *Capitalize on your talents and skills, because long-term those will make you money.*

Another example – I do not come from money. My dad worked his ass off for every dollar he earned, and it is called hard-earned money because he had to work hard to earn it. Every dollar mattered. *Education was not pushed on me, and if it had been, I may not be educated today because I may have taken advantage of my parents' resources with the attitude of entitlement that I witnessed among my peers.* Between a lack of money and a lack of educational motivation, you could say my future looked bleak, and it was. For me, life was *fundamentally unfair* and disadvantageous in that regard.

Don't allow your disadvantages to cripple you. This is a choice you can make for yourself. As limited as I might have been, I did desire to take personal responsibility and **ownership** of my future. That **ownership** of my future is what the spoiled little entitled kids lack, which is why they still live in their parents' basement at 40 years old making less than $20 an hour doing a job they hate. That **ownership** of my future literally saved (and made) my life. I had the sense, combined with internal motivation, skills, talents, and moxy, to get out there in the world, figure out my damn problem, and start making shit happen.

Did it happen overnight? Hell no! Did it happen in a decade? Hell no! Was it as painful as all hell? F*ck yeah! ***<u>Pain is not a bad thing like most people think.</u>*** Pain is fuel. When you experience pain, you realize you don't want to be in pain anymore, so you *take action* preventing future painful experiences. A lack of money, resources, and opportunity caused me great pain, so instead of sitting on my ass bitching about poor little me, I got up, marched my ass up to the community college, enrolled in two classes, worked 60 hours a week while going to school full-time and *made a dream come true.*

The journey is painful but rewarding. If you are looking for an easy route, you won't find it. If you are looking for a quick fix, it doesn't exist. You must be willing to fight, and you must be willing to bleed. Between work and school, I was working 14–16-hour days while crying every single day because my life was so difficult, and I had no support. ***My village was only I. Independent to a fault.*** My life today is **beyond blessed** because of all that long-suffering. Do not be afraid to suffer. Do not be afraid to do arduous work. It does pay off in the end. And finally, everyone is responsible for themselves. ***No one can make anything happen for you except for you.*** Life does automatically privilege some people while it systemically deprives others (***fundamentally unfair***). Minorities treated poorly and women oppressed just because of who they were born to be is fundamentally unfair, ***but you do not have to be a victim of circumstances. You can and will be a champion of change. A Titan of Transformation.***

If you are a born male, you won the first lottery.

If you are born a white male, you won the second lottery.

If you are born a white male with economic privilege, you won the third lottery.

If you were born in the United States, you won the fourth lottery.

If you are born a white female, you won the fifth lottery and so on.

Be fully cognizant that we are all different. Life does not discriminate, only humans do. If you act discriminatory, in any capacity, you are NOT operating from a place of humility, love,

The Matilda Advantage

One of the hallmark movies of my childhood growing up in the nineties is Matilda. Many people are familiar with the story of Matilda. She comes from a family who don't value and appreciate her, and they also don't value education and learning. While her family is busy watching TV every night, she is always reading. The reading disappoints her father, and he rips pages out of her books, calling them trash and throwing them on the ground. Matilda has no positive role models in her family.

From a young age, she starts reading and she continues reading constantly. She is always reading, and she has a zest for learning. She expresses the desire to go to school until her parents finally and reluctantly enroll her. This is where she makes many new friends flourishing as a student of potentiality. *Reading gives Matilda an advantage.* It makes her smart. The books take her on adventures that she doesn't get to go on in real life.

Because she has this "gift" of reading and learning, she discovers through her intelligence that she has magical powers and can maneuver objects with her mind. She discovers the magic deep within herself that learning and knowledge offer. Matilda has always been one of my favorite movies of all time for this beautiful comparison.

My advice to you is that you never stop reading, growing, and learning. **Knowledge is the most powerful tool you have.** Always be reading. Never make excuses not to read. Reading will take you places, whereas watching TV and endlessly scrolling social media will not. When you gain knowledge, you gain power just as Matilda did. That internal power lies within you. **When you are knowledgeable and competent, there will be no stopping you. You will become a force of reason and potentiality.**

I couldn't read until I was eleven years old. Now I consume an average of 4-5 books per month consistently. It was a teacher I had and no one else who discovered this problem of mine before it was too late. She took personal ownership teaching me comprehension, and to this day she has no idea concerning the magnitude that has made in my life. My writing exists because of her. My business exists because of her. My degrees, opportunities, and amazing life exist because of her. **Never underestimate the power of reading.**

Take your education and learning into your own hands, and when you read and develop your competency, there will come a day when everything you touch will turn to gold. That is your magic. Dr. Seuss says in *Oh, The Places You'll Go*, "the more that you read, the more things you will know, the more that you learn, the more places you'll go." And another quote by Dr. Seuss, "You have brains in your head. You have feet in your shoes. You can steer yourself in any direction you choose." And lastly, "Things may happen and often do to people as brainy and footsy as you."

Dr. Seuss encourages a love for reading and learning, instilling in readers that anything is possible for those who educate themselves. It is not the richest or the most well-equipped or spoon-fed who succeed; it is those most hungry, and if you're hungry, you'll read.

Those who don't value learning and growth will forever be a prisoner of their own minds.

Sister – You are a beacon of brilliance.

Chapter 2 Takeaways

> - Pain and suffering are universal constants.
> - You cannot choose which family you were born into, but you can steer your future.
> - Always self-soothe and provide yourself with **emotional nurturance.**
> - Embrace your pain and use it as fuel to accomplish your goals.
> - Reading is an advantage and will take you far in life.

Share Your Story:

In the space provided, it is time to share your story. How have you turned your disadvantages into advantages? What steps will you take to educate yourself more often?

Chapter 3
Throne of Authority

"How could I ever author a book about self-esteem if I didn't spend 2/3 of my life not having one?"

Offense Vs. Defense

Living a good life is all about choice and strategy. **You must choose first to live a good life.** Tell yourself that you deserve a good life. Construct the exact life you want to live. **The key is strategy.** For those of you who play sports you have heard the terms offense and defense. Allow me to define these terms: offense means to attack something or to strike, whereas defense means to defend against or resist the attack. In life, there will be circumstances and situations where you need to play offense and situations where you need to play defense.

Playing Offense

Most of the time you will be playing offense. **Offense means action.** It means to do or to attack. You were born with significant power and potential. However, for most of us, our power and potential are taken from us by other people and situations outside of our control. **When we learn that, yes, we possess profound power and potential within ourselves, <u>the door of enlightenment is opened,</u> and we can achieve all that we deserve and desire.**

Playing Defense

Playing defense is our defensive strategy. Most of the time, people attack us from all angles. Criticism and negativity are rampant in society. People abuse us, use us, mistreat us, disrespect us, belittle us, insult us, etc. By playing defense, we protect and defend ourselves against the bullies of society.

The Sleeping Dragon

Understand something before we move further in this book. You are a human being. This is your life. I feel bad for women. Men are permitted to chase after the women they want, and women are not afforded this same luxury. Many women end up with men who claim or choose them, but they do not choose these same men for themselves. According to societal rules, if a woman likes or wants a particular man then she is not permitted (traditionally) to chase/pursue him; otherwise, she will be perceived as a chaser/pursuer, and he may get scared and run away. Pause for a second and think about HOW F*CKED UP THAT IS. Do you understand what this is suggesting to women? That we are **LESS THAN** humans— that we are NOT ALLOWED to chase/pursue the person of our desires— that we should be available for capturing but not dare do the capturing ourselves.

It is sickening. *This is a LIMITING BELIEF.* It is a social belief and a social problem, and right here, as you read these very words, we will ***ANNIHILATE THIS LIMITING BELIEF TOGETHER.*** You are going to put on your big girl panties and go after whoever you want. I recently went on a date with a man I asked out, and he agreed. We had this very conversation on the date, and he agreed with me concerning how messed up this is. He told me (he was 35 years old) that I was the first girl to ever ask him out on a date. *Why do men have all the power, and we have none? Why? Who made these moronic "rules?" Who?*

When I was a teenager, I knew of this older woman in her forties. She was my Mary Kay consultant at the time, and the topic of dating and marriage came up in our conversation. She was talking about her husband, and she became so excited, she told me, "I couldn't believe it; someone wanted me, someone finally wanted me!" As I look back at this situation today, I think, "are you really this less than that you believe someone FINALLY

WANTED you? Did you believe you were unworthy of love and commitment prior to this man marrying you?" We wait our whole lives. *We wait our whole lives for someone to finally want us.* We wait our whole lives to be good enough for marriage, to be good enough to be someone's wife. Then he makes us his wife.

In many cases but not all, over time (by a little or a lot), things change, he changes, what once was no longer is, and then comes the abuse, the neglect, being taken advantage of, turned into a house slave, a maid, a sex object, or lack thereof, a personal secretary or assistant. You go from lover to mother to slave as you watch yourself fade slowly away into the **Abyss of Misery.** *You lose most or all your self-esteem and self-worth in the process.*

Inside every human being lies a sleeping dragon. This *sleeping dragon* is a metaphor for your subconscious mind. Prior to your relationship, your dragon was alive and active; it had goals, dreams, ideas, wishes, desires, thoughts, and ambitions, and it achieved great and mighty things. It kicked ass in all areas of life. You won awards, had a career, and excelled academically, athletically, and creatively. You did whatever you wanted to do and more because of the power of your **subconscious mind.** Once you get into a relationship, either your partner, yourself, or both of you put your dragon back into a deep sleep where it lies today sleeping and breathing air out of its large nostrils. It is asleep, useless, and inactive. **But it is hungry,** and you haven't fed it in years. Your life became your partner's life as you faithfully supported him in his hobbies, interests, activities, and career. His life became yours. **You both live his life.** Your life no longer exists. You gave it up. You said in your head, *"my need to be loved is so great that I am willing to do anything to receive love, including giving up my entire life, self-esteem, and essential personhood."*

Let that sink in, please, for just a moment. This is a huge concept I am teaching now. Where is the love? Do you feel love right now? Is he spending time with you? Does he cherish you? Is he faithful? Does he spend time with you in the evening, or is he gone most nights? Does he make love to you and treat you like a queen, or does he ignore you? Where is the love that you gave up your life and personhood for? Where is it? You put your dragon to sleep. Your dragon is so powerful that you cannot even comprehend its magnitude and capabilities unless you intensively study the workings of the subconscious mind. **Your subconscious mind has horsepower that is unstoppable, untamable, irresistible, and almighty. You have so much power and dynamism within you, but you euthanize it.**

You've heard it said people only use 10% of their brain. You have the power to use 100% of your brain. It is always accessible for usage if you acknowledge and tap into it. Your conscious mind (rational mind) makes up 10% of your brain, and your subconscious mind (irrational/creative/emotional mind) makes up 90% of your brain. Anything you create originates in your **subconscious mind**. That is why it is so powerful.

Power

Just like Ariel traded in her beautiful voice for love, you ladies trade in your self-esteem for love. That is disturbing. Your self-esteem is all you have! You are so powerful. You literally can do anything; I know that sounds cliché, but it is true. You cater to and accommodate your whole life around one man to get love that he doesn't even give to you. Do you understand how much you are risking? *Take your dragon, wake her up, and unleash her.* She is so powerful. *She can do anything. She is all-wise, all-knowing, and all-powerful.* She will lead you, guide you, direct you, and give you all the answers needed to solve your problems. Unleash her. She will breathe fire unto the world because you are **FIRE WOMAN**. You were not born to sit on your ass watching football with your man on Sundays (unless you love football, sorry not knocking genuine football lovers, but to those of you who cannot stand football and could be using that valuable time for achieving your dreams and goals but aren't). *Unleash her.*

STOP LIMITING YOURSELF.

STOP SLEEPING YOUR LIFE AWAY.

STOP WATCHING SPORTS YOU HATE.

STOP BENDING OVER BACKWARD TO PLEASE OTHERS.

STOP GIVING UP YOUR GOALS AND DREAMS FOR OTHERS.

STOP ACCOMMODATING OTHERS.

Love yourself. Unleash your sleeping dragon. Breathe fire to the world and give them hell.

Learned Helplessness

Every dating book I've read teaches women that men love to be heroes, need to be heroes, and need to be needed. That they have a so-called "Hero Complex." They want to come in, save the day and solve some problem, large or small, and if you let said man solve your problem, then he will love and cherish you for all eternity, and you will be the girl he obsesses over and will marry someday. Ummm… what? **This is asinine. This is what is called Learned Helplessness. Women learn from the time we are little girls that it is attractive and appealing to men if we are incompetent and helpless.** This screams LESS THAN to me. Just another way for society to make women feel like we are LESS THAN. Society is always architecting ways for women to feel worthless and LESS THAN until we begin understanding and accepting that we are LESS THAN. Who makes this shit up? For real.

You were not born to be helpless, sister. You were born to learn, to grow, to evolve, and to thrive. Yes, there will be things you are good at and things you are not good at, and it is perfectly okay to ask for help if you need help. But to *"put on a show for guys"* by playing helpless so he can feel like his c*ck is five times its actual size is farcical. Once again, we are catering to a man's ego while **NO ONE GIVES ONE F*CK ABOUT OUR EGO AS WOMEN!** You'll never hear anyone talking about a woman's ego – because we are NOT ALLOWED TO HAVE ONE! And that depresses us. **That submerges us.** That obliterates our true potential and worth as fully equal human beings. Men are allowed to have egos, and we aren't. INSANE. **It's as if we don't really matter, isn't it?** We are here to breed, be sex objects, cook, clean, cater to, bend over backward for, lose ourselves, chauffeur, wipe asses, organize everyone's lives, invent the most creative Valentine's Day boxes that make you look like mother of the year, buy matching PJs to wear on Christmas to show the world how perfect and put together your family is, because that is what a good woman is supposed to do… attend PTA meetings and volunteer at the school, and lose yourself, lose yourself, lose yourself, **become an unperson.**

You don't really matter, do you? You are just simply put on this earth to please, serve, agree with, submit to, and wipe asses – that is what a good and noble woman is to do with herself. Dr. Penelope Russianoff explains in *When Am I Going to Be Happy,* "another negative habit that our culture encourages in women is helplessness. We are taught it. My female patients tell me repeatedly that they feel helpless. How well I know what they are going through. In my day, women were virtually trained to be helpless as a seductive asset… learned helplessness is just another form of social suicide. The woman who practices it is deliberately killing off her capacity to grow."

Are you screaming yet? If you aren't, start screaming and let it all out.

YOU ARE NOT PUT ON THIS EARTH TO SERVE AND TO PLEASE OTHERS DAY IN AND DAY OUT – THAT IS CALLED WALLOWING IN THE ABYSS OF MISERY. YOU ARE HERE TO GROW, LEARN, DREAM, ACHIEVE, PROSPER, KICK ASS, ANNIHILATE FEARS AND LIMITING BELIEFS, AND DO WHATEVER MAKES YOU HAPPY AND GIVES YOU PURPOSE.

<u>YOU WERE PUT ON THIS EARTH TO KICK ASS NOT KISS ASS.</u>

Damsel in Distress

Stop shrinking yourself. Stop lessening your brilliance and magnificence. You aren't helpless. You aren't a Damsel in Distress. This is not an attractive quality whatsoever. It makes you look like a little girl and not a woman. You don't deserve love because you act helplessly, stupid, or needy. **You deserve love because you are a human being, damnit.**

Beliefs

Every person has a unique life based on her or his experiences and environment. We are so different in countless ways, and that is why it is unfair and inappropriate to judge and or criticize others. Beliefs are powerful. Beliefs suggest that whatever I believe to be true is true, and whatever I don't believe to be true is not true. This is your **Map of Experience.** Who you are today is an accumulation of ALL CHOICES (or lack thereof) you have made in your life. **You get to CHOOSE what you believe.** Everything is a choice except for feelings. Your beliefs are a choice, and you can choose to believe differently at any time. We tend to believe whatever our parents and early teachers taught us without ever truly questioning reality. It is easier and less effortful to believe what we were taught growing up— accepting everything as an absolute truth. I often wonder if our early beliefs limit or even harm us. Brian Nox tells us in *Fuck Him, Nice Girls Always Finish Single*, "many people are brought up as a so-called Nice Guy or Nice Girl. They believe if they are good to the world and anyone in it, the world will be good to them, too. That's not how the world works. So, these well-meaning people are often left frustrated and feeling helpless."

Self-Esteem Versus Narcissism – is there a difference?

There is one reason why I chose to write a section on self-esteem versus Narcissism, and that is because there seems to be a general or possible universal confusion between the two: two distinctively paradoxical realities of human experience. ***What you must first understand is that each of us is fundamentally narcissistic.*** It is impossible to call yourself a human being without some existence of **central narcissism** within you. This is because we all have an ego or identity. Your identity is your ego, and vice versa. Narcissism involves the self or the ego.

However, as with anything else in life, Narcissism exists on a spectrum or (to a greater or lesser degree) with extremes on both sides. Narcissism is a predominant awareness of our own human existence. Without this knowledge, we couldn't call ourselves human. **Narcissism acknowledges the self.** Although some of our own Narcissism is so unnoticeable that you cannot perceive it in certain individuals. These individuals are lower on the spectrum. **Whereas Narcissism is natural and unachievable, self-esteem is not.** Self-esteem is not natural, and it is achievable. This is the first essential difference between Narcissism and self-esteem. **Narcissism naturally exists without effort, whereas self-esteem develops over time through a process.** Therefore, self-esteem can be achieved. Narcissism is natural-born or infantile. Psychologists refer to Narcissism in babies and toddlers because until a certain age, children only have awareness of themselves and their own needs, and everyone in their internal orbit simply revolves around them.

The most disturbing part about Narcissism is that many (especially so-called narcissistic individuals) never seem to evolve out of their *fundamental Narcissism,* which suggests they remain (sometimes indefinitely) in an *infantile state* and, more disturbingly, an emotionally infantile state; these are the "if I am not happy, ain't nobody happy" individuals who can also be classified as the misery loves company people. *No one else exists for them in their own world.*

As a Self-Esteem and Human Empowerment Coach, it is challenging to get others to achieve self-esteem when they believe that they will be perceived by others (or themselves) as narcissists for having self-esteem. They are terrified to be perceived as arrogant, cocky, prideful, or conceited. There is healthy pride and unhealthy pride, as pride also sits somewhere along a spectrum, and the secret is about balance between acceptance and permissibility. I sometimes struggle to get my clients to accept that self-esteem and Narcissism are two contrasting curiosities, I thought it might be fruitful to delineate the inherent polarities between them.

The largest divergence assumes empathy or the recognition of other people and their emotional states. Narcissists only have the recognition of themselves, which is a distinguishing fact of Narcissism. Narcissists lack empathy. In other words, they only recognize the importance of themselves and not the importance of other people. This is the most eminent distinction. *Individuals with self-esteem regard themselves as being important but simultaneously also regard others as equally important.* Individuals with self-esteem easily recognize, appreciate, and respond to the emotional states of others.

Another factor is that narcissists lack self-esteem. They may appear to be high and mighty and think very well of themselves, but that perception is only a distortion of self-esteem. Self-esteem is the process a person naturally evolves into overtime, whereas narcissists do not truly invest the time in bettering themselves because they are naturally the best without any effort... or so they believe. Individuals with self-esteem are highly self-aware and deeply introspective, cognizant of their own self-worth. They have overcome many, if not all, of their insecurities, and they surely do not mind taking responsibility admitting when they have made a mistake. *A narcissist would never admit to a mistake.* A narcissist believes they are a know-it-all, while an individual with high self-esteem is continuously educating themselves, learning, and growing while expanding and gaining a deeper understanding of life and how to function within it.

Self-esteem is a journey, and Narcissism is not. Self-esteem is progressive, and Narcissism is regressive. If you are a narcissist, you either act like an infant or are regressing back to an infantile state of me me me and everyone must tiptoe around you walking on eggshells. If people in your life are tiptoeing around you, then you are an infantile narcissist, and you must evolve asap. Self-esteem is not natural, but narcissism is. A child with low self-esteem may not have the fondest of relationships with her or his parents. It is quite possible, unfortunately, that your fundamental concepts of self-love and self-esteem were literally beaten out of you as a child. There is no such thing as a bad or misbehaved child. *Children are simply children and act accordingly.* Adults, on the contrary, are angry, ill-informed, and unhealed, carrying around crucifies of pain on their backs (like Jesus), *and they beat their children as an opportunity for release and control.* Most often, parents invent reasons to punish (beat) their children. Or children are beaten over trivial matters often committing no domestic crimes at all. *You do realize that the volcanic eruption of problems permeated throughout our world is a result of many beaten, mistreated, and molested children.* Punishment back in the "good old days" was archaic, barbaric, and passed down from generation to generation, making it thus a *social and cultural issue*. This is why today many of you *walk around unhealed.* Look at the reality. *Instead of sweeping shit under the rug like you were taught, address problems head on.*

The most heartbreaking reality of it all is when the adult realizes that they never did anything wrong as a child, and their suffering is the result of unhealed parents' anger and former childhood humiliation. Why do I even bother talking about childhood abuse and neglect? It is the reason problems and suffering exist in the world. *If children were loved better, they'd never end up in toxic, poisonous relationships that annihilate their self-esteem.* Patterns of behavior are repeated until **CONSCIOUSLY BROKEN**.

Self-esteem is a journey, a path, a choice. Self-esteem is a decision. Self-esteem is your concept of yourself viewed in a positive light, whereas Narcissism is a concept of yourself viewed in a negative light. A narcissist must kick and scream for blessings to come their way because they don't believe they are worthy of good things. Their self-concept is distorted; it is a negative self-defeating view (although seemingly high on the outside – that is a façade, a mask). Those with self-esteem have a positive self-concept and believe good things are due to them, and blessings will come their way without all the kicking and screaming. Gabrielle Bernstein has this to say about worthiness in her book *Super Attractor*, "there is not a source outside of us that can save us from our sense of unworthiness. When we truly accept that we embody the power of love, then we can start to realign with the belief that we are worthy of feeling good...accepting our greatness is the key to being a Super Attractor."

I am an advocate for becoming more human, and the primary way to become more human is first developing healthy and positive self-esteem. When your self-esteem is fully developed into a healthy and positive entity, it will be impossible for another individual to shatter that <u>because it is precisely at that point that you become indestructible.</u>

For example, I used to believe that my sense of security could only come from my romantic partner, and I rotated on whatever security or lack thereof that other person provided for me. ***Eventually, those other people obliterated my self-esteem and, with it, my sense of security.*** I had **allowed** myself to become destroyed as a human being. I would cry out with almost an exorcist sort of scream because the pain of it hit my core, my essential personhood. Once I exiled old romantic partners from my life, I slowly but surely regained my self-esteem and learned that security can only come from inside of us and not from other people. I learned how to rotate on that internal backbone of security. The next time someone attempts to wreak havoc on my self-esteem, they will be destroyed (figurately) by me before they can destroy me. ***All of life depends on what we will or won't tolerate.*** Many of us have a high tolerance for bullshittery, and it makes me incredibly sad because what could you really become if someone else wasn't murdering your self-esteem?

Childhood abuse and emotional neglect have the power to obliterate self-esteem in children. If you look around you, it is easy to see how many suffer from low to no self-esteem. This is a common social issue. You will not have to swim oceans or climb mountains to find individuals who suffer from low-to-no-self-esteem. In *For Your Own Good*, Alice Miller says, "the way we were treated as small children is the way we treat ourselves the rest of our life. And we often impose our most agonizing suffering upon ourselves. We can never escape the tormentor within ourselves." This will create a myriad of problems within us. In addition to low self-esteem, a few include self-hatred, lack of empathy, caring and loving too much, people pleasing, perfectionism, self-flagellation, constant need for external validation, abandonment issues, negativity, fear-based thinking, poor grades and or poor performance, trouble making friends, trouble in social settings, and struggles in romantic relationships to name a few. *Having low to no self-esteem is your biggest problem.*

What is self-esteem? *Self-esteem is respect for oneself.* I do not believe narcissists can demonstrate respect even for themselves because respect means holding something or someone in high regard. Someone with self-esteem has self-love, and someone with Narcissism has self-hatred, so they ruin everyone around them, making themselves feel better. Whereas someone with self-esteem would not feel the need to do that. *In other words, self-esteem includes confidence, dignity, morale, self-respect, self-assurance, and worth.* Self-esteem is a choice; it is a state of mind. Narcissists cannot choose to be narcissists; they just are narcissists, but they can choose not to be narcissistic anymore. Narcissists can develop healthy and positive self-esteem or an essential awareness of their self-worth. Self-esteem is a state of mind, which is why I said earlier that you must develop it. *How exactly can you do this?*

1. **STEP 1:** Take total and complete **ownership** of your healing. There is a high probability that you are walking around day in and day out unhealed. *No one can heal you. Healing is a self-induced, self-guided journey toward the end of suffering.*

2. **STEP 2:** Tune everyone else out. Everything and everyone are a perception in your own mind, which means what they think about you doesn't matter. If you are listening to other people, you are no different from someone who hallucinates in their mind. People are

often put in our paths to hold us back or keep us from progressing. ***The reason I know success is because I do not give a rat's ass about what people think or say about me. I have learned to tune everyone out.***

3. ***STEP 3:*** Put all energy and focus on you. As women, we are notorious for putting energy and focus on everyone else except for ourselves, which is usually to our own detriment. This is your life, and it begins and ends with you. This is your show, baby!

4. ***STEP 4: Embody undeniable, indestructible self-worth and self-love.*** When we recognize, accept, and appreciate our own value, we become invaluable. ***Children who come from emotionally neglectful and abusive homes do not learn self-worth and self-love, so many turn to self-defeating habits numbing the unwanted pain of existence.***

5. ***STEP 5: Continuously ascend.*** Ascension is a state of mind. It is a forward upward moving direction – forward and up where you continuously soar ever higher. There are many activities that can help you ascend; let me name a few until you get the idea: ***read books (learn), engage yourself in hobbies and interests, make new friends, meet new people, get out there in the world, learn new skills, earn a degree or certification, start a business, create something, write a book, etc.***

Some women (because of social conditioning), unfortunately, do not believe there is more to life than marriage and babies, so they put themselves into the marriage and baby box fixating on those goals until they are accomplished. Not only do they put themselves into a box, but they also allow society to put them into a box. Little by little, this can bring them down, robbing them of healthy and positive self-esteem. ***This is the elimination of our essential personhood, our journey of becoming an unperson, or the loss of identification with who we are, what we need, and most importantly, <u>what we might</u>***

become _if we never lost those fundamental elements of ourselves, namely our self-esteem._

Your only job here on earth is **_to make the most of yourself._** _This is known as_ **_self-actualization._**

A person who makes life all about herself or himself, the narcissist, will never go very far because **we need other people to become successful.** No one wants to help someone who makes life all about themselves. However, a person with self-esteem values themselves and others equally; therefore, others will want them to be successful, and when one person wins, we all win. If I won by authoring this book, and you won because it resonated with you and helped you overcome certain problems, then we both won, and the engagement is mutually beneficial. I got to share my knowledge, and you got to consume it. My blessing was to give, and your blessing was to receive. We both won. **_In summation, please understand that the difference between Narcissism and self-esteem is that narcissists are only about themselves and lack community, and those with self-esteem are about themselves and all others embodying community. Those with self-esteem acknowledge the worth and value of every human being, while narcissists do not._**

How to Cure Depression in 60 Seconds

All Depression has a cause. Depression comes with legitimate reasons. One cannot inherit Depression since Depression is a state of mind like any other reality. Depression is a Hell-State, which I will cover in greater detail later in this book. If your parent or caregiver suffered from Depression, then you might also, since emotion is contagious, that is known as **_emotional contagion._** When I was 16 years old and had seven suicide attempts, my psychiatrist called me **_The Happiest Depressed Person_** he had ever treated. I call this aberration **_The Shining Light Within,_** which means that I have an internal light always glowing inside of me no matter the **external circumstances** around me. I was depressed. I had zero self-worth, zero self-love, and lacked self-esteem. I was an unperson, eating, breathing, and sleeping with zero meaning and purpose. That light inside burns bright, and it will never extinguish. *That light inside makes us human.* Our **internal warrior** ready and willing to fight no matter how many times life punches us in the face. *This is our human mystery, an inexhaustible will to live and become fully human.* It was my way of communicating to my psychiatrist that I didn't really want to take my own life; I wanted to live and live fully, but I didn't see any productive way to do so, so I assumed suicide was my only chance at ending misery. That light is the human spirit, and it is so powerful. We all have possession of it, but most of us do not bother with it because we worry that if we do, then we might be judged by others.

If you are depressed, you are only experiencing 50% of your life while the other 50% is hiding in the basement, locked tightly in a safe. The 50% you are experiencing is the bleakness and blackness of your everyday existence. You are living, but you certainly are not alive. That missing 50% is the treasure chest of life filled with gold, riches, gifts, and mystery. Depression is the 50% known or experienced, and the 50% unknown or mysterious are the treasures and gifts of life. *Every human being is infinitely intelligent, creative, and productive.* Allow me to explain:

<u>Infinitely Intelligent:</u> *Within you lies an intelligence greater than yourself, which means you are boundlessly smart.* There is no end to your smarts. You might have the lowest IQ possible, yet you possess infinite wisdom and problem-solving abilities inside of you. For example, I grew up being placed in all the "dummy classes" yet got a PhD and graduated at the top of my doctoral class. *Once I <u>recognized</u> my own infinite intelligence, the entire game changed for me.* I went from "Can't Read to PhD" overnight. That revelation revolutionized my world.

<u>**Infinitely Creative:**</u> Everyone has talents and skills that differ from person to person. Tap into your creativity. ***As humans, we are natural creators.*** Just look around you: would buildings, houses, movies, music, artwork, businesses, entertainment, and more exist without human creativity? Could you author a book someday? Well, maybe some of you think you don't really have anything to say, that nobody cares about what you have to say, or that every topic has already been written about. But that shouldn't stop you from writing a book. ***You do have something to say – everyone does; that is precisely why you were given a voice-to speak!*** What if someone doesn't like your book or doesn't agree with you? Just because I have a PhD, you are allowed to disagree with me. I will always share my knowledge with you, but I am not a know-it-all; I do not know it all. In fact, I know very, very little, but I do believe in infinite wisdom in the universe. Of course, there may be some women who hate my work and criticize it, and others crying the entire way through reading it because it completely revolutionized their lives as they know it. The content resonates deeply with them and their experience. ***Everything is about perception.*** I've read books that made me cry the whole way through, and that is precisely what gave me the gusto to author my own book series. My thinking was, "If this author's work can change my life and inspire me, then perhaps my work can change and inspire others, too." ***Writing and knowledge become gifts that keep on giving.***

You might be thinking, "Dr. E, I have been on Prozac for ten years and have been sitting in my therapist's office twice weekly for the past three years. It is preposterous to believe I can cure my Depression in just 60 seconds!"

You just answered your own question. ***Everything comes down to BELIEF.*** Depression is a state of mind; it is a Hell State because it is a state you would rather not be in. Nobody chooses to be depressed, and nobody votes to remain there, either. No one is a glutton for Depression, but many are a glutton for punishment, which is partly what causes Depression and suffering in the first place.

The story goes, something happened to you, or it was a chain of events that caused you to become depressed. *Everything in life has both a cause and an effect.* Depression is a disease of the mind, a disease of lies and distorted beliefs. Depression is directly linked to low self-love, low self-worth, and low self-esteem. When I think of the word Depression, I picture someone taking their hand and pressing down on someone else, thereby depressing them; *Depression is a psychological and emotional lowering of the self.* And it is **YOUR HAND** that is pushing you down regardless of whether it is another human being or not who could be causing your Depression.

How exactly do you cure Depression in 60 seconds?

BUILD YOUR SELF-ESTEEM.

Easier said than done, I know, *but remember the development of your self-esteem is A PROCESS, which means it will NOT happen overnight.* You cannot snap your fingers out of Depression. You must have a revelation from within coming to terms with your own reality and know what you can do to strategically turn things around and dramatically revitalize your life.

STEP 1: Try to remember when it was that you first experienced pain or experienced some kind of *Depression or psychological lowering of the self.* What did that feel like, and how long did that feeling last?

STEP 2: What kind of person were you before you became depressed? What was that person like? What did she or he like? What did she or he dislike? What were her or his hobbies, interests, and preferences?

STEP 3: Who do you want to become? I am convinced that all of us have a dream or another. Has it been actualized? Maybe not. This can also lead to Depression. Did you know that if you believe, you can become anyone you want? (More on this in my third book). Every person has all the resources inside to actualize all dreams and accomplish anything.

STEP 4: Recognize your own self-worth and respect yourself. Do not allow other people to treat you less than or push you down. Cultivate and develop self-love, self-worth, and self-esteem.

STEP 5: Fully understand that you exist for a reason. You have passion, purpose, and potential, and your life has significant meaning.

STEP 6: Set goals and work towards them. When you are focused and busy, you do not have time to be depressed because you are not wallowing in emotional suffering.

STEP 7: Accept that suffering is a natural part of life and that no one is immune from it. If you are not willing to suffer well, then you are not willing to be human, and part of being human is learning how to suffer well. ***This is called productive suffering.*** For example, if I hadn't learned how to suffer productively, then I would have never received my PhD, never started my own business, and never would have authored this book. I have done and achieved all these things specifically because of my own suffering and Depression. It was "as if" my suffering and Depression where the ingredients I needed to become successful. ***Make suffering your salvation.***

STEP 8: Create a beautiful life with your beautiful mind.

Back in my teenage emo suicide days, I think I was prescribed every anti-depressant under the sun (not all at once, of course) and saw a handful of different therapists. No one or nothing could cure me. No one had the answers I was looking for. I found the answers myself. Because I was desperate to heal and didn't want an 8th suicide attempt, I went to visit a Faith Healer. The Faith Healer gave me a purple stone and told me to hang on to it tightly. She looked at me and saw all these wonderful things inside of me that I hadn't the slightest clue about because I was clouded by my own Depression and misery. She told me that I would go on to live a beautiful life and become highly successful. She told me money would never be an object for me and that I would have lots of friends and love in my life. She told me I would become an author and that my voice and talents would bless and inspire many. All these beautiful things she saw in me, at the time, I hadn't seen within myself, but they did exist inside of me; I just hadn't recognized them yet. How could she see these things that 20 years later have ALL come true? A miracle, isn't it? *It is because this woman filled me with hope and not fear. She focused exclusively on the positive and spoke my future into existence. Her words created such a powerful reality for me that she was able to project me into the future, convincing my subconscious mind that I could and would have all those wonderful things she spoke of. She took time with me and noticed me. She recognized the importance, creativity, intelligence, and potential inside of me, and she spoke it all into existence.*

When I left, I put the purple stone inside of my pant pocket. She told me to carry it around for a week and then release it. I remember crying hysterically the entire way home, as if a huge burden had just been lifted off my shoulders. When I got home, I immediately reached for the purple stone in my pocket, but it wasn't there. I ferociously searched my car, looking everywhere for it, but it was nowhere to be found. It was as if the stone had magically vanished. I became worried and immediately called the Faith Healer telling her what had happened to the stone, and a gentle voice on the other line smiled and said, *"do not worry, my dear, the lost stone means you are already healed."*

And just like that, in a matter of what felt like 60 seconds, 10 years of Depression had been instantly cured, and from that day forward, nearly 20 years ago, I have never suffered from Depression since and never had another suicide attempt, ___all because some perfect stranger saw my value and worth in the world.___

I don't know your story. I don't know if you were born addicted to drugs or if your family was poor and you went to bed hungry at times. I don't know if you were beaten or molested. I don't know what your grades were like or how many boys broke your heart. I don't know what kind of conditions you suffer from or what surgeries you've had. But I do believe it is safe for me to assume that throughout your life you have suffered in many ways. You may or may not have Depression, but even if you don't have Depression, this can still apply to you for those times you do become temporarily depressed. **Depression is a state of mind based on your own perception of your experiences and the external world.** The external, in other words, impacts the internal (your mind). I will tell you, perhaps because of my own suffering and Depression, **I do see the value, worth, and potential in every human being, no matter your background or where you came from.**

It is no coincidence that you are reading this book. Some divine reality brought you to these very words at this specific time in your life. I do not know you personally, and I do not know what you are going through, but I do know that you are a human being. I do know that you were once a little baby born into this world who asked for nothing other than love and acceptance. **You want to feel and know that you matter**—that you are somebody. I know because that is what makes you human. Imagine that I am sitting next to you right now in the room that you are in. Imagine me taking your hands and putting them in mine and looking into your eyes; this is what I would tell you –

"I see you. I hear you. I am listening to you. I see your humanity. I acknowledge your essential personhood. I understand your need to be loved and cared for. I embrace your need to belong and be accepted. And right here, right now, I am speaking into existence a beautiful life for you with a beautiful state of mind / sunshine in your mind. I am speaking into your life health, wealth, happiness, abundance, lots of friends, love, good times, accomplishment, joy, peace, and good fortune. <u>You will have these things. You are these things.</u> Take personal ownership of yourself and your life. You are now in the driver's seat, and you can make the best and most judicious decisions for you. Your Depression now leaves your body. I command its removal from you. Go now in peace; you are whole, and you are healed."

Sister – You are the hero you have been searching for your whole life.

Chapter 3 Takeaways

- In life, there will be situations where you need to play offense and situations where you need to play defense; leverage both to your advantage.
- There is a dragon sleeping inside of you (your **subconscious mind**), waiting to wake up and assist you in achieving your goals.
- **Learned Helplessness** is a tactic taught to women keeping them restricted, oppressed, and unhappy. **The hero you need is yourself.**
- Power is leveraged, helping you gain control in any situation.
- It is important to build strong, secure, and stable self-esteem.
- There are big differences between Narcissism and self-esteem. Do not confuse the two.
- The recognition of your own essential personhood is a step in the right direction toward curing Depression.

Share Your Story:

In the space provided, it is time to share your story. What steps can you take to boost your self-esteem and begin to heal deep wounds?

Chapter 4
Your Magic Zone

"If you give people permission to walk all over you... they will."

Every person is born with a myriad of gifts, many of which are never realized. We spend more time trying to fit in and be like everyone else than we do discovering what our special gifts are. ***We spend more time gossiping about others and judging them, putting all our focus on other people instead of ourselves.*** Can you imagine what would happen if that energy were redirected off other people and put where it belongs, on you? Some would rather waste these gifts. Some would rather spend their entire life chasing men who cannot give them what they really want instead of tapping into their own holy grail of unimaginable greatness.

Whatever it is that you do exceedingly well is your Magic Zone. When you are in your ***Magic Zone,*** you create magic because this is your special power. A power bestowed upon you that not everyone has. Have you tapped into your ***Magic Zone***? What is it that you do exceedingly well? Do you spend all your time serving other people, trying to make them happy instead of focusing on the magic you could be creating?

You have an unlimited number of special skills and talents. Some of them you may be conscious of, and some of them you may not be conscious of. You have no idea just how powerful you are because you let so many people tell you that you are nothing. Why? Why do you listen to naysayers? Why do you care so much about what others think of you? Why do you focus more on other people than on you? ***Why do you allow your dreams to pass you by?***

As children, we formed our earliest values and belief systems, habits, ideals, norms, and behaviors, much of which were taught to us by our parents who shaped our early thought patterns. You think the way your family thinks. And you do not want to stray from that because you do not want them to ostracize you. These values, belief systems, habits, ideals, norms, and behaviors are carried with you into adult life and shape who you are and what you can and cannot do as an adult.

Because you may have been abused and or neglected to a greater or lesser extent in childhood, you spend your adult life chasing validation from others that you never received from your parents. It is like a constant high you are chasing after, always concerned about what someone else is doing or thinking, putting all the attention on them and not you.

The Plight of Women

Women are instructed to be caretakers and nurturers because that is a "woman's role." *Caretaking and nurturing are called human qualities, and NOT feminine qualities.* Men are perfectly capable of being caretakers and nurturers, yet instead, they have been given a get-out-of-jail-free card by society so that they don't have to be burdened with caretaking and nurturing responsibilities in the same manner women are.

It's fascinating how men love their freedom and alone time. Men do not like to be bothered. Men have no problem getting enough sleep, having me time, relaxing and unwinding from a long day, and getting out of daily responsibilities as often as they wish. *While on the other hand women never get to relax.* They constantly move, run, and serve. Many have trouble sleeping, have no peace, have minimal to no me time, have no unwinding, and cannot escape daily responsibilities. *Women and men incessantly punish women.*

Why do the children and husband not help more? Because the woman will do it. She will always pick up the slack even if she works 60 hours per week. A woman's goal in life is to serve and please everyone. **Women are notorious people pleasers.** Women want to make everyone happy and are the glue that keeps the family together. Dr. Barbara DeAngelis, in *Secrets About Men Every Woman Should Know*, discusses how often women fill in the blanks in relationships, "I call what I used to do, and what so many women do, "filling in the emotional blanks" in a relationship. We have a picture in our mind of what we think a good relationship should look like, and we find a man and go about creating that relationship without much participation on his part…the danger in doing this is that we often end up practically having a relationship with ourselves. We work so hard to make the relationship look good that we get tricked into believing it's a mutual creation, when it's a solo performance, and the man has a front-row seat."

Women bend over backward and do backflips to catch and then keep a man. We have been conditioned from the time we were infants that the **acme of existence** for us is to find a man, get married, and have babies. It is ingrained in us. We are pushed and pressured by society and our families to marry and have babies whether we want to or not, whether we are ready to or not. **Whether we will be caring and effective parents or not.**

We spend our whole adult lives desperately searching for a man, worrying ourselves sick at every little detail, and overthinking every interaction with a man because we have this **determined goal to get married.** Then, if it wasn't bad enough already, we must be **chased and won** by a man as if we are a **carnival prize to be won and purchased with a ring, as if we ourselves are a piece of jewelry and not a human.** To have our parents pay for our wedding because, finally, someone has taken us off our parents' hands, so we can live in a cage of perpetual servanthood and self-sacrifice until we find ourselves sitting in front of a therapist or magistrate, wondering why our husbands are cheating on us and no longer find us attractive.

This is what I call the plight of women.

Do you understand what is happening? All the emphasis on the man and no emphasis on ourselves. ***A man will invest all his energies into himself, making him more prone to Narcissism, and a woman will invest all her energies into a man, making her more prone to Depression.***

Ever notice how easily they move on? How fast? While you get stuck with the kids, they can put themselves out there, date, and maintain a social life while you remain in your motherhood cage indefinitely. You spend your entire life cooking, cleaning, managing a household, raising children, managing their lives, raising your husband, managing his life, and you wonder why you have no friends, interests, hobbies, or talents ***of your own***? Why? Why does this happen? Why do we do this to ourselves, gals? ***Let me break it down for you.***

1. ***Social Conditioning:*** Men are taught to become someone and have a career, and women are taught to become wives and mothers, with a career being only optional but not necessary. ***Naturally, the burden falls on the mother because this is where the expectation lies.***

2. ***The Preferred Sex:*** Having a boy has been preferred over having a girl transculturally throughout all of history. We are regarded as less than and weak compared to men. A boy is regarded as superior compared to a girl. Society and religion have given ***all power*** to men as leaders inside and outside of the home. This places women in a secondary or lesser position underneath the authority of a man. Many families prefer to have a boy first and then a girl. Ya hear that, sisters? We are not regarded in the same way as men. Shocking!

3. ***Family Dynamics:*** Many fathers feel distant and detached from their daughters as if they cannot relate to them, so daughters grow up sometimes with neglectful father-figures. This can also happen if the father feels attracted to his daughter. He will specifically distance himself from her to avoid crossing the line, which is a good thing in this context. Mothers typically wallow in their own self-pity, drama, and trauma, and sometimes mothers also ignore and neglect their daughters. This creates a **burning need to be loved and seen** in the daughters. ***Daughters then spend their whole lives chasing men who give them the attention that their parents should have been giving but didn't.***

A woman spends her entire childhood **being reduced**, so she grows up with no to low self-esteem attracting men who have no capacity to love and only care about themselves. This leaves the woman relentlessly trying to win his love and attention, believing that her unending service will eventually render her the love she is desperately seeking but never gains. She plummets further and further into Depression, becoming less and less of a person with all that power and potential just dormant inside of her.

Turning Tables

Sisters, the tables are turning. No more kissing everyone's ass. Wake up and realize you are a full, whole human being with thoughts, feelings, and dreams of your own. It is time to take ownership of your life and discover your **Magic Zone**. Tap into your unlimited power and stop acting like a damn maid. You were not put on this earth just to clean up baby spit, wipe asses, wash dishes, and clean toilet bowls. **You were put on this earth to make it a better place offering your special gifts to others.**

The People Pleasing Peasant

When you spend time cooking and cleaning day in and day out that is time that could be spent working on your dreams and making them come true. Some of you would rather sit in a mommy group, hating on other women spewing negative energy out in the world, because you have been unconsciously informed by society that you are nothing unless you are a wife and mother. It is time to reclaim your personhood, your throne of impact and authority. Only do what you want to do. Your parents have no control over you anymore. ***You are controlling you!*** You are stopping you! ***You are preventing yourself from greatness because you believed the lie that you are never good enough.*** Not being a good enough child, not a good enough student, not good enough in sports, or not being a good enough mother. These become your beliefs, and your beliefs determine your behavior and the way you live your life.

Why We Ascend

If I could summarize life in one single word, I would call it bullshittery. Bullshittery means suffering. We all suffer. Life is hard. There are no easy roads. Each of our Bullshitteries look different, and each of our experiences are unique to us. ***We ascend because Ascension is the ANSWER.*** Descending is not recommended. And staying asleep, although neither bad nor good, isn't the most viable option. When there is pain in your life, all you can do is rise above it. That is why we ascend so that we can transcend our pain and walk in alignment with our highest purpose. Always remain in your ***Magic Zone*** or Zone of Brilliance. Do what you were put on this earth to do. Dr. Scott Peck in *The Road Less Traveled* says, "it is only when one has taken the leap into the unknown of total self-hood, psychological independence, and unique individuality that one is free to proceed along still higher paths of spiritual growth and free to manifest love in its greatest dimensions."

Sister – You are uniquely talented.

Chapter 4 Takeaways

> ➢ Everyone has a **Magic Zone** of infinite talent; tap into yours.
> ➢ Think of how much you could achieve if you stopped cooking, cleaning, and caring for everyone.
> ➢ People pleasing is not the answer to your problems; it has the exact opposite effect.

Share Your Story:

In the space provided, it is time to share your story. What are your unique talents, skills, and gifts?

Chapter 5
Slow Ya Roll – The Power of Patience

"Patience is something you need all the time in every situation."

Everyone knows we live in a society of instant gratification. Most of life is arguably painful. We will spend more time being uncomfortable and downcast in life because humans have a negative proclivity, and negativity is all around us in various forms. ***We desire instant gratification because we seek to consistently lessen the uncomfortableness we feel. We run toward pleasure and run away from pain; that is what we do.*** I am convinced we will experience far more pain in life than pleasure. Instant gratification is a slippery slope to self-destruction. Instant gratification looks shiny and bright on the outside, but on the inside, it's ugly and painful. ***Instant gratification is a band-aid. It does not solve any real problems you struggle with.*** It is a temporary fix. Instead of chasing instant gratification, use that energy instead to solve the ***real problems*** in your life. ***Delay gratification, a concept I will introduce called Deprivation.***

Plan for the Future, but Live in the Present

We live in the present but should always consider the bigger picture in life, the long-term effects, and not the short-term gains or losses. If I had to guess, I would say that no one likes being patient. ***Being patient is not a comfortable state of mind.*** Being patient can be downright painful. ***However, in patience is significant power.*** Patience is the ability to give up control, allowing the natural flow of things to fall in order. ***When we stop trying to control everyone and everything in our lives, we open ourselves up to receive an abundance of blessings.*** When we give up control, we are truly ready to receive all that is coming to us. ***Much good is coming our way if we are simply prepared to receive it.*** We cannot receive all the good if we are incessantly chasing our next fix, whatever that "fix" is for us. For some, it's drugs and alcohol, others sex and or porn, others relationships and or romance; for others it could be adventures and or risky activities. We all have something or someone we want. ***We all have an insatiable desire for something or someone. This keeps us hungry for more.***

After Kelly's divorce, she had a burning desire to rush into another relationship asap. She didn't know how to be alone, and she was not good at being alone. She had a natural propensity to catch another man as quickly and painlessly as possible. Having been with her ex-husband for ten years, she had no idea how to date. Everyone rushed into everything. This is what society conditions us to do because society wants us not to be fully evolved human beings. When Kelly asked her guy friend for dating advice after her divorce, he gave her the best dating advice she had ever received, and that was to ***"slow ya roll."*** Slow down. Breathe. Slow down and appreciate life. Keep things light and fluffy. However, because Kelly was conditioned to get married and have children, her subconscious mind was telling her rush into the next relationship as quickly as possible because her only worth as a woman is being someone's wife and mother. I don't know who needs to hear this today but ***slow ya damn roll.***

Kelly did date after her divorce, but only casually. It took 18 months post-divorce before she got into another relationship. She took those months to heal. ***She learned how to be alone, appreciate it, and like it.*** Kelly mastered being alone and loved every minute of it. She unf*cked herself from society's conditioning of her self-worth and the value she brings to the world. During those 18 months, she experienced a complete transformation into her highest potential and most potent personhood. Understand that haste makes waste. **Nothing worthwhile is achieved or gained overnight.** This is why we live in a here today gone tomorrow society- nothing feels sustainable **because no one is willing to be patient.**

Become what I call **perpetually patient. What this means is that you will never have the luxury of not having to be patient anymore**. Live in a state of patience for the rest of your life. **Patience is continual, ongoing, and perpetual.** You will never receive the carrot dangling in front of your face because **something** will always be dangling in front of your face. Even when you do receive what you want, there will be other things that you must be patient with. **Bask in limitless patience**, my darling. **Revel in your own misery of discomfort.** Learn to be uncomfortable and learn to relish pain. **Massive healing happens when you allow yourself to wallow in your own pain.** You will fight like all hell overcoming everything in your life because it will not be easy. Nothing worth gaining is ever achieved without considerable effort and resistance. **You can either master patience or allow impatience to master you.**

Patience is something you master. No one is naturally born with patience; patience comes naturally to no one. Patience is part of your personal development and revolution as a fully evolved human being. Rushing leads to inevitable destruction, whereas patience leads to lasting results and benefits. **There is power in patience.** Learn to delay gratification. The best things in life are worth the wait. **First praying, then waiting, and then gaining in that order.** Remember, life is all about strategy. **Those without a solid strategy and game plan will always lose. Winners have a slow, patient, and sustainable strategy that will beat their opponents.** Always **slither like a snake**. Snakes are patient and strategic; they wait for the perfect opportunity to strike and **slither slowly** so as not to be noticed.

When we master patience, we allow good things to naturally enter our lives. We are no longer forcing and manipulating to get what we want. When things are forced, they are not enjoyable, like sex, for example. You cannot force good sex. Sex is either good or not; there is either sexual bonding and chemistry or nothing at all. You cannot force good sex; similarly, you cannot force and manipulate situations to get the outcomes you want, but you can work toward them. *Action is more sustainable than force.* If you want to do or achieve something, then act, but don't force things to happen; allow them to happen organically for you. *Life is all about learning, mistakes, and experiences.* At the end of the day, you want more wins than losses; you want more successes than failures. You want more joy than sorrow. You cannot be out there winging it.

Patience is a Virtue

We have all heard that *Patience is a Virtue,* but do we really understand what this means? Since we know the definition of patience, let's explore the definition of virtue. According to the dictionary definition of virtue, virtue means "of moral excellence and righteousness." Arguably, moral superiority. *A rectitude of calm and faith.* The adage *Patience is a Virtue* means the ability to wait in stillness for something without becoming unsettled. *To live free from the anxiety of the unknown.* Stillness and unknown are keywords here. Most of us are not still. Most loathe *the unknown.* We like knowing what's coming next. We like knowing WHAT TO EXPECT. *There is ONLY ONE thing we should expect, and that IS THE UNEXPECTED. Uncertainty is a natural part of life, and you should embrace it.* <u>*The only certainty we have in life is uncertainty.*</u>

DO NOT EXPECT ANYTHING IN LIFE....EXCEPT....FOR THE UNEXPECTED.

Life is very much here today and gone tomorrow. As much as we try to hold on to things and people, we cannot. We try to hold on to relationships, jobs, possessions, obsessions, addictions, and all kinds of other things. But we should not. *We should free ourselves. We should let go.* BUT WE HOLD ON. *We endlessly hope for the hopeless. We endlessly fix the unfixable.*

LET GO – easier said than done, I will be the first to admit. But let go. *It is okay NOT to HAVE what you so desperately want. It is okay.*

FREEDOM – letting go frees us. Holding on imprisons us, catapulting us into the *Abyss of Misery.*

Divine Love

I am going to presume that all of us want what I call *Divine Love.* I am also going to presume that women and men crave *Divine Love* equally. This is not just a woman thing. *Divine Love* embodies several components; let's define each.

Physical Captivity – we are initially attracted to physical or outward appearance. Men and women equally. It is difficult to have sex with someone that you do not find physically attractive; it can be done, but it is not as satisfying. *We are all attracted to beauty.* Beauty is how a person looks. *We want to feel the butterflies for someone. We all want to fall in love and become emotionally captive by someone.* This is what most of us think *Divine Love* is. This act of falling in love and being psychologically obsessed with another. *We all just want to f*cking matter to someone.*

Sexual Connection – *sex is the acme of life; without the act of sex, none of us would be here.* Sex is as necessary as eating and sleeping. As humans, we connect through sex, and it should provide a means of *emotional nurturance* in a perfect world.

Emotional Connection – the ability to open, share, express, and speak freely without judgment or condemnation. The ability to be one's unapologetic self in the presence of another. To be seen, heard, and listened to deeply, fully, and completely. *It is to feel as if you are a human being, and it is perfectly okay to have needs without manipulation and game-playing.*

Whimsy – the ability to be careless and spontaneous. To enjoy life for what it is with your partner, *to dance around in fields of gold with fire in your soul.* To be engaged, delighted, and elevated in a myriad of activities both mutually experienced with your person.

Safety – an internal and external sense of security. To fully know that you are needed, wanted, and desired. You could never do anything to mitigate your person's love and commitment.

Freedom in Choice – that you are an active and conscious participant in choosing Divine committed love. You are not bound by commitment or obligation but instead freely choose to love, cherish, behold, and give to your person without bitterness, resentment, fear, and anxiety.

This is the embodiment of the kind of love each of us wants, but only a few of us have. What prevents us from having this kind of love? Two words: *selfishness and (loss of being in) control.*

As a hopeless romantic myself, there is nothing I want more than this **Divine Love,** and I know for a fact that I deserve nothing less because this is the kind of love I give. Every man wants the kind of love I give. BUT is he equally willing to give me the kind of love I give? You also give good love, but do you receive it in return?

Is there a Cure for the Heebie-jeebies / Collywobbles?

When I fall head over heels in love, I experience what I call the *Heebie-jeebies* and *Collywobbles*. These two words mean the same thing. I equally love both words. **This is the feeling of existential goosebumps raging with sexual and emotional tension. It instills an instant sense of panic and produces clutchy behaviors.** Systemically pushing away exactly what we want the most. I am not someone who falls in love often, but when I do fall, I fall so hard and so fast. With Jordan, it was love at first sight, and my first thought upon meeting him in person was, **"This guy is way too good-looking for me; he will never like me the way I like him."** This was my first thought! **This was a major limiting belief. Stemming from my own subconscious unworthiness.** When we acquire the collywobbles, our thoughts of "not being good enough" begin to surface, and so we start bending over-backward proving our worthiness and good enoughness to the other person. We begin to unconsciously exhibit "wifely and clutchy behavior," **which is the beginning of our relationship's downfall.** We work hard proving ourselves by showing off and winning the person of our lusty desires. We dress to kill, we fervently clean our homes, we make the most complicated dinners, we give too much, love too much, accommodate too much, and eradicate our own uniqueness becoming the version of ourselves that he most prefers or what we believe he most prefers if we do not directly know what he prefers us to be.

We put ourselves through a physical and psychological shapeshifting, becoming exactly what the man wants us to become, completely losing our unique and individual sense of self. We lose ourselves and become an extension of him **because of the collywobbles.** The collywobbles make us attach to him. When I was with Jordan, I used to clean his apartment all the time without him asking and buy him stuff he needed, such as hand towels and dish soap. I should never **have done**

any of that. It triggers a man's commitment phobia. He picks up the clue that we are trying to prove our worthiness as potential wives, and his internal alarm system goes off, and he gets scared. ***Our noble behavior and good intentions make him feel suffocated and trapped in the relationship.*** They have the EXACT OPPOSITE effect that they should have. ***If someone buys us gifts, replenishes basic household supplies, cleans our apartments, or makes us chicken noodle soup when we are sick, we should feel grateful and loving toward that person, but that doesn't work on men. For men, it makes them feel like you are giving and loving too much, which in turn makes them repel you, and thus, their confusing and contradictory behavior wounds you deeply.***

I was so nervous around Jordan that I would sweat and shake. I wanted him so badly that the anxiety paralyzed me. I was in ***emotional paralysis***. The inability to contain oneself reasonably and controllably. My emotions were getting the best of me and controlling my behaviors and interactions with Jordan. I just wasn't used to falling so hard for someone, so I didn't know how to act normally. I was subconsciously pushing him away because I didn't know any better. ***I wasn't armed with the knowledge that I am armed with now.***

Save Something for the Next Time, A Now and Later Kind of Woman

My grandpa used to have this saying, ***save something for the next time,*** and it always made me think of the candy, ***Now and Later.*** I used to love those as a kid and would eat one now and then another one later. ***This is how patience works.*** You get some blessings and good times now, and then you save some for later. ***As humans, we have an insatiable desire for the things we want and value.***

Think of it this way. You finally meet a great man, and you want to spend every second with him or, at the very least, the whole weekend with him every weekend. But too much of a good thing becomes a bad thing, and familiarity breeds contempt and complacency. **Your objective with men is to become _a Now and Later kind of woman._** Give him some now, then remove yourself from the situation and come back later and give him some more. Attraction and desire are built in space (distance). **_Make yourself scarce and valuable._** You have a full whole life, and he is only one slice of the pie in your full whole life. He is NOT, nor should he be, the entire pie.

Do not spend every day with him, and do not spend every weekend with him. Seeing him once a week when the relationship is new is more than enough – allow time spent to grow with time. **_Save something for the next time._ _Do not take all the satisfaction and happiness right now, leaving no room for the relationship to grow and expand down the line. Relationships grow with time and space._** Haste makes waste, and slow and steady wins the race – lock these two sayings into your head and say them over and repeatedly.

Men move impulsively fast in a relationship if they like you. **_They do not think at all._** They act on impulsive emotions. They favor crash-and-burn relationships that do not last and are not sustainable. **YOU must be the brain FOR THEM.** Do NOT think they are leading you. Yes, they are leading you; they are leading you right into the **Abyss of Misery, aka emotional hell.**

Always always always stretch out your happiness – save something for the next time. You are a **Now and Later,** an effervescent, timeless, emotionally grounded, logical, riveting woman deserving of high-class and high-quality everything life has to offer you.

Heebie-jeebies / Anxiety

I have wrestled with this so much: how to cure myself of the Collywobbles for someone I like. This feeling of anxiety is crippling and paralyzing. It makes me feel immobile harnessing its grip on me. BUT if there is a will, remember there is a way.

I punished myself endlessly over Jordan. I fell so hard for him and begged and pleaded with God to remove my feelings for him, but feelings did remain for a long time. I needed to feel this gut-wrenching, heart-wrenching, **PSYCHOLOGICALLY TORMENTING PAIN.** There is a way to naturally get over someone. Now, if you are ANYTHING like me, I suffer from my own **Cycle of Chaos**, my own **Abyss of Misery**. That is why I cannot get over Person A without falling in love with Person B. It takes falling in love with someone else to get completely over the previous person. **What this suggests is that I am perpetually in love.** I am always in love WITH SOMEONE. Without fail. Oh, how I wish I could be in love with no one – wouldn't that be bliss? I could just focus all my mental and emotional faculties on myself and my goals. But I am who I am; I feel how I feel, **and I accept myself for the way I am.**

My pain was necessary. If I didn't feel deeply, I know I wouldn't be a writer. **I write from a sacred place of pain and passion.** I write from the heart. I connect deeply with my reader because I know I am not the only woman in the world who feels the way I do. I am willing to bet that most of what I discuss in my books can resonate with you to a greater or lesser degree.

Here are steps to getting over someone and removing the anxiety you feel about them:

STEP 1: Understand that it is perfectly okay to love and love well. There is no crime in loving who you love. **To love is to live, and without love, there is no life.**

STEP 2: Own, accept, and embrace your feelings. Do not suppress what you feel. Allow those feelings to permeate your body.

STEP 3: Heal your insecurities. The collywobbles come from having an *Anxious Pre-Occupied Attachment Style*. You like the said person so much that you are petrified and (expect) them to leave you at any moment since you *have a significant fear of abandonment*.

STEP 4: Stop abandoning yourself. You must change now. You cannot live the rest of your life as *an insecure, abandoned woman*. Yes, your parents abandoned you, yes, ex-boyfriends abandoned you, *but by golly, do not abandon yourself.*

STEP 5: Let go. You will not die without romantic love. Love is all around you. Let go of whatever is plaguing you. I know this is far easier said than done but remember that your life can and will be full and rich, with or without a partner.

Gifts

Life wants to bless you abundantly. Life wants to pour miracles and gifts into your life. Small and large treasures are both tangible and intangible. I suffer from love addiction and abandonment issues, so I embrace all gifts involving love. I embrace the love gifts of Jordan and Asher because I would have rather had those experiences than not have had them. Gifts and blessings are all around you. Look for them and be open to receiving them. Open your hands up in a receiving motion and receive all the abundance of the world. Never limit yourself. *Expect good things to happen and come for you.* Be grounded and be blessed, dear sister. Women love so hard. There is nothing wrong with loving hard or well. Love is all around you like a river flowing from and back into you. Embrace love for all that it is and embody a loving and gracious presence.

Final Words on Patience

Patience isn't pretty. It is not fun. But it is a virtue. It is a noble and diplomatic pursuit of embodiment. To embody a calm, still, and patient presence. To own your own power through patience. Nothing worth having is given easily or quickly. This is why rushing into relationships doesn't work. Control the pace. Understand that patience is perpetual, and you will never have the luxury of NOT having to be patient anymore. You will always have to be patient. You will always be waiting for whatever the next thing is for you. Learn this level of quiet, stillness, and self-mastery. Learn that it is okay to be without and *learn that it is empowering to be deprived.* I want more than anything to find my person. All the success and accolades in the world will not replace sharing my life with a special someone. But I too, must be patient in complete and total faith. *I am deprived of romantic love, but I do not deprive myself of love.* I am open to receive *Divine Love.* I know there is someone special out there for me, just as there is someone special out there for you, too.

Sister – You possess infinite patience.

Chapter 5 Takeaways

- ➢ There is power in patience.
- ➢ Patience is perpetual. You will never have the luxury of not being patient anymore.
- ➢ Crash and burn relationships are never successful; as they say, "only fools rush in."
- ➢ It is okay to love and love well. Love is all around you.

Share Your Story:

In the space provided, it is time to share your story. Have you ever had a relationship end abruptly because it started fast? What happened? What did you learn? What will you do differently next time?

Chapter 6
The Fight of Your Life

Overcoming Anxious Preoccupied Attachment Style

"Abandonment of the self is the worst type of abandonment."

The worse I feel inside, the better my writing. I know I produce my best writing when I feel the most like shit. And right now, I feel like shit, so buckle up. If I could describe the emotions I feel at this very moment when writing these very words, they are scared, fearful, and insecure. I am the **Queen of Insecurity**. Why do I feel insecure? I have been dating a new guy for two months now, and things are going incredibly well between us. Things are moving forward, but he hasn't texted me all day, and it is 7:26 p.m. Ugh. Feeling all the feels. And I only feel this way because I *like-like* this man, which is rare for me because it takes a lot for me to *like-like* a guy. Dr. Scott Peck, author of *The Road Less Traveled*, was an instrumental author in helping me finally overcome my insecurities. He says in his renown book, *The Road Less Traveled* (which I highly recommend you read), "the only real security in life lies in relishing life's insecurity." ***Make your insecurities your security because insecurity is the only security any of us really have.***

Where Attachment Styles Come From

Anxious Attachment Style develops in childhood in a relationship with your parents when their love for you is not given either consistently or regularly enough because, let's be honest, parents are busy with their own lives and have their own needs and cannot love on their children 24/7 in the way that child needs and craves love. Women tend to run toward men (anxious or activating behaviors), and men, for similar reasons, tend to run away from women (avoidant or deactivating behaviors). ***The social conditioning of women molds them into becoming anxious, and the social conditioning of men molds them into becoming avoidant.*** Men can be anxious, and women can be avoidant, but the ***most common pattern is the anxious woman and the avoidant man.*** In *Bad Boyfriends* by Jeb Kinnison, he has this to say about the Anxious-Preoccupied Attachment Style: "People of the anxious-preoccupied type (who we will call the Preoccupied) are the third-largest attachment type group, at about 20% of the population. Because their early attachment needs were unsatisfied or inconsistently satisfied, they crave intimacy but tend to feel doubtful about their own worth, making it harder for them to trust that they are loved and cared for. At the extremes, and with a more secure or dismissive partner, they are viewed as "needy" or "clingy and can drive others away by their demands for attention. Many have never been able to come to terms with memories of parental failures."

Women historically lean more anxious, and men lean more avoidant. The reverse can be true: men can be anxious, and women can be avoidant. ***However, the most common pairing is the anxious woman and the avoidant man.*** *This is a crucial point in this book.* Remember this. ***This is why women are far more likely to get emotionally abandoned compared to men (not that the reverse isn't true, but it is more common for a man to abandon a woman than vice versa).*** When a man is pursuing you and thus "into you," he is operating from a place of anxiety or a need to **get you / capture you.** Any resistance you give him will flare up his anxiety even more. ***<u>This anxiety or tension is how men fall in love.</u> Keep them in this anxious or tense state to keep them into you. <u>Once they lose their anxiety for you, often with it goes their love.</u>***

When a relationship first begins, the man/pursuer is anxiously chasing the woman, and she is resisting him (she is avoidant); then he finally "wins" her over and gets her to fall in love with him; once she does it is game over for her because the roles switch, she then becomes the anxious one, and he becomes the avoidant. There must be this balance in a relationship. You can't really have two avoidants or two anxious. The key to any relationship with a man *IS TO ALWAYS BE THE AVOIDANT PERSON* and never the anxious one. *As soon as he detects that anxiety in you, he's running away to Africa.* This is the precise psychology behind the chase. And why men are incessantly chasing women. They love the "high" feelings or anxiety that the heebie-jeebies over someone gives them. They want to feel "crazy" about you. *But in most cases, the reverse is true, which is why women have been perpetually hurt and emotionally destroyed by men.*

More Than Anything

I write this paragraph with tears in my eyes now. More than anything else in the world, I want a loving, supportive, giving, caring, and reciprocal relationship with my "special person." I am on my knees praying that my current boyfriend is the person for me, but we've only been together for two months, so it is way too early to tell. If you read my first book, *GIRL GRIT: SAVAGE NOT AVERAGE,* I was single the whole time I authored it, but now, writing *GIRL GAME: BALLS OUT,* I have begun this new relationship, and in summation, it is going super well, and I am so afraid of f*cking it up, why? *Because I am so f*cking insecure, that's why.* I cannot help but be honest because I am sure there are a plethora of women reading these very words who know exactly what I am talking about and understand exactly how I feel right now. I wasn't planning on writing tonight, but because I feel this way right now, I knew I wanted my emotions to be authentic for you. I know damn well you can relate, and I know damn well my words bring comfort to your soul this very second because empathy is the thread of support weaving our humanity together. *More than anything, I want to feel fully secure. More than anything, I want to be fully loved,* *respected, and accepted. More than anything, I just want to be held. I just want to f*cking matter to someone.*

You'll Fight Like All Hell

As you are fighting to overcome your insecurities, you will fight like all hell. You will fight the fight of your life, and it will be rotten to the core, but every day, you will improve, and every day, you will get better and overcome more. I have made noteworthy progress at overcoming my insecurities with love and men, but I still fight every day.

With ***Anxious Attachment Style***, you feel like you could be discarded at any moment. Other characteristics of this attachment style include emotional discomfort, avoidance of being alone, fear of abandonment (huge one for me), feeling unworthy of love, always needing external validation, intense desire for intimacy, feeling jealous, people-pleasing, low self-esteem, sensitivity to the behaviors and words of others, tolerance of unhealthy behaviors and relationships, co-dependency, needing constant contact (texts or calls at regular intervals), constant need for reassurance, hypersensitivity to rejection, negative view of self, difficulty setting boundaries, emotionally reactive, overanalyzing every interaction or non-interaction, and overthinking everything. Sounds fun, doesn't it?

It is a horrible existence to say the least. When a child's emotional needs are left unmet, a child will develop ***Anxious Attachment Style.*** I am willing to bet that at least most women (I do not want to speak for men since their experiences are different) have this attachment style, hence why women are known to be notoriously overemotional, clingy, needy, and desperate. If you are not like this, then you know a woman in your life who is. This is why I call ***overcoming insecurities the fight of your life.*** I feel as if I have been locked in a cage with no key in sight, and I am banging and yanking like all hell to break free from the prison of my own insecurities.

Attached by Amir Lavine and Rachel S.F. Heller is an exceptional and well-respected resource on **Attachment Theory**. For the **Anxiously Attached** individual, we often feel like we are on an emotional roller coaster within our romantic relationships coupled with highs and lows and lots of mixed signals, "every time you get mixed messages, your attachment system is activated, and you become preoccupied with the relationship… you now live in suspense, anticipating that next small remark or gesture that will reassure you. After living like this for a while, you start to do something interesting. You start to equate the anxiety, the preoccupation, the obsession, and those ever-so-short bursts of joy with love. What you're really doing is equating an activated attachment system with passion." The authors go on to explain activating versus deactivating strategies for intimacy and passion. Avoidants will deactivate, while Anxious will activate. ***If you want to make a man crazy over you, you must learn how to activate his attachment system. <u>You can do this simply by not giving a f*ck about him.</u>***

I have massive fears of abandonment. Massive. I grew up with no self-esteem, not low-self-esteem, no self-esteem. I overthink and overanalyze everything. I default to negative and worst-case-scenario thinking. It is now 748pm, and my boyfriend still hasn't texted me – what could be the reason? Instead of throwing myself onto my bed crying my eyes out like a scared little girl, I decided to write this chapter of this book and hopefully help millions of scared little girls out there who are DYING inside just to be held and loved. In **GIRL GRIT: SAVAGE NOT AVERAGE,** Chapter 1, I discuss how the need to be loved is our greatest emotional need of all time. ***How many little girls and big girls are moving through life totally sad, afraid, insecure, and lonely?***

If I can offer any encouragement to either of us, I would say this fear and this insecurity just lives in our heads. A man not texting you for a day is not the worst thing in the world, far from it. I am making a much bigger deal out of this situation than is necessary. I sit here completely freaking out emotionally that my boyfriend hasn't texted me all day. Rewind to 48 hours ago, when we were together in person, and everything was fine. He met some of my friends for the first time and had a great time. He told them we were together and discussed things he wanted to do with me this summer. Why am I freaking the f*ck out about one small insignificant incident? **Why do I torture myself so badly?** Why? Because there is a little girl still inside of me crying, begging anyone to love her, begging anyone to hold her, listen to her, just to be held, *just to f*cking matter to someone.*

I needed to heal that little girl; I needed to nurture her, and I needed to give her the love she never got before. **You will never have a good relationship with anyone if you don't first have a good relationship with yourself.** Every day, I fight, but every day I do improve. I must remain on the **Positivity Train** no matter what. *Before I came home from my walk to write this very chapter, I spoke these words to myself out loud:*

You are an amazing person.
You are a great woman.
Anyone would be blessed to have you as his girl.
You have so much to give and offer anyone.
You have so much love to give.
You are beautiful inside and out.
You are worthy and deserve love.
You deserve respect.
You deserve a supportive and reciprocal relationship.
You deserve happiness.
You deserve success.

Learning to love and accept myself was the greatest lesson I ever learned. I hated myself as a kid. I had my first thoughts of suicide at **seven years old**. I just felt like I didn't matter, and no one would care if I died. I felt like nothing. For too many years, I beat myself up living a self-defeating, self-loathing life, feeling unworthy of everyone and everything.

And amidst it all, I can be so damn confused when it comes to modern dating in 2023. Dating isn't what it used to be, so the same rules do not apply. I don't know about you, but I was raised with men being in perpetual control of everyone and everything. For example, the words of wisdom I was taught include, "let him chase you, let him pursue you, let him call you, let him text you, men like a chase, men are the hunters. If he doesn't call you, don't call him, don't chase him, play hard to get, be a mystery, don't respond right away." And you know what all of this feels like to me? **One big giant game!** That's right, dating is **one big giant f*cking game**!

Someone please tell me why we are giving men all the power and control when it comes to dating. Why are men the "chasers" and "pursuers"? Why do men like "hard to get?" Why do we have to be "a mystery?" Why do men get to make all the moves and call all the shots? Oh, that's right, we live in the patriarchy where women are nothing. Women are less than "un-persons." Picture this:

He makes the first move.
He asks for her number.
He invites her on a date.
He pays for the date.
He makes the first sexual move.

She's supposed to resist sex, or she's "too easy," and he won't "like that."

He's supposed to propose to her. **He's supposed to buy her with the ring.**

A woman cannot initiate a marriage. Only a man can (but women are more likely to initiate divorce; funny how that works out, huh?) …

I just look at all of this and think, "Wow, this is so f*cked up." We give ALL RELATIONSHIP POWER to the man. Sadly. We women must sit back, kick back, and wait (and pray) to be chosen, to be worthy enough and good enough. **And we wonder why our self-esteem is so messed up.** We wonder why we struggle to move ourselves. **We wonder why we are so damn insecure.** Why we feel like we are nothing without a relationship. Why do we put all our emotional eggs in a man's basket? Are you starting to see the problem now?

Parents have issues. Parents are insecure. Parents fight emotional battles. **A great many parents were abused and neglected by their own parents.** Parents have children when they are themselves unhealed, burdened, and struggle with abandonment issues. When you have so many issues of your own, it is so difficult to love your own child and tend to their emotional needs.

Pushy Patty, Desperate Debbie, Needy Nancy, and Anxious Annie.

A woman's four worst enemies are **Pushy Patty, Desperate Debbie, Needy Nancy, and Anxious Annie**. A great majority of us women have befriended these four women and have allowed them to penetrate our souls. Think of times (in relation to men specifically) when you acted like **Pushy Patty, Desperate Debbie, Needy Nancy, and Anxious Annie**. If you have an **Anxious Preoccupied Attachment Style,** then you should be familiar with these women, especially Anxious Annie, who makes you feel anxious in your romantic relationships with men. Pushy Patty is a chaser. She is a pursuer. She chases men. A big no-no, right? Not only does she chase men, but she is also pushy about it. Pushy means forceful, in a hurry, in a rush to make things happen and get her way. In fact, Pushy Patty is so pushy that she pushes men away. No man finds Pushy Patty attractive. **No one is attractive when they are pushy. Pushy Patty doesn't even like herself.**

Desperate Debbie, on the other hand, is desperate for a man. She just wants someone to choose her finally. She will do anything to catch a man as quickly and painlessly as possible. **Her desperation is unattractive.** Men do not like desperate women. Desperation is unattractive in general. Desperate Debbie grew up with the belief that she would be an insignificant and incomplete human being if she did not get a man.

Needy Nancy is very insecure. She needs incessant external validation and reassurance from everyone outside of her. **She has no internal backbone of security.** Her security comes in spurts in those little moments when someone does validate or reassure her, but those little moments are short-lived because that old familiar feeling of insecurity always creeps back in eventually.

Unfriend these women. Block them. Cancel them. They are not your friends. They are your enemies, and they will stab you in the back. They do not bring light and life to you. They do not enhance your life and make it more complete. They limit you, reduce you, cripple you, and sabotage you. You must DECIDE to block and unfriend them now. YOU CAN DECIDE TO CHANGE. YOU CAN CHANGE. **BE WILLING TO FIGHT LIKE ALL HELL BECAUSE IT WILL NOT COME NATURAL TO YOU. It will not be easy for you.**

Start Holding

I have a daughter, and I have struggled to nurture her. I have struggled to nurture her because I was battling my own insecurities, which made attending to my daughter's emotional needs hard for me. I was suffering so badly myself. There would be nights I would just hold her close as she slept while I wasn't holding onto anything at all except for the invisible hand of God. The good news is that I am self-aware enough to recognize my weakness and struggle in nurturing my daughter in the way she needs and deserves to be nurtured. This was not easy for me to overcome, but I did recognize it, nonetheless. I accepted how I was and made a very **conscious decision** to do something about it and to do better because I knew better. I held her, I just held her. I stopped consuming myself by trying to be the perfect parent or trying to run her around to all these different sports and activities, and instead, I just held her. *I just held her when I had nothing to hold onto or no one to hold me; I just held my daughter, knowing in my heart of hearts that the greatest need any of us have is simply to be loved and to be loved well. To just f*cking matter in the world.*

What to Do

When you are in the cage fighting like all hell to overcome your insecurities, just love yourself. Hold her. Nurture her. Give her exactly what she needs at that moment. Know just how precious and worthy she is. A beautiful baby girl who has been through hell and back in her life, who has weathered all the storms, a little child with a heart of gold, so loving, so forgiving, just wanting to live and live well. Baby girl, please keep fighting. Fight for yourself. Fight with me because I am fighting like all hell right now, all hell. When my mind jumps on the **Negativity Train** with worst-case scenario thinking, I must choose to switch to the **Positivity Train** and say I deserve the best love in the world. I deserve the world. I am deserving of all love. I fear being discarded by my new boyfriend with whom I am deeply in love. That old familiar feeling of being less than not good enough. But remember that it is them and not you. You are worthy of all the love, and you deserve healing from your insecurities. *It is a battle you will continue to fight until your brain finally believes that, yes, you are fully worthy and deserving of the most divine love known to humankind.*

Go hug that baby girl still living inside of you. Go mommy her right now. Tell her how awesome she is. How powerful, radiant, magnetic, seraphic, and ascend child. This is your life. This is my life. **With or without a man, life is worth living.** With or without a man, life is wonderful. With or without a man, you are so dearly loved. With or without a man, you matter to the world. And with or without a man, you will move mountains in your own life and the lives of others. **With or without a man, you matter, dear sister.**

As I close this chapter, I pray you find a healing love. I pray you overcome your deepest, darkest demons. I pray this book gives you the answers you are desperately seeking. I pray you feel less insecure. I pray you will give yourself the love your parents were not capable of giving to you. And in my hour of sorrow, my weakest, my most vulnerable place, I hope you understand just how deep this pain runs but that this too shall pass, and we should always expect the unexpected. ***As you heal yourself, the world will heal little by little as well.***

The Outcome

I had nothing to be insecure about. I went out with my good friend for karaoke to try and take my mind off my boyfriend not texting me for **three days**. Although my heart was aching, I still needed to live my life. *I couldn't let this boy become the center of my existence.* I have other friends and hobbies that I enjoy. I went to karaoke with a good friend, and we talked and sang together. Later that evening, around 1015pm, I missed Jordan. I went into our message thread and typed "Jjj" by accident and accidentally sent it! I did not mean to send Jordan a text that night, especially a goofy drunk text with just the letters "Jjj." I was so embarrassed that I sent another text right afterward and said, "I am so so sorry that was a boo-boo." He read the text immediately. And he replied immediately with "Jjj," and I responded with a ? and he responded immediately and said, "just kidding, how are you doing?" From there, we exchanged a handful of nice texts, talking about our work week and catching up. *I immediately felt better; I had the reassurance I needed.*

I slept well that night; no more anxiety over him. His text messages were kind and considerate. I decided without delay that my *outmoded beliefs* were no longer serving me. In fact, they were hurting me. Terribly. No more bullshit. Let him make all the moves, let him do all the chasing, be a mystery, play hard to get, and play all the blah blah mind games. I knew these beliefs were no longer serving me because they made me feel weak, insecure, and most unfortunately, an un-person. Like I was some deer to be chased, hunted, and captured by a man. Prey. F*ck that. *Archaic beliefs do not serve us in a modern egalitarian world.*

I know it is okay for me to text him first and or reach out first if I am not doing it all the time. I know it is okay for me to chase him a little. *There is a healthy balance of relationships.* Don't call or text him all the time, but don't be afraid to call or text him either. It is okay to have balance and initiate contact some of the time. I told myself I would reach out the following day and invite him over for dinner, and I did that. *Relationships are all about reciprocity. No reciprocity, no relationship.*

He responded after work and said, "what time," and that he had stuff to do but would try and make it work. It was a Friday, and we both got up early for work on Fridays, so he called me that evening at 730pm and said he couldn't come over because it was getting late, and he wouldn't make it over until 9 pm. He was tired, and it was okay with me because I was tired too. He was kind on the phone and asked me what I was doing on Sunday. We made plans for Sunday. I planned on taking my daughter to the Lego Fest, and I invited him to join us. *He said yes immediately*, which shocked me because I didn't know if he would be willing or wanting to join my daughter and I for a kid activity.

When Jordan was okay with going to Lego Fest, it meant the world to me. Jordan came and had a blast with us. My daughter absolutely loves him, and he is good with her. He pays attention to her and talks to her, making her feel seen, heard, and listened to. He's engaged and was taking photos with us. After Lego Fest, I dropped my daughter off with her dad and went back to Jordan's apartment. He made me dinner, rubbed my feet, gave me attention and head kisses. We talked for hours just enjoying each other's company.

Up until that point, I let myself get massively carried away because of my own conditioning. I jumped on the *Negativity Train* based on references (past experiences) where I had gotten hurt, and then I compared apples to oranges. *Do not ever compare apples to oranges.* Do not base current events on events that happened in the past. New day, new drama, new people, new circumstances, don't punish yourself like that. This is why it is so important to be secure in who you are taking action to heal your insecurities. I discussed actionable steps to heal insecurities in my first book, *GIRL GRIT: SAVAGE NOT AVERAGE.* Jordan is different in every way. Jordan does not love bomb me. Jordan does not regard me as an object or as less than men. Jordan is not misogynistic. Jordan is accepting, loving, attentive, caring, and considerate. This is unfortunately not what I am used to, so my mind went to the worst-case scenario thinking. *I needed to unlearn and relearn what love is.* What healthy love looks like.

It was perfectly OKAY for me to text Jordan and initiate a date. I didn't need to be insecure, *waiting by the phone*, endlessly nervous for him to text me. ***It is okay to be human and demand that other people treat you as such.*** Dating is so much work for hardly any return. I am thoroughly convinced that dating and marriage punish women, yet we all desire commitment so badly. *What is it that we want?*

Later that night, when I got home, I sobbed uncontrollably for two full hours blowing my nose into tissue after tissue. The fact that Jordan came to Lego Fest with us had me ugly crying for two hours straight. This gesture touched me in a way I had not been touched before. It felt like I ***just f*cking mattered to someone.***

Blowing out the Flame

My intuition is stronger than I'd like to admit. I was insecure because deep in my subconscious, I knew Jordan would abandon me, and he did. It became a self-fulfilling prophecy. One Sunday, out of the blue, no one saw it coming; *Jordan dumped me via text.* He told me he really liked me; I was a great girl; he couldn't find anything wrong with me, but he had *lost the spark*. He was hoping it would come back, but it did not, so he broke up with me.

Somehow, I knew all along. Some weird psychic ability told me I could never have Jordan. I fell so hard for him. I didn't even like him at first, but he pursued me hard (annoyingly hard). I gave him a chance just to get my heart ripped out of my chest in the end. When men are done with you, it is like *blowing out a flame. Once they blow out the flame, that is it; you are done.*

Stalking

For years after the breakup to this very day, Jordan still stalks me hard on social media. Like the song *Every Breath You Take* by the Police. ***He watches every single one of my Snapchat stories without missing any TO THIS DAY. What does that tell you? The man cannot let me go, for some reason or another.*** At the time, I could not figure out why he watched every single one of my stories if he discarded me; ***it made no sense***. I wanted him to text me more than anything. My sister told me to take a photo of me holding a sign and post it on Snapchat, saying, "Jordan, stop watching my snaps and text me, damnit." I thought that was a great idea but didn't do it.

Mind Blown

I had gone out with my girlfriends' post break up, and I told them about this book and Attachment Theory. ***They informed me that they date and marry men who are more into them than they are into the men.*** I was entirely baffled. They proceeded to inform me that it is common for women to involve themselves with men who are more in love with them than they are with their men. My mind was blown. ***This makes so much sense from an attachment perspective.*** The women chose men they were ***not in love with*** for stability reasons and because the men would kiss their ass. It is interesting that the men were ***more into them*** when ***the women were not in return***. Since men want what they cannot have, it made perfect sense to me. I felt bad for the women. They were denying themselves what they really wanted for what they thought they wanted. This also creates the ever-present lean-in / lean-out roller coaster where the ***leaned in partner*** causes the other to ***lean out*** and vice versa. Each partner rotates and takes turns. Partners cannot be equally leaned in all the time; there is usually some level of leaning out / leaning in exchange. This is why when I am leaned out of a relationship, men are on me like flies on shit. When I am leaned in as I was with Jordan, then they are running to Africa completely leaned out.

Sister – Understanding is the gateway to healing.

Chapter 6 Takeaways

> ➢ Attachment theory helps us understand the dynamics with our parents and romantic partners.
> ➢ Women tend to lean more toward an **Anxious Attachment Style**, which is why we often get abandoned by the men we love.
> ➢ Jordan was the catalyst forcing me to heal my insecurities head on. Jordan made me feel super insecure to the point I thought something was dramatically wrong with me. I had the collywobbles bad over him, which was only an activated attachment system. **Once I healed my insecurities for good, the whole game changed.**
> ➢ External validation is only a bonus. **Internal validation is all that matters.**
> ➢ **When a woman learns to accept, love, and validate herself, the whole game changes fully, completely, and permanently.**

Share Your Story:

In the space provided, it is time to share your story. Do you have an **Anxious Attachment Style?** What activates it? **Have you noticed men breaking your heart when you are more "insecure?"**

Chapter 7
Orbit of Love

"Cast a wider net; stop fixating on only one person."

Everyone has an **Orbit of Love**. An **Orbit of Love** is a giant bubble with you in the center and everyone else in your life orbiting around you. The **Orbit of Love** is who you allow or don't allow into your personal love world, your **Orbit of Love**. When we think of love, we often think of romantic love as what the media portrays as love: love songs, movies, TV shows, books, social media, happy couples, etc. **Love is deeper than romantic love.** Love is like an ocean: boundless, endless, full of mystery, intrigue, depth, and oneness. When you cannot have romantic love, you can still have love. I live and die for romantic love. **When I do not have romantic love, I am still fully capable of receiving and giving love to myself and others.**

The primary person in your **Orbit of Love** is you. Love yourself completely in this life. Put yourself first always. Men often put themselves first while women prioritize their partners. Stop it! **Put yourself first always. You come first and he comes second.** Secondly, in your **Orbit of Love** is your love for a Higher Power, The Divine, The Source, God, The Universe, or whatever it is you believe in. **Connect with your higher authority and its love for you.** Thirdly, nature, animals, the earth, friends, family, colleagues, acquaintances, and all interactions you have. Every experience and interaction you have is an opportunity to give and receive love. Everyone and everything matter. Without love, none of us would survive. This is why love is our greatest emotional need. **Love is at the center of all emotions.** You feel because you love. You love because you feel.

Connect with all that is and feel love in this very moment. It doesn't matter if you were neglected or abused as a child, it doesn't matter how many people broke your heart, it doesn't matter how many people hurt you; you are fully capable of giving and receiving the most authentic love there is. In my own healing journey, I had to prioritize myself. I used to be a people-pleaser. I used to believe that to love others, I had to sacrifice myself and put myself on the back burner so that I could serve and tend to everyone else while everyone else walked all over me like a doormat. Playing the role of **Old Faithful** will not render you the love you need. ***Give yourself the love you need.***

Emotional Friendships

Friends are good for you. ***Cultivate lots of friendships with both women and men.*** You can get the emotional nurturance you crave from friendships. ***You should surround yourself with good solid friendships and stop fixating on one person. That one person cannot fulfill all your needs.***

Stop having emotionless relationships and start forming emotionally rich friendships. ***An emotional friendship is between two persons: woman and woman, man and man, or woman and man where both parties feel equally seen, heard, listened to, and respected.*** Understand that we must have meaningful and life-giving relationships. ***Diversify your friend groups*** (diversity is key). The solution isn't becoming fixated on one person for the rest of your existence but rather cultivating and nurturing meaningful opportunities to experience emotional connectivity with a diverse circle of friends. To experience more of life and more of people. ***I am not anti-relationship, but when we close ourselves off from friendships, we notice both our self-esteem and self-respect begin to suffer because everyone in our lives provides value to us in innumerable ways.***

The song *You've Got a Friend* by James Taylor reminds me of my good friend, Lou. I've known Lou for ten years as we worked together at one point and then lost touch. In the past year, Lou and I have become close friends. He lives in another state, and I haven't seen him in ten years, but we talk every day. We send voice messages to each other. Lou and I have what I call an **emotional friendship.** It is steady, grounded, and stabilized. We love each other dearly. We mostly talk about our days, sharing what's going on in our lives and the various struggles we face day by day. We are each other's therapists because anytime I need advice, I go to him. Lou is a few years older than me, so I look up to him like a big brother and consider him to be wiser than myself. ***Lou and I provide for each other emotional nurturance through talk, acceptance, love, and genuine care.*** We send each other pictures of what is going on in our lives, and he has this thing where he always plays songs for me that remind him of me. Oftentimes, it was exactly the song I needed to hear that day. The songs always bring a smile to my face and brighten my day.

Although Lou and I don't spend time together in person due to distance, I consider him my best friend, and our bond is real and unbreakable. He is a kind, generous, thoughtful, and a secure person, bringing a lot of depth, truth, and consideration to our conversations. He is conversant in many topics and is willing to discuss. I share some of my deepest sorrows with Lou, and I never once felt judged or discarded. We accept each other for who we are. We both hope to find partners to share this deep, connected emotional bond of love and meaning. ***Lou meets certain needs of mine that other men could never meet.***

Healthy Relationships

We live in a modern time where authentic relationships are increasingly rare. That's not to suggest that they don't exist, but we can agree that individuals don't hold onto relationships the way their grandparents did in past generations. We are way less tolerant and a more selfish society (and for good reason). ***We are less tolerant of bullshittery.*** Many women divorce their husbands because they reach the breaking point of dealing with bullshittery, and that is the predominant reason why many women divorce. What exactly is marital bullshittery?

Marital Bullshittery is:

> Dealing with an alcoholic or drug addict
> Dealing with a man who physically and or emotionally abuses you
> Dealing with a man who has sex addiction
> Dealing with a man who won't work or hold down a job of some kind (the legal way)
> Dealing with a man who acts like a helpless child
> Dealing with a man who has no emotional control or maturity about him
> Dealing with a narcissistic man
> Dealing with a man who is avoidant and dismissive
> Dealing with a man who is clingy, needy, possessive, controlling, and or jealous
> Dealing with a man who plays video games all day or watches TV instead of being productive around the house
> Dealing with a man who does not participate in domestic duties

And the list can go on another mile, but I think you get the idea. All of this can be classified as marital bullshittery, and more specifically, **bullshittery is anything you must "deal with" or "put up with" that you normally and otherwise probably wouldn't put up with. You must put up with it because you made your bed and now you must sleep in it** (another way is saying a **glutton for punishment**).

Pre-marriage, Kelly considered herself a **bullshit-free woman.** Once married, she became a **glutton for punishment.** She knew she was putting up with bullshit to sustain her marriage, whereas in other circumstances, she would not ever tolerate such behavior, such bullshittery. Become a **bullshit-free woman** because a **bullshit-free woman**, in most cases, has very few, if any, problems. **_It is the bullshit that is the problem._**

Take note that everything listed in the above-bullet list is not just bullshittery but also classified **as unhealthy.** None of those above-listed behaviors are healthy in any capacity. If your man is any one of those, then you are in an unhealthy relationshit. **Relationships are either healthy or unhealthy.** Unhealthy relationships are known as relationshits, and you should not be in one of those. My desire for you is healthy living. Lying, cheating, and degrading are not healthy behaviors; do not convince yourself otherwise.

What does a Healthy Man Look Like?

As humans, we are either healthy or unhealthy, and I will provide specific definitions for each.

Healthy Individuals – Healthy individuals are always ascending. **_They have first and foremost taken complete responsibility and ownership for their lives._** They place blame on no one and understand that they create their own realities. More importantly, they always move forward and never backward, which means they are hungry for learning and spiritual growth. They never remain stagnant. They accept who they are, love themselves, love others well, and continuously evolve, becoming the best and brightest version of themselves. **_They expand their horizons, creating solutions, not problems._** They admit when they are wrong seeking higher wisdom. They are not doormats. **_They have firm boundaries, high self-esteem, and a great sense of self-worth._**

The Struggling – The struggling are individuals who fall between healthy and unhealthy. They were formerly unhealthy struggling to achieve healthy status due to things such as fear, doubt, self-sabotage, limiting beliefs, negative emotions, and unresolved issues plaguing them. If there is a will, there is a way. ***All is not lost for the struggling.*** With time, patience, and gentleness, they too will become emotionally healthy individuals.

Unhealthy individuals – Unhealthy individuals are aplenty. Venture outside and you will find them everywhere. There is no shortage of unhealthy and unstable in the world; please do not be one of these poor souls. They are descending in life, but if they are lucky, they may be sleeping aka living their life on cruise control without significant purpose or direction. ***They are the lost and the selfish. They are plagued by their own blindness and inability to see clearly the world around them.*** They are often self-centered, jealous, controlling, manipulative, defeated, excuse-making, constantly complaining, abusing people and substances, questionable behaviors and intentions, insecure, self-loathing, others-loathing, unproductive, unreasonable, unwilling, lacking understanding, lacking personal ownership and responsibility, and pleasure-seeking. It is true that unhealthy individuals make up most of the dating pool, so trust me when I say the problem isn't you. Women can be equally unhealthy. This isn't gender specific. ***Making judicious decisions compared to emotional decisions is non-negotiable.***

Family Man

If you want a solid and sustainable relationship, you will need a ***Family Man***. I am not saying the ***Family Man*** is perfect and will not cause any problems, but you've got a better chance with the ***Family Man*** than the bad boy on the motorcycle who highly cherishes his me time (away from you and the kids). <u>A ***Family Man*** is a man who has his **head in the game**.</u> He does not spend excessive amounts of time playing video games, watching TV, or participating in any other hobby or activity away from the home and the children. He is actively involved with his children and is present when he is home, engaging with his partner and children while sharing domestic responsibilities equally. Choosing a **Family Man** is a choice. Mr. **Family Man** may not be **Sex Himself** or have a torpedo for a dick, but that is why we have vibrators, ladies! You need a man with his ***head in the game*** (and I don't mean video games; I mean giving as much, if not more, than you give to the relationship and household).

What does a Healthy Relationship look like?

Unfortunately, a healthy relationship does not always look like good sex. You can have good sex in a healthy relationship, but sex itself does not make a relationship healthy. ***A healthy relationship is all and only about reciprocity, and that's it.*** If you are doing all or most of the work, then you are NOT in a reciprocal relationship, which means that you are NOT in a healthy relationship. Relationships are 50/50 with give some and take some. Relationships are partnerships. ***A healthy relationship is a partnership.*** Furthermore, healthy relationships look like:

> - Equally loving each other
> - Equally caring about each other
> - Equally giving to each other
> - Equally being available for each other
> - Equally communicating and listening to each other
> - Equally respecting each other

Egalitarian relationships are healthy relationships because nobody feels overburdened.

Male Friends / Value & Respect

Many of my closest friends are men, and I value and cherish those relationships. Being a full human being is important to me, and a full human being is friends with both women and men fueled by diversity. ***Every individual is both a student and a*** *teacher, which implies that we all learn from each other.* How can you ever expand your horizons if you only surround yourself with the same handful of people for decades? *You will outgrow certain people who are not walking in the same direction in life, and that is okay.* Just because you grew up with someone doesn't mean you have to be friends in adulthood. Most of my closest friends are people I met recently because they are aligned with who I am and the direction my life is heading.

Your friend group should demonstrate variety. Have a diverse group of friends with varying demographics, skills, beliefs, values, philosophies, learning styles, and lifestyles. *This will prove invaluable to you, adding greater meaning to your life.* You do not need to agree with everyone. Disagreeing while still respecting each other is tantamount to spiritual growth and personal ascension. Variety and diversity are what make life. Your job is to learn from every person you interact with, whether it is for just a minute or a lifetime. Equally, your job is to teach every person you interact with; this is a healthy and valuable exchange between two human beings. This is also a representation of give and take. *That value is being transferred between two beings. <u>Notice the value in every human being.</u>*

Different Types of Love

Many people confuse "being in love" or "having feelings" as love. It is not. Being in love or having feelings for someone is called **limerence**. Other words are infatuation or obsession; in Dr. Elinsky's personal dictionary, I call it the Heebie-jeebies or collywobbles, as literally liking someone to the degree of obsession makes me extremely anxious. It is also called **The Spark.** This **state of anxiety for another** is what most people consider love, but it is not. Therefore, it now becomes necessary to distinguish the distinct types of love.

1. **Limerence** – the Heebie-jeebies or having butterflies for someone commonly referred to as *The Spark.* If someone says they lost the spark for you, that implies that they lost feelings or fell out of love with you.
2. **Love for children and parents** – This type of love is steadfast and enduring, commonly known as *unconditional love.*
3. **Love for friends and community** – this is more of what I consider deep casual love where you genuinely care for the well-being of others.
4. **Love for hobbies/interests/career** – this type of love keeps us focused and motivated toward our goals and life mission.
5. **Love for God** – this is an everlasting love for God's omnipotence in the universe.
6. **True love** – true love has nothing to do with butterflies or collywobbles. *True love is a decision. You choose your mate every single day, and do not leave that person just because you "fell out of love."* This is precisely where most people get tripped up. They leave their girlfriend or boyfriend, wife, or husband when they no longer "love" them, aka *no longer IN LOVE with them.*

The truth of the matter is if you base love solely on feelings, you are in for a rude awakening because feelings come and go as quickly as hours do. Feelings are not permanent, and they do not last. Therefore, it is preposterous to choose a partner based exclusively on feelings alone, and this is where all, if not most, of us make major life mistakes in selecting the wrong partners. *We choose people we are in love with and not people who make good partners.* I will illustrate this point with a story in a moment. Before I give you the story, I want to discuss the different emotional needs we have.

Different Types of Emotional Needs

We all have different emotional needs. These include the following:

The need to be loved
The need to be accepted / belong
The need to be cared for
The need to be taken care of
The need to be supported
The need to be encouraged
The need to be listened to and acknowledged
The need to be seen and heard
The need to be important and matter in the world
The need for significance and meaning
The need for connection and community
The need for social interaction
The need for fun and excitement
The need for consistency and stability
The need for variety and mystery

ONE human being WILL NOT BE ABLE TO meet all your emotional needs. You will be lucky if one person could meet 3 or 4 on this list. Some of the best advice I ever heard was from Steve Harvey in his book *Act Like a Lady Think Like a Man* where he says, "the only way a woman can truly be completely satisfied is to get herself four different men – an old one, an ugly one, a Mandingo, and a gay guy." In his book, he discusses how it is impossible for one man to meet all your needs and that every woman should have four different men, because together and combined they can meet all her needs. This is genius advice. **We get too fixated on one man only to be massively let-down by him eventually.**

Cassidy's Story – Caught Between a Rock and a Hard Place.

Cassidy is your typical girl. In fact, it could be assumed that she represents many of us as women. It is common knowledge that women love bad boys and that nice guys finish last. You are familiar with these realities, and they may apply to you. Cassidy loves bad boys. *She loves their mystery and their emotional unavailability.* She indirectly loves the hot and cold games as they keep her forever on the edge of her seat waiting for his next move. She is madly in love with Randy (who is your typical bad boy). Randy wants NOTHING to do with Cassidy, but that is precisely why she wants him so badly, because she cannot have him! She wants what she cannot have! Sound familiar? Rick on the other hand is obsessed with Cassidy and throws himself at her incessantly. Cassidy senses Rick's clinginess and has no feelings towards him whatsoever. However, in reality, Rick makes a far better partner because Rick is emotionally available, he communicates with Cassidy everyday (she doesn't have to wait days or weeks for his replies), he buys her flowers, offers to clean her house, cooks her meals, babysits her cat, drops off medicine when she is sick, offers to take her on expensive dates, never lets her pay, will do, or buy her whatever she wants. Because Rick is there and wants her, she doesn't want him. Just like Cassidy, Rick also wants what he can't have and what he can't have is Cassidy.

Randy only offers good dick – that's it. Randy is not a partner. Randy only cares about himself and hardly ever communicates except for when he's horny and wants to use Cassidy; yet isn't it ironic that he is exactly who Cassidy REALLY wants and who Cassidy has feelings for? Cassidy has zero feelings for Rick and places Rick in the friend zone. Rick gives Cassidy the ick.

Someone or something is far more valuable to us (psychologically) when we cannot have it (because we psychologically feel like we are not good enough for whatever it is, creating the never-ending chase). Cassidy values Randy far more than Rick because Randy is unavailable to her. Randy is edgy and mysterious. Rick is like a puppy dog practically begging for love and attention, therefore there is no excitement with Rick, there is only excitement for Randy. *This creates a need within us or an ache for someone we want so badly but cannot have.*

Men love to chase women who are hard to get and who they cannot have. I read something once that said couples who made it past 20 years of marriage and how they do that, and the article said, *"because he never really got her."* 20 years of marriage, and the man was still chasing the woman; she *still never fully gave herself to him.* What I mean is having a hold on someone. *When someone has a hold on you, that means you are deeply infatuated with that person, and subconsciously, the other person knows it, and because they caught you or got a hold on you, they also subconsciously no longer want you.* They lose feelings for you. However, if they don't have a hold on you, they will want and chase you forever. Randy has a hold on Cassidy; therefore, Randy does not want Cassidy. She possesses less value in his eyes, and similarly, Cassidy has a hold onto Rick; therefore, Cassidy does not want Rick. Rick has less value in Cassidy's eyes because she got him. *Human beings psychologically want what they cannot have.*

In my research for this book, I read 20+ renowned dating books, and they all fundamentally said the EXACT same thing, *"men want what they cannot have."* This statement reads as if it only applies to men; that is untrue, the same is true of women. This is precisely why people who you DON'T WANT want you, and people who you DO WANT don't want you. It is all psychological and backed by the emotion of *desire. You simply CANNOT desire someone that you possess. You can only desire a person if you DO NOT possess them.* Desire is the feeling linked to *limerence* or being in love. *Desire is an obsession.* It is a forever ache sunken in the pit of your soul. You know my own heart is bleeding as I write these very words. Because I am in limerence with two men, Jordan and Asher, both of whom I deeply desire simply because neither one of them want me. Desire is not a pleasant state. **Desire is unbearable.** This is why so many songs are written about the pains of love and heartbreak.

*I authored this book for one reason: I wanted to write something F*CKING REAL! I wanted to write something that would acknowledge the human in all of us. I wanted to write something that women could relate to. I wanted to write something that, just maybe, would help a lot of hurting women heal... for good...*

The sex with Rick sucked for Cassidy. She got nothing out of it, *and she felt nothing at all.* There was no attachment to Rick. The sex with Randy was EVERYTHING. It was pure magic. *It made her feel so alive and complete. The truth is that different people meet different emotional needs.* Randy met Cassidy's sexual needs, and Rick met mostly everything else. Rick was the rock in her life. Rick loved her, accepted her, cared for her, and took care of her; he supported and encouraged her, listened to her, made her feel important and significant, was consistent and stable. He lacked excitement; he lacked mystery, thrill, lacked a great dick, and he didn't give good sex. Rick was boring, and Randy was exciting.

Don't put all your eggs in one basket, sis. Randy will never make a good partner. He cannot give Cassidy anything other than good dick. *However, Randy represents the guy we all want.* Randy represents our desire, our crush, our perceived true love. Rick represents the guy we are unattracted to, but Rick makes the better partner. Here is what happens to most women: they choose the Randys of the world and make babies with them. Randys eventually leave. These Randys make awful husbands, boyfriends, and men. They usually give far less and demand far more. ***They are the true heartbreakers of the world.*** They are the ***I don't give a damn about anyone but me types.*** Yet woman after woman falls in love with the bad boy and ends up sad, lonely, and depressed, forever spiraling further and further into the ***Abyss of Misery***. The Ricks make great partners and husbands, but you don't want them. They are willing to do backflips in the street naked for you, but that is precisely why you don't want them. You don't want the man who throws himself at you or the man who would do anything just to see you smile. ***<u>This is the phenomenon of desire. The longing, the loss, the can't have, the not good enough.</u>***

What is the solution?

1. ***RECOGNIZE YOUR OWN F*CKING WORTH!*** Take ownership of your life now. Stop wasting time and waiting around for others. Stop hoping and praying that he changes and one day wakes up, and things turn around. NEWSFLASH – THEY DO NOT CHANGE. THEY DON'T CHANGE! THEY DON'T! ***Kelly spent years of her life DOING BACKFLIPS IN THE STREET NAKED for a man who wouldn't even do a jumping jack for her.***
2. ***HAVE YOUR CAKE AND F*CKING EAT IT TOO*** – Date BOTH Randy and Rick. Take Steve Harvey's advice – ***different men for different needs.*** Shit- if men can do it, we can too.
3. ***STOP BEING A GLUTTON FOR PUNISHMENT.***

Doing more, loving more, and giving more DOES NOT MAKE YOU MORE VALUABLE IN SOMEONE ELSE'S EYES – it does THE EXACT OPPOSITE!

It's the guys you DON'T CARE ABOUT – YOU DON'T LOOK AT – YOU HARDLY ACKNOWLEDGE – YOU DON'T MAKE TIME FOR who will send you flowers, wash your car, make you dinner, buy you expensive purses, and take you on lavish dates. ***IT IS ALL ABOUT WINNING SOMEONE'S LOVE AND NOT HAVING***

SOMEONE'S LOVE. When he has your love, you become less valuable to him. ***This is why it is YOUR PSYCHOLOGY that needs to change, girl!***

The day I stopped being a F*CKING DOORMAT is the day men jumped out of bushes and started worshipping and treating me like a queen. Women embody what I call ***Doormat Syndrome.*** We all want to be the perfect wife or girlfriend, so we make the fancy meals, wash the clothes, clean the house, pack the lunches, ask for incessant reassurance (do you still love me, am I still attractive? Blah blah blah) ***THAT IS WHAT MAKES YOU A F*CKING DOORMAT! NOBODY respects a DOORMAT because a DOORMAT does not respect herself, because she IS TRYING TO WIN OTHER PEOPLE'S LOVE, RESPECT, AND APPROVAL.*** Change your psychology!

The 5 Foundations of Fundamental Self-Esteem

If you don't love yourself – nobody else will love you.
If you don't respect yourself – nobody else will respect you.
If you don't value yourself – nobody else will value you.
If you don't like yourself – nobody else will like you.
If you don't treat yourself like a queen – nobody else will treat you like a queen.

Self-esteem starts with THE SELF. It starts with YOU. Some of you don't even know who you are anymore! Six months before I started writing ***GIRL GRIT: SAVAGE NOT AVERAGE***, I was an ant. I allowed someone to dismantle my self-esteem, and I became an unperson. ***That was because I based all my self-worth on the acceptance and approval of others.*** Whether or not I was attractive, beautiful, desirable, lovable, respectable, valuable, and likable depended on what other people thought of me and not what I thought of myself. ***That is exactly where I went wrong. And just like that, the entire GAME CHANGED, and my world turned right-side up. At that moment, I said TO HELL WITH YOU- and I packed my bags along with my dignity and marched***

right out the front door, never looking back. My entire personhood now depends exclusively on me, and how I notice, accept and value myself. As a result, I made hundreds of friends and have what seems like hundreds of men desiring me again (not to brag, just showing an illustration of what can happen for you too). My life will NEVER be the same. The only thing that makes my life sad right now is wanting those two men I cannot have, but at least I accept myself, and I refuse to reject myself again. *The only person who can reject you is you. Read that AGAIN!*

On Rejection

The worst emotional pain is the pain of rejection. We've all been rejected at one time or another. Rejection goes both ways. Just as others can reject you so you too can reject others. How should we deal with rejection? *Firstly, never reject yourself.* Change your entire internal programming. *Accept relationships as they are AND NOT what you IDEALIZE them to be. <u>Detach from the outcome.</u> Marriage, children, and happily ever after should no longer be your relationship goals.* Cassidy envisioned her relationship with Randy as much more than he could realistically offer her. *Secondly, hold space for yourself. Holding space means to always acknowledge the human in you.* You are allowed to be human, forever, and always. Which means you are allowed to feel and have emotions. You are allowed to get angry and lash out. *You are allowed to have a mental breakdown.* You are allowed to get your heart broken and to break others' hearts. *You are allowed to make mistakes. You are allowed to have sex AND enjoy it. You are allowed to feel guilt-free and shame-free.* You are allowed to do what is ALWAYS in your best interest. You are allowed to divorce disappointing husbands. *You are allowed to become the best, brightest, and most effervescent version of yourself. You are allowed to believe whatever you wish and not just what your parents taught you as the absolute truth.* In *When Am I Going to Be Happy,* Dr.

Penelope Russianoff addresses rejection, "you cannot reject somebody who is not available for rejection. You cannot put down somebody who is not available to be put down."

Heal fully and completely. Do not abuse or emotionally neglect your children. ***Befriend people instead of gossiping about and or judging them.*** If you can help someone else with your time, services, or money, you should be generous and do it. You should always be a real human being no matter who devastated you or broke your heart. You will hear me talk a lot about Jordan and Asher in this book because this is a book about human emotion and healing, and those two are the most emotional parts of me right now. They are the two men who are making me most human because my own feelings come from the result of loving and losing both. ***If I don't accept and acknowledge my own humanity, then how could anything I say in this book bring any value to your life?*** If we are not truthful to ourselves and others, then essentially, we are living a great big lie.

Always hold space for yourself and others. Acknowledge humanity in everyone. ***No one is better than you, damnit! No one is less than you, damnit! We are all worthy, we all matter, we are all capable of prodigiousness! Remember, if you act like an ant, others will step on you, but if you roar like a lion, others will surely hear you.*** The choice is yours. We are all made for love, and we are all worthy of love.

Design your ideal relationship. ***Believe this person exists.*** Write down all of her or his qualities and characteristics. Be as detailed and specific as possible. ***Never ever settle.*** Being alone is far better than settling. You cannot change the unchangeable, nor can you fix the unfixable, but you can CHANGE and FIX YOU! Put that energy back where it belongs ON YOU. ***<u>When you are whole, when you are healed, when you</u>***

<u>are magnificent and magnetic, you will have whatever your heart desires.</u>

Sister – Never fixate on one person – always have many friends and diversify. Cast a wider net.

Chapter 7 Takeaways

> ➢ Create your **Orbit of Love** carefully delineating who is and isn't allowed in your orbit.
> ➢ Develop and nurture relationships with both women and men, cultivating diversity and variety in your social circles.
> ➢ Everyone is a teacher. Relationships should be a constant exchange of value between two people. *If someone is not reciprocating, then they need to go.*
> ➢ All humans want what they cannot have. **This is what makes desire so tempting.**
> ➢ You cannot desire something or someone that you possess.
> ➢ All people are either healthy, struggling, or unhealthy. Healthy people are healed, and unhealthy people are not healed. The struggling are fighting to heal, and they are moving forward.
> ➢ Your best chance at having a noble partner is a **Family Man.**
> ➢ Love exists all around you. Romantic love is not the only type of love for you.
> ➢ *The only person who can reject you is you.*

Share Your Story:

In the space provided, it is time to share your story. What steps will you take creating and nurturing your **Orbit of Love**? How will you surround yourself with people who value, cherish, encourage, and champion you?

Chapter 8
Your Allstar Players – Emotion and Logic

"Every game consists of one winner and one loser – your job is to not be the loser."

The ability to think and feel is exactly what makes you human, and it is perfectly okay to be human all the time. There is power in feeling and equal power in rational thought. Men are conditioned to suppress emotion, and women are taught to express emotion. Why? Why is it acceptable for women to express an array of negative emotions, but the ONLY emotion socially acceptable for men is anger? Does anyone ever ask these pertinent questions? ***Why are we setting ourselves up to be so incongruent with each other?*** It is criminal to teach and encourage men to not express emotion as you are removing the very fabric of what specifically makes them human. ***<u>We do not need tough men; we need empathetic men.</u> <u>We need men who feel, men who listen, men who understand, men who relate, and men who cry.</u>*** *We desperately need men who cry. If we had men who cried, then wars wouldn't have happened, and so many innocent lives wouldn't have been lost. There are better ways to solve problems than war.*

If men were allowed to express emotion, then they wouldn't be angry all the time. Men outwardly express anger as a form of any negative emotion, including sadness, hurt, frustration, insecurity, and loneliness. Instead of expressing those emotions, they resort to anger expressing anger when deep down, they are not angry but rather sad, frustrated, or insecure. You get sad first, then angry. ***<u>Perhaps if men are allowed to express sadness, then their anger might not exist.</u>***

Your Players

Life is a game about strategy. You need a strategy to succeed in anything you do. You cannot just wing it. Emotion and logic are your all-star players. *Leverage both to your advantage by controlling them, so they don't control you.* Emotions are hard to control. Emotions hit us at certain times throughout the day based on external circumstances we experience through the thoughts we have. *Emotion is hard to control when met by overwhelm.*

The Differences Between Loving and Being in Love

Everyone loves to be in love. It is a wonderful feeling because being in love is equivalent to being high. When you are in love, your brain is on drugs, hence the saying love is a drug. There is no difference between being in love and being on drugs. *It makes you feel good and anything that makes us feel good, we naturally chase.* Being in love is only a feeling, and feelings themselves are fleeting meaning that feelings cannot sustain themselves. This is why you have been in love with several different individuals throughout life.

Being in love is your emotional brain in the driver's seat because you cannot control your emotional brain. Emotions are not a choice. They are a feeling, and feelings cannot be controlled because they come and go. Next time you find yourself in love just know that your emotional brain has taken over. This is why you've heard the terms madly in love, crazy for you, or obsessed because your emotional brain is impacted significantly with a force equivalent to a car crash. You literally feel like you have gone mad when you are in love because you do not feel normal. Being in love clouds your mind, removing your focus on important things and tasks, while carrying you away from reality. *Being in love is an escape from reality. Being in love is an illusion which is why the object of your affection can do no wrong only in your eyes.* You have completely idealized and romanticized this person, and you cannot get them off your mind. You think about them 24/7. Seduction is so powerful, because you are taking someone away from reality. Everyone wants the feeling of being removed from the mundane of existence.

It is not psychologically healthy to be in love. You feel crazy, and when you are crazy, you are not psychologically healthy. Being in love is not a normal state because your mind is on the love drug, and when your mind is on drugs, you are not in a normal state. ***A normal state is a state of equilibrium or resiliency when you are not emotionally clouded by another individual.***

Let me give you two examples.

Matt was madly in love with me. To my knowledge, he has been in love with me and has been chasing me for years now, and I am constantly rejecting him because I do not see him that way. It is unrequited love on my end. Matt refuses to give up on me because I am a challenge, and he is determined to win me over. However, little does he know that even if he gave me a million dollars, it still wouldn't happen. I am not in love with Matt. Matt texted me all the time over days, weeks, months, and years endlessly pursuing me with no reciprocation on my end. The few times I attempted to give him a chance because he treated me so well, it didn't work out because he would eventually demonstrate signs of jealousy, control, and possession which are red flags ***(and unattractive qualities in general).***

He'd buy me gifts. Buy me anything I want. Take me on nice dates. Wine and dine me. Not letting me leave the house without rubbing my feet for 30 minutes. Offer to come over and clean my entire house free of charge. Drop off flowers on my porch once a week. Support me, champion me, and compliment me. He was my #1 fan, it was all about Alex, Alex, Alex. I mean, you'd be sold right? There was only one problem: I did not see him that way, I was not in love with him. I did care about him. I did like him as a person, and I did try to befriend him, but that was not good enough for him; if he couldn't have me, then he wouldn't stop trying. He called me goddess. He called me his **one true love**.

I will forever be his Femme Fatale. I will forever be his Firewoman. The girl he was unable to win. **The uncapturable girl.** The object of his desire. His obsession.

Matt only wanted me because he couldn't have me. **Nobody treats you better than someone you don't want.**

Jennifer's Story

Jennifer is a good friend of mine and gave me permission to share her story in this book. She has been married for ten years and has three small children: nine, seven, and three years old. She has had problems in her marriage and lost all attraction to her husband. In her mind, her marriage is over. However, she faces a great dilemma: **her children and their best interests.** Jennifer is a good mother, giving, and unselfish. She never wants to take any action that will jeopardize and upset her children. She considers them before her own needs.

She puts on the façade of a big happy family. Her own needs, hopes, and dreams go entirely unmet. She is unhappy in her marriage and has psychologically left it. She concluded that she will not divorce her husband only because of her children. She considers them more important than her own happiness and is old-fashioned (hanging onto the marriage at all costs).

She met a younger man at work (10 years younger) and developed a secret affair with him while staying in her marriage for her children. The affair makes her happy and puts the spunk back in her personality. It keeps her sane because it is something she wants for herself. Her boyfriend is Tony. Their relationship is sizzling and passionate. She is in love with Tony.

She loves her husband, but she is not in love with him anymore. Tony meets the needs of hers that her husband is unable to fulfill.

However, to complicate matters, her husband is in love with her. He is crazy about her, so he acts like the picture-perfect husband winning back the affection he lost from her. He would do backflips in the street naked for her, which is exactly what Matt did for me. He buys her gifts, including brand-name handbags, perfumes, and clothes. He makes her breakfast and dinner every day. He cleans the entire house and doesn't let her do any domestic work other than care for the children. He is willing to give her massages to relieve her stress. He takes her on nice and expensive dates, but she refuses to go. She doesn't want him. She wants Tony. Her husband could move mountains and swim oceans for her, and it still wouldn't be good enough simply because he is not the man SHE WANTS. She WANTS Tony. She is in a predicament. She is legally married to her husband, and together, they have three beautiful children, but she is not in love with him. However, he is in love with her. It is another unrequited love situation.

Why does Tony want her? Because she is **uncapturable**. Tony cannot truly have her. She is married to her husband. Therefore, the idea of her is an illusion to him, so he wants her only because he can't have her, and equally, she wants him because he is an illusion to her. She wants him because she also cannot have him. Being in love is wanting what you cannot have. Once you get it, you don't want it anymore. It is human nature to want and desire only what we cannot have. Some relationships are one in and one out. *That means one person is often leaned in while the other is leaned out, and it can be either the man or the woman. The leaned in person is leaned in because subconsciously they feel they cannot "have" the other person so that yearning makes the other more desirable. The leaned out person feels like they have the other person wrapped around* *their finger.* Cheating usually begins with the leaned-out person going out and seeking what they feel they cannot have. It is human nature to fall in love, and falling in love, as good as it may feel, is unfortunately toxic to our mental health and emotional wellbeing. ***Let's consider what it means to love.***

To Actually Love

Loving someone and being in love with someone are two entirely different realities. Being in love is directly linked to your emotional brain, whereas paradoxically loving someone is linked directly to your logical brain. These are two totally different and separate experiences. Your logical brain is your decision-making brain, whereas your emotional brain influences your subconscious mind, which is why you cannot choose who you fall in love with; it simply just happens to you without conscious choice. There is no decision-making process when falling in love. ***Loving a person has nothing to do with being in love with them.***

Love is an action. It is a choice. People who are together choose each other every day because love is a choice, a decision, and not an emotion. Once you conceptualize these ideas, you will make better and healthier choices. Everything in life is a choice, and every choice produces either life-giving or life-taking consequences. Jennifer must make a choice. Go with her heart, aka her emotional brain, and leave her husband to be with Tony, or go with her logical brain and stay married to her husband for her children's sake.

Choosing Partners Based on Logic and Not Emotion

This is the reality that nobody likes: choosing romantic partners based on logic and NOT emotion. Many of us choose toxic partners simply because we are in love with the toxic person and our emotional brain has taken over. People make decisions based on emotion and not logic. Consider your past for a moment and the partners you have chosen for yourself. Would the people you have chosen for yourself be good for your own daughter? At a certain time in history, parents chose their daughter's future husband, and attractiveness had nothing to do with the person they selected for their child. It had everything to do with the man's ability to provide and be a good long-term partner for the daughter. It was a logical decision made by the parents on behalf of their daughter. They were choosing a partner who would be good for her and not the partner she was in love with. ***Being in love didn't pay the bills back then, and it doesn't pay the bills now.***

Being in love:

> ➢ Doesn't pay the bills
> ➢ Doesn't wash the dishes
> ➢ Doesn't do the laundry
> ➢ Doesn't take the kids to school and pick them up
> ➢ Doesn't pack lunches
> ➢ Doesn't make dinner
> ➢ Doesn't manage the household
> ➢ Doesn't mow the lawn or take care of the cars

Choosing partners based solely on emotion is detrimental to your mental health if and only if that partner is not a good partner for you. You may be lucky and be in love with someone who does all these things and shares the load with you 50/50, acting like a real partner but consider those circumstances the exception and not the rule.

Choose a person willing to be an active and equal partner for you. Some men (and women) willingly have children without ever considering that they must be a parent and put in 50% of the work to raise a child. Some men (and women) get married or move in together without ever considering that they must be a reciprocal partner and contribute 50% of their time and resources to pay the bills, maintain and clean the home, procure and cook food to eat.

The next time you make a decision, ask yourself: am I making this decision based on emotion or logic? If you said emotion, I would carefully consider the circumstances before officially moving forward. I cannot stress enough that you are only responsible for yourself and that all your decisions are entirely your own. ***Above all, protect yourself.*** No one can or will protect you. There is no such thing as an external hero in your story. You are a woman warrioress and must always protect yourself and your mental health. There is no reason for suffering emotionally. ***You have complete power and authority to solve 100% of your problems at the snap of your finger.*** Let me give you an example: Lisa was in a tumultuous long-term relationship. For many years she lived in a tornado of frustration and confusion based solely upon her partner's words and actions. She was what I consider to be a ***glutton for punishment.*** Having been raised **old school**, Lisa was instructed to work things out at all costs. She endured the worst pain of her life simply because she made a promise in front of 200 people to an individual who did not give a rat's ass about her mental and emotional health. That is called being a ***glutton for punishment.***

If you are willingly in a relationship with a man who treats you like shit, you are a ***glutton for punishment.*** I don't care if the man has a magical dick and works it like a torpedo. When Lisa finally mustered up the courage to leave this individual for good, 100% of her problems all melted away OVERNIGHT! ***Yes, 100% of her problems dissipated just like that.*** What shocked Lisa the most was that 100% of her problems were due to him, and without him, she had no more problems. Lesson learned: whatever you do, do not be a ***glutton for punishment***. A man may be a **Dick Wizard**, but if dick is all that he brings to the table, then trouble is aplenty.

Good Versus Bad Sex

Have you ever considered what makes sex good or bad for you? What are the differences? I don't know about you, but I am crazy for avoidant and dismissive men, better known as the bad boys. A man does not need to wear a leather jacket or ride a motorcycle to be considered a bad boy. A bad boy is hard to get, mysterious, enigmatic, hot and cold, and not needy. The bad boy is more psychological versus physical. It's not about his appearance; *it's about his behavior.* This is why nice guys and girls finish last. <u>*It is not advantageous to be nice, it's advantageous to be bad because everyone wants what they can't have.*</u>

You can say that the sex is better with bad boys. I know plenty of girls who love bad boys and do not find nice guys attractive. A guy who is willing to do anything for you is not going to win your affection, whereas a guy who acts like you don't exist will. Now I understand that not everyone is like me, but many of you can relate.

The truth of the matter is that sex will either be good or bad or mediocre at best. You will not have sexual compatibility with every person you go to bed with. You will have sexual compatibility with some. However, it just depends on the person, the circumstances, and the degree to which you like or love the other individual you have taken to bed. Good sex and bad sex in both instances are all about our perception concerning the acceptability and enjoyment of that sexual experience with that person. What that suggests is the following: just because you think the sex was great and you feel sexual compatibility with your partner DOES NOT MEAN he or she thinks and feels the same way about it.

Comparably, your partner may tell you they thought the sex was great and that they feel sexual compatibility with you, but you feel the opposite about them. One person likes it, and the other does not. One person thinks it was great, and the other person thinks it was horrible. ***Different individuals bring different sexual experiences and expectations to the table.*** Different people like and tolerate different things. No two individuals are the same. What one person finds to be kinky and fun, another may find to be gross and intolerable. ***There can be significant incongruency in the bedroom because of two different sets of needs, expectations, fantasies, fetishes, and preferences.*** Whereas one person may be vanilla, another person may be Neapolitan, and another person might be the kitchen sink flavor. Sexual congruency and incongruency are simply realities. The important takeaway, however, is that sex is only one of your needs. Sex can also be both a physical and an emotional need. Our human needs can be physical, emotional, and sexual.

No One Person Can Meet All of Your Needs

The person who best meets your sexual needs may be lacking in other need areas. This is why selecting a man with only a good dick is not advantageous for you, because he cannot meet those other needs you have. Similarly, a man willing to cook for you, clean for you, babysit your dog and cat, put oil in your car, run errands for you, and buy you gifts may be meeting your physical needs, but he may not be meeting your sexual needs. He might love you well and be emotionally available, but if he sucks in bed, sis he sucks in bed! ***You must learn to accept that no one person can meet all your needs, which is why it is important to cast a wider net and create your own Orbit of Love.***

Sister – Equally leverage the powers of your emotional and logical brain.

Chapter 8 Takeaways

> ➤ You have two components that make up your brain: your ***emotional brain*** and your ***logical brain.***
> ➤ Your ***emotional brain*** is your ***subconscious mind,*** and your ***logical brain*** is your ***conscious mind.***
> ➤ ***It is better to make decisions based on logic versus emotion.***
> ➤ Understand the difference between loving and being in love.
> ➤ Choose ***healthy partners*** who are good for you. ***Heal the parts of you that chose unhealthy avoidant partners.***
> ➤ No one person can meet all your emotional needs.

Share Your Story:

In the space provided, it is time to share your story. How much of your decision-making has been based on your emotional brain? What types of consequences has it rendered?

Chapter 9
Romance is an Illusion

"Romance is a tool men use to lure women into their web and discard them when they lose interest. That is why if something seems too good to be true, it is."

The dismissed little girl is forever chasing the heart of the avoidant man.

My stomach is in a thousand knots. I have not heard a word from my boyfriend in almost 72 hours, and my insecurities have flared up once again. I was raised on Disney movies, fairytales, happily ever after, and **Love Will Rescue Me syndrome.** I live and die for romantic love. But here I am, alive, waiting by my phone right now like some idiot who can't let go of the idea of love. I wish I could throw my phone away. And as the seconds, minutes, and hours roll by, the pain in my stomach worsens. I can't eat or sleep. Why does this happen to us? Why do we fall in love? Why do we need someone? What is wrong with me?

We all want lovebombing that lasts forever. We all want the honeymoon phase to last forever, and in a brand-new relationship, sometimes we think it will last forever. But it doesn't. Therefore, romance is an illusion. ***It's like every time you are about to touch romance, it moves further away from the palm of your hand.*** You get just close enough, close enough to almost touch it, and then it moves away again out of reach....

Women grow up believing that their *acme of existence* is marriage and children, and so they fixate on men jumping through hoops trying to catch a man and then keep him at ALL COSTS, even to their own detriment. Women chase commitment, and men run from commitment; ***how are you supposed to have a loving and healthy relationship with the*** *opposite sex if one gender runs toward love and the other away from it?* It is IMPOSSIBLE. You are better off having a romantic relationship with a pillow.

Romance is Deception

Many men know exactly how to romance a woman, and many women eat it up every time. Even the most intelligent, responsible, and independent women still fall for this bullshit often. Romance is bullshit. I am going to use the words romance and love bombing interchangeably since they are the exact same thing. Romance, aka lovebombing, is nothing more than *a manipulation tactic* men use to seduce and thus destroy women. And the scary thing is, it works. Many men are *master manipulators.* They will do and say anything to get exactly what they want out of you, and once they achieve whatever that is, then poof, they disappear. It is what I call *The Cycle of Chaos.* Think about it for just a second, you have been manipulated repeatedly by different men in your life. I need to make something abundantly clear before we move any further 1) you did NOTHING wrong. Do not ever assume you did anything wrong because you didn't. It is him and not you, and I will prove that all throughout this book 2) This is a *male behavioral pattern* that a great majority (not all but many) men have; therefore, it is a *societal issue* the way men are conditioned in the early years of life. 3) never blame yourself, this has ***NOTHING TO DO WITH YOU AND EVERYTHING TO DO WITH HIM.***

The Cycle of Chaos

Boy meets girl. Boy likes girl more than girl likes boy. Boy pursues girl with extreme interest. Girl is minimally responsive because she does not yet trust boy and has been hurt in the past. Boy pursues harder with zest and passion, showering her with interest, attention, affection, gifts, dinners, and time until he has sold her on himself. The second she becomes interested in him and therefore is "sold," he pulls away, creating an unwarranted distance between them. Girl is outrageously confused by his bewildering behavior, wondering why his intentions are so poor. Everything he did screamed commitment and long-term, only to suddenly end things with her.

A month, two months, three months, or several months later, he comes back, and the cycle starts all over again, thereby creating the perfect storm or **The Cycle of Chaos** with the girl becoming more hurt, confused, devalued, and discarded in the end. Brian Nox, in *Fuck Him, Nice Girls Always Finish Single,* says this about men and relationships, "men start to take a woman for granted and start to give her less attention the moment they are sure she will stick around. This has everything to do with his hierarchy of needs. Most men want to be with a great woman. So, finding her is very high on the hierarchy of needs. They'll put in a lot of time, money, and effort. Once the mission has been completed, that great woman has been found, attracted, dated, and now "relationshipped," he can focus more on his other needs again... like Netflix indeed." He goes on to say, "nagging is like bluffing. A woman who nags has just proven that she won't run. She'll wait. And that's the exact opposite of what he needs. He needs you to withdraw a bit without an explanation!"

This pattern of **common male behavior** is extremely harmful, deceptive, manipulative, and abusive, and we women are falling for it often. What does that suggest about women? *It says we are easily deceived. We believe so much in fairytales, marriage, relationships, and happily ever after that we even perpetuate our own misery by becoming hooked on hope.* Hoping that someday things will be different, and he will change, or that some man will see the real value in us and will not discard us after the so-called honeymoon phase has run its course. Steven Naifeh and Gregory White Smith have this to say in *Why Can't Men Open Up,* "in relationships, as in game-playing, men need a goal to give their efforts shape and meaning. Thus, the emphasis on conquest among young men. Responding to the challenge of a goal, a man can summon up whatever is required to achieve that goal – even a sort of emotional honesty. But once the prize is won, once the woman says yes, once the relationship is consummated (sexually, emotionally, or maritally), problems begin. All too often, because there is no longer any clearly defined goal, a man's interest wanes, and with it his desire. The arrangement often continues – from need, convenience, or simply familiarity – but his heart isn't in it." *This is why game playing is essential and never allowing the game to end even more. Once the game is over, it is game over for you girl.*

The Parallel

The **Cycle of Chaos** never ends. Abusive men love drama (as much as they will not admit it). They love thrills, mystery, unknowns, unpredictability, and excitement. You will never find the word **STABILITY** or **NORMALCY** in a manipulative man's dictionary. The more chaos and drama manipulators create in your life, the more thrilling and exciting it is for them. And if everything is going well, and things are looking up, and everyone is happy they will purposely cause drama and upset for no reason at all. That is boring to a man, and abusive men do not do boring. They do excitement, unpredictability, and tension. They are like five-year-olds who never grow up and become adults. *It is constant games, drama, and playing on people's emotions.* The only reason why women become overemotional is because men make us that way. Women do not become overemotional because they are innate drama queens. We are often provoked by our five-year-old boyfriend or husband looking for more excitement in his life. *When men become bored of you, they will be done with you.* These types do not value relationships. You cannot have a relationship with someone who does not value nor want a relationship or work to improve it. **Women constantly work to improve the relationships that abusive men are systematically destroying.**

Let's say you finally got him to commit to marry you. In many cases, as evidenced by the literature referenced, abuse will settle in, subtle at first. **Women are forgiving that they do not even recognize they are being abused.** Many women still believe that abuse is only physical. **Emotional abuse enrages us as it should. You have every right to be angry as hell. Your feelings matter.**

Now you are married, all is well in the world, and then comes the subtle shift in his attitude toward you. He may criticize, blame, gaslight, stonewall, leave every night, talk incessantly, pick fights, downgrade, belittle, or find a myriad of other ways to emotionally punish you, gaining control over you. And eventually, the discard will come. Even some married men are not committed. A committed person doesn't put their spouse down, ignore them, or manipulate them. A committed person does not lie or cheat on their spouse. Yes, he is married, but since he is cheating on you, that is not a commitment. A committed person would not do this. Therefore, your cheating and abusive husband is not committed to you and is still running away from commitment even though he is married to you.

It is the same shit repeatedly with no reprieve. It is **The Cycle of Chaos.** You keep believing he will change, and you keep forgiving him. Therefore, you are allowing him to dupe you repeatedly. The never-ending crazy-making drama cycle **THAT HE IS THRIVING OFF OF** while it is **PUNISHING/DESTROYING YOU**. He is being rewarded for his shitty behavior while you are being punished for it. WAKE UP. STOP BEING SO INSECURE AND DESPERATE, SISTER. YOU ARE BETTER THAN THIS. No human being deserves to be treated like this, and until we start **REPRIMANDING ABUSIVE AND DESTRUCTIVE MALE BEHAVIOR,** these abusive men will keep getting away with this for generations to come without change.

What has society done to abusive men to make them act out like this? This is not how relationships work. However, I want to make one thing clear, since this book is about you. Underline this and write it in your mirror.

<u>THE ONLY WAY TO HAVE A HEALTHY RELATIONSHIP WITH AN ABUSIVE MAN IS TO HAVE AN UNHEALTHY RELATIONSHIP WITH HIM.</u> Steven Naifeh and Gregory White Smith explain in *Why Can't Men Open Up*, "many relationships resemble a Marx Brothers movie in which the characters chase each other through a labyrinth of doors. Each time one enters, another exists. One exits here but enters there, another is suddenly caught alone with all the doors closed. People cross each other's paths, stumble over each other, catch disappearing glimpses, then disappear themselves. Despite the confusion, the closed man's relationships, controlled as they are by the fear of dependence, do tend to follow a simple pattern: attraction, withdrawal, and stalemate."

Since the time you had your first boyfriend, men have been psychologically mind f*cking you, and you didn't even know it. How are you going to win this never-ending mind game of his? Sister, are you ready for this?

YOU ARE GOING TO LEARN HOW TO PSYCHOLOGICALLY MIND F*CK HIM AT HIS OWN GAME.

<u>The best way to f*ck a man is to NOT f*ck him.</u> That means don't give in. Don't give him what he wants. The men who chase me the hardest and call/text me incessantly are the ones I just don't give a f*ck about!

You will dish out to him what he dishes out to you. You will give him a taste of his own medicine. I understand that this may not make sense to you. As humans, we should not be toying with each other's feelings, mind f*cking each other, abusing each other, manipulating and lying to each other, and ripping apart each other's self-esteem, **BUT ABUSIVE MEN DO THIS TO US!** Do you get it yet? **ABUSIVE MEN DO THIS TO US!** I am sick and tired of seeing you hurt! I am sick and tired of screaming into a pillow because some guy broke my heart when I did nothing wrong. Rachael is sick and tired of being abused by her husband when all she was was the perfect wife cooking, cleaning, and picking up after him.

THE GAME HAS GOT TO CHANGE!

I am sick of the oppression we experience. We live in a completely gendered society where women have been severely disadvantaged for centuries. I am sick of living in a society where women want relationships and men don't, where women want big happy families and their husbands run off on them, where children grow up in a one-parent home because the man is abusive and won't quit it, where women have to go to therapy every damn week because some men psychologically ruin them, where men treat women like objects, where women do the bulk of the domestic work and childcare because abusive men are lazy and indifferent.

SHIT IS GONNA CHANGE NOW!

Masochism doesn't work. Being a **glutton for punishment** doesn't work.

Even in marriages, men are still running away from commitment. It is a war that we as women cannot win – or can we? Understand that we have lost for so long. We are still losing. We are still disadvantaged in many ways. Change starts with us, and it begins with changing our attitudes and shifting our mindsets.

He Knows What You Want

He knows you want love and romance, and he will only give it to you when he wants something from you in return. He does not give it freely out of love the way it is supposed to be. Remember, familiarity breeds contempt. Once he is familiar with you, contempt will settle in eventually. How do you combat this? **You become smarter than him. You learn to beat him at his own game.** You take back your power, control and manipulate him without him realizing what you are doing. This is the premise of **GIRL GAME: BALLS OUT.** This is why the lovebombing or honeymoon stage doesn't last forever. It could last forever if men never stopped trying, but eventually, they stop trying when in their minds, the pursuit is over. *Men only use romance to chase you, and once they've sold you winning you like some prized animal, it is GAME OVER, sister.*

Never believe the lie of romance again. Yes, we all want romance, and yes, we all want love-bombing. I will even go as far as to say it is a psychological and emotional need in us, but it will not last forever. *Learn to romance yourself. Learn to give yourself exactly what you need to meet your own needs.*

De-Duping Ceremony

If you have ever been romanced by a man and then days, weeks, months, or years later dumped by him out of the clear blue, then you have been duped by him, and you are a dupe. Do not beat yourself up. *Firstly, you did not know any better: no one does. Secondly, I am the queen of getting duped.* It has happened to me countless times, so chances are it has happened to you at least once. Why? *Because we want to believe in love.* We want to believe in good pure intentions. We want to believe in romance and bliss and the good feelings that accompany it. *But we are getting duped, and that is indeed the problem.* Brian Nox in *Fuck Him, Nice Girls Always Finish Single* has this to say about weak women, "players, narcissists, bad boys, manipulators, douchebags, losers…all seek out women who are weak. Women they *can* play and manipulate."

Do not blame yourself; we have all been there. We all have wanted to believe the man who said he loved ***and yes, he did love you IN THAT MOMENT***. But those moments don't last forever, and this is where we need to put on our **Judicious Brain**. Most people act out of emotion only. They do not think rationally; therefore, they do not make rational decisions. You cannot rely on your emotional brain as it is not a reliable source; it is catapulting you into the **dupchuary**. The **Dupchuary** is a sanctuary for dupes. It is where you go when you use your emotional brain and you get bamboozled (duped) so you go to the **Dupchuary** where you will have the opportunity to have a **De-Duping Ceremony** to forever de-dupe yourself (or unf*ck yourself). ***Let me walk you through the steps of your De-Duping Ceremony.***

De-Duping Ceremony:

STEP 1: Forever a Romantic Skeptic; romance needs taken with a grain of salt. It is completely acceptable and permissible to indulge in romance for the sake of fun, adventure, and affection but keep it at that. ***Do not expect ANY MORE than what is being offered at face value.*** And certainly, **do not** believe that…. ***THIS IS FOREVER.***

STEP 2: Detachment; never allow yourself to become attached. You can love. You can love hard. And you can indulge in romantic and sexual pleasures, but you will remain aloof and always detached (this is precisely where your power lie and why men have had more of an advantage your entire life – men are masters at aloofness and detachment). ***Wise up and start acting like that too.***

STEP 3: Chanting: meditate daily and chant to yourself, "I refuse to be duped. I will no longer be tricked, manipulated, lied to, ambushed, or bamboozled by any romantic buffoonery and ill-intentions."

STEP 4: Pray for your personal transformation; with the help of your higher power and my words, you can revolutionize your life and the way you respond to love, sex, men, and romance.

STEP 5: Do not blame yourself. Forgive yourself. And move on. Wash your hands of the duping.

Chalanting Versus Nonchalanting

In simple terms, Chalant means to care, and nonchalant means to not care. If you had to embody one of the two, which do you suppose you should choose? ***If you answered nonchalant, you would be correct.*** Our problem as human beings (especially as women), because I do believe we have it worse, is that we care too damn much, and when you care you get hurt. <u>**When you don't care, you don't get hurt.**</u> You have been programmed and conditioned to care as a woman because you have been programmed and conditioned to be caring and to take care of others because that is your gender role. You walk around chalanting all the time, and that causes feelings of anger, frustration, angst, misery, sorrow, and defeat. Men do a far better job of nonchalanting. Men sleep better at night. Men worry less about kids, finances, the household, etc. Men don't strive to be perfect like women do. ***Overall, men carry a more "I don't give a f*ck attitude."*** I am not saying all men are like this, and I am not saying that all men don't care. ***I am not generalizing, but we would be kidding ourselves if we did not agree that men in general have an air of indifference or "nonchalanting" about them.***

Remember in **GIRL GRIT: SAVAGE NOT AVERAGE,** women are everybody's everything, so of course you feel like you must care too much about everyone and everything, but the problem is that that type of behavior and way of thinking is both ***hurting*** and *harming* you. It is ***crushing your self-esteem***, frustrating you to no end, making you feel like you aren't a person, and like a hamster spinning on a wheel while never making any actual progress or solving any real problems. ***The best way to chalant is to nonchalant. The best way to care is to not care.***

Sister – Always nonchalant, never chalant.

Chapter 9 Takeaways

- ➢ Romance is an illusion robbing women of true happiness.
- ➢ Every man knows what every woman wants, and he often uses romance (lovebombing) to manipulate, control, and sell the woman on himself.
- ➢ Once she is sold on him, he will often discard her and move on to the next conquest, ***starting the process all over again.***
- ➢ Women are often duped by men, because we want to believe in love, romance, and happily-ever after. We want the white-picket fence and abusive men want drama.
- ➢ We get trapped in the **Cycle of Chaos** perpetually repeating the lovebomb, devalue, and discard stages.
- ➢ Perform a **De-Duping Ceremony** and never get duped again lest you end up in the **Dupchuary.**
- ➢ The best way to care is to not care – ***it is better to be nonchalant than chalant.***

Share Your Story:

In the space provided, it is time to share your story. In what ways have you been bamboozled by a man? What types of romantic gestures were demonstrated to you only to be removed days, weeks, months, or years later?

Chapter 10
The Three-Course Meal: Exploring a Woman's Sexual Needs

"Every woman has sexual needs, but society tells her that she is not allowed to have them."

Dr. Scott Peck does not disappoint when addressing sex or what he calls (the Universal Problem) in his book *Further Along The Road Less Traveled*, "sex is a problem for everyone. Sex is a problem for children, sex is a problem for adolescents, sex is a problem for young adults, sex is a problem for middle-aged adults, sex is a problem for elderly adults. Sex is a problem for celibates; sex is a problem for married people, sex is a problem for single people, sex is a problem for straight people, sex is a problem for gay people. Sex is a problem for bricklayers and plumbers, sex is a problem for dentists and lawyers, sex is a problem for surgeons and therapists and psychiatrists.… God built into us a feeling that we can solve the problem of sex and be forever sexually fulfilled, that we can get over the obstacle. Indeed, for a couple of weeks or a couple of months, or even for a couple of years, if we are lucky, we may feel that we have solved the problem of sex. But then, of course, we change, or our partners change, or the whole ball game changes, and once again we are left trying to scramble over that obstacle with this built-in feeling that we can get over it when we never can." Sex is truly a problem for everyone.

Does anyone care about a woman's sexual needs? Do you care about your own sexual needs? If you grew up in the church like I did, the idea of sex has two essential meanings: 1) first and foremost, it is only reserved for marriage (no ifs ands or buts), and 2) it is nasty and something only men want and need. ***Cool, so we have been programmed from day one that women are not***

human because our sexual needs do not matter – awesome! You may not even know what your sexual needs are because you may not have been allowed to have any! I equate shame and guilt with sex because I was raised to believe that all sex outside of marriage is both shameful and sinful. You have Christian and religious women saving themselves for marriage who have zero clue what their sexual needs are when they are well into their thirties, forties, fifties, and sixties. ***<u>The only kind of sin we can commit is a sin that directly and intentionally hurts another human being.</u>*** Read that again. ***If having sex is completely consensual, and you are not directly and intentionally hurting the other human being in that process, then I would consider that to <u>not be a sin.</u>***

This is the same religion (Christianity) that has conditioned us to believe that we are going to hell if we do not conform to its beliefs, ***the biggest manipulation tactic in the world.*** This goes to show how powerful fear is. ***<u>If you can evoke the emotion of fear in someone, you can influence them to do or believe anything you wish.</u>*** The God they preach of and who I still very much believe in would not send his people to hell. God loves all people equally, no matter our sins, because we are forgiven. Furthermore, no one can prove hell exists because no one has been there. ***<u>Hell, as is everything else, is only a state of mind. We should recognize and champion the good in everyone and not tell them that they are bad and sinful for that ideology lowers self-esteem.</u>*** We should uplift each other. Telling someone that they are sinful is like telling a child she or he is bad and unworthy of love. ***<u>There is no such thing as a bad human being, only negative and harmful behaviors.</u>*** No person is inherently ill-intentioned; it's just our ***own selfishness*** that makes us operate that way. If you ask people, most of them want to help others and make an impact on the world. We all have dark sides stemming from selfishness and the need to fulfill our own ***infantile wants, needs, and desires.***

Sex is physical and biological. Without sex, none of us would exist. Sex is a reproductive function and a transfer of fluids between bodies. Sex is a basic need as is eating and drinking water, sleeping, socializing, and safety. ***There are several arguments when it comes to sex, let's consider some.***

1. The recognition, first, that as humans, we are all sexual beings. You are a sexual being. You were born with sexual organs that do function. Do not discount your fundamental need for frequent sexual release. You were taught that sex is dirty and gross, therefore sex became dirty and gross to you.
2. Sex should always be consensual between two agreeable adults who are of age.
3. No means no, and sex can cease at any moment one of the partners declares it.
4. Sex is an action.
5. ***It is okay, acceptable, and normal to have sexual needs and desires.***

The reason I always have a chapter about sex in my books is because sex is a large part of who we are as human beings and sexual homo sapiens. You exist because of sex. How can we deny sex and act like it isn't a big deal? Many of us as women spend 80-90% of our lives as caretakers caring for our children, husbands, boyfriends, and parents that we often do not even recognize our own human needs, sexual and otherwise. ***We make life more about others and less about ourselves, which on the outside appears to be entirely selfless, and to an extent it is, but at what expense?*** What price must you pay to be entirely selfless, to have all your own needs and desires completely unconsidered because other people are helpless without you?

Deeply consider your own sexual needs. I do not take this chapter lightly. I do not take any of my work lightly, as I know that my work transforms lives and heals deeply suffering women. Really think about this reality and your own needs, both sexual and emotional, because we know there is much emotion that is related to our sexual experiences.

Is It Really All About Him?

I grew up with the idea implanted in me that women don't like sex, don't need sex, shouldn't initiate sex, shouldn't want sex, and that sex is all and only about fulfilling and satisfying a man. It was understood by me as a young child that women are not sexual beings themselves, but only sexual objects used to satisfy the male sexual appetite. Sex was forbidden, secretive, and allowed only within the parameters of marriage. *If this topic makes you uncomfortable, good!* Your needs matter just as much. *You are not less than anyone, ever! Since I was raised to believe a woman's only true worth is in marriage and motherhood, I learned to hold onto every relationship for dear life because maybe "he could be the one."* Whatever the f*ck "the one" means. When you are an object, you don't really have the capacity to feel like a human, *because <u>everyone</u> has reduced you to an inanimate object.*

As described in **GIRL GRIT: SAVAGE NOT AVERAGE**, sex is *emotional nurturance.* We have sex more for the emotional than the physical. We seek partners because we are seeking *emotional nurturance* from them. Even if you have a one-night stand or a bunch of one-night stands **IN THAT MOMENT** for those very brief seconds, you are still acquiring some level of *emotional nurturance* from that other person simply because it is human-to-human contact. *The act of sex is physical, but the* **INTENT OF SEX** *is 100% emotional.*

Marriage Versus Divorce

 Looking at Kelly's marriage, it gave her a lot of things (see below):

- ➢ Massive earth-shattering anxiety
- ➢ PTSD
- ➢ Low self-esteem
- ➢ Crushed confidence
- ➢ Weight gain
- ➢ Loss of freedom
- ➢ Loss of friends
- ➢ Turned her into a fuddy-duddy
- ➢ Turned her into a workaholic (most of the work being unpaid and unappreciated)
- ➢ Hours of therapy
- ➢ Alcoholism
- ➢ Dependent on anti-depressants and anxiety medications
- ➢ Single motherhood
- ➢ Unending and unsolvable frustration
- ➢ Held her back and slowed her down
- ➢ Made her unrecognizable to friends and family
- ➢ Made her subservient
- ➢ Removed her independence and badassery
- ➢ Made her an expert in misogyny, emotional, and narcissistic abuse

…and marriage is supposed to be the happiest day of our lives; it is supposed to be the "acme of existence" for women.

Divorce, on the other hand, also gave Kelly a lot of things (see below):

- ➢ Healed her anxiety and PTSD
- ➢ Skyrocketed her self-esteem
- ➢ Regained her confidence
- ➢ Lost weight
- ➢ Regained independence and freedom
- ➢ Homeowner
- ➢ Life of the party
- ➢ Hundreds of new friends and old relationships restored

- ➢ Work-Life Balance
- ➢ Hired a cleaning service
- ➢ Stopped drinking
- ➢ Stopped taking prescription medications
- ➢ Crushed all goals
- ➢ Made her a badass bullshit free woman
- ➢ Brand new wardrobe and sense of style
- ➢ Self-love like never before
- ➢ Restored faith

…and divorce is something we are supposed to avoid at all costs, but what a high cost so many of us pay.

Know Thyself

I want to assume that men understand their sexual needs. If you don't know what your sexual needs are as a woman, then it is time to **KNOW THYSELF.** What makes you feel sexy? How do you best connect with another human being? What makes you feel good? What makes you feel loved? What makes you feel alive? What makes you feel cherished? What revs up your physical and emotional engines?

Know yourself emotionally and sexually since sex is related to your emotional life. **Define what you like and need.** Write it down and say it out loud. It is OKAY TO LIKE SEX. It is OKAY TO WANT SEX. It is OKAY TO DESIRE SOMEONE. It is OKAY TO HAVE SEXUAL NEEDS. It is OKAY TO LONG FOR SOMETHING OR SOMEONE YOU DON'T HAVE. SEX IS OKAY. Sex isn't dirty or secretive. Sex isn't only for men to enjoy.

Why don't you go put on something sexy right now just to see how it makes you feel inside? I love to put on some sexy lingerie and admire my beautiful plus-sized body in the mirror while playing a love or sexy song adding to the atmosphere of sexuality. **The sexier and more confident YOU FEEL the more your man will be into you.** It doesn't matter if you weigh 200+

or 300+ lbs. Men love ALL sizes of women, *and confidence is the SEXIEST TRAIT OF ALL.* Straight facts – Kelly got laid more, weighting 275 lbs. than 175 lbs., because her confidence at 275 was at its peak. *No one saw the damn numbers on the scale.* All that bullshit about weight and body image is all fake news ingrained in women to keep them pregnant, miserable, self-loathing, in abusive marriages instead of out there in the world kicking major ass at every opportunity.

Why do you think Marilyn Monroe was the most famous movie actress of all time and every guy wanted her? Because her spirit was ON FIRE, her confidence was off the charts; she was flirty, fun, and fully ALIVE. She was magnetic and effervescent, and YOU CAN be that type of woman too. No guy wants a fuddy-duddy. No guy wants an insecure, self-loathing, self-defeated woman who bitches about her weight and looks. Guys like fun and action. They like excitement and newness, they love surprise and spontaneity. They want to be kept on their toes. *The mystery is what matters to men.* Change things up. Start dancing around. *Start acting like every guy wants you. Shake your booty a little, smile more, kick up your heels, laugh, joke, and work on becoming wittier.* Don't take life so seriously. Stop WORRYING about when you are going to get married and have kids. Life isn't all about marriage and kids. *Life is about feeling and being ALIVE.* Reinvent yourself, sis. You can be the Marilyn Monroe of this era. *You can have every guy drooling over you with that UNSHAKEABLE self-love confidence.* Put on that sexy lingerie, look at that sexy bitch in the mirror, put on some Marvin Gaye, and shake it, sister! *We can all use some sexual healing; after all, two rounds a day keeps the bitchiness away.*

Who's Hungry?

When I really began understanding my sexual needs and prioritized myself over men, I discovered that my sexual needs could be broken down into what I call *The Three Course Meal.*

Course 1: The appetizer: talking, foreplay, role-play, kissing, slow dancing, teasing, laughing – course 1 is very playful in nature and ramps up feelings of desire inside of each partner. ***This is the intensity buildup.***

Course 2: The main entrée, the physical act of intercourse.

Course 3: Dessert or after love love. Closeness, holding each other, talking, and laughing.

I cannot have one or two minutes of passionate intensity and then be done with it. That model doesn't work for me. I need the **Three Course Meal.** The excitement leading up to the act and then the dessert. ***I need to know and feel that sex is more than just an act and that it is an exchange of energy between two emotional beings.***

Sex Herself

It is okay to be a sexual being. ***You are Sex Herself!*** This is an acceptance and embodiment of your own sexuality, which is normal and healthy. You should feel pretty, attractive, and desirable. That is a fundamental human need. It is a fundamental need to be wanted and desired by others. We have been lied to our entire lives. We have been told that sex is

1. Only for men
2. Dirty
3. Shameful
4. Sinful
5. Lustful
6. Only to make babies

And on and on and on.......

How can you be a full human being if you don't accept and understand certain critical aspects of your humanity? My books are about helping women evolve into full human beings. Many women evolve into perpetual caregivers, never resting, only working themselves into the grave. My prayer is that you become a full human being accepting and embodying all of who you are.

If you've been taught that men don't like women who are too sexual or easy, well, f*ck them; men are easy too! **Men are the easy ones.** Embrace your femininity and sexuality. Hug it, hold it, and squeeze it. Pour yourself a glass of wine, throw on some sexy lingerie, play your favorite sexual tune, and dance for yourself in front of that mirror!

Sister – You are a Sexual Goddess.

Chapter 10 Takeaways

> - It is okay to like, want and need sex. You are human.
> - Understand yourself and your sexual needs.
> - Stop denying yourself because you have been told all your life that it is wrong.
> - Sex isn't only about men.
> - Put on some sexy lingerie, play a sensual song, and dance in front of the mirror. **Admire the gorgeous effervescent sexual being staring back at you.**

Share Your Story:

In the space provided, it is time to share your story. How have you been lied to about sex? Have you ever considered your own sexual needs, or have you been in service of pleasing others?

Chapter 11
You're Still Expected to Live

"Love is pain, not pleasure."

Have you ever been so heartbroken over a boy and thought to yourself, ***"f*ck, I am still expected to live, aren't I?"*** When you just want to crawl into a little ball wallowing over the heartbreak for centuries.

Yes, sister, YOU ARE STILL EXPECTED TO LIVE – AND YOU WILL LIVE!

This chapter takes you through a cerebral deep dive into **the emotion of desire.** What is desire? **Desire is the most intense pain-inducing emotion of them all.** Desire is a wish. It is an all-consuming longing. A hunger, an appetite. Desire is hopeful. It is covetousness cupidity, yearning, lust, weakness, mania, madness, intensity, craze, fondness. It is the exciting feeling on Christmas morning running down the stairs to open presents only to discover you've been given nothing but coal. When you desire someone, nothing can stop you. Nothing can diminish that aching desire. Nothing. It is a freight train running full speed, full throttle, in my mind constantly. Yes, I push through work, motherhood, paying bills, maintaining friends, a social life, having fun, doing my meditation, writing this book, and serving my clients, but the freight train keeps on running, electricity flooding my body, mind, and soul. **A longing that can never be satisfied.**

Death of Desire Awaits You

I wish I could bang my head against the wall and forget him for just 10 minutes. Forget the images of him on top of me, kissing me, looking into my eyes, holding me, desiring me, coming toward me, biting his lip, that look of love, that look of desire, those deep beautiful blue eyes. Was I just dreaming? Or did this all really happen? Was this reality? This was everything. *Whatever TF this was, it was everything. I felt so visible to him. So desired. So seen, so heard, so cared for, and so wanted. Wanted! I felt wanted!* I wish I could just block it all out of my memory forever and erase every conceivable image from my mind. In those moments of heated passion, the emotional nurturance I received from him was overwhelming; you cannot imagine the euphoria unless you have experienced that feeling. How could I make this last? How could I keep his interest in me? As I write this chapter right now, I am bawling my eyes out. The rain tears flow so heavily I can barely see through the water to the words on the computer screen. A pain so significant you just feel it 24/7. No relief. No escape. This is desire. *Desire is death.*

A soft dreamland, intoxication, I am high on him. I am high on this. Like entering the gates of heaven itself seeing the most wonderous sights imaginable, utter bliss, complete magnetism. How can I make it last? *How can I make it reality?*

Of all emotions, desire is undoubtedly the most painful because desire is never fulfilled. You cannot fulfill a desire. *The object of your desire will never be yours, and that is precisely why you want it so badly.* It causes you so much pain because you cannot have it. You never will. You ache. You starve. Anger, frustration, euphoria, and other emotions can be intense, but they are not as intense as desire because anger, frustration, and euphoria come and go. They usually only last minutes or hours, *but desire is ongoing.* Desire is every second, every hour, every day, every week, every month year over year. The desire to be wanted is so profound that it permeates your psyche clouding your rational thought. Therefore, you often make emotional decisions rather than logical ones. *Every... second... hurts...*

The plight of every single woman is the total emotional dependence on a man until resolved. This is an unsolvable problem, an ever-aching need never satisfied. *Even you married women... still wait by the phone. When are we going to learn? When are we going to heal?*

It's Over

I sat there frozen behind the text message of him dumping me after three months of dating because he *lost the spark.* My stomach sank, my heart raced, and my brain turned on panic-mode. I couldn't believe it. He said, "you look great on paper. I couldn't find a thing wrong with you, and I like you as a person, I really do, but I no longer have the spark to continue dating you. It's not fair to you or your daughter."

I cannot write this chapter without tears falling down my face, but I know I need to write it for you (and for myself). Without saying more words, you know exactly how I feel right now. I love him so much. I am so devastatingly in love with him. I feel like I would do anything to be with him right now. You know what this is, *this is the feels.* A very intense and powerful emotion, infatuation on fire; the burning desire, the longing, the inner pleading, the wondering how you will go on another day without this person. Why? Why does this happen to us? Why do we fall so madly in love? Steven Carter and Julia Sokol hit the nail on the head in *Men Who Can't Love*, "the beginning: fearless pursuit. This stage is typified by the hard sell. He is obviously taken by you and is trying desperately to make you feel the same way. To accomplish this, he pulls out all the stops. How long the Beginning lasts depends upon how long it takes him to make the sale and what he perceives as the commitment point of no return." *I made only one mistake with Jordan... I fell for him.* He got me. I was sold. *If you want the honeymoon phase to last forever, never fall for him, or at least NEVER F*CKING SHOW IT.*

I feel like I cannot go on. I know I must, but I don't want to.

The ability to feel is a human quality. It is precisely what makes us human. And this longing feeling that I am talking about is ***desire.***

Sexual and emotional attraction for another human being is what makes us human. We are sexual and emotional creatures. It is impossible to understand these terrible emotions we feel. I say terrible because I do not like the feeling of desire when I cannot have the object (person) of that desire. To me, it is the most painful feeling in the world. It feels like you are being dragged by a train against tracks for miles and miles with no break or stopping. Not for a single moment does this feeling leave your mind. There is no Band-Aid, no cure. Just an incurable sorrow of lost love, no pill to remove the pain, and no firefighters to cool your desire. **You are on fire.** Like an electromagnetic wave rushing through your body distracting you from all other imminent matters in life. You feel like you cannot go on, like you cannot live without this person you love so much.

I remember the first time he kissed me. We went out to dinner and had a lovely evening. The plan was to go to the movies. On the car ride from the restaurant to the theater, he said that he needed to use the restroom and did not want to go to a public one. He asked if we could make a quick stop at my place so he could go and then we would be on our way to the movies. He went inside my home, and honestly, I cannot recall as to whether he used the restroom, but all I know is two minutes after being inside my house, he came up to my face and kissed me gently. The next thing I knew, I was on my back. A few minutes later he whispers, "let's go upstairs."

That is all I remember from there. The electrifying rush. It was exhilarating. It was as if someone put me on a **roller coaster,** and I was flying at speeds of 150 mph. There was no thinking happening. No logic. No thought process, *only intense emotions.*

A day later he drove 45 minutes over to my house at 11pm and spent the night with me after I had a big work event that day. This would be our third date. We cuddled and watched a movie together. It was very sweet. The next morning, he took me to breakfast and then we walked around at the beach and talked for an hour. During this date, he set up our fourth date; he invited me over to his place because he wanted to cook dinner for me – bacon-wrapped scallops. *Who is this guy?*

Heaven

The memory of him will haunt me for a while. He had the most beautiful blue eyes I'd ever seen, a perfect jawline, ashy hair, and a slender masculine body. The devil couldn't get a hold of me type of deal. He was breathtaking. He's so handsome, it hurts. I break down and cry, looking at photos of him and I together. His blue eyes are like a mysterious unchartered ocean filled with intrigue and emotion. They are so deep you would get lost inside of them. I was lost in him. No one made me feel the way he made me feel, not even Boyfriend from *GIRL GRIT: SAVAGE NOT AVERAGE. Jordan is his name.*

Friday came, and he was cooking bacon-wrapped scallops for dinner for me. *I remember how I felt about him.* I am a strong, self-assured, and confident woman which is entirely true. However, there is always a but right? *He made me weak. Like on my knees.* I couldn't walk or talk, I couldn't eat or sleep, I was in deep. I lost all control. All strength. I have never felt like this before. *Who is this guy?*

Bacon Wrapped Scallops – The Kitchen on FIRE

As he was cooking for me, I think I just stood there drinking my drink while frozen and talking anxiously. He knew he made me nervous when I was around him, and he told me to calm down (LOL). I remember he approached me with a soft intimate kiss, and I melted. Then he'd go back to cooking and conversing for a few minutes. Then a few minutes later, he pinned me against the wall while the scallops were sizzling in the pan and pressed himself against my body. *I felt the heat of desire sizzling inside of us.* I couldn't eat a damn thing. I forced myself to eat. Mind racing, heart beating, head spinning, crotch soaked.

The emotion of it all was mind-bending. No greater excitement. In my mind, I was picturing us burning down the kitchen, breaking every glass and plate, pots and pans banging against each other, utensils flying, throwing each other around, destroying the room. Have you ever felt this way about someone? Have you ever had this type of relationship before?

Three Months of Heaven

Rewind three months, and it was early April. I had lost much hope and faith in dating since our modern dating landscape is a shit show. There he was on the Bumble app. I have no idea why I swiped right on him because I did not find his photos attractive. Sometimes I just swiped right on random people to generate more matches. I matched with him and figured what the hell, another three-message exchange that will go nowhere. Then we started talking, and he was *actually RESPONSIVE.* I don't give anyone the time of day, why was he any different? He was different. He was responsive, inquisitive, and thoughtful. I wasn't used to this.

A Real Date

So, like a boy, no a man wants to take me out on a real date. Wait, what's a date? Who goes on dates anymore? We matched and started talking on a Wednesday, and by Friday, he asked me out on a date for Saturday. *I did not want to go out on a date with him. He did not look good in his online dating photos.* BUT, because he ACTED LIKE A REAL MAN and asked me out ON A REAL DATE, that in and of itself impressed me because he took on that male leadership role, and so I agreed, but not for Saturday. I made him wait until Tuesday because I was playing a hard-to-get little shit. He picked out a nice restaurant for Tuesday AND MADE A RESERVATION (insert mind-blown emoji)! I don't think anyone asked me out on a REAL DATE in over 10 years! *I was more than impressed by him. Big mistake of mine. I should have acted like I didn't give a shit.*

We continued to talk every day leading up to our REAL DATE and on that Sunday, which happened to be Easter Sunday, he sent me a lovely selfie of himself, and I almost fell off my chair. I was instantly smitten. Instantly in love. This photo of him and the man on his dating profile could not be the same person. He sent me a good photo, and I couldn't stop looking at it. *His eyes instantly electrocuted me.* I was confident about our first date; he knew about me writing *GIRL GRIT: SAVAGE NOT AVERAGE*, knew I had a PhD, and knew I directed beauty pageants. He encouraged me and was impressed by my achievements. I did not have to lower myself for him, as I was accustomed to doing with other men. He was happy about my successes and seemed to like me for them. I figured any man who was okay with me having a PhD and being a beauty pageant director must be the one because some men would not be okay with all of that.

When I met him in person on that first date, I melted instantly. He was absolutely striking. A total heartbreaker. I do not understand why he doesn't have better photos on his dating profile, because the photos on his dating profile do not do him any justice. He looks like a celebrity! He's perfect. *And he was into me! He was really into me!* Our first date went great and lasted five hours. We hung out three times during the first week and then subsequently once or twice a week thereafter, depending on our work schedules.

He was the perfect guy. He checked all the boxes in my book. He had a good job, a college degree, and had his own place. It is, in my opinion, very hard to find a man nowadays with all three of those qualities. You are lucky to get two out of the three. He had his shit together, and it was IMPRESSIVE. I couldn't believe my own luck. This is a guy who prioritized me, paid for every single date, spent tons of money taking me out, made reservations for dates, cooked for me, planned fun stuff for us to do, made date suggestions, was AMAZING IN BED, attentive, great with my daughter – he was a dream. *I had to have been dreaming.*

I've Been Waiting All Week to See You

It was a Friday night, and I had just dropped off my daughter with her father. I headed over to his place for our Friday evening plans, and the second I stepped into his place; he immediately pulled me close, and he softly kissed my lips. I knew he loved me from the way that he kissed me, so gentle, so soft.

He sat me down. He looked into my eyes. Those deep blue perfect eyes and he whispered into my ears, ***"I have been waiting all week to see you."*** He captured my heart. I do not think I have ever felt like this before. I have loved and I have been in love, but this was so different. Why? Because **HE WANTED ME**. I was wanted by him. I wanted him too. *I just wanted to f*cking matter to someone...*

He pursued me hard for three full months. I have NEVER been pursued like this before. It caught me off guard and came from the left field. It was all so fast; it was all a rush. As fast as he made me his girl, he broke it off fast too. It wasn't me rushing the relationship, it was him. All him. I went along with it all, so that is where I made my mistake because I should have been more judicious in my approach and guarded my heart carefully. I was a bit reckless with it all because I wasn't used to this. In fact, I did not want to rush; I do not believe in the immediate relationship; I voiced to him the day we met that "I was not determined for marriage and children like many women. I am open to the idea, but they are not goals of mine."

He did all these things that signaled he wanted something long-term with me. He told his parents about me (you would not tell your parents about a booty call), spent thousands of dollars on me, gave me his time consistently, courted me, set up fun dates and made reservations, met my daughter and was great with her (you wouldn't meet someone's kid if you knew it was only short term), and BEST YET, he moved his $1000 inflatable hot tub into my house! **You would NOT be doing that unless you saw long-term potential with someone.** You would not move a big-ticket item into their home. Three weeks after he moved the hot tub in, he broke up with me because he **"lost the spark."** All that passion, all that lust, all those fancy dinners, all those deep philosophical talks, all those little adventures we had enjoying each other's interests, all because he lost the electricity he had for me. **He "fell out of love."**

Desire is painful. I desire him because I cannot have him. He did something to my body and mind. My nervous system was all out of whack. Sweaty palms, racing heart, racing mind, trouble breathing, collywobbles and butterflies, anxiety, panic, fear, loss of appetite, loss of sleep, loss of concentration, and trouble relaxing. This is what I call the heebie-jeebies. **It is a physiological response to the emotion of desire. The most powerful and painful emotion to ever exist.**

I will not fall out of love with Jordan until I fall in love with the next guy, unfortunately. That is just how I am, and that is just how this works. The best way to get over someone is to get under someone else, right? I want to rid him of my memory. Those emotional discussions over fancy dinners, how he attended kid events with my daughter and I, the look in his eyes, the gentle kisses. I want it all gone… SO BAD. I cannot get the images out of my head. Everywhere I go, everything I do, I see him. He haunts me. ***His ghost follows me everywhere.***

Live Regretlessly

Do I regret meeting him? No, no I do not. If I could do it all over again, I would, but this time, I would do things differently now that I have learned some valuable lessons. I write this because I know you know this feeling well. I know you have similar feelings of love for others. I know you have felt or do feel desire for someone right now. Emotion is part of being human, and desire is a powerful emotion.

These three months were the best three months of my life. I have no regrets. Like the adage goes, ***"it is better to have loved and lost than to have never loved at all."*** The day he broke up with me, he let me come over to his place for a few minutes to talk and say goodbye. I cried humbly in his presence but then collected my things and walked out of the door with dignity and not desperation. ***You don't want me anymore? Cool, awesome, goodbye.***

I walked out that door and cried uncontrollably for an entire week. I still worked, I still conducted my sales calls, but I cried in between each call, then held myself together again to execute the calls confidently. I got it all out of my system. I went no-contact with him. For years thereafter, he stalked me on social media. We were connected via Snapchat, and he viewed every one of my stories. Many times, he would be the FIRST PERSON to view my stories. He was consistent in stalking me, which confused me. I did consult friends on the matter. The feedback I received was:

He misses you and wants to see what you have been up to. He cares about you; I don't look at people's stories who I don't care about.

It could mean nothing; he might be routinely looking at everyone's stories.

The conclusion I came to is this: he's interested. To what degree, I am uncertain. Is he romantically interested? I have no clue. He said he really likes me as a person and wants to remain friends. There is something to this post-break-up stalking. It might not be as big a deal as I hope it is, but nonetheless, he is investing time clicking on my stories to see the content I post. Four weeks to the day after we had no contact, I reached out to him. Here is what I said:

Hey Jordan,

I hope you are doing well and enjoying your summer. I wanted to check if you're still interested in being friends. I have had time to reflect on everything and would like to be friends with you. If not, I completely understand. You won't hurt my feelings if you don't want to remain friends. The ball is in your court now.

I left things light and fluffy, completely giving him the option to "opt-out" if he wished. (Side note – I have overcome my fears of rejection; I accept rejection now).

He responded almost immediately (within 10 minutes), which is very good. A fast response is always reassuring, and he texted back, "yes, we can still be friends." Then I asked him how he's been lately, and he filled me in on the updates (keeping it very casual which was perfectly okay). Once he responded… I didn't respond back for four days! Got to play mind games, right? You must be unpredictable, right? Got to keep them guessing, right? Got to keep them wanting more, right?

After another two weeks, I asked him to come pick up his hot tub and he asked, when? I put him off for a whole week saying that I had something every night this week and that he could come the following week. I did this for three reasons 1) I was truly busy that week, although I didn't have something every night, I had something almost every night 2) I was playing some mind games, wanting him to think I was going on dates with other guys 3) I needed a week to mentally prepare myself just to see him again since it would be very hard on me.

The Power of the Mind

I spent a week mentally preparing and getting myself into my Zen zone and zone of resilience. I sought counsel from friends, family members, and online dating coaches. I had a foolproof plan and strategy in place. I even set out roses another man recently bought me in plain view so he might spot them when he was over. I wore an elegant and classy work outfit (since he knew I was on coaching calls all day), it was simple, not overdone, small earnings, a nice blouse, red pants, no makeup, and hair done. Subtle yet beautiful, *I cannot give myself away again.*

I was instructed to be friendly, polite, and cordial but remain aloof and indifferent as if nothing happened to **keep him guessing** if I had moved on or not, if I was seeing someone else or not, or if I still liked him or not. I was nervous and scared inside. I didn't want him to be indifferent and cold toward me. I prayed. I ensured that I could get through this and maintain my composure completely, acting cool, calm, and collected. *I could not give myself away at all.* I could not show any weakness. *I could not give him my power like that again.* I had to get him in and out swiftly. Inside I felt weak. Inside I was crying. Inside I was crumbling, but I had to be strong AF. I had to pull myself together and get through this because I am a strong woman warrior.

He came over to take apart the hot tub. He was nice, friendly, and respectful. We both acted like old friends, like nothing ever happened between us, good or bad. I assisted him with the deconstruction of the tub, which gave us the opportunity to catch up and chat casually. He asked me some questions, which I was pleased about like 1) how have you been 2) how is your summer going 3) how is work 4) how is your daughter doing? I am always impressed when someone asks me questions because it tells me they care and are taking an interest in me and what I have to say. As we said goodbye, he said, "see you later."

I went balls out and asked him, "would you like to hang out sometime as friends? Maybe go for a walk or grab a coffee." He hesitated for a second but said yes. He said in a couple of weeks since he had plans over the next two weekends (I think he was going out of town for one of them), and I said sure, no problem. He asked if we could meet halfway since it was a 40-minute drive, and I said no problem, halfway is fine. He could have said "yes" to be "nice" and not reject me since I had asked in person (another one of my carefully planned moves). I wanted to ask in person rather than via text. I used this situation as an opportunity to ask.

He mentioned meeting halfway, that told me he is serious about hanging out again.

The Master Plan – The Snake, The Lioness, and The Shark

GIRL GAME: BALLS OUT is about having a solid strategy to win in life, love, and business. If you don't have plans in place, then it is hard to make things happen for you. I created a master plan to reengage with Jordan. I must act slowly, carefully, and judiciously because if I mess up, my plan might backfire, and I might lose my chance.

Be patient leveraging time to guide you. *Everything in life is all about timing.* You don't earn a degree overnight, you don't become successful in a year, you don't write a novel in a week, you don't train for a marathon in a day, and you don't master guitar in an hour. Everything in life takes time. Therefore, you must act wisely and carefully to win. You need a solid game plan.

My plan was to wait another 3-4 weeks. Why that long? Couple of reasons 1) I want to give him the space to possibly reach out to me first (which would be very good) 2) after three weeks have passed I wanted him to wonder if I am going to reach out to him or when I am going to reach out (building attraction is all about being mysterious and unpredictable with men, men love uncertainty it drives them crazy… for you). If after three weeks of crickets, I will make my Lioness move and reach out to him. I will ask him to hang out via text and attempt the reconnection.

The Foundation of Friendship

This relationship was the very definition of a crash and burn, which, unfortunately, is how most, if not all romances and affairs go. ***Everyone wants to be in love, so they rush into everything hoping it will work out and last.*** And most often it doesn't. It is possible, but haste is not an advantage; patience is. If I had used my brain instead of being carefree with Jordan, then I might still possibly be with him today. He was leading hard, and I was following hard. ***I went along for the wild ride he took us on.***

I never built a friendship with Jordan to start. This was my opportunity to start over with him. This was my second chance with him. It may not be successful, and it may fail but so what? ***It is far better to try and fail than to not try at all and live with regrets.*** At this point, my intention is not to get back together with Jordan. Is that what I want and desire? Yes, very much so. However, I am a smart girl, and I know that just getting back together quickly will render another crash-and-burn situation. The only shot I have with Jordan is establishing a real, authentic friendship with hin, completely leaving sex and romance out of it for a while.

If I see Jordan again in person for a friend date or hangout, then it will be just that, a hangout/friend date.

We will naturally and organically build a healthy and lasting friendship. One of four things will happen.

1. I will never see or talk to Jordan again (worst-case scenario).
2. I will see him again but for one reason or another it may be the last time (either on his end or mine).
3. We will establish a true, authentic friendship and remain good friends for a long time (very good outcome).
4. We will establish a true, authentic friendship and emotional bond deciding to get back together in a committed relationship (best-case scenario).

I am hopeful that #3 or #4 will happen. I would be okay with #3, as I genuinely value having solid and meaningful friendships in my life. Only time will tell, right? I regret absolutely nothing. I lost absolutely nothing. I had a wonderful relationship with Jordan. *I experienced being deeply desired and wanted by him.* I learned many valuable life lessons through this experience that can be applied to other areas of my life. I regret nothing. I am thankful to know Jordan. I am thankful he was in my life. *I am thankful for the time I had with him and the memories I get to keep in my heart forever.*

Rejection is Okay

No one likes rejection. I think we can all agree that rejection is one of the worst things to experience. Many people decide not to act on something simply because they cannot bear the thought of being rejected. **They protect themselves by never trying.** Others have the power to reject us, and similarly, we have the power to reject others; this is just part of life. After the hot tub pickup, I waited five weeks before reaching out to Jordan. I wanted to make him think I had completely forgotten about him and moved on. All my moves were carefully and strategically planned. I needed to make him wonder if I would ever reach out or if he might ever hear from me again. I prayed and prayed. I just kept praying, strategizing, and scheming not to mess up my foolproof plan. Then after five weeks, I reached out via text and sent him this message.

Hi Jordan,

I hope you are doing well.

I know you said you wanted to remain friends with me, and I'm unsure if you only said that to be polite or if you genuinely care about sustaining a real friendship with me.

Either way, I hope all is well and I'd like to get together soon.

I knew Jordan had the authority to reject me, and I got to a place where I was completely okay with it. I knew that he would either say yes (ideal), no (not ideal) or no response at all (even more not ideal). I had mentally and emotionally prepared myself for rejection because Jordan had the right to reject my offer.

He waited about eight hours to respond but I did get a…. *POSITIVE RESPONSE!* He said:

Hey, sorry I have been so busy with work and was out of town last weekend. Yes, I would like to get together how does Monday sound?

I sent the text to him Saturday afternoon and he is requesting a date for Monday! Less than 48 hours away! I felt that was a bit urgent on his part – why would he suggest Monday of all days? I was unavailable on Monday, so I told him I could do it on Thursday, and he agreed.

Sister – It is okay to get your heart broken.

Chapter 11 Takeaways

> Being in love sucks if it is not reciprocated.
> Being in love and feeling electricity makes one ***feel alive – feeling is a good thing.***
> Excitement is good for us.
> It is okay to love, and it is okay to get your heart broken.
> Rejection is not the end of the world.
> ***Learn to accept and embrace rejection; rejection is a natural part of life.***

Share Your Story:

In the space provided, it is time to share your story. Describe a time when you had a love like this; how did it make you feel? What was the outcome of that relationship?

Chapter 12
Becoming a Man
Women Have no Power in a Relationship

"It is alarming how many heterosexual relationships are all about the man and getting his needs filled, while a woman consequently never gets hers filled. Relationships often become one-sided, with one person giving and the other taking - there is no reciprocity."

Have you ever considered how privileged men are? Think about all the ways they have been throughout the decades.

- Women have supported them throughout law school, medical school, or college.
- Women have aided them in building their careers while forsaking their own.
- Women have served them and raised their children (oftentimes alone).
- Men have all power and authority in romantic relationships (I will discuss this later).
- Men have power, authority, and control in many areas of their lives, especially in love.
- Men are deemed head of household (in a traditional sense).
- Men are conditioned to make something of themselves and pushed toward achievement and success.
- Men usually do not give up careers to raise children.
- Men get to relax after work (video games, TV, the bar, etc.).
- Men are paid more than women just because of their gender.

- ❖ Men have been given authority to make decisions in their home, financial and otherwise.
- ❖ Men are the chasers, pursuers, and hunters (always going after the women they want whereas women are not allowed to go after the men they want as it is socially unacceptable).
- ❖ Men (some of them) take credit for other people's work and efforts.

Men are perceived as strong and powerful whereas women are perceived as weak and insecure. Men have been historically regarded as the first sex and women the second (hence Adam was created before Eve, biblically speaking). Men are given opportunities often without effort because they have "families to support." The scariest thing of all is that they have total and complete power in relationships. Women have no power in a historical sense. I do believe times are changing and tables are turning, and women are increasingly gaining more power, but the powers that be still conquer heteronormative relationships.

Dating today is so weird. ***Who is supposed to pursue who? Who is supposed to take that initiative, that leadership role?*** Let's examine how dating and marriage have traditionally evolved here.

Man likes a woman.

Man asks a woman out on a date.

Man takes that leadership role, sets up the date, and pays for everything.

Man sets up a second date.

Man is "leading" the relationship from conception to completion.

Man proposes to a woman (buys her).

It is the man's decision and ONLY the man's decision as to whether he marries her. It is not her decision at all. She is at the mercy of his proposal which may or may not ever come.

Historically, from the first date to the marriage proposal, the man has initiated and led the entire ordeal. It is all and only and entirely **his decision** from A to Z. The only thing the woman can do is either go along with him or not. That's it. She has no power. No control. No say so in anything. And if she dares pursue him, chase him, or take initiative then she is emasculating him supposedly. She is taking the male role. Relationships are 100% about power dynamics with the man having total power and total control and the woman going along with him while being submissive. We know there are cases where the woman is leading and initiating and cases where men expect to be chased by women, but keep in mind I am speaking in a **traditional or historical sense**. We are discussing the rules, not the exceptions.

The woman adapts to the man's life. She forsakes her own hobbies, interests, and often friends rearranging herself to fit perfectly into his life bubble under his authority. She no longer has a life or identity of her own. They both live **his life**. Furthermore, she is usually happy (at least at first) to give up these sacred parts and pieces of herself because she so wants his love and approval, and she will do anything, **including reducing her personhood,** to achieve that end. Her goal is marriage and kids because she has been conditioned by society to believe that marriage and kids are the **acme of existence** for her. Her greatest purpose is to be a wife and mother living in **perpetual servitude of giving** until her arms break off her body. She gives up so much getting so little in return. Why? What is so lacking in her that she surrenders to these realities? Dr. Penelope Russianoff, in *Why Do I Think I Am Nothing Without a*

Man, articulates the harmful reality of gender roles and the traps they place both women and men in, "but the solution to dating (and mating) problems is not role-reversal. It is role-dropping. If men and women would interact as plain people, there would be less "Him Tarzan, Me Jane" thinking and no need for "Him Jane, Me Tarzan." Women wouldn't cling; men wouldn't encourage their clinging. Desperate dependence, on both sides, would give way to more humanistic (rather than male-female) ways of interacting."

We are all insecure (to a greater or lesser degree). Most believe they need a partner, spouse, or lover because they believe they cannot function on their own. ***We would rather look for someone else to heal us when we are responsible for doing the healing ourselves.*** Many of us live in the most f*cked up of situations because we are insecure and worried about being alone (along with some other situational factors). We allow ourselves to be used and abused because we believe having someone, no matter how abusive they are, is better than being alone and having no one at all. ***Many of you in relationships are lonelier than us single people.***

Do you understand how heartbreakingly destructive this is? YOU ARE A PERSON! You are purpose. You have power. You have potential, but you waste your life away living under the thumb of some man who treats you like you are invisible. Treating you like you don't matter to him. Familiarity breeds contempt is 100% true. Remember how he used to be in the beginning? Now how does he treat you? Do you wish you could change him and have him return as the man you once knew?

Men have succeeded due to the efforts and hard work of women. Men have taken credit for our labor. Men have made us their maids, servants, assistants, helpers, and secretaries. You don't see women out here with maids, servants, assistants, helpers, and secretaries, do you? ***Yet, WE ARE THE ONES WHO ACTUALLY NEED THE HELP!***

The Accommodation Queen

As women, we are notorious for twisting ourselves into a pretzel for men to love us, want us, and value us. We are the ***Accommodation Queens***. We accommodate his every need. We walk on eggshells for him. I hear about women walking on eggshells all the time for men, but I never hear about men walking on eggshells for women! If you must walk on eggshells around someone then you are babying that person. You are accommodating their weaknesses. You are tiptoeing around their feelings so as not to cause them any upset because God forbid you disturb what little inner peace they don't have! Let that man tiptoe around you, sis!

You are jumping through hoops and doing backflips naked in the middle of the street for him, so that you don't offend his little male ego. You are reconstructing your essential personhood to please and appease him. You want so badly for your relationship to last. You have so much hope when all you are really doing is wasting your precious time and energy that could be better spent on going out there in the world, achieving your own dreams and fulfilling your own potential. Women and men are not as different as people make us out to be. We are both human. We all think and feel. We can all accomplish, achieve, serve, conquer, overcome, and heal. ***However, we attribute certain traits and characteristics only to women and others only to men. Bullshit.***

Dr. Penelope Russianoff wrote a book called *Why Do I Think I Am Nothing Without a Man*. It really changed the way I view relationships because the title of her book alone is so true for so many women. Here is a passage from the book: "If you don't have a man, you operate (or put off operating) on the premise that when you get one, you'll be and do and have everything you dream of being and doing and having. You postpone genuine enjoyment of work and play. You do not make life commitments-such as deciding where you want to live permanently or buying real estate or establishing any kind of roots. Because you have made everything contingent on the man you're going to have. He will not only help you make it through the night; he will determine your daily routine and even your lifestyle. If you are married or living with someone, chances are that you still don't escape the role of lady-in-waiting. Still, your enjoyment of life depends on the presence of a man." She goes on to express, "I find it so sad that so many women spend so much of their lives on hold – waiting for Mr. Right to come along, waiting for him to come home, waiting for him to make them feel complete instead of allowing themselves to be who they are, to emerge as themselves, to give themselves the right to enjoy, to feel complete in themselves."

Dr. Russianoff's work is brilliant because it is so true. If you are not one of these women, you know someone who is. She said they spend much of their lives on hold, waiting. Waiting to be chosen, waiting to matter, waiting to be seen, heard, listened to, f*cked, touched, loved. And the list goes on. They even wait for their men to change. ***Imagine what they could achieve in their lives if they would just stop waiting on a man.*** This illustrates my point in Chapter 1, when I discussed ***hiding from the world***. Men make you hide from the world. ***She puts herself into hiding because she is waiting on a man to rescue her when she needs to rescue herself from all this madness.***

Individuality Vs. Possession

Understand that each human being is, first, and always, an individual. You are an individual. You came into this world alone as an individual. We are all fed this lie that everyone must have someone. That is simply not true. I am not anti-relationship or anti-marriage. *I am anti-making everyone think they need to do something when they don't.* There is nothing wrong with being in a relationship or having a partner. Nothing. But how many of you really have partners? Equal contributors in the relationship? It is no secret that women do far more in and for relationships. Women are conditioned for relationships and men are not. That is why, as women, our sole emphasis becomes hooking a man. Men go out there and build careers. Men are not consumed by relationships the way women are. Men do not feel like they will combust if they don't have a woman. *Gender role conditioning is so programmed into our heads that it is almost impossible to escape it.*

Dating is Nothing but Mind Games

Don't text him first. Don't call him first. Let him be the one to reach out first. Don't initiate sex. Don't bring up marriage. Don't be too needy. Let him come back to you. *We have no power. Do you understand how disturbing this is?* Please think about it for a minute. We are powerless as women. There is nothing we can do but hope and pray. *We hope too much, and we pray too much for changes and miracles that never come.* Then we watch as he gives to the next woman all the things we wanted but that he refused to give to us.

I have completed extensive research considering the psychology of dating, and I have come to the sobering conclusion *that it is nothing but a giant mind game with one winner and one loser. The men are often winning, and the women are often losing, and you know EXACTLY what I am talking about.* I am speaking on how to date a man as a woman and not how to date a woman as a man. This is not advice for men (although maybe some can relate) this is advice for women dating men in the game. It is called the dating game because it is a game.

Now as for my own opinion on the dating game - it is malevolent and frightening. I do not believe in playing games, but unfortunately, when it comes to dating, they do work. Not all men love mind games, but enough do to make this a major issue for us women. I have listened to, studied, and bought the books of renowned dating coaches and experts, and what I am delineating in this chapter aligns with the advice they give. This is a complex subject, and it is much to digest.

Eat or Be Eaten

Men do the eating and women are eaten. Men are the hunters, and women are the hunted (the prey). Men are the chasers and women are captured by the chase. *Men fall in love fast and out of love faster.* Women are left discarded and heartbroken, and you see this pattern happen repeatedly to the point where it is *The Same Story.* I discussed *The Same Story* in my first book, *GIRL GRIT: SAVAGE NOT AVERAGE.* **You have two options here, okay? You can either eat or be eaten.** If I had to guess, you have been eaten by men. Chewed up and spit out like a fish caught and released back into the wild. Sad. Cold. Hard. Truth. So…. the secret revealed is to eat. I am going to teach you exactly how to do that. *Most of life is a pattern of you having your hooks in others or others having their hooks in you – don't be the one with the scars because you will always lose. It is far better to catch a fish than be the fish caught.*

Nice Versus Mean – Strength Versus Weakness

If you were born a female, then I am willing to bet you were taught to be "nice." Nice does not mean what most people think it means. Nice means "take advantage of me, I am weak." *Nice does not earn respect, praise, or adoration. People do not respect nice.* Yet, women have been instructed to be nice for centuries because it is in our supposed "nature." *You were not BORN nice! Nobody was born anything.* Character and personality are developed by the environment and social influences. ***Being nice is not adding value to your life, it is taking away value.*** I am encouraging you to be mean. Now by mean, I mean put yourself first and establish strong boundaries. Do not be a people-pleaser and do not allow others to walk all over you.

We are all weak and we all have weaknesses. Weakness is the refusal to be strong because strength is a supernatural ability. ***Strength comes naturally to no one.*** We are naturally weak because humans are fallible. Strength is something that is developed and refined over time. It is not innate. This is why many suffer from mental health issues because they are not naturally strong and resilient. ***Strength is a choice. It is a decision.*** You choose to be strong, or you remain weak. ***Strength is a mindset.*** Be mean and strong. Have the audacity in you. ***People respect audacity.*** People respect the brave and fearless. ***<u>If you remain weak and indecisive, you will face many struggles in your life.</u>***

Charlotte and Her Web

We all know the beloved story of Charlotte's Web. When it comes to relationships between women and men it comes down to value and whether a man values a woman or not. In a traditional sense, women put their men on a pedestal. He does not deserve to be put on a pedestal. You need to put yourself on a pedestal because that is how he will perceive you, the way you perceive yourself. Theresa Mummert says, "The moment you put someone on a pedestal, they will look down upon you. The trick is respecting each other equally." ***When we put others on pedestals, it is often because we fail to recognize and understand our own worthiness.*** He will value you the way that you value yourself and many of you devalue yourselves for men, and it never works.

Repeat these words now to yourself:

I AM A HIGH-VALUE WOMAN
ANYONE WOULD BE LUCKY TO HAVE ME
I PUT MYSELF ON A PEDESTAL AND I REMAIN THERE
I WILL NOT ALLOW ANYONE TO DEVALUE ME
I NEVER DEVALUE MYSELF
I AM EXPENSIVE
I WILL BE EARNED AND NOT GIVEN FREELY
I AM ALWAYS THE RIGHT CHOICE
I AM A QUEEN AND A GODDESS, AND I WILL BE TREATED AS SUCH

Never devalue yourself and never accept piss-poor treatment from a man. Men love to test women, okay? Be smarter than them. ***Be five steps ahead of them, and that is what I am teaching you in this book: how to play the game and win it.***

In the classic story of Charlotte's Web, the main character, Wilbur, a pig, is going to be slaughtered and cooked as bacon. He meets an unlikely friend, a spider named Charlotte, who notices and understands Wilbur's value; Charlotte understands that Wilbur is much more than a piece of meat, AND SO ARE YOU, SWEET SISTER! She **BUILDS HIS VALUE** as an individual by writing four words on her web speaking to Wilbur's worth making the townspeople not want to slaughter him.

Know this, understand this, envision this, and embody it. Embody and radiate the qualities of light, love, purpose, passion, and potential in your life. ***You are taking back control of your life and developing your personal power.*** Every day you are becoming more confident, secure, and self-assured. ***Every day you are becoming a better version of yourself.***

Envision yourself now as Charlotte the spider and create your own spider web always in alignment with what you are attracting into your life. Things will get caught on your web.

Your web will attract things into it, but we want to ensure that these are desirable and not unwanted things. Capture a man into your web, but not just any man. It is your distant avoidant husband, it is an ex-boyfriend you want back, or some other man you have your sights on. ***Your goal is to trap him into your spider web, and I will show you how.***

Sister - It's time to take back your power and control.

Chapter 12 Takeaways

> ➤ Traditionally, women have had no power in romantic relationships, because romantic relationships are about power and control.
> ➤ In most cases, you cannot get married unless a man proposes to you; this gives you no direct authority to get married if you want to.
> ➤ Men have been privileged and advantaged because of their gender for centuries, and women have been disadvantaged because of their gender.
> ➤ Know your worth, create a web, and attract all that you desire into it.

Share Your Story:

In the space provided, it is time to share your story. In what ways have you been disadvantaged specifically because of your gender?

Chapter 13
MVP – Most Valuable Player

"If you want to be oppressed, objectified, manipulated, and disadvantaged, all you need to do is be born a female."

The Most Valuable Player – MVP

Historically, women are what I consider **_Selfless to a Fault._** Being selfless to a fault means you are a doormat. **You were raised to be a girl; therefore, you were raised to be good, kind, loving, selfless, giving, caring, nurturing, and agreeable.** You might have had an abusive childhood. You may have experienced abusive relationships as an adult. Now you have a history of abuse and mistreatment, first at home, and second in the home you made as an adult. You are a good girl. You love too much, give too much, care too much, sacrifice too much, you give until your arms break off because that is what you are supposed to do. That is how good noble girls behave. You don't question a man, you don't challenge a man, you don't disrespect a man, and you never ever emasculate a man. **A good Christian girl would never do that.**

You let everyone walk all over you because you are a doormat. They can do anything they want to you, say anything they want to you, and the only thing you are allowed to do is to take it and accept intolerable behavior as normal behavior. Let me stop right there – **intolerable behavior is not normal behavior.** You have been programmed to believe that **boys will be boys** and **men will be men** and it's just the way it is, and our problems will continue to perpetuate themselves.

How to develop GIRL GAME.

1. **GROW A PAIR OF BALLS (metaphorical balls) –** *This means you must be brave.* **AUDACIOUS.** Kick fear to the curb, as it is not a productive emotion. What you are afraid of is holding you back because of ***Limiting Beliefs.*** Being afraid serves no purpose in your life. All it is doing is holding you back from greatness.

2. **DEVELOP A BACKBONE –** *This means you will not be treated like a doormat anymore.* You will also become a secure individual and heal/remove all your insecurities (your insecurities, like fear, are also holding you back). You will operate and rely solely on your central core of security, as security comes from within you, and not from external sources. *External validation is only a BONUS and nothing else.* You cannot acquire or sustain security from another human being. *Develop a backbone and refuse to be treated like shit.*

3. **SELF-LOVE –** *You put yourself first, but you are not selfish.* Self-love has nothing to do with being selfish. Being a self-absorbed human being who does not concern herself with others is selfish. *Putting yourself first is not selfish.* This is where many women get confused; they think by demonstrating more self-love, they are being selfish. *You can only be selfish by being an unemphatic asshole who only cares about herself.*

4. **DETACHMENT –** Here is where true power lies *in detachment.* As humans, we want more than anything to attach. We are wired for attachment and to develop healthy attachments to our parents, significant others, and loved ones. ***When you learn the art of detachment, you maintain a sense of power and control over your life.*** You need you. Getting attached (especially prematurely) will only lead to devastation as so many of you have experienced in the past. I will discuss detachment later.

5. **EMOTIONAL MATURITY** – Many individuals, I will go as far as to say most individuals, both women and men, are *emotionally primitive*, which means they react in hostility or despondency to their circumstances at any moment when triggered. *Learn to RESPOND and not to REACT.* It is natural to react. In fact, reacting requires no thinking at all, it just happens. You get mad so you blow up. Someone hurts your feelings, so you cry. Feelings are uncontrollable; therefore, our reactions are also uncontrollable unless we harness the power and learn how to RESPOND instead of REACT. We can develop *emotional maturity* within ourselves by becoming mentally healthier individuals. Emotionally mature women learn how to control their emotions no matter how intense they are in the moment.

6. **WILLPOWER AND DEPRIVATION – A crucial aspect of emotional maturity is the concept** *of willpower and deprivation. Deprivation is the art of learning to delay gratification. We can use our willpower depriving ourselves of pleasure in the moment heeding greater pleasure in the future.* All humans run toward pleasure and away from pain. That is human nature. By learning to strategically deprive yourself of your heart's desire now, you are creating greater strength and emotional maturity within yourself through willpower. That level of patience will reward you justly when the timing is right.

7. **REJECTION –***Never give someone the opportunity to reject you.* Every man who has ever rejected you has rejected you because you consciously or subconsciously gave him the power to. No one should have this level of power over you. It is unnecessary and unproductive. We have the power to reject others and others have the power to reject us. That is 100% true, but no one can reject you if you do not give them the opportunity.

Control yourself, control your life, and learn detachment now.

8. **MAINTAIN YOUR MYSTIQUE** –Always remain an unsolvable puzzle. No man should ever understand you nor should you ever act or react in a predictable manner. Always give a regal air of mystery and intrigue. Keep him guessing. Keep him wanting more. Never give yourself away. Never show your hand. Always maintain your poker face and never tell a man how you feel about him IF he is playing games with you. ***The goal is to outsmart the other player.*** You have been duped too long now you get to do the duping. ***Playing men are endlessly mysterious, puzzling, and intriguing which is why we can't figure them out, why they are so fascinating to us, why we are so fixated on them, and why we get our hearts broken by them.***

9. **LET GO – *Give up the ghost of the fairytale. It doesn't exist.*** Act as men do. Treat them the way they treat you. You treat him like a king while he treats you like a servant. ***You are fixated on commitment.*** If you are single, you are likely chasing commitment. If you are married, you are likely chasing your husband and trying to fix an unfixable marriage. Give up the ghost. Divorce yourself from the idea of commitment. ***Learn to fear commitment. Equate commitment with servitude and slavery because that is what your life becomes in marriage anyway, to a greater or lesser degree. Learn to think like a man. To beat your opponent, understand their every move and motive.***

10. **THE DECEIVER –** Playing men have been conniving against you your whole life. You have been manipulated several times over, lied to, cheated on, abused emotionally, physically, and possibly sexually while you have done nothing but be a "nice girl." ***Sweetheart, nice girls get abused. <u>You are now a daredevil.</u>*** You are a daredevil and not a doormat. You will deceive playing

men the way they have deceived you. You will gaslight them the way they gaslit you. You will dish out to them what they dish out to you, **and you will discover THAT THEY LOVE IT.** They LOVE the Femme Fatale treatment. **This behavior screams RESPECT ME – VALUE ME – LOVE ME – CHERISH ME – SPOIL ME. <u>Men spoil women who treat them like shit; men treat women like shit who spoil them.</u>**

Distortion and Reverse Psychology

Playing men, I talk about playing men. I DO NOT include all men. **Not all men act the way I describe just as not all women act the way I describe. There is enough of a common pattern, theme, and problem suggesting that many men (playing men) and many women (doormat / insecure women) act this way or that.** We are paying attention to certain realities that, unfortunately, many have experienced to a greater or lesser degree.

Women are relationship experts. Ask any woman, and she can tell you how to have a wonderful, communicative, reciprocal, and life-giving relationship. Many men don't have healthy relationships. Remember, many men love chaos and inconsistency. Many men need the thrill, the excitement, the mystery, and **the bamboozlement.** Many women want stability and predictability. Playing men despise those things; they are boring to them. This is why the adage goes, "men love the thrill of the chase," and unfortunately, the chase never ends, which is why they create **The Cycle of Chaos <u>to keep the chase going indefinitely.</u>** It also explains why playing men have no peace; you cannot have peace when you are forced to live in constant chaos. Think of a cyclone – that is what playing men do to relationships they exude chaos, whimsy, and debauchery. This also explains why women are wildly attracted and addicted to bad boys. Bad boys are more exciting because they exude these things.

The only thing that truly works on playing men is **reverse psychology**. That is what every dating book under the sun says to a greater or lesser degree. **Nothing about reverse psychology is normal; that is why it is called reverse psychology.** I do not agree with the game. **I am not in favor of the game.** I am not in favor of emotionally manipulating people whatsoever, but what I want you to understand is that it does work. Whether you want to believe so or not, it is exactly what playing men want and crave. **What feels normal and natural is the exact opposite for playing men.** Let me give you a few examples.

1. *A guy is more likely to commit to you if you tell him that you don't want commitment (reserve psychology).*
2. *If you tell him to pick his dirty clothes up off the floor, he won't do it – but if you pile your dirty clothes on top of his then he will eventually pick them up (reserve psychology).*
3. *If you tell him you aren't interested in him and you don't think this is working out, he will convince you otherwise (reserve psychology).*
4. *If you ignore him and treat him coldly, he will buy you flowers and treat you like a queen trying to win your love (reserve psychology).*
5. *If you act indifferent toward him, he will become more affectionate toward you (reserve psychology).*

To win against playing men, understand their behavior and what drives their emotions. **The primary driver in male behavior is this: MEN WANT WHAT THEY CANNOT HAVE. The trick here is to never fully give yourself to him. <u>The chase can never end.</u>** He should never be able to capture you. The second he captures you; he's gone. **Become an Unattainable Girl.** This will leave him wanting more from you forever.

The other psychological trick is to get a guy hooked on, obsessed, and addicted to you by remembering these important principles. **It works on the reward centers in his brain.**

You can reward him in intervals, but not consistently. Be as *inconsistent* as possible. ***This is called Intermittent Reinforcement.***

Something is only desirous to us if we don't have it. If you are showering a man with too much attention, love, and praise ALL THE TIME, your love will become less valuable to him. He will eventually discard you because there is no excitement. ***If you breadcrumb him with (little rewards), you will keep him hooked for life because he will get so excited every time he gets a reward. He will be begging for more of where that came from.***

This practice also works on women. Even though women have been conditioned for relationships and family, they too want what they cannot have, which is why we love the bad boy so much. We want him because we cannot have him. We want what we cannot possess. Imagine there is a bad boy in your life that you are in love with, and he texts you in very unpredictable patterns. Week 1, he texts you once, then he goes two weeks without texting you, then a month without texting you – ***you become addicted*** (because of the reward system in your brain). Every text you do receive from him will be a reward. It will feel like Christmas morning because it comes so rarely and sporadically. Play men with ***intermittent reinforcement. I cannot say this enough: do to them what they do to you.*** I hate saying this, but it needs to be said, ***"abuse a man, and he will never abuse you."*** Dish out to him what he dishes out to you. ***He loves it more than you realize.***

Abusive and narcissistic men do not have a concept of the golden rule, and in your relations with them, neither should you.

THE GOLDEN RULE WITH ABUSIVE / NARCISSISTIC MEN:

Treat abusive men the way that abusive men treat you.

Historically, women treat men better than men treat women. Shit is going to change now, DAMNIT. I am sick and tired of the way abusive men treat women. If you want a man to love you, then hate him. You want him addicted to you, so you must learn to psychologically mind-f*ck him the way he has psychologically mind-f*cked you. ***The best way to f*ck him is to not f*ck him.***

In *When Love Goes Wrong* by Ann Jones and Susan Schechter, they describe the overall pattern of male control and dominance or what I have termed **The Cycle of Chaos,** "if controllers were simply "bad" people who do "bad" things, our relationships with them would be a lot less complicated – and very brief. But many controllers manipulate by doing "good things."

This pattern of good versus bad creates an emotional cadence in the relationship with the man doing all the punishing and the woman doing all the suffering. ***Until the woman understands and accepts that this is a never-ending pattern and cycle of abuse, she will continue subjecting herself to his cruel treatment in the hopes that he will someday change.*** Change never happens, his abusive behavior toward you is rewarding him far too much for him to change. And it all relates to control and Attachment Theory. The more invested or leaned in the woman is, the meaner and less invested the man will be. ***There is no relationship, only the removal of the woman's self-esteem. Women are not more emotional than men. They display emotional behaviors because the men in their lives are provoking them to overemotionalism. This is destroying their essential personhood.***

The unfortunate conclusion I have reached after conducting extensive research is - ***when a man loses feelings for you, he tends to become mean.*** When he has feelings, he will be nice. His feelings come and go; they fluctuate, and so does his treatment of you. Where you are consistent and stable in your affections, he may not be. His behavior directly impacts what he is feeling for you at that very moment. This is why men will do backflips in the street naked for you during the honeymoon period. When you fall for them, as soon as you are "sold" you just lost the game, sweetheart. Treat them mean, and you will keep them keen just as they do to you.

The more you ignore him, the more he will want you.

The colder and indifferent you are, the more he will see you.

The more you treat him like he is invisible, the more visible you will be to him.

The more you act like you don't care, the more he will care.

Playing men do not respond to anything other than being ignored.

Do not try to have a conversation when there is a problem; he will likely not listen to you, and it will be like talking to a wall. Simply withdraw, walk away, and ignore him. He will come crawling back eventually and act like nothing happened at all.

Whatever feels natural to you – <u>do the exact opposite.</u>

You want him weak, begging you for more.

Deploy the *Teeter-Totter* when necessary. The *Teeter-Totter* suggests that in romantic relationships things can never be equal because when gender differences are involved, power dynamics are at play. When a man has the upper hand, he is typically abusive, controlling, demeaning, unloving, and cold, and his wife works overtime trying to appease him with her unending labor and love. In this scenario of *Teeter Totter*, she is down, and he is up. This is the common and usual case, but I am suggesting something different. When women take back their power in heteronormative relationships, refuse to be a doormat, refuse to allow abuse, and detach, they assume the man's position of power. ***This is why when women threaten to walk away, men express that they will change.*** It is all about power and control, learning to maneuver the situation to your advantage.

Confidence and Dark Femininity.

A woman can only take back her power if she **embodies confidence.** Many women lose confidence because they give all the power to the man (as they were programmed to do). I am convinced that every man secretly or openly loves a **Femme Fatale.** A **Femme Fatale** is a bullshit-free woman exuding confidence, power, mystery, and sexuality. She is the woman he can never capture **because she is uncapturable.** Therefore, he desires her indefinitely. **Desire only exists when you don't have what you want.** You cannot desire something that you possess, that is not how desire works. A desire is a wish, so create that desire within your man making him want you. ***You can do this by creating anxiety in him. How do you create anxiety in a relationship?***

1. Be entirely unpredictable
2. Do not give a shit (act like you don't care, ever – **chalanting versus nonchalanting**)
3. Never give yourself away
4. Detach
5. Do not want for or desire him (at least do not show it)
6. Take hours or days to respond to text messages (**intermittent reinforcement**)
7. Ignore him
8. Do not give in
9. Occupy yourself with things that are **not him**

10. Have your own life and plenty of friends outside of the relationship
11. Keep him guessing (never let him see your hand)
12. He should always wonder where he stands with you and even if you still love him (incorporate drama demonstrating slight interest in other men)
13. Withhold your love and give it to him sparingly (*intermittent reinforcement*)

Do you know what men do with a boring and predictable wife? They cheat on their wife, and they go after something more exciting *because they always need the chase. The chase does not dissolve just because you got married.*

Many marriages end in divorce because mostly everyone walks around unhealed, and people do not take an honest look at their lives and problems. Playing men do not want to solve their problems because if they did, they would lose their power. This would require having to admit they are causing a myriad of problems in the relationship. Let me expound. Playing men are prideful. These types seldom take responsibility for their actions and instead act like children blaming other people with zero accountability on their side. *This explains why they do not go to counseling because they would have to take responsibility for the chaos they caused in the relationship. If the problem got solved, the chaos would dissipate (since chaos and drama are the problems to begin with). There would be no more chaos (since it got solved), and playing men would get bored because the relationship would go back to normal.*

Playing men cause frustration and anguish in our lives to feel a sense of power and control. It leaves women angry with no emotional peace. Women want emotional stability for the sake of their mental health and the upbringing of their children. Playing men do not tolerate the mundane of stability. When you were growing up, was Dad ever particularly a Grinch on holidays? Did your father systematically make holidays miserable for all?

Steven Carter and Julia Sokol describe this misery in *Men Who Can't Love* concerning men who feel trapped in relationships and the lengths they will go to sabotage the relationship, "this man is so perverse that he is happiest when the relationship is in shambles because then not only does he have a good reason for leaving, he can blame it on the woman." They continue, "such a man is rarely rational. All he knows is that he is feeling acute discomfort, which he cannot understand or discuss. When this man is involved, everything that happens between the couple revolves around his trapped feelings and what he does about them. How the relationship progresses or falls apart, the children, the sex, the fighting, the building, the destroying – all revolve around his need." The literature gets fascinating, "however because he also needs the security of a woman's love, his conflict is enormous. When the woman gets fed up and withdraws, he often reverts to his pursuit/panic tactics, chases her down, and the whole process begins again. These men play a constant cat-and-mouse game with commitment, and any woman who gets involved with one of them is bound to suffer an amazing amount of pain."

Because of your deep-rooted need for love and attention as a woman, you systemically enslave yourself to a life sentence of domesticity, forever fixing an unfixable relationship while raising your children, usually on your own with limited to no help from him.

By being born, **you are automatically sentenced to a life of domesticity because of gender and no other criteria. And because of gender, men are automatically granted a life of choice, freedom, power, control, and excitement driven by purpose, passion, and potential while you are getting shit on** *(literally and figuratively) in domestic entrapment. Men fear entrapment, and women experience it.*

Women ARE NOT more nurturing than men. We are programmed and conditioned from the day we are born gendered to be and act only male or only female with preconceived ideas concerning how we should think, act, behave, relate, operate, perform, and feel as a woman or a man. If we were all raised like men, then we would all act like men. If we were all raised like women, then we would all act like women. However, we were not raised equally. We were gendered. Men are raised like men, and women are raised like women.

Do you know women who are not nurturing? I do; I am one of them. Nurturing does not come naturally to me. The characteristic of nurturing is not naturally programmed in women from the womb. *Being nurturing is a learned and acquired skill.* One can be taught nurturing. Not all women are nurturing. *The influence of your childrearing impacts you now as an adult, which brings us to the next chapter on Emotional Infantilism.*

Sister – If you want to keep a man hooked, do the opposite of what you think you should do.

Chapter 13 Takeaways

- ➤ The more I interacted with, dated, and learned about men, the more I understood that the trick to win with men is *reverse psychology.*
- ➤ Unleashing your inner *Femme Fatale or Dark Femininity* will have many men worshipping the ground you walk on.
- ➤ You come first before anyone else – as a woman, you cannot pour from an empty cup.

Share Your Story:

In the space provided, it is time to share your story. Which beliefs will you unlearn to become a *fierce Femme Fatale* garnering the unending love and respect you deserve?

Chapter 14
Emotional Infantilism

"Most people walk around unhealed and wonder why they have so many problems."

Within each of us dwells this concept of **Emotional Infantilism**. We came into this world as infants and were entirely dependent on our primary caregivers for our **emotional needs**. As infants, some of us had our emotional needs met, some of us did not have our emotional needs met, and some of us had our emotional needs partially met with inconsistencies and conditional love. We were and are **emotionally dependent**. We all have emotional needs; that is what makes us human: the ability to feel and express emotions of varying intensities.

Emotional infantilism is an emotionally primitive state existing in adults. Many adults seek romantic relationships and life partnerships to meet their emotional needs. ***We all need to belong. We all need to be loved, looked at, touched, listened to, admired, longed for, needed, wanted, and desired.*** It is human nature to be in close connection and intimacy with one another. Adults have the same emotional needs as infants do because our need for closeness and intimacy never disappears.

Adults are just grown infants. ***The needs developed in infancy never dissolve.*** We never grow out of our primitive needs. We cannot exist in solitude all the time. Solitude is beneficial at times, but perpetual solitude would harm us. This is why people stay in destructive relationships because they are terrified of being alone. ***Many of us are emotionally immature, acting like children when things do not go our way. Many of us are reactionary.*** Was your dad a yeller? Did he explode about trivial matters? Then your father was emotionally immature. When we react from anger and impatience, we are emotionally immature. It is okay to have emotions, and it is okay to express emotions, but to act out on emotional whims is a sign of **emotional infantilism.**

Something happens to us in infancy and childhood that is not desirable. No parent is perfect. No parent can be there for you 24/7, and no parent can meet all your emotional needs, it is not possible. We do not live in a perfect utopian society. Your parents had their own share of emotional needs that went unmet by their parents and lovers. It could have been difficult for them to meet your emotional needs, which leads us to **Attachment Theory. Attachment Theory** suggests that the way you formed attachments or lack thereof with your primary caregivers as children will impact your adult romantic relationships when you form attachments with significant others.

It is suggested that if you form secure attachments with your parents in childhood you will grow up with a **SECURE ATTACHMENT STYLE.** This is the ideal attachment style. However, there are three other **insecure attachment types**, and they are 1) Avoidant; dismissive - indifferent behavioral patterns 2) Anxious; preoccupied - behavioral patterns and

3) Disorganized - fearful-avoidant or a combination of avoidant and anxious behaviors. You will have any of the latter three attachment styles if your parents fully or partially neglected you unable to meet your emotional needs in childhood. If you look around, you will find that there are many insecure people in the world. Many suffer from insecurity, because they had dismissive and emotionally neglectful parents who subconsciously implanted within them insecurities around not being good enough or lovable from an emotionally vulnerable age. **Emotional neglect is more common than anyone wants to admit.**

Like I said, parents are not perfect. You are not a perfect parent. As much as we do for our children, some of us are equally messing them up without realizing it, and I am going to say it louder for the people in the back: if you lay a hand on your child, you are a physical abuser. Physical punishment is no way to punish a child. *You can discipline your children in other, more loving, supportive, and productive ways.*

When you were a kid, did a punitive device touch your body? If the answer is yes, you are a survivor of *physical abuse.* Hitting someone is not punishment. *Hitting is abuse.* Some of you are emotionally traumatized because someone laid a hand or an object on you. *You cannot lovingly attach to a child if you abuse that child.* That child will come to fear you and feel unsafe around you rather than feel bonded, secure, and protected by you. This is where your insecurities started. *If that parent couldn't love you, how could you love yourself?* This is the first time you felt bad. This is the first time you have felt not good enough. *That there must be something wrong with you.* You are unlovable.

The reason you acted out, the reason you were bad is because you just wanted mommy or daddy to pay attention to you. You acted out for attention, and instead of getting their attention, you got hit. All you wanted was for mommy and daddy to pick you up, hold you tightly, and say, *"I love you; you matter to me,"* but instead of that, you got beat, the exact opposite of what you needed.

Why Did They Do It?

They did it because they are just like you. They were an innocent little baby once with emotional needs of their own that went unmet by their mom and dad. Therefore, insecurities built up and festered within them too. They are simply acting on their conditioning. *If they hit you, they were also hit.* You can be certain of that. *If they neglected you, they too were neglected.*

You can be certain of that. They are hurting just as much as you are, but that still does not excuse their behavior. They still made that choice, the choice to abuse you – an innocent little child who wanted nothing more than mommy and daddy's attention. This is where our insecurities are rooted and grounded, because we did not receive sufficient love, nurturing, and security from our parents, we endlessly, passionately, and psychotically look for it in adult romantic relationships. We are searching for our parents in our significant others. *I am not sure if I ever met a secure person, to be honest.* I know they exist, and I do know some of us did form secure attachments in childhood. However, many did not, and now it is a social issue impacting romantic relationships.

We create an ideal or perfect partner, and we have convinced ourselves through disillusionment that this person exists. This is why fairytales are so powerful on women. Women believe in a so-called Prince Charming or Knight in Shining Armor and that one day he will come and rescue her. Even the most intelligent of women believe in this horrible lie that this perfect Prince Charming archetype exists somewhere out there in the world. Only to be let down horribly. I am convinced that the Prince Charming or Knight in Shining Armor we are seeking is Daddy. *Since we could never fully capture Daddy's heart, we endlessly chase the cold and distant man resembling in behavior our own father.*

Men also believe in a Dream Girl or Perfect Woman embodying all qualities he loves. She also does not exist because eventually, he will find fault in her when the rose-colored glasses come off. We create dramas in our minds, fixations, distortions, dream-like states, fairy tales, and fantasies keeping us hooked, suffering, and longing for that which we could never have-*our Mommy's and Daddy's attention. The reason why men love cold, distant, and indifferent women is that those women model their own mothers.* He could never capture his mother's love because her love was often cold and indifferent. ***Hence, the chase.*** He is chasing his mother's love in his romantic relationships, creating an obsession in him. This is why men want what they cannot have. They couldn't have their mother's love – so they chase it romantically. However, if you give playing men your love, it will turn him off, and he will discard you. ***Turn into his cold and indifferent mother, and he will be hooked on you... FOR LIFE.***

The Pattern: The Anxious Woman and The Avoidant Man

In my studies on ***Attachment Theory***, I notice a pattern. ***Women gravitate more to the Anxious Attachment Style, and men gravitate more to the Avoidant Attachment Style.*** This is not to say that women cannot be avoidant, and men cannot be anxious. I know plenty of anxious men, and these qualities of anxiety and detachment can be triggered within all of us depending on the environment and circumstances. My natural curiosity made me question why many women tend to be anxious, and many men tend to be avoidant.

The reason for these natural gravitations toward anxiety and avoidance has to do with the social conditioning of the sexes. Women are conditioned toward love, romance, marriage, family, and relationships. Men are conditioned to prioritize independence, social status, accomplishment, and career. Therefore, relationships are not so much a priority for men as they are for women. It is easy for men to dismiss relationships and become avoidant. They are avoiding the very thing they were not programmed for. Women take more ownership to process emotions; they experience more anxiety; they live more with their emotions than men do. Men are instructed to repress and ignore emotion; therefore, their aloofness is more natural to them. The paradox creates this dichotomy of yin and yang, with the woman usually moving toward the man with anxious tendencies and the man moving away from the woman with avoidant tendencies. ***Women have the power to trigger anxiety in men creating desire.***

This is why some relationships end badly; no one is on the same page because they were not conditioned (raised) the same way. Therefore, both sexes do not want and need the same things. It is creating chaos and inconsistency. This is why women are far happier single because they don't have to put their own human emotions on a never-ending roller coaster of up and down, good and bad, and in and out. This ***anxious/avoidant death trap*** is the perfect storm perpetuating relationship abuse and subsequent divorce. ***It is a common social pattern.*** This is why some women have had two, three, or four marriages. Each time, they hope the man will be different and things will finally work out, but usually, it is the same situation with a different person. The definition of insanity is doing the same thing and expecting different results. Until we fix these social issues, and people fix themselves plucking out their own toxicities, we will never have happy marriages. ***The only way to solve this problem is to do something about it.***

The Ice Queen: Deploying Emotional Weapons

Women and men are both emotional beings. However, men do a better job of concealing their emotions since it is not socially acceptable to express any emotion other than anger. Women are labeled overemotional all the time. Both genders need to learn the power of ***emotional containment and control***. We must harness control over our emotions.

How can this be achieved? It can be achieved by putting yourself through an ***emotional exorcism.*** We all harbor intense feelings, and the worst thing we can do is keep those emotions bottled up until they inevitably explode. Men explode because they have not mastered their emotions. You owe yourself an ***emotional exorcism.*** Allow yourself to suffer for a pre-determined amount of time.

The Zen Room – An Emotional Sanctuary

A **Zen Room** is a room in your home used as an **Emotional Sanctuary,** a place of rest, solace, and mindfulness. I use my **Zen Room** only for prayer, relaxation, meditation, and reading. Every woman needs a **Zen Room.** Try and designate a bedroom in your home and turn it into a **Zen Room.** A closet will also work. It should be a clean and quiet space just for you and your emotional health and well-being. I painted my **Zen Room** an olive-green color with the word **Relax** written on the wall. I decorated it with plants, flowers, ambient lighting, and other embellishments. It is clean and smells wonderful bringing tranquility and stillness every time I enter it.

You are going to experience emotions. Allow yourself to experience emotions completely. Do not suppress them. Allow yourself an **emotional exorcism** or several. An **Emotional Exorcism** is when you lay still fully experiencing all emotions as intensively as possible, no matter how painful they are. If you need to cry, then cry. If you need to scream, then scream. If you need to roll around or punch a pillow, then do that. Let it all out when no one else is around. To experience an **Emotional Exorcism,** be by yourself. You will only gain healing and clarity when you are alone and not when surrounded by others. Feel deeply and completely. Embody the full force of your **Emotional Exorcism.**

Zone of Resilience

Once it is over with, then it is over with, no need to perpetuate your emotional trauma. This is what is building your **Zone of Resilience.** Your mind is the most powerful asset you own, so use it completely and intelligently. Remain in your **Zone of Resilience** as often as possible. It is hard to be resilient all the time, and you will fall out of your **Zone of Resilience** sometimes. Return to it as quickly as possible. Think of your **Zone of Resilience** as being a spectrum. One on the far-right side are intense negative (feel bad) emotions, and on the far-left side are intense positive (feel good) emotions. Your **Zone of Resilience** is center. Circumstances of varying kinds will move you to the right or to the left, but again, you are not to remain there forever; let the emotion of the good or bad experience run its course and quickly return to your **Zone of Resilience**. It is in your **Zone of Resilience** where you are most grounded, logical, and powerful. Leverage emotions to your advantage; do not allow them to punish you forever.

Mom Grump

I have what I like to call **Mom Grump**. I do not have it all the time. It affects me primarily in the morning when I am getting my daughter out the door for school. As an anxious mother who has much on her plate all the time, I am tired and zombie-like in the morning, crabby, sulky, and bothered. I have **Mom Grump**. I have precisely 30 minutes to get my kid dressed, ready, hair and teeth brushed, bookbag and lunch packed, and out the door by 7am. I have trouble sleeping and am not well-rested in the morning. Remaining in your **Zone of Resilience** can help you fight **Mom Grump**.

Some people lack information and resources. You don't know what you don't know. I read 4 to 5 books per month consistently feeding and arming myself with knowledge. One of the most important things you can do for yourself is arm yourself with knowledge. **Learning is a powerful tool.** To not learn new things is to deprive yourself. Learning brings with it understanding and understanding brings healing. Like I have said throughout this entire book, life is a game of strategy, carefully plan every move with patience and tenacity.

In life, you can eat or be eaten. Overcome or come undone. Take control or be controlled. Master your emotions or let them overwhelm you. It all comes down to choice. We are all susceptible to deception. Women can be gullible; we can be easily duped, especially when it comes to love and romance. Do not allow yourself to be duped anymore. Arm yourself with knowledge. Always remain cautious and judicious exercising discernment. Guard and protect yourself, especially from the people who claim to love you the most. **No one can protect you better than you can protect yourself.**

Sister –Master your emotions so they don't master you.

Chapter 14 Takeaways

> ➢ Most people react instead of respond to problems.
> ➢ Mastering your emotions is a sign of strength and character.
> ➢ Emotional control will guide and protect you always.
> ➢ There is no problem that cannot be solved.
> ➢ Think before responding.

Share Your Story:

In the space provided, it is time to share your story. How can you gain control over your emotions becoming a more powerful you?

Chapter 15
Wanted

"He never took his eyes off me."

Parents

Having your own children is a wonderful idea, and I believe most people share this sentiment. We are supposed to be fruitful and multiple, right? Many of us believe we will one day have our own children when we grow up. *Many adults should NOT be parents, and many adults have children when they shouldn't.* You do not need to be perfect to be a parent, but you should do your best. You should be healed BEFORE you have children (ideally). *Many are not capable of handling the responsibilities of parenthood; thus, <u>they should not be parents.</u>*

Society does not openly discuss childhood abuse and emotional neglect. Many parents who abuse and emotionally neglect their children will say that they do not abuse or emotionally neglect their children. This is called *gaslighting*. Gaslighting creates an alternative reality based on a new narrative distorting facts and experiences, making the victim question their own reality and memory of those lived experiences. Parents deflect blame retaining their god-like social image making their children feel more ignored and invalidated than they already feel. Those parents have convinced themselves that they are good parents by society's standards. In fact, many children who are beaten with hard objects are just simply being "punished" after all – *that cannot be classified as child abuse.... or can it?*

Did you know that children are never bad? The only reason children act up behaviorally is because they want attention; they <u>want you to notice them.</u> Did you know that parents who emotionally neglect their children to a greater or lesser degree (and yes, there is a spectrum to everything) do so because they have better things to fill their time. This includes their jobs and careers, their own problems, concerns and troubles, other more problematic or attention-seeking children, overly devoted and concerned for their spouse, hobbies, interests, activities, emotional apathy and personal burdens.

Have kids, they say!

This chapter was specifically written for the **emotionally neglected little girl (and little boy).** Is she you? Were you emotionally neglected? Abandoned? Unwanted? Discarded? A burden? I wrote this chapter for you. I know your being and your essence. I know your thoughts and feelings. …. I know. *This is why women especially suffer from Anxious Preoccupied Attachment Style, you are forever chasing avoidant men, because you are forever chasing your <u>avoidant parent.</u>*

You want so deeply to catch what you cannot have. You will NEVER have the avoidant parent, and you will NEVER have the avoidant man, but you chase them both because you desire what you cannot have. You are in love with toxic people. **You chase toxicity in people.**

When the avoidant man is treating you like you are invisible, it mirrors your earlier relationship with your parents. You will always get more of what you've always gotten until you break the cycle recognizing the patterns. Invisible children become invisible adults and visible children become visible adults until the issue is resolved head on. This is simply the Law of Attraction, like always attracts like. The famous adage, "children should be seen and not heard," has messed up so many of us. You are running on a rat wheel, sweet girl. Constantly chasing something that does not want or cannot want you. **Therefore, you feel unwanted.** A precious baby girl wanting nothing more than to be loved, nothing more than to be seen, heard, and listened to. To be held closely and for your parents to look deeply and lovingly into your eyes like you are so wanted by them. I wish this for every baby girl. However, the truth is that it does not happen to every girl. That baby girl grows up to love, desire, and chase toxic and avoidant men. **_She is chasing these men, but who she is really chasing are her parents._**

In Love with Toxic

Some women suffer from **Love Addiction** and a wild, ruthless attraction to toxic, unhealthy men. Why? **_Because the love they received as children was insufficient._** I am NOT saying that your parents did not love you. Many of them did to a greater or lesser degree. What I am saying is that their love or lack thereof was insufficient for your actual love, belonging, and attention needs. Your parents may have loved you **_more superficially or at the surface level_**, but it was not the deep emotional love you needed.

Human beings are fragile. **_We are all so fragile._** _WE ALL NEED TO BE LOVED. WE ALL NEED TO BE HELD. WE ALL NEED TO BE NOTICED. WE ALL NEED TO BE CARED FOR. WE ALL NEED ATTENTION. WE ALL NEED TO FEEL GOOD ENOUGH. WE ALL NEED TO FEEL LIKE WE JUST F*CKING MATTER TO SOMEONE. WE ALL NEED TO BE ACCEPTED. DESIRED. WANTED. LOVED UNCONDITIONALLY._

I am going to say this loudly, and I am going to say this clearly:

CRIME exists because the one committing the crime WAS NOT loved sufficiently.
DIVORCE exists because one or both spouses WERE NOT loved sufficiently.
ADDICTION exists because the addict WAS NOT loved sufficiently.
BULLYING exists because the bully WAS NOT loved sufficiently.

SUICIDE exists because the person who ended her or his life WAS NOT loved sufficiently.

Love is our ultimate source of life. WE CANNOT EXIST WITHOUT LOVE. We do not thrive or survive without love. Attention. Belonging. Every single human being has a love/attention threshold, some stronger than others, some of us require more love and attention than others do. I assure you that all of us, without exception, require a significant and sufficient amount of love and attention. However, for many of us, those love/attention thresholds are not met. We suffer significantly in a myriad of ways. We attach ourselves to toxicity because, truthfully, *that is all we know.* That is all we ever had. Pain. Misery. Negativity. Toxicity. *We are deeply, passionately, and innately attracted to toxic men because we are forever chasing what we never had.*

The Gift

Life has a way of blessing us when we least expect it and when we are fully open to receiving blessings. Life will give you what you need. Even if you did not or do not have sufficient love and attention in your life. Watch closely and listen for it.

More than anything else, we all want to matter in the world. We want to belong. We are just little babies, just little infants, and we want our parents to look deeply and lovingly into our eyes like we are enough, like we are God's gift to the world, because we are, we absolutely are God's gift to the world. You are God's gift to the world, but some of you turn your backs on all the gifts he's given to you. *You've shrunk yourselves.* You've allowed others to hurt and bully you. *You've accepted abuse and mistreatment from friends, family, and partners.*

You have given up your goals and dreams to raise your children. You've put yourselves on the back burner to give more to others than you receive back for yourself. You've become a doormat that everyone can easily walk all over. You wallow in your own misery and self-loathing. You cling to your emotional bad habits and insecurities like they are the only comfort you have. You've kissed all your dreams goodbye just to receive one kiss from a boy. You've watched yourself wither away day after day, year after year, until you do not recognize the girl staring back at you in the mirror anymore. She's gone. *The ultimate sacrifice – the complete and total loss of the self. You can do anything, truly anything.*

If you were abused – you can do anything.
If you were emotionally neglected – you can do anything.
If you were unloved – you can do anything.
If you had nothing – you can do anything.
If they hurt you – you can do anything.
If they told you, you can't – you can do anything.
ANYTHING - ANYTHING – ANYTHING.

But you sit. And you sit. And you sit. And you wait. And you wait. And you wait. And when you wait… IT WON'T EVER COME. *IT NEVER COMES WHEN YOU WAIT!*

Why?

BECAUSE YOU HAVE THE POWER, GIRL! *THE POWER LIES WITHIN YOU!*

But you laugh in God's face!

She made you so beautiful – and you laugh.
She made you so talented – and you laugh.
She made you so intelligent – and you laugh.
She made you so funny– and you laugh.

She gave you every emotional and mental tool to move mountains – AND YOU SIT THERE AND LAUGH IN GOD'S FACE!

I laughed in God's face, too.

I laughed in God's face – when I tried staying with a man who ripped apart my self-esteem.

I laughed in God's face – when I tried to take my life seven times.

I laughed in God's face – when I gave up my dreams to become a wife and mother.

Everything comes and goes through YOU. That is it. No one else. STOP COOKING, STOP CLEANING, STOP BEING EVERYONE'S BITCH, STOP SELF-LOATHING, STOP MAKING EXCUSES, STOP SELF-SABOTAGING, STOP CRYING OVER THAT BOY, STOP TRYING TO MAKE IT WORK WITH YOUR HUSBAND WHO DOESN'T GIVE A RAT'S ASS ABOUT YOU ANYMORE.

GO OUT THERE IN THE WORLD. GET OUT THERE IN THE WORLD. YOU ARE CAPABLE OF ANYTHING. STOP LAUGHING IN GOD'S FACE – GOD DOES NOT MAKE MISTAKES SO YOU ARE NOT A MISTAKE!

I digress. Your life depends on you changing your thinking and transforming your life for the better; only you have the power to do this.

Life gives us gifts. We are filled with gifts, but sometimes we do not recognize them. What are the gifts life has given to you? Here are examples of gifts in my life that may resonate with you.

> Caring and invested friends
> A listening ear
> Healthy food
> Exercise
> A warm bed

- ➢ My beautiful home
- ➢ Wonderful appreciative clients
- ➢ My businesses
- ➢ My hobbies and interests
- ➢ A warm smile
- ➢ A friendly hello
- ➢ Good sex
- ➢ A date with an adorable guy
- ➢ Coffee
- ➢ Music
- ➢ Safety
- ➢ Self-esteem
- ➢ Love
- ➢ Generosity
- ➢ Patience
- ➢ Trust

I could go on forever, but you get the idea. My life isn't perfect. It was never perfect. In my life there has been much hell, much pain, much sorrow, much devastation, much disappointment, much Depression, much anxiety, much discouragement, much heaviness, and much burden. I grew up too fast, much too fast. I held my own hand more than others held it. I have been given so many lemons in life that I could build a **Lemonade Factory**! and so…. that is just what I did! I built a **Lemonade Factory** with all the lemon's life has given to me. We have many flavors now! What do you like? Blueberry? Strawberry? Peach? Mango? Raspberry? Blackberry? ***Each lemon has a purpose! Each lemon has potential! Each lemon has such beauty! Each lemon has such magnificence.*** Each lemon, splendor…. ***because each lemon has made me who I am today.*** How many lemons do I have to thank? Endless! Endless lemons! ***Each one perfectly constructed me into the strong, resilient, ass-kicking, trailblazing, badassing, bullshit-free woman I am today!***

Each lemon is a magnificent gift. Be wise enough to see its beauty. Sometimes we are blind. We are blind to the beauty of life that lies right before our very eyes. Our vision clouded by hatred, jealousy, negativity, defeat, emotional burdens, Depression, anxiety, circumstance, doubt, fear, and shame. Recently, life has given me a magnificent gift that even thinking about it fills my eyes with tears.

I share my story with you. My story about *Electric Blue*. The writing style is different and could be difficult to interpret; that is the point. *Follow as best as you can.* I wrote this section completely from my heart, with *themes and purpose woven into the beautiful story.* I pray you capture the beauty I am creating. I pray that you know a love like this in your lifetime. The **Gift** is what *Electric Blue* gave to me – *he saw me. He wanted me.* The gift of being wanted – indescribable! And similarly, the **Gift** I gave to him – *the gift of listening and empathy. The gift of being heard! The gift of just f*cking mattering to someone.*

… … … … ….

Electric Blue

Magnetic. Absolutely breathtaking. *There was just something about him.* I cannot put my finger on it. Looking through his Bumble profile, he has this bright magnetic smile stretching across his striking face. *Every single photo, smiling. Every single photo, happy. Every single photo, angelic.* He completely enraptured me. I did not even know the man. A salient man with arresting eyes, an inviting smile, and shaggy white/blonde hair, he was the best-looking man I have ever laid eyes on. Unusually charming, his smile so vibrant just sucked me in like a vacuum mesmerized and captivated by his mystery. At the time, he was only 22 years old, and I was 32 years old, and for the first time in my life, I became a cougar.

Now if you had asked me when I was 10 years old what my idea of a fairytale was, I would have told you that by 32 years old, I would be married to a rich corporate executive, with 2-3 children, living in the suburbs with a white picket fence and golden retriever. A stereotypical American Dream family. Never did I imagine at 10 years old that I would be a divorced single mother, sad, and far stronger than I ever wanted to be. Plot twist, I did get my fairytale after all, but not in the way I had imagined. At 32 years old, my fairytale was *Electric Blue*, the most beautiful man I ever laid eyes on. Eyes as blue as an ocean piercing the core of my heart with electric shock waves. I call this man with arresting qualities, *Electric Blue*. Never did I dream that my life would turn into a romance novel, but here I am…. living the dream.

Hiding Behind That Pretty Face

Electric Blue's real name is Asher. My 10th birthday party was Backstreet Boys themed with a Backstreet Boys cake back in the late 1990s. The cake had all five of the Backstreet Boys' heads on it. My favorite BSB was Nick Carter, so naturally, I claimed his face and ate it. Each of the other little girls also claimed their favorite BSB and ate the piece of cake with his head on it. Pretty cannibalistic of us 10-year-old girls already batshit crazy about boys. Asher was just being born while I was having my 10th BSB birthday party. I was robbing the cradle by an entire decade. Savage at 10 years old… still savage today.

I matched with Asher on the dating app, and we started exchanging messages. After a few days, he asked for my number, and then we started texting. Asher was transparent with his intentions concerning dating. Here is what he told me, "I really like you. You are a beautiful woman, but I do not want to let you down. I am not seeking a relationship if that is what you are looking for. I am only here because I am looking for an *Affection Buddy,* and I would love to have one as gorgeous as you." **Affection Buddy**…huh…that is a pleasant way to say friends with benefits, f*ck buddies. And so, I was down with it because you only live once. Right?

I informed Asher that I wanted to be his **Affection Buddy** and that I was not looking for a relationship. Owning my own business, it was convenient to date casually than be tied down and fixated on only one person. I could accept an **Affection Buddy** if that affection was not a one-night stand. **Acting as if we are in a relationship without being in one.**

It was settled. Asher and I would be **Affection Buddies** because the single thing we both needed more than anything in our lives was…well…. **affection.** Asher asked me when I was available for our first date, so we had set one up for a Wednesday evening. We would meet at this cozy pizza bar then go on a walk. Wednesday came, I had **the collywobbles.** I was excited to meet my **Electric Blue** …and then he canceled on me. He claimed he had to help one of his friends and asked if we could reschedule for Thursday night. I said sure, no problem, and so it was settled for Thursday night. Thursday night came, I had **the heebeejeebees** excited to meet this man who took my breath away…and then he canceled on me again! Claiming he had to help his other friend. Okay, fine, cool, be like that Electric Blue, play hard to get. **That made me want him…. EVEN MORE!** There is nothing I love more than a man who is unavailable. **I love challenges, and so it was game on.**

Just F*cking Do It, Reprised

Remember **just f*cking do it** from **GIRL GRIT: SAVAGE NOT AVERAGE**? This was the perfect opportunity for me to make a complete ass out of myself and scare a man away…. or so I thought. I had no contact with Asher for about 5 to 6 days. I wanted to convince him that I had forgotten about him and lost interest. After no contact, I sent him a 50-second voice message with intention but kept the message succinct. *I prepared myself for rejection.*

Hi Asher,

I hope you are doing well and having a good week.
Sorry, we didn't get a chance to see each other last week.
I was hoping we could reschedule again. I want to meet you.
If you are interested in me, let me know and if not, I completely understand.
I hope we can be friends and **Affection Buddies**, and if not, then I wish you nothing but the best life has to offer.

He responded immediately…

And said **yes**, he was still very much interested and asked for my availability.

We set up a date for the following night, and he texted me all day. He would text me, then like a savage, I would wait 3-4 hours to respond (so he wouldn't think I was desperate)…then I would text him after 3-4 hours, and he would respond immediately every single time. I maintained my *savage composure* by spacing out the texts. *I got to make him think I am unavailable.*

The next day came, the day of our 3rd rescheduled date. I worried he would cancel on me again, but I assured myself that I am a secure and confident woman and that any man would be lucky to go on a date with me. I felt better and more secure. I texted him that morning with my address and the time to be over at my house. The plan was for him to come here to park his car, and for us to go take a walk down the road to the Metroparks. I would then take him to the beach by my house.

He confirmed my morning text. I was all excited. Like over-the-moon excited. *I felt like I was meeting a celebrity. An Icon.* Three hours before the date, he texts me…my stomach drops…he doesn't cancel, but he is giving me a myriad of reasons why he shouldn't come over tonight. Some of these reasons include: I think you want a relationship, and I cannot give you that (when did I say I wanted a relationship?), I am afraid to hurt you, I don't want to use you you seem so sweet, you live too far (it was only 40 minutes not horrible), I am just afraid, and I have reservations.

He was not about to cancel on me a 3rd time. *I was about to completely freak out and lose my shit when I remembered that I am a confident, self-assured badass bull-shit free, FIRE WOMAN who can get what she wants out of life.* I went *balls out*. It took me the next 60 minutes of convincing him why he should come over that night to be with me. I sent him a voice message so he could hear the sincerity and intention in my voice.

Hi Asher,

I completely understand. I get why you feel the way you feel. It is a valid feeling. First, *we can all use a friend.* All of us. Sex or no sex, all of us can use more friends. We all need each other to survive. You cannot hurt me. *You can only hurt me if I give you permission to hurt me.* I told you several times that I am not looking for a relationship; I know this is just a friend-with-benefits situation. I really want to meet you. I was really looking forward to it. I really want to see you. If, after the first hour, you aren't feeling me or I'm not feeling you, we can end the date, and you can leave – no feelings hurt. We will say goodbye. You don't know unless you try. Can we please give this a try?

He did respond.

It took more convincing. He felt bad about the situation because he felt like he was using me, and he felt like I wanted a relationship when I didn't. He had reservations and was in his own head being his own worst enemy. *He made the situation far more complicated than it needed to be.*

At last, he said he was sold again and would be on his way at 3pm. *He was excited to see me, but he was also nervous.* Once we both knew he was going to come over, we both got so nervous, and I was running around my house like a chicken with my head cut off, trying to get ready. *The intensity and tension between us were absolute fire.* I couldn't think of anything else other than him.

He pulls into my driveway. I freeze. We are both shaking. He is way more nervous than I. He told me to take the lead and that he would follow me. *He gets out of his car.* Time stands still. I was enchanted by him. *Ethereal.* He's shaking. Poor thing is so nervous. I walk up to greet him with a big warm smile making him feel at ease and comfortable with me. We hug. *He pulled me closer, and he didn't let go for two whole minutes.* For two whole minutes, we hugged in my driveway in front of all my neighbors… like we had been in love for 100 years and hadn't seen each other in ten years. ***And for the first time in our lives, we both felt so wanted, so held, in that moment.***

There is no greater need than human to human affection. A little baby longs to be adored. Looked at. Admired. Held tight. Cuddled. And during that two-minute hug in my driveway, we were both adults looking at the other (our infant other), completely comforting our infantile selves, *and all our pain melted away quickly.*

The Best Day of My Life

We hopped in my car. The poor thing was still so nervous and hardly spoke; I had to carry the initial conversation. However, he opened up quickly within the first 10-15 minutes together. We drove to the Metroparks down my street. As the minutes passed, he became increasingly comfortable around me and then suddenly dominated our conversation, which I was completely fine with. It was magic, an instant bond, like nothing I had ever experienced before. **Something about him.** I needed to know him. I needed to experience him, and I knew, I intuitively knew, that more than anything else in his life, he needed me too. He needed me so badly; *his infant self was never held. Never looked at. Never adored. I knew him. I knew him so well.* I instantly make people feel seen, heard, listened to, and noticed because I am non-threatening and I do not judge anyone. He opened up to me like a book, and we talked as old friends. *Never had I bonded with someone so intimately before after only knowing him for 30 minutes.*

He can't look at me. Every time he does, I disarm him. He smiles. He looks and smiles. He can't take his eyes off me. *I am hiding behind this pretty face.* I listened to him talk. I took him in. *He was in pain.* Deep emotional pain. *And in those hours, I got to be there for him, and it was the best thing I ever got to do.* After 30 minutes of walking in the Metroparks, we came upon a secluded area among tall grass and beautiful colorful flowers. He spins me around, pulls me close to his body, and kisses me excitedly for ten minutes. During those ten minutes of romantic passion, I could feel him pressed up against my leg, and I knew he was ready to go right there on the tall grass. *Never have I been so wanted. Never have I been so desired. Never have I been so seen, so heard, so noticed.* The parent looking into my eyes longingly, I love you, I adore you, I want you, you're mine, you are my sun, moon, and stars, I prayed for you. And me, *in my own infantilism*, looking up at him… *knowing I am wanted.*

Pure magic. It was everything. I was everything. He was everything. Life was everything. Time stood still. Only time. You cannot rush time. You can only pray for miracles, more heavens, and fewer hells. This was heaven. Wait, no, it couldn't be I had to have been dreaming; none of this could be real. His eyes are not real. His magnetic smile is not real. His shaggy white, blonde hair was not real. Our bond was not real. He looked into my eyes with desire and longing, not real. Pressed up against my leg—not real. **Real life is not this rich. Real life does not feel this good.** Real life is painful, and this is a pleasure. Mommy, mommy, look at me. Daddy, Daddy, notice me. Don't you love me, Mommy? Daddy, why is work more important than me? **Discarded.** We are too busy for you, because we have our own pain to deal with. We cannot deal with your pain. We cannot handle your emotions, child. Discarded. But, mommy, daddy, you brought me into this world. **But we didn't know you would feel. We didn't know you would actually need us.**

Are you hiding behind that pretty face? Frozen in time. You are wanted. You are wanted, Asher, you are wanted, Alexandra. I have never been desired so badly. He has never been wanted so badly. Asher discarded, but in that sovereign sacred moment as the heavens themselves opened to us, he filled me with himself. But not at that moment, not yet.

I pulled him off. If I hadn't, two minutes later, I would be lying down in a flower bed with a man I had only known for 40 minutes on top of me. Only time. Thank you, Universe.

What does it mean to be wanted? What does it mean to be desired? What is desire?

Desire is hell.

Our smoldering lust did not end there. We could have sexually slayed each other. His blue eyes electrocute my soul. Only time. No longer discarded. Wanted, not unwanted. **Are you hiding behind that pretty face?**

Things return to normal. The collywobbles remain. I took him to the beach by my house. **We are teenagers.** I am cold and he offers me his jacket. We are playful. He takes selfies with me. We look like we have known each other our whole lives– *time* *is relative.* I have known him for 100 years; I am correct. **We look very much in love.** Very much wanted by the other in this picture. Passion, lust, limerence, bonding, sex, wet, heat, fire, desire. I let him chase me. He likes it. He likes playing cat and mouse. Well, technically, in this situation, it would be cougar and mouse (he's the mouse, wait, no, I am the mouse, he is chasing me, he is the cougar), no, I am the cougar, and he is the mouse, he is chasing me. **He consumes me.** I look inside those electric blue eyes. The adrenaline shocks my body. I am not a mother. I am not an adult. ***<u>With him, I am only a child.</u>*** He is also a child with me. Our adult bodies have left us, maybe forever. **Time is relative.** Discarded. I want you. You are loved. You are enough. **He holds nothing back. Are you hiding behind that pretty face?**

My Life is a Scene Out of a Movie

I am dreaming. This doesn't happen to people. Life is painful, not happy, not pleasurable, not this easy. **He spins me around and around playfully.** I am so dizzy. My head spinning. Am I really 32? Am I even alive? I think I died last night. **This feels like heaven.** This cannot be real, no, no, no. Mommy, where are you? Hello? Daddy, are you in there? Daddy……don't call me daddy, I am not your daddy. But I am an infant. He is an infant. He never got to be an infant. He was born, and the very next day, he had to become an adult. I am your lover, not your daddy. Be my baby. **Electric Blue.**

Around and around, I went, laughing, joyfully, playfully laughing. Why was I born? **Discarded.** You are everything. **You are everything.** I give you everything. Suffer now, cry later. Scream now and reap the rewards later. This is Heaven, Nirvana. Ecstasy. I don't do drugs. **Are you hiding behind that pretty face?** Laughing. Joy. Magnetic. Bond. Chemistry. **Electricity.** Electricity. Wow, this is reality. Thank you, God.

Unwanted. I did this. I put you here. No, No, I cannot do this. Mommy? Daddy? Asher? *Is anyone there?*

Asher pulls me close. Kisses me fervently as if time stands still. I am embarrassed because I wonder if anyone can see us. The Energizer Bunny is ready to go right there on the beach in broad daylight for the voyeurs to see. I stop him. Slow it down, Bunny. Let's save those teenage-like hormones. *Are you hiding behind that pretty face?*

Snow Globe

We left the beach. *He is hungry, but not for food.* I had to know this man. We go to dinner. It is a 1950s theme diner. I order us Reese Peanut Butter Cup milkshakes because why not. Infantilism. We order the cheeseburger meal. He tells me everything. He holds nothing back. ***I knew it all before he even opened his mouth.***

A beautiful baby boy, unwanted. Daddy works so much and never has time. Mom cares more about constructing the perfect little boy instead of loving him. He has no love. Not from mom. Not from dad. Not from anyone. Just as I suspect, *are you hiding behind that pretty face?* The most magnetic smile, the most electric eyes, a beautiful baby, unwanted, discarded. Mommy are you there… silence. Daddy are you there…. silence. He retreats to his room. *I wish I was never born.* What am I even doing here? Suicidal thoughts.

I give him something he never had before. *Why am I telling you all of this, Alexandra?* Because you trust me. Because I want you. *I see you, I hear you, you are valuable.* You are so valuable, never forget it. You are going to do amazing things; I see it in you in those electric blue eyes, that magnetic smile. *Smoldering.* Is any of this even real? *I have known you for 100 years.*

He was forever changed. Not just changed. ***Healed.*** Really healed. I love you. Transformed by love and listening. We ate the food and drank the milkshake. What is desire? Wanted. ***There is no greater need than to be wanted.***

On His Knees

We go back to my place. I make our drinks, and we sit on my porch and laugh. He talks; I listen. He is the child I am the parent. I give him that matronly love he never received. Unwanted. ***Discarded. It is better to raise a perfect child than to love a child.*** A beautiful baby boy. I want to cry. I hold back. I listen. I mother him. He needs it. I mother by listening by looking into his eyes. Wanted. Desired. Infantilism.

He kisses me. Wanted. Desired. ***The man did not once take his eyes off me. He never took his eyes off me.*** Life is only pain. Life is mostly hell. Where is Heaven, Daddy? We are children. Infants. Being held and looked at for the first time ever. ***He never takes his eyes off me.***

He holds me there. ***Wanted.*** Desired. Is he real? Am I real? Is life even real? ***I am a better human being when I am loved, wanted, and desired.*** I am just an infant, after all, in a woman's body. Held. Close. Wanted. Desired. Infantilism. Bliss. ***Are you hiding behind that pretty face?***

I start to cry. I have never had a reason to until now. I hide my tears from Asher; I do not want him to see my weakness. ***He discovers my tears.*** With a concerned look on his face, he asks, "why are you crying?" He asks me softly and gently, "why are you crying? Is something wrong?" No, I say, no, no, no. ***Everything is perfect.*** You are perfect. This is perfect. Life is perfect. A whole moment in time held so close, so loved, so cherished, and so filled with every ounce of joy. Mommy?

Mommy is here now. Daddy? *Daddy is here now. Mommy and Daddy love you so much.* They would never ignore your **emotional needs.** They would never treat you like you are invisible. ***Are you hiding behind that pretty face?*** Yes, Asher is hiding. Alexandra is hiding. We are hiding because it is not safe for us out in the open. He was abandoned, left, and discarded. One boy, one girl, *time standing still…….forever locked away…in a Snow Globe…*

Absence Makes the Heart Grow Founder

I get up at 5am for work. Okay, I say. Asher gets **on his knees** and holds my hands, **not taking his eyes off me.** "Alexandra, thank you. Thank you so much for today, I mean it. I needed this so badly. **Today was the best day of my life, you have no idea.** You are so special, so wonderful, such an amazing person" …. I look at Asher and thank him. "Thank you", I said. "You can come over here anytime, I am not going anywhere." ***Then I said, "absence makes the heart grow fonder," and he gives me a sweet smile as he walks out the front door and says, "it sure does make the heart grow fonder."***

What a gift! All my pain melted away. It was healing. It was everything. When we open ourselves up to receive such gifts, life has a way of giving them to us. ***I never saw Asher again, but I can joyfully say that was the best day of my entire life. And when I am an old lady, laying on my death bed, minutes away from taking my final breath, I will remember this very day and my Electric Blue; <u>to have known and experienced what life truly means.</u>***

What was the gift Asher gave to me?...

He made me feel…. alive.
I AM….no longer hiding behind this pretty face.

Sister – Life is magical.

Chapter 15 Takeaways

- ➢ Life has a way of giving us what we need.
- ➢ We attach most to people who resemble our relationships with our parents.
- ➢ Be open to all new experiences – life has a way of surprising us.
- ➢ Live like a child; you don't have to be an adult all the time.
- ➢ It is okay to live and to live well; **life is full of blessings.**
- ➢ Relax, take a deep breath, **and stop hiding behind that pretty face.**

Share Your Story:

In the space provided, it is time to share your story. Explain the most magical day of your life. What was it like? What made it so special?

Chapter 16
Exposed: Decoding the Dating Game

"What's the point in dating when many fear commitment"

Dating is a game. A horrible game. I have spent months researching dating, the psychology of men, getting ex-boyfriends back etc., and I am about to unravel many things. Did you ever have a guy really pursue you, and everything was going so well, and then out of thin air, he dumps you for no reason at all? ***The second you started falling for him?*** This story, **The Same Story,** has happened to all of us. I am about to tell you the truth behind this because this situation has happened to me countless times, and I am sick and tired of getting played. Most of this has to do with the way boys and girls are conditioned into gender roles as children (and Attachment Theory), something that has already been explored throughout this book.

To summarize the game, men want who they can't have. Women also want who they can't have. This is why the people you are interested in are not interested back, and the ones you have zero interest in want you. This is why women are wildly attracted to bad boys and men are wildly attracted to confident, self-assured women. ***And this is why I authored this book: to help you become a fiercely confident, self-assured woman.***

Men value the chase way more than the capture. The second they capture you; it's game over. **How can you win?** In my vast amounts of research into dating and the psychology of men and how men fall in love, it comes down to men falling in love with the woman they feel that they cannot have. This is why many men cheat; they are incessantly chasing women, seeking one thrill after the next – it's all game for men, with men winning

216

and women losing. ***Women constantly lose this game, and men win. This is why women get their hearts broken and men move on quickly to the next woman.***

This argument points no fingers of blame at anyone since what I am describing is simply ***human nature,*** but if you sit down and ruminate on this for a moment it is absolutely sick that we as women must play games to hold a man's interest for the long-term. You know you've had men get bored with you quickly. For some men, their love, lust, and desire for you comes and goes in cycles, which means one minute they love you, the next they don't and back and forth forever. Their passion for you is like a pendulum constantly swinging back and forth, which is why they are quick to break up with you returning weeks or months later because they miss you again. Do not be surprised if he says he lost the spark for you or fell out of love because it will come back eventually ***depending only on your attitude and actions.***

Women are taught to play games from day one – does any of the following sound familiar to you?

> ➢ Don't call him first
> ➢ Let him text you
> ➢ Don't make the first move
> ➢ Take hours to respond
> ➢ Don't chase a man
> ➢ Let him make all the moves

You aren't some prized prey to be captured and won. ***You can never be in love for real. The second you give yourself away, the second you fall in love, the second you fall head over heels is the second he is done with you.*** Men do not bond through sex; women bond through sex. Men bond incrementally through friendship, which is why it is paramount to be friends with them first taking the relationship slowly. ***Men crave mystery, unpredictability, and excitement…women who make them nervous and uneasy they find insanely attractive and irresistible.***

Desperate, needy, clingy women with low self-esteem are unattractive to them. ***Become emotionally grounded and resilient. Develop a backbone, a central core of security.***

If you want men to become batshit crazy about you, then you need to become a Femme Fatale. Why? Why do we have to twist ourselves into a pretzel to capture the man we really want? ***Never let him know how you really feel; you should always keep him guessing because this creates tension, and tension makes him desire you.*** Leaving him on the edge of his seat makes him want you. Playing men do not crave relationship stability and normalcy the way women do. They want the woman who drives them crazy. The **Dark Femme** who is mysterious, ambitious, confident, self-assured, and never falls in love. Falling in love is a sign of weakness and playing men do not like noticing emotional weakness in women, which is ***why they pull away. When it comes to relationships, less is more.*** Never give too much. One person in the relationship always gives more. ***<u>Be the one giving less.</u> When you give more, he gives less. When you give less, he will give more. Place yourself in a position to receive more.*** He should pour into the relationship as much as you pour into it.

Dating baffled me. I could not understand puzzling behaviors or how to keep a man hooked. I was adept at attracting or catching a man but not keeping him interested. Keeping a man's interest for whatever reason seemed to be an ***impossible feat. When Jordan broke my heart unexpectedly, that is when I knew something seriously needed to change, so I read every dating book that I got my hands on. Now I have men swimming in oceans and climbing mountains to be with me.***

In *Men Who Love Bitches* by Sherry Argov, her primary thesis is the more a woman does for a man, the less he will appreciate and want her. She says, "the women who have men climbing the walls for them aren't exceptional. Often, they are the ones who don't appear to care that much." This is what Sherry Argov says about **Nice Girls**, "the nice girl makes the mistake of being available all the time. "I don't want to play games," she says. So, she lets him see how afraid she is to be without him, and he soon comes to feel as though he has a 100 percent hold on her." And most compelling, she states, "women are conditioned to give themselves away." A few more quotes from this book that I love are, "men don't respond to words. They respond to no contact." And "most women are starving to receive something from a man that they need to give to themselves."

Some ideas to consider:

1. Don't be nice.
2. Don't be over-giving, over-caring, and over-loving.
3. Give plenty of space.
4. Don't even **want** a relationship or make it appear as if you do.
5. Don't be available 24/7.
6. Don't bend over backward.
7. ***Put yourself first.***
8. Don't make the relationship all about him and his needs; make it about you and your needs.

Her second book, *Why Men Marry Bitches* is equally interesting; here are a few of my favorite quotes, "in romance, there's nothing more attractive to a man than a woman who has dignity and pride in who she is" .... "He doesn't marry a woman who is perfect. He marries a woman who is interesting." **This one is important, "once you start doing the same thing *he* was doing, suddenly, the bad behavior will magically disappear."** As I love to say, ***dish out to them what they dish out to you.*** If they make you suffer, make them suffer back. ***Punish bad behavior with more bad behavior, not good behavior.***

Relationships are for Women

We've heard that words are for women. *The idea is to strike a careful balance between hot and cold.* Women do not like playing games, but men do, so if women refuse to play games with men, then women will always lose and walk away with a broken heart. Let me ask you a very serious question here – are you sick and tired of being played? I DO NOT AGREE with what I am teaching you! It is all *reverse psychology*, and it is all a mind f*ck. But IT WORKS! What I am teaching you will make you WIN and not LOSE. *You have been experiencing these same patterns your ENTIRE LIFE.* Man chases you; you fall in love, and boom, he's gone as quickly as he came into your life. Playing men fall in love fast, and they fall out of love faster. Everything playing men do is with heated intensity, which is why they attempt to get inside of your pants as fast as possible.

Relationships are for women. Sure, yes, men do commit. Sure, yes, men do get married, but how many married men cheat? And if they don't cheat, they may have contemplated it from time to time. *Women bend over backward doing backflips in the street naked trying to hold their marriages together.*

Why do you think playing men are commitment-phobic, or if they aren't, it still takes them forever and a day to commit? Why do you think playing men have a *Don Juan Complex* where they incessantly chase and pursue, only to eventually discard? **WHY IS THIS A PATTERN?** What makes playing men act so insensitive and cold toward women? *(Answer – they are CHASING A FEELIING (A HIGH) AND NOT A PERSON.) Why are playing men treating women like objects and prey instead of human beings to love and cherish?* Why is he so nice and sweet when he likes you/is pursuing you, but when he loses interest, he turns mean and cold? Mean! Why does he turn mean when he loses interest? WTF! Understand this stuff because *IT WILL SAVE YOUR LIFE!* How many times I have cried and screamed over a boy! Wondering how the hell I could be his entire world one minute and the next completely discarded?

Power, Control, Destruction & Revenge

Create a sense of scarcity around men. You are a high-value, respectable, lovable, worthy, and well-intentioned woman. All you ever wanted was a normal fairytale life; you aren't even asking for much. Learn the art of making yourself scarce. Men value and desire who they cannot have. *The more they cannot have you, the more they will want you.* Men for centuries have had total power and control, but I am here to tell you that the tables are turning. *Women now have power and control, and we must claim it.* We have diminished ourselves for years, and shit is about to change now. Remove yourself from gender roles and expectations. You are not a maid, slave, servant, helpmate, chef, or nanny. *YOU ARE A HUMAN BEING. YOU ARE AN EQUAL. Gender roles perpetuate relationship abuse.* You perpetuate your abuse through compliance of bullshit expectations. *If that man you live with cannot shape up, then he needs to ship TF out.* This is YOUR life. You are in control now. *<u>Reclaim what has been taken from you.</u> <u>Get your power back.</u>*

Femme Fatale

Whether they openly admit it or not, the shocking truth I have discovered is, men love POWERFUL WOMEN. You become POWERFUL by taking a stand, building your confidence, and stop tolerating bullshit. Become a *<u>Dark Femme and Femme Fatale woman.</u>* In summary, a *Femme Fatale* is a fiercely confident, self-assured, bullshit-free woman who is ambitious, inspiring, riveting, and mysterious. A *Dark Femme / Femme Fatale* has men wrapped around her finger. The problem is, in childhood, women are taught **Light Femininity** which contributes to and perpetuates the abuse of women. *Women are raised to be nice, which is utter bullshit on all fronts.* If on the contrary, women were given *a voice in girlhood* to become a *Dark Femme* with **strong boundaries** they would never experience abuse. *Life is all about what we do or do not tolerate.* Simple.

Women don't know this stuff until they learn about it. I was misguided my whole life when it came to dating and relationships. No one knows what they are talking about. People do not know how to date and get married until they invest the time to learn.

Understand that true relationships, whether in friendship or romance, are built on genuine kindness, connectivity, mutual understanding, respect, patience, empathy, sincerity, good intentions, openness, active listening, and effective communication. However, these are not the ingredients for making a man obsessed with you. Understand how messed up and dark this really is. I am calling out the sickness in the game. ***Like I mentioned before, I do not believe in manipulating or destroying men emotionally, but it does work, and that is the concerning part.***

Backflips in the Street Naked

This is why the men you don't want, want you. Those men perceive you as a cold, stoic, hard-to-get woman, and they will do backflips naked in the street just to talk to you! I will give you an example... Matt and I had been on and off for years due to my always being the asshole every time and breaking his heart. I did genuinely like Matt as a person and friend, but I did not have feelings for him. I felt that by giving him an honest chance and spending time with him, my feelings would grow. I did believe Matt to be a good guy for me because he was always willing to do nice things for me. Matt would always blow his chances by eventually becoming too needy, clingy, and desperate. That was a turn off. This went back and forth for three years with intermittent periods of talking and no contact.

They say the third time is a charm, right? Wrong! I wanted to give Matt a chance, and he truly loved me or at least was insanely obsessed with me. The more I pushed him away the more he wanted me. On the third year of talking again, he bought me three bouquets of flowers in ONE WEEK! Yes, in one week I received THREE bouquets of flowers. Every time we hung out, he had tons of gifts for me. I got flowers, heart necklaces, snacks, energy drinks, socks, perfume, makeup, edibles, flowers, anything. He did backflips in the street naked trying to win my love. He even offered to come over and clean my entire house and drop off cough medicine on my front porch when I was sick. I told him we could date but that I didn't want to rush things or be exclusive. Honestly, if I had given him the green light, he would have gone out and bought a diamond ring and proposed to me.

His parents met me and my daughter, and they loved both of us. They always took us out and had us over for dinner. I loved his parents too and wanted to give this relationship a fair shot since I was excited about who my future in-laws would be. But then his needy, clingy, and possessive side would always sooner or later emerge. When I posted two selfies on Snapchat because I was going to my friend's Bridal Shower, he got upset and questioned my intentions, saying that I was soliciting attention from other men instead of sending those selfies directly to him. I put him in his place telling him he cannot cage me, and I am who I am, and he conceded. The possessiveness didn't cease. He would question me if I took longer than two hours to respond. He texted me all day long. The more possessive he acted, the more turned off I became, even after I had slowly started developing feelings for him. One day, he posted a shirtless selfie to his story in his boxers with a caption that read, "This is for my one true love." Guess who his one true love is? Do you see what I mean? In some cases, it is the WOMAN acting like Matt needy, clingy, desperate, and possessive of her man. *As she continues to pursue him, he* *continues to run away from her.* This is why men have been running from you your whole life. You are either consciously or subconsciously exuding behaviors of clingy, needy, desperate, and possessive. And playing men act like me; cold, distant, aloof, not giving a f*ck, indifferent, not wanting to go exclusive.

If you want men or a certain man to desire and obsess over you, then act the way I did toward Matt, which is what playing men do to you driving you crazy and making you obsess over them. The reason I desire Jordan so badly is because I cannot have him. Jordan is the cold, distant, and aloof guy. *Being cold, distant, aloof, and detached gives off an air of mystery and confidence naturally drawing people to you.* This is why women love bad boys and men love detached emotionless women. Matt will forever love, respect, and obsess over me. I will forever be his *Femme Fatale.* He still texts me sometimes, and I never respond. Four years later, and he is STILL PURSUING ME! Why? *Because it is all about the chase!*

Listen closely – if your marriage is struggling right now, then implement these principles on your husband. *I guarantee he will respect you more, value you more, cherish you more, stop leaving you, stop cheating on you, and even pay attention and listen to you.* If you want to relate more with men, then start acting the way they do. Get on their level. Do not act like a woman, act like a man, and watch as the tables turn in your life.

Harness Detachment

Our natural proclivity is for attachment. When we are born, we form attachments to our parents and primary caregivers. Sometimes these are healthy attachments, and sometimes they are not. However, true power lies in the ability to learn effective detachment. *Everything I am teaching you right now goes against everything you have been taught or believed in.* I am 34 years old authoring this book, and I have only learned about these things from about age 31 on. I wish I knew all this stuff at 18 years old; I could have avoided significant heartache.

We are wired to attach to others in healthy, productive, and life-giving ways. The problem is that women bond through sex, and men bond through time and talking. This is why there is no emotional connection for men in sex because sex for men is just sex (nothing more and nothing less). Sex for a woman, however, is EVERYTHING. Sex is the acme of our existence as women. This is also why men can easily cheat on their wives, dump the mistress, and continue to love and stay married to their wives because they do not bond through sex. His wife is the woman he is bonded to and loves. *This is why men do not typically divorce their wives.*

Our power as women is in detachment because we want more than anything to attach. The story of Electric Blue. That is a story of attachment related to **Attachment Theory** and our early relationships with our parents. We attach to our partners because our parents never truly attached to us. Many of us were abused and or emotionally neglected by our parents to a greater or lesser degree. Not everyone was abused or emotionally neglected, but a great many were. *I illuminate our earliest heartbreaks so we can begin to understand now why, as adults, we have so many problems and experience such significant pain and suffering in our lives.* Many parents are too busy to be parents. Too busy providing a living that they have nothing left over emotionally. *Moreover, a great many women suffer considerable emotional traumas from the past and present and cannot be fully present attending to the emotional needs of their children.*

Learn to become detached. You will be perceived as more valuable, esteemed, and rare in other people's eyes. *You will be perceived as strong, powerful, and independent.* You will succeed wildly in your professional career and love life. Remember this statement always:

And with him, she was mildly successful, and without him, she was WILDLY SUCCESSFUL.

Kelly was successful when she was married to her ex-husband, but after their divorce, she became even more successful with opportunities falling out of the sky and directly into her lap, unexpected and unsolicited. *By removing the toxicity and letting go firmly, Kelly opened herself up to an abundance of blessings. I am not an advocate for divorce; I am an advocate for women recognizing their worth and not allowing men to treat them like shit. Too many marriages are not salvageable because it is only the woman who wants change.* It is only the woman seeking counseling while the man resists and fights when he is the one that needs therapy for treating his woman like shit!

Therapy does not work with narcissistic men because they do not think anything is wrong with them or the relationship; therefore, they do not change, and if they do not change, then the relationship is not salvageable. Period. These types must take ownership of their actions and behaviors just as women do. *You cannot go around abusing your partner expecting things to always go your way – relationships do not work like that.* Please remember that abuse is not about abuse, abuse is about control. Playing men need to be and feel in control. But then they act like children, which is emotionally rudimentary. Men also need to learn how to properly control their emotions. The idea is RESPONDING and NOT REACTING to emotionally charged situations. ***Learn to deploy your emotional weapons, and the art of detachment is the most powerful.***

No Contact

No contact works brilliantly on men simply because they hate it. *Whatever they hate drives them crazy, and whatever drives* *them crazy, they want – including you.* Learn how men think. Do you like it when someone ghosts you? No, you don't. No one does. When you need to punish a man because he is being an asshole or acting like a buffoon, the simple solution is no contact. *It wakes them the f*ck up, which is what they need.* Playing men don't know what they have until it is gone.

You can use no contact with boyfriends, husbands, and anyone, really. *When it comes to love and relationships, less is more.* True love is established in friendships and not romance. The key to making someone want you is to be kind, warm, loving and then, without warning – ghost them. Become cold and distant. This will keep them on their toes always wanting more of you. It's all about making them want more. *Become the girl that every guy wants but nobody can have; that is your power; that is a true Femme Fatale.*

Breakups

Jordan broke up with me for one reason only: he lost the spark. He fell out of love. He likes me as a person, and he even wants to remain friends. These are all his words, not mine. Nothing bad happened in our relationship other than the loss of attraction on his part. Given the nature of the breakup, there is still hope for Jordan and I to get back together someday, but I needed to devise a carefully planned strategy. At the breakup, I remember being puzzled by his sudden loss of interest. I never saw it coming. I couldn't believe that a man could chase me so hard, climb Mount Everest to impress me, express sincere interest with long-term intentions and then just end things abruptly. *What I came to understand through my research is that Jordan's loss of interest had nothing to do with my physical appearance.* Jordan still found me physically attractive, BUT no longer did he desire me. I became too predictable to him, and thus, the mystery of me had been solved. Then came the discard. When a man tells you he lost the spark or fell out of love with you, it's not because he no longer thinks you are physically attractive. It is because of the **change in your attitude toward him.**

When he first started dating you, you were confident and effervescent; you didn't need him. You were aloof and even played hard-to-get, but layer by layer, you became more comfortable with him and let your guard down because you fell in love with him. Therefore, you gave yourself away and unknowingly killed his desire for you. Do you want that man crazy over you? **Then be as cold as he is. Mirror his behavior. If he abuses you, abuse him.** Being a doormat of a woman does not work. Women have been oppressed and pushed around by men for centuries because we haven't amassed the balls to stand up for ourselves. We accepted their abuse and shitty behavior psychologically encouraging them to discard and disrespect us by acting weak, insecure, desperate, and emotional.

I knew I could win Jordan back, but it would take precision on my end. I implemented a 30-day no-contact rule and then only reached out to give back the hot tub. In his presence, I was polite and respectful maintaining my composure; I also acted aloof like I was completely over him. Never tell a man how you feel about him; he needs to guess your feelings and intentions always as this will keep him off balance. He is not expecting this kind of behavior from you. He is expecting you to obsess over him, which will feed his ego. I let him pick up the hot tub, I asked him out, never planned a date, and let him leave. Let his mind wonder if I'd ever follow through on reaching out to him again. **Playing men need the challenge and the chase, and it is an exhausting act for women, but if you want to win the game, you must learn to play it.**

Presence Vs. Absence

It is better to be absent than present. Men fall in love with a woman when she is not in his presence. *Your absence speaks louder than your presence, and your absence is more valuable than your presence.* Use your presence sparingly, creating an air of scarcity about you. People should have to earn your time and attention; it should not be given freely. Men value your absence. Absence makes the heart grow fonder. *You can only be missed when you are not around.*

The truth is women are taught from childhood to become obsessed with romance, but romance does not actually exist; it is an illusion of the mind. If someone falls in love with you and then falls out of love with you, that is not true love. We chase love, men, and romance our entire lives. Men chase sex and purpose. Chasing love, men, and romance leads to nowhere at all… no my apologies, it does lead somewhere. It leads you to your therapist's office right on the couch. *Chasing sex and purpose is powerful, and it is fuel.* Sex is a gift. Why be in a relationship with a man who refuses to have sex with you when there are countless men out there who would love the chance to be with you? The problem is you are fixating on one person for your happiness. *Disappear out of someone's life and notice how important you become to them. Your absence speaks volumes; your presence says nothing.*

The Solutions

There are two solutions to weather the shitstorms of this reality.

1. Always remain **ABOVE THE BULLSHIT** first and foremost
2. Affection Buddies

Many women are consumed by bullshit. These women are in the thick of the bullshittery of dating, marriage, and or abusive relationships. Most of it is bullshit. Not all. Not everyone, but many. There is nothing wrong with you. ___You are not purposefully attracting toxic, negative, and narcissistic people.___ Everyone attracts these people because there are millions of them all over the world in every culture. **This is a transcultural issue.** One human being treating another like absolute dog shit is a **transcultural issue**. It is a **human issue**.

Deliberately rise above the bullshit. Rise above the nothingness of low effort, dead-end, heartbreak and buffoonery. When will you learn? The loss of your self-esteem? **CHOOSE TO ASCEND NOW AND RISE ABOVE THE BULLSHIT.** This is a **DELIBERATE CHOICE.** This is not magic, and there is no easy or simple way to do it. It is a choice based on your limiting beliefs and early conditioning. Many were raised believing we must get married and have children. We were raised to be in a relationship with one another, and being alone is the ultimate punishment and a great sign of unworthiness. ___Being alone is not a sign of unworthiness; allowing someone to tear apart your self-esteem is a sign of unworthiness because only someone who rejects themselves would allow that.___ The only person who can reject you is you. Allowing someone to treat you like shit means you are rejecting yourself. You have a fear and limiting belief of unworthiness locked deep within your soul.

Form **AFFECTION BUDDIES.** An **Affection Buddy** is a pleasant way to say **friends with benefits**, but it doesn't just mean sex. **Affection Buddies** provide affection to each other in countless ways such as **1) spending quality time together, 2) having deep chats, 3) watching movies and cuddling, 4) hanging out and exploring, and 5) experiencing life together.** This is not exclusively about sex. It is about being a human being and sharing the human experience with those you love and value.

Divorce yourself from relationships. **Women are fixated on committed relationships, and it is destroying us.** Men do not have this fixation like we do, that is why it is easier and more convenient for them to leave. You are in a relationship with him, but he is not in a relationship with you (even if he says he is – in his head, he isn't, which is why he cheats, lies, makes up stories, and convinces himself and you that he is faithful when he isn't).

Affection Buddies are commitment-free with no strings attached, and you can have as many as you want. You are in control. This gives you power, authority, influence, and control. *As women, we sometimes give all power, authority, influence, and control to everyone else except for ourselves, and this is precisely why we get shit on.*

Cast a wider net, open your **Orbit of Love**, and start collecting **Affection Buddies** because they do it to us. You will be surprised by how much power this new arrangement gives you, brings you more peace of mind, and you don't have to worry about who is cheating and lying. You never worry if you lose an **Affection Buddy** because you should have an arsenal of other Buddies to call upon when you need Affection. You need affection, do not deprive yourself of it. Get an **Affection Buddy** today!

Final Thoughts on Dating and Relationship Hell

The Dating Game is a game of Tag with one always the runner and one always the chaser. **Be the runner always. Always run away but never too far.** Strike a balance between constantly running and allowing small dosages of being caught. Always be on the run again. Think about men for a minute and what they do. Men are ALWAYS running. They are either running towards you or away from you, but they are always RUNNING. Always run away and not toward.

Many romantic relationships are what I call **Crash and Burns** because it is only a matter of hours, days, weeks, months, or years before you **Crash and Burn** literally. Romance is not sustainable unless BOTH PARTNERS are sustaining it. Take your **Crash and Burn** and turn it into a **Slow Burn**. Burn the frog slowly by putting it in cool (not boiling) water first. Patience is a virtue remember? **Narcissistic men have PhDs in Crash and Burn relationships; they fall in and out of love faster than you can say sex.** One minute you are the bees' knees to them, and the next you are getting stung. Stop being DUPED! This is the definition of **EMOTIONAL EXPLOITATION. Emotional Exploitation** is f*cking with someone's feelings making that person believe you like/love them only to remove that like/love out of nowhere ripping the rug out from underneath them without warning. That is **emotional exploitation,** and playing men love to emotionally exploit women because it gives them a powerful ego boost. That's all they want out of you. **This is why you must perform the De-Duping ceremony, so you will not be Emotionally Exploited anymore.** These men do an excellent job of playing the role of The Deceiver, but in **GIRL GAME: BALLS OUT**, the tables are turning, and **YOU ARE NOW THE DECEIVER**. You can have sex, you can like sex, you can enjoy sex, and you can want sex, but **ALWAYS DETACH FROM SEX.**

Utopian Relationships and Fantasy Worlds

Everyone lives in a **Fantasy World**. This **Fantasy World** takes us away from normal life. Normal life is monotonous. No one enjoys the everyday drudgery we all live in. We all fantasize and romanticize. Ideal relationships, ideal families, ideal careers, ideal lives etc. We have images of what we want our lives and relationships to be like. Everyone has a dream guy or a dream girl. We have all (at least at one point and to some degree believed in a Utopian Relationship). If you believed in fairy tales as a little girl, then you believed in the Utopian Relationship. **A Utopian Relationship is your perfect relationship, whatever that means and looks like for you.** You design it exactly as you wish based on your needs, wants, hopes, and desires. I believe relationships can be good and healthy, and I believe we can find the right person for us, but I do not believe in **Utopian Relationships**. Jeb Kinnison in *Bad Boyfriends* has this to say about Fairytales, "many people straight and gay men and women-still believe the Fairy Tale of how unions form and stay together. The Fairy Tale is that "we're in love, he would never hurt me, she will never get sick, we will own a home and two cars and we'll always have enough money and be safe and the sex will be really great and we'll never have a gloomy day."

Our Fantasy Worlds only live in our minds. The problem with narcissistic men and women is that they only want and value these supposed **Utopian Relationships** that do not exist because everyone has weaknesses and baggage. This means that the Narcissist enters a relationship idealizing (worshipping) the partner. Perceiving the partner as all good. Ignoring red flags and wearing rose-colored glasses. However, this perfect image cannot be sustained as nobody is perfect, **but the Narcissist expects you to be** because all that matters is what lives in their head. The minute you disappoint them, or they begin to see the real you, they suddenly start devaluing instead of idealizing you, as they become aware of all your **perceived** flaws. These are not your real flaws; these are only your flaws, **according to them.** Whereas you were once a perfect angel in their mind, they have now convinced themselves you have some devilish qualities that they simply will not tolerate because in their mind (they only deserve the best), their perception of you completely changes in a matter of hours, days, months, or years. ***This is why women have a horrible habit of twisting themselves into a pretzel, walking on eggshells, shrinking themselves, and becoming the Accommodation Queen because they would rather be or become the girl they think the man wants than who they truly are.***

They would rather lose themselves gaining his (***perceived favor***), which is only breadcrumbs of love at best. ***They would*** *rather allow him to berate and negate them because their fear of losing him and being alone is worse than death itself.* They were conditioned to believe that being alone is a sign of worthlessness. These women are allowing themselves to become unworthy before a man in an attempt to become worthy (which backfires 100% of the time) because they fear **unworthiness** (being alone). What they don't realize is that the only way they become unworthy is by allowing a man to treat them like they are unworthy of love and respect.

After the Narcissist devalues you, he will eventually discard you. *He eventually discards you (rejects) you because YOU FIRST rejected yourself. Because you rejected yourself (and deemed yourself unworthy), <u>he was only mirroring you.</u>* You gave him permission to discard and reject you because you first rejected yourself. Your need for his love and approval was greater than your need for your own love and approval. You got it all backward, girl. Once he rejects you, he will move on to the next (seemingly perfect) conquest wearing those rose-colored glasses, but eventually, he will find fault with her and discard her too. *He can never be happy. This is a pattern. He needs to heal himself.*

AI Orgasmo: The Tension Tamer

Tonight, my older sister and I were out to dinner, and we invented *Orgasmo, The Tension Tamer* (his nickname is Stiffy, btw). He is our *AI Love / Boyfriend Robot*. We were discussing the modern-day dating landscape and how dreadful it is. Non-monogamy is in. It appears that no one is faithful anymore. It appears that beautiful, wholesome, happy, and monogamous relationships don't exist anymore. We know that they do, but from a modern-day perspective, they don't because of hookup culture. Online dating apps give you access to hundreds of people; everyone has access to many people with too many choices and options. Why would anyone settle when the *grass is greener* on the other side, right? It is hard to find a guy who wants a relationship (not saying they don't exist) but it is hard. With cell phones, social media, and dating apps, getting sex has never been easier. Hooking up is at our fingertips. ***And if you do get into a relationship, there are absolutely no guarantees that your man will be faithful to you. It is a risk every single time.***

Low / No Effort

Moreover, we now live in a society of ***Low / No Effort.*** Back in the good old days, men would date you and you wouldn't have sex until the third date or later. Back then you would go on real dates and men wouldn't send you dick pics. They also wouldn't ask you for naked photos upon first meeting. No one wants to try anymore. If there is effort, often it is low. They do not need to work hard to get sex. ***It is instantly accessible.*** People have become so lazy. I know even in my own friend groups, if I don't do the inviting and initiating, then I don't get invited out. I do get invited out occasionally, but it feels like I take the most action and do most of the initiating/inviting with my friends. ***People put minimal effort into relationships.*** This is not true of everyone, but it is felt in modern society. Dating is not what it used to be.

My sister and I are sick of the bullshit, so we invented ***Orgasmo, The Tension Tamer***, our AI boyfriend robot. Orgasmo is everything you could want in a man. He gives the best foot rubs, his two favorite words are "yes dear," he loves completing his honey-do list, he enjoys long walks and talking, he'll even say to you, "Girl, you look good in those jeans, have you lost weight?" ……. you'll just have to get used to touching metal. You can order his cock in any size you want; (that part isn't metal, BTW)- he will give you complete pleasure. He will cook for you, clean the house, and not throw his dirty clothes all over the floor. He will plan fun and romantic dates for the two of you, keep track of the kids' school activities, and will even buy you a bouquet of flowers every week.

Jordan – Annihilating Limiting Beliefs

On my first date with Jordan, upon meeting him for the first time, my very first thought was, "he's too good-looking for me." *This is a Limiting Belief. Before Jordan could reject me, I had first rejected myself.* I put him on a pedestal, and I put myself on the ground. *I made him more important and worthy than myself.* I said he was too good for me, and my subconscious mind believed it. My subconscious mind believed Jordan was too good for me, because that is precisely what I had told my subconscious mind. Your subconscious mind remembers and believes everything you tell it. *At that moment, because I first rejected myself, I gave Jordan all the power and authority to reject me too.*

Jordan and I had a wonderful three months together. He treated me so well. He wined and dined me. He invested money and time in me, and we had wonderful adventures together. *I had never seen someone so turned on by me in all my life.* That man was undoubtedly physically attracted to me. But sooner or later, Jordan was bound to discard me because I first had discarded myself. I declared myself unworthy and unlovable subconsciously and subconsciously projected those *limiting beliefs* onto Jordan who also believed them and did the job that I told it to do from day 1. I was crushed at the breakup. Devastated. I loved Jordan with all my heart. I felt so connected and bonded with him. I fervently enjoyed all the passion and love that I got to experience with him. *I had one and only one very powerful limiting belief, and that limiting belief was – I am unworthy, I am unlovable.* My entire life, I believed I was unworthy and unlovable, and I repelled all attempts of love by first rejecting myself. *What are your limiting beliefs?*

Whatever we tell our subconscious mind about ourselves, it believes them to be true and will bring them to fruition. If you have harmful and negative thoughts about yourself, then your subconscious mind is manifesting those beliefs, and you are probably not having good luck in friendships, relationships, and careers.

Your NEW BELIEFS are:

I am worthy
I am lovable
I am more than
I am awesome
I am amazing
I am brilliant
I am creative
I am a badass
I am a daredevil
I am courageous
I am strong
I am capable
I am competent
I am deserving
I am social
I am brave
I carry myself with assuredness and diplomacy
I have a mind of my own and I think for myself
I am not easily influenced by others
I do not accept subpar behavior
I do not tolerate bullshit
I am important
I make my presence known
I am blessed
I am surrounded by love
I am worth the effort
I am not a doormat

I am not a people pleaser
I am not lazy
I am not unproductive

I AM ALWAYS THE RIGHT CHOICE

Sister – The only thing holding you back from greatness are your limiting beliefs.

Chapter 16 Takeaways

> ➢ Dating is a game with one winner and one loser.
> ➢ Learn to play the game if you want to win.
> ➢ Your **attitude and psychology** will either keep a man hooked long-term or make him repel and eventually discard you.
> ➢ **Detachment is your new best friend.**
> ➢ Master your emotions and never reveal too much of yourself – remain aloof and mysterious forever.
> ➢ **Eradicate your Limiting Beliefs.**

Share Your Story:

In the space provided, it is time to share your story. What have you learned so far? How is this material different from other dating advice you've received in the past?

Chapter 17
Alaska

"Healing is the greatest gift we give to ourselves."

This chapter is about your personal healing journey. Most people walk around unhealed. If you take the time to heal yourself, you are at a huge advantage. People bury their pain most often, hardly recognizing that it exists at all, because to think about it would only cause more misery. ***What kind of world would we live in if everyone got healed? What kind of parents would we be to our children if we healed ourselves fully and completely?*** A major social problem is that many individuals have children and never heal themselves, so all their unhealed behaviors and emotions are passed on to their innocent children, which is precisely why so many children are emotionally neglected and or abused.

Abuse and emotional neglect would not even exist if parents healed themselves BEFORE bringing children into this world. Think of the kind of person you would be today if your parents held you MORE than they laid their hands on you. Think of how different your life may be. Think of how your past choices could have been impacted. Think of how the trajectory of your life may have gone or what you could have achieved but didn't. When a parent lays their hands on a child, the message they are conveying to that child is, "you are bad, and therefore you are not good enough." ***From day one, some are told by the people who supposedly love them the most that they are unworthy and not enough, and they carry these messages with them into adulthood for the rest of their lives.*** Children should be nurtured, held, and loved; they are not human punching bags.

I am **not** insinuating that every person was emotionally neglected and or abused. However, many were and some situations worse than others. ANY act of PHYSICAL PUNISHMENT (hand or object on the body of the child) to any degree of force is considered, without a doubt, physical abuse. *You were not put on this earth to be neglected or hit. You were put on this earth to be loved, acknowledged, listened to, soothed, nurtured, and comforted. You are supposed to experience peace and not chaos.* Alice Miller, in *The Drama of the Gifted Child*, says this about the healing journey, "the damage done to us during our childhood cannot be undone, since we cannot change anything in our past. We can, however, change ourselves. We can repair ourselves and gain our lost integrity by choosing to look more closely at the knowledge that is stored inside our bodies and bringing this knowledge closer to our awareness. This path, although certainly not easy, is the only route by which we can at last leave behind the cruel, invisible prison of our childhood."

Many grew up in dysfunctional homes. Chaos was considered normal. Your first sense of self and essential personhood shattered before your eyes, and your attachment style developed. *The other problem with childhood abuse and neglect is that nobody talks about it.* It is considered a taboo topic, and children love their abusive and neglectful parents just as if those parents had not abused and or neglected them. Children easily forgive their parents as if nothing happened at all. They accept their abuse as punishment. It is not until they have deep revelations and full understanding conceptualizing what was done to them as children. *Only through these revelations can we even begin to heal.* Consider the totality of the situation and all your interactions with your parents, including the type of people they are and what their problems and traumas were. *Trauma is passed down, which is why it scares me when unhealed people have children. We continue to perpetuate problems instead of solving them.*

An excellent description of trauma passed down and on is the Holocaust. Alice Miller in *For Your Own Good* says this, "against the backdrop of the rejection of childishness instilled by our training, it becomes easier to understand why men and women had little difficulty leading a million children, whom they regarded as the bearers of the feared portions of their own psyche, into the gas chambers. One can even imagine that by shouting at them, beating them, or photographing them, they were finally able to release the hatred going back to early childhood. From the start, it had been the aim of their upbringing to stifle their childish, playful, and life-affirming side. The cruelty inflicted on them, the psychic murder of the child they once were, had to be passed on in the same way: each time they sent another Jewish child to the gas ovens, they were, in essence, murdering the child within themselves."

The reason anger exists is because of child abuse and lack of **emotional nurturance** in childhood. When a child is abused and or emotionally neglected the child learns to hate herself **and if you look around you, more people hate themselves than love themselves.**

The Screams

I work with many clients who were abused and or emotionally neglected as children. One client shared her story with me. Her name is Cynthia. Cynthia every so often has nightmares about her childhood. She does not beat her own children, but she has had dreams of beating them because she was beaten. She shared her most recent dream with me. She was in a room, and in another room, she could hear a small child, maybe six or seven years old, being beaten. She could not identify the child in her dream; she was not sure who the child was. She could hear the screams coming from the child. She got up and locked the door that the child was in, and then she woke up.

She doesn't understand why she locked the door. She doesn't understand why she didn't rescue the child and stop the beating. *It is plausible that the screaming child was her, and she locked the door instead of rescuing her because <u>she couldn't save herself.</u>* She wanted to defend that child so badly. *<u>I will say this a million times over, there is no such thing as a bad child, only unhealed adults.</u>*

Surface Level Love / Obligatory Love

Some of you had what I call *Surface-Level Love or Obligatory Love*. This means your parents only loved you on a surface level or out of obligation, and if this was the case, then it probably showed. A parent who loved their child would never scream at them, beat them, belittle them, or criticize them. *Screaming, beating, belittling, and criticizing are all <u>projections.</u>* It is the parents' way of hating themselves and then transmitting that self-hatred onto you, their child. *These parents do not demonstrate love; they demonstrate fear.* A child should not live in fear. I will ask my clients what they did to deserve a beating, and usually, they will say, *"I did nothing wrong."* Understand that you were the child in this situation and not the adult. The adults were in control, and they exercised that control over you. *They put you in a fear-inducing situation which was traumatizing for you.*

Children have nightmares when they are constantly in fear for their lives. The adult is the adult, and it is the adult's responsibility to *exercise emotional control* and not beat their children. *This is why unhealed adults should not have children in the first place.* Alice Miller, in *The Drama of the Gifted Child*, has this to say about many childhoods, "I sometimes ask myself whether it will ever be possible for us to grasp the extent of the loneliness and desertion to which we were exposed as children. Here, I do not mean to speak primarily of children who were obviously uncared for or totally neglected and who were always aware of this or at least grew up with the knowledge that it was so. Apart from these extreme cases, there are large numbers of people who enter therapy in the belief (with which they grew up) that their childhood was happy and protected."

If your parents didn't hold you or say, "I love you," you might have felt this surface-level or obligatory love I speak of. Most parents do love their children, but to what capacity is the question? There is deep empathic love, and then there is surface-level or obligatory love. It is I love you because I must love you. I love you because you are my kid. It is not - I love you because you are a human being whom I deeply cherish. *Imagine if your parents wanted a boy and you were born a girl, or if they wanted a girl and you were born a boy. Do you understand what that does to a child's self-esteem? It annihilates it. Right off the bat, the child is not good enough or less than because they are not the sex the parent wanted.*

Parents also sometimes have "favorites" the child or children they love, and then the obligatory or surface-level love children. If you had obligatory or surface-level love, you did not have real love. If you did not have real love, you probably don't love yourself. If you don't love yourself, you probably think you are unlovable. If you think you are unlovable, romantic partners probably enter and exist your life often. And the cycle keeps repeating itself.

Holidays can be difficult for these children. Why spend it with people who don't even love you or just pretend that they do? There are so many mommy and daddy wounds that sometimes holidays become unbearable, and it is just something we must do out of **obligation with no real significance.**

Learning is your new parent. Let understanding become your new parent and reparent yourself.

On School Shootings

School shootings are an interesting and unfortunate phenomenon. How does a person go from not shooting up a school to shooting up a school? How exactly does one conclude that it is somehow advantageous to shoot up a school and kill innocent lives? In a school shooting, everyone blames the gunman, the murderer, and yes, it is partly but only partly (his) fault. The remainder of the responsibility is society. This is not to negate the horror, tragedy, and loss of the victims and their families, *but stop for a moment and acknowledge the human inside of the gunman.*

When ugly exists inside of us, we then project ugly onto others, and obviously, there is much ugly inside of the gunman. There is ugly inside all murderers, all homicides. The question is, how did that ugly get inside of there? Humans are not born ugly or evil. Evil develops inside of us based on external circumstances and our internal world. My question to the gunman is: what happened to you? Who or what turned you evil? *When calamity exists within us, we project it.* This is why I spend so much time talking about childhood abuse and neglect. As a psychologist, it would be preposterous not to acknowledge the existence and prevalence of it in society. *Childhood abuse and neglect are topics largely swept under the rug because they make people uncomfortable.*

I cannot say with certainty that every gunman was abused and or neglected, but it is certainly plausible. What I can say with almost certainty is that someone or something did something unfathomable to the gunman for him to seek revenge on others. The human in me recognizes, acknowledges, and accepts the human in him. We are to hate the sin but love the sinner. I believe love will transform the gunman because it is evident he is without it and may have never experienced it in childhood.

Those individuals who take their own lives never experienced the resounding true love, peace, and joy that I know. Their worlds came crashing down around them, and they had no idea how they could ever make it better, so they ended their misery. *The truth is we are SUPPOSED to SUFFER; we are SUPPOSED TO feel; that is what makes us human.* Without feelings and suffering, we would not be human. Instead of taking our own lives and shooting up schools, *how can we turn our pain into power?* How can we let our pain transform and transcend us? How can we take our deepest misery and revolutionize it into good for all humankind?

To the Gunman and the Suicidal Individual, here is what I have to say to you:

*I see you, I hear you, I'm listening to you. You are a human being. You are loved beyond measure. You are valuable, worthy, and priceless. You are cared for and appreciated. You F*CKING MATTER. Your purpose and potential here on Earth extend far beyond the vastest oceans. You are important! Please do not kill yourself, and please do not kill others. There is a better way, there is a better path; let my love and embrace hold you tightly, knowing that you are safe and whole now and forever.*

Admission

I do not consider myself Mother of the Year. I am not a motherly mother. I am not a cookie-baking, class-volunteering, field trip-going, dance mom, soccer mom, or helicopter parent. *I want my daughter to learn independence and not cling to me.* However, I am aware that my daughter has **attachment needs**, and her security is developed in childhood. You won't see me decorating the state-of-the-art Valentine's Day box. If there is one thing I do well, it is *I just hold my daughter*. I work 7 days per week, sometimes 12–18-hour days; I know my daughter does not have 100% of my attention. I am the only provider in my home; it is just me and her. I call us the **Dynamic Duo**. There is no village. *I am the village. I am her rock. I am my rock.* When all else fails, when I feel like a bad mother because my kid didn't have the most inventive Valentine's Day box or the most ingeniously decorated pumpkin, *I just hold her. I just hold her. I just hold her. I hold her as much as I can. As if I am offering her the greatest gift anyone could ever offer another human.*

Nobody is holding me, and it is hard to hold my daughter when nobody is holding me. It is hard to love a child well when you are not loved by anyone (romantic partner). I pull strength out of my ass, and I hold that child as if both of our lives depend on it because they do. I will never win **Mother of the Year,** but at least my daughter will know that I love her with all my heart and that I am attentive to and cognizant of her attachment and security needs. May she never grow up feeling unloved, unworthy, not enough, or less than. May she always know she is fully, completely, and entirely loved simply because she is a human being, and all human beings are worthy of such love and attention.

Every child indirectly says, "just hold me, just love me."

Murderers, rapists, serial killers, and mass genocide leaders once looked up to their parents as little girls and little boys and thought, "love me, hold me, please love me." Only to receive a cold shoulder...

Remember that our greatest emotional need is the need for love. We cannot survive without love.

All Aboard the Negativity Train

Look around you. People are hurting. People have problems. People are negative. People are rude, deceptive, self-absorbed, broken, confused, anxious, and unhappy. Many of us live our lives as if a black cloud follows us around everywhere we go with no sunshine in sight. Many of us hide in shells, afraid of the outer world, afraid of getting too close to anyone, afraid of being our true selves. Worried about being judged or misunderstood. Constantly unsettled by other people's opinions of us. We board the **Negativity Train** with a one-way ticket into the **Abyss of Misery**. The **Abyss of Misery** is a state of mind; it is our own personal hell. Why are we so negative?

Negativity is perpetuated and passed down from generation to generation. Abuse and neglect also make people negative. If your parents were negative people constantly spewing negativity onto you and your siblings, then you will likely adopt their state of mind. This is another **Cycle of Chaos** because there is no reason for it. People do not get their way, so they decide to throw an everlasting tantrum. Misery loves company. We feed ourselves negative thoughts for breakfast, lunch, and dinner. We take baths and showers with negative thoughts. We clothe ourselves in negativity. We have this abiding propensity for negativity. **Negativity attracts negativity, and positivity attracts positivity.**

Not everything will go your way. Many things are outside of your control. People you love may not love you back. You might be overlooked for a promotion. Your parents may have neglected or abused you. Your friends might gossip about you. Your kids might hate you. This is life. There are endless blessings and there is equally endless pain. Your life will be an amalgamation of emotional heaven and hell states. You will experience significant pain and earth-shattering ecstasy. Your life will not be perfect. You will learn many lessons and make many mistakes allowing yourself to live completely. **Allow yourself to experience joy and pain equally, for that is what makes you a complete human being.**

Many people ride the **Negativity Train**, but the **Positivity Train** has fewer passengers. It comes down to choice. People who are negative are choosing to be negative because you can get a

FREE TICKET to ride the **Positivity Train.** Make that switch. You don't have to fall deeper and deeper down into the **Abyss of Misery.** It is not uncommon to suffer from abuse and or neglect. Many of us have been **emotionally abandoned** as children because our own parents were preoccupied with their **Abyss of Misery.** They could not fully give to us in the ways we needed them to. Your parents did the best they could with what they had, but given their own sorrows and personal hells may not have been able to give you the time, attention, and love you deserve. Similarly, they may have raised you with limiting beliefs and other cognitive distortions. They imprinted ways of thinking, relating, and behaving into you that you now struggle to divorce yourself from. They programmed you the way they were programmed and made you believe what they believe because teaching is passed down.

Children need an abundance of love and attention. Children need **emotional nourishment and emotional nurturance.** It is likely that your own father was avoidant and severely neglectful because this is how society conditions men to become. Society teaches men to become cold, closed off, and stoic, so that is what many men become. Society has ruined some men. Your mother could have also been justifiably neglectful to you. I use the word justifiable carefully because she too also likely suffers from abandonment and **emotional malnourishment.** Many of us suffer from **emotional malnourishment.** When your emotional needs go unmet, it is extremely onerous to give what you lack within yourself to your own children. Our emotional needs go unmet, which causes many to board the **Negativity Train** and ride it until the day they die.

Multiple Children

In an ideal world, all siblings within a family unit would be loved, regarded, and treated equally. That does not always happen, unfortunately. You will notice some siblings are independent and others dependent. You will notice some siblings with behavioral issues, often acting out and causing more disruption and problems compared to their siblings. Some parents may **unintentionally give more attention** to the needy child while neglecting the seemingly independent child. ***That does NOT mean the independent child requires less love and attention compared to the needy child.*** However, the parent is blind to the problem because the parent is ill-informed concerning the issues at hand. Children also compete for their parents' love and attention. Some children are more attention-seeking than others and will perform outrageous acts to render a parent's undivided attention. The independent and neglected child will **emotionally withdraw**, roaming further and further away from the family unit.

Parents should be cognizant that all their children have equal emotional needs for love and attention, but they may express them differently. Parents should strive to love, regard, and raise all their children the same. Parenting should be equitable for all children in the family. Have you ever noticed how two, three, four, or five kids can all be raised by the same two parents but turn out so differently?

Those independent, well-behaved children who did not cause disruption or upset in the family will grow up becoming more independent self-sufficient adults who thrive. These independent children will be more disciplined, focused, driven, successful, and likeable. They understand what it means to sink or swim. They will take care of themselves without dependent entitled attitudes. They will become everything their parents were not. Their sheer success and drive overcompensate for the lack of love, attention, and emotional support they did not receive from their parents. Their overabundance of success becomes their childhood savior.

The dependent attention-seeking children come with behavioral problems adopt entitled, selfish, and dependent attitudes. They feel the parent **owes** them love, attention, emotional support, financial support, a roof over their heads, and whatever else they need. The dependent child cannot stand on her own two feet. They do not work for anything. They are not motivated, lacking determination and focus. They expect their parents to parent them even at 30+ something years old. *We all know people like this.* These individuals may or may not ever leave the nest, and the parent (usually the mother) has a self-sabotaging need to care for the dependent child well into adulthood. She needs to be needed because she has not let go and healed herself of her own issues.

The Fade Away into Self-Mastery

The independent child can rely on no one except herself, so she learns to do just that. She becomes everything because she once felt like nothing. *She is more imaginative in nature because she uses her imagination escaping her pain and feelings of abandonment.* In this alone space of hers, she develops the skills and internal powers by becoming wildly self-sufficient and successful in everything she does. *She learns to master herself and takes full ownership of her successes and failures.* She learns all that life wants to teach her because she is not held back by anything or anyone. She spends time on self-reflection and self-awareness, not relying on anyone except for herself. Their opinions mean nothing to her because obviously those opinions refuse to pay her bills.

In this book, I dissertate **Attachment Styles** and childhood upbringings. Much of our pain as adults originates in childhood and is carried into adulthood, influencing the ways we relate to our partners in adult relationships. This causes significant pain that we carry around in adulthood.

You need a major revolution, transformation, metamorphosis etc., in your life. Being on medication and going to therapy might help, but many people do those things and still never heal. **You cannot suffer forever.** You must heal. Release this pain, and when you do, you will be free to fly like a bird. You will become unstoppable and indestructible. Nobody or nothing will be able to touch you ever again. Commit this time now to heal. Take the necessary steps and go through this painful process of healing.

My Personal Healing Journey

I am going to assume that we all need some kind of healing. We've all been hurt by someone or something. **If your life is perfect, then you are lying to yourself.** Somewhere, somehow, someone or something hurt you.

For my entire life, I have suffered with low self-esteem and Anxious Attachment Style. It wasn't until I was 34 years old attending a Tony Robbins event live that I learned for the first time (and believed it too) that I am worthy of love and lovable. I held a limiting belief for years that I was unworthy of love and thus unlovable. All I did was attract avoidant men into my life who further hurt me triggering all my insecurities. I knew I had a mental disease, as I called it, because it honestly felt like something was wrong with me. **I was constantly sitting on the edge of my seat with paralyzing anxiety.**

I went on vacation to Alaska with my best friend. Although we had a lot of fun together, I also spent a sizable portion of the trip alone so I could heal once and for all. Being one with nature in Alaska was the best place for healing. Surrounded by water, animals, and greenery is the perfect scene of serenity and surrender. There is a certain hush about nature, a calming yet powerful presence whereby nature itself welcomes the absorption of our pain and suffering, our most traumatic moments. ***Nature wishes to free us, durable enough to remove our pain and cleanse us.***

As a planner, I refused to plan this trip. I wanted to fully live in the moment, whatever happened in Alaska, as carefree as possible. I wanted to fly by the seat of my pants and let the wind take me where it may. We had the best week and vacation of our lives. I could write another book just regarding the memories of this trip. One of my favorite memories was arriving at the Anchorage Airport at 11pm. We had no idea how we were going to get from Anchorage to Seward, a 2.5-hour trip at midnight; we had no prior plans of arrangement. It was literally wherever the wind took us.

First, we tried renting a car with zero luck because Seward is a small city and there was no port to get the rental car back to Anchorage from Seward. Renting a car was entirely out of the possibility. From there, I called every train and bus at 1am, rejected by all because I had to schedule that in advance. We investigated taking an Uber. The Uber would be $250 to get from Anchorage to Seward, but we didn't care because we just needed to get to Seward. We were lucky a driver was willing to pick us up from the Anchorage airport at 2am and drive us 2.5 hours to Seward. Under the influence of majesty, I became mesmerized by the Alaskan coast; one road for the entire 2.5 hours to Seward. A perfect view of serene tranquility and quintessential arcadia.

What did I learn that week? F*ck planning! ***Sure, planning is a good thing, but sometimes overplanning robs us of the opportunity to really experience the moment of just being.*** That first day in Seward (without any prior planning) we went dog sledding. ***Dog sledding was the most thrilling experience of my life.***

The Voice of God

I knew it was time to heal when I could hear the **Voice of God.
God will speak if we are willing to listen.** Even though I am an
Air sign, water is my healing element. It was while I was alone
in the hot tub that I heard the **Voice of God** calling my attention
by repeatedly saying, **"Focus on me."** I had to **focus on God**, The
Creator, to heal. Although the skies were gray, the heavens
opened, and light appeared in only one area. With the bubbling
motion of the hot tub, I could feel chains of bondage breaking
from my body. The chains of trauma held me hostage all my life.
With my anxiety and **Anxious Attachment Style**, God said, **"Be
still, be still, and focus on me."** I looked behind me as the ship
sailed forward witnessing the trail of water left behind,
watching my pain released and left behind in Alaska, absorbed
by nature.

And the **Voice of God** declared, **"Do you not know who I AM? Do
I make mistakes? Do I not know exactly what I am doing? Have I
not called you by name? Have I not created you IN MY OWN
IMAGE, instilling in you numerous talents, skills, and abilities? Do
you understand how badly you hurt me WHEN YOU BELIEVE you
aren't good enough or lovable enough? That's like saying I am a
fool for creating something PERFECT! I made you for love. To
bless and inspire people, but you sit there AND BELIEVE that you
are less than other people!"**

How To Heal:

The healing process is painful but necessary.

1. *Only you can recognize that you need healing.*
2. Your healing journey IS YOUR JOURNEY. Do not involve
   others in this matter. Unless they are a spiritual healer
   guiding the journey (that is the only exception).

3. Be willing to heal. Be ready to let go. If you are not ready to let go, give yourself more time until you are ready to do so.
4. Create a calm and safe space to heal (free from distractions and other people).
5. Have your emotional exorcism. Fully experience all emotions to their full capacity and release them.
6. Calmly nurture yourself. Give yourself exactly what you need (only you know exactly what that is).
7. Restore yourself, reclaim your essential personhood, and build your temple of resiliency.
8. Beget a life of peace and tranquility as your daily norm; learn to keep yourself centered, balanced, and always stable no matter what happens to you. Always ensure the inside is calm and resilient.
9. Heal other people.

Healing the Parental Wound

Parents are invincible. No one holds them accountable for the pain and suffering they may have caused their children. Children are quick to forgive their parents or prefer instead not to recognize the abuse and neglect they may have endured at all. Parents can do anything; they are gods to their children. The commandment "Honor your father and mother" bothers me because how can a child honor their father and mother when she or he is being weaponized, neglected, molested, screamed at, or harmed in ANY CAPACITY? Abuse and neglect research is not widespread. Knowledge and understanding are limited in this area.

You cannot change what was done to you. No one can. It is a memory that lives in your mind. All you can do is CHOOSE to move forward. The first step is healing yourself. When we need to heal, it is usually because other people hurt us. It is ONLY AFTER others have hurt us FIRST that we go and hurt ourselves.

I believe there is only one sin in the world, and that is the sin against someone else. When a person psychologically, emotionally, or physically harms another in an INTENTIONAL manner, that is sin. When you hurt yourself, that is NOT sin, you only hurt yourself because others FIRST hurt you. If others hadn't hurt you, you wouldn't have hurt yourself. Other people hurt us because other people have hurt them, pain is never-ending; it is part of the **Cycle of Chaos**. People would rather cause problems than solve them. It is easy to cause problems and chaos. *We shouldn't have problems at all.* People cause problems. Problems exist because of pain. There is no problem that cannot be solved, so if you have a problem that is impossible to solve, IT IS BECAUSE the other in the situation DOES NOT WANT TO solve the problem because then their fun would cease to exist.

Parents do the best they can with what they have, but that statement gives them NO RIGHT OR PERMISSION to abuse and neglect children. Raising children is difficult; it takes so much of your emotional and physical energy, and you live for your children and not for yourself. I get it, but that gives parents no right to mistreat their children. Just because you as a parent are frustrated and angry gives you no permission to hurt your innocent children who do not have the life experience you have.

What can we do then to heal our wounds? It depends on the severity of the hurt. Abuse and neglect fall on a spectrum, some of which is so minor you would not even consider it abuse and neglect. If you provide for your children but neglect their emotional needs, then you have neglected your children. If you do not hug or hold your children, that is also a form of neglect. If you berate or belittle them, that is a form of neglect and abuse. Some adults do not talk to their parents or hold onto those relationships at all, and that is your choice and right as an individual. However, if you choose to maintain a relationship with your parents, then I would advise you to forgive them and establish boundaries for yourself. I know forgiveness is hard, but it is also necessary. When you fully heal yourself, forgiving others becomes more tolerable. It is still a process nonetheless and will take time. Give yourself what you need. **Give yourself time and forgive when you are ready.**

You cannot change what was done to you, but you can take ownership of how you move forward. **You can choose the person you want to be and how you treat and interact with your own children.** This creates a higher level of awareness and consciousness. When you have this level of understanding, you will not pass on to your own children what was done to you. **Your parents did not take personal ownership to heal themselves and give them what they needed. They took their pain out on you; you then became their scapegoat and took the revenge meant for their parents who hurt them. You became the substitute for your grandparents.** You will break the cycle because you are wiser and more emotionally equipped than your parents and grandparents combined.

Dr. Susan Forward is an excellent resource on toxic and abusive parents. In her book *Toxic Parents*, she describes how parents typically feel toward the children they abuse, "toxic parents are never willing to accept responsibility for their destructive behavior. Instead, they'll blame you. They'll say that you were bad or that you were difficult. They'll claim they did the best they could, but you always created problems for them." Parents are in denial because of the godlike image afforded to them by society. A child who was beaten learns that she was "bad" and "unworthy" and not that the parent was unhealed projecting their anger onto the child. Many parents are not emotionally mature enough to reflect inward analyzing their own shortcomings. She goes on to express, "most children of toxic parents develop a high tolerance for mistreatment. You may have only a vague awareness that anything out of the ordinary happened to you as a child." *If you are an angry person, just remember that anger is an emotion that must come from somewhere. No one is ever angry just for anger's sake.*

Many of my clients are perfectionists because many children are raised to be perfect. They are not allowed to commit minor indiscretions. It's not that the child does anything wrong, it is THE PARENT who does not have any emotional control. Forward says, "perfectionist parents seem to operate under the illusion that if they can just get their children to be perfect, they will be a perfect family. They put the burden of stability on the child to avoid facing the fact that they, as parents, cannot provide it. The child fails and becomes the scapegoat for family problems. Once again, the child is saddled with blame." *That child learns to hate herself or himself.*

We aren't all born into loving families. Even in families where your parents did love you, often that love is obligatory or surface-level, it was not the *emotional nurturance* you needed as a child. These children who experienced obligatory-level love usually have abandonment issues because their parents' love was inconsistent at best. In these situations, the child is more like the parent, and the parent acts more like the child because the parent lacks empathy due to their own unmet emotional needs as children, making it impossible for them to give their children what they never received themselves.

Abuse and neglect are on a spectrum. On one extreme, abuse and neglect are obvious, and on the other extreme, they are hardly noticeable. Then there is everything in between. *Many of us have experienced this in-between stuff where it is hard to articulate if what we experienced can be considered child abuse and emotional neglect or not.* For example, most children who were beaten simply consider themselves punished for (perceived) bad behavior.

The Only Way to Forgive Your Parents

You do not HAVE to forgive your parents. Forgiveness is a choice, and it must be EARNED. *I believe abuse and neglect can be forgiven under one condition: the parent must <u>acknowledge</u> THEIR wrongdoing and ask for forgiveness. In most cases, parents are in denial due to generational trauma.* Most parents would not dare consider themselves abusers. Abusers rarely take any personal accountability at all. They simply "did their best" with **no consideration** for how their behaviors impacted their children in the present or the future. The problem many people experience is that the parent never reflects inward. In their eyes, they are perfect, and they did the best they could with what they had. They don't understand what they did would be considered childhood abuse and emotional neglect. They simply do not have enough education on the topic, or they believe "that's just the way things are, this is just the way things have always been."

As uncomfortable as it might be for them, they must **acknowledge and accept** their wrongdoing. They cannot continue lying to themselves while sweeping issues under the rug. They messed you up. They traumatized you. The least they can do for you now is **acknowledge their wrongdoing.** This points no fingers of blame. No one is perfect. If we are willing to lose the façade, we can all become more human in the process.

Confrontations can be effective, but they can be hard on everyone and don't always go as expected or planned. The most powerful thing childhood abuse and neglect survivors can do is ***<u>heal their parents.</u>*** What they did to you was detestable, but for just a second, put yourself in their shoes. They were once the scared little children facing abuse and neglect, and they are not mad at you (their child). They are mad at their (parents) for abusing them. If you can understand how similar they are to you, you will understand the scared little child inside of them. That does not make what they did to you acceptable, but it does give you the opportunity to understand abuse and neglect on a comprehensive level. You can be the beacon of light and hope in your parents' lives by demonstrating this sacrificial compassion for them. ***The solution to our healing is to heal others, especially those who have hurt us.***

Your parents believe they were punished for being bad. They don't see beating a child as abuse. Those criticisms and putdowns are simply modeling the behaviors and words that were modeled on them. ***This is their conditioning.*** This is what they consider good parenting. ***They do not know any better.***

If you acknowledge the human inside of them, you can win them over with your empathy. You have gotten on their level. Teach them what you have learned in this book. Make them realize that the mistreatment and neglect they experienced is abusive behavior. ***People don't understand what abusive behavior is because they were not taught how to recognize abuse.*** Back in the old days, children were beaten with a myriad of objects. Today, we have more awareness of childhood abuse, but it still happens. Some parents still believe in a good-ass whooping, tragically.

There is no situation that ever warrants a body part or device used on a child. If you are an emotionally mature and resourceful adult, you will find a more productive and efficient way to correct your child's behavioral problems. ***Mostly, they act out for attention, so give them what they want and watch what a difference it makes.***

Heal your parents, and you will be healed. When we can be more human toward one another, we will all become more human.

To Stone the Woman- Historical Trauma from a Biblical Lens. The Blame is Always Carried by Women for No Reason at All

It is ironic to me and rather disturbing that only women in scripture were stoned for adultery. There are two major issues with this, besides the one Jesus himself declares (he who is without sin, cast the first stone) ...

1. It is suggested that men did not commit adultery (because if they did, they were never punished for it). You don't hear about a man being stoned for committing adultery. This also suggests that only women were sexual sinners (of course they were, right?) It is no different in today's world (the double standard, men can sleep around, and women cannot).
2. It suggests that the woman committed adultery. Well, what proof do they have? What if she didn't? What if she is being wrongfully accused? What if they are using her as an example because of how historically misogynistic men have been? Isn't the killing (hatred) of women misogyny?

The story deeply disturbs me from a feminist perspective. Again, suggesting men are high, mighty, and perfect and women are dirty, shameful, and scornful – the same message we STILL receive today. We walk around dirty and filled with shame **BECAUSE OF WHAT OTHER PEOPLE DID TO HURT US.** Although I do not carry a victim mindset, it is true that we, as women, are victimized and oppressed, stoned, and whipped by everyone else into compliance, submission, and servitude. *Because others punish us, we punish ourselves.*

Recharge Your Batteries

As *everybody's everything,* we never stop moving, caring, and serving. We hardly ever sit down, take time for ourselves, get time alone, or watch TV. We are incessantly on the go. If something happens to us, our homes fall apart. We are not allowed to be sick, but Daddy is allowed to be sick. Furthermore, no one gives a shit when we are sick. We must attend to the sick individuals around us because we are the nurturing caretakers, after all. Women are not naturally nurturing. Both women and men have a natural propensity for nurturing, as nurturing is a human quality, not a feminine one. Men can absolutely be nurturing. It's just that, unfortunately, men choose not to be because they can get away with it, whereas women cannot.

Stop assigning gender to skills, as this is causing unfair advantages and division. Gender roles are bogus. The thing I hate most about being a woman, for myself and for women in general, is that we spend a significant portion of our lives as caregivers. We go to school, go to college, become caregivers forever, and then die. There is nothing wrong with caregiving. I am not belittling it at all. I am simply stating that it is a disadvantage that we are assigned caregiving responsibilities. It is a 24/7 job with no breaks, rest, and often little to no help. A woman is largely her own village. I praise the men who do step up and help but be advised that there is no need to step up and help. **SIMPLY RECOGNIZE** that you are an equal partner and are therefore **EQUALLY RESPONSIBLE** to share in the task of caregiving. ***Learn how to become more selfish. Men- learn how to become less selfish; this is why narcissism is more common in men – women simply do not have time to be narcissists. Narcissism isn't even an option for us in this respect.*** If this were to happen, finally, ***we would experience real balance.***

Stop running yourself to the ground. You don't have to be supermom. ***You are allowed to be human.*** You are allowed to make mistakes and mess up. You do not have to be perfect. You are allowed to be forgetful. If I can offer any parenting advice, and trust me, I am no parenting expert and will never author a book on parenting, BUT what I can advise is please **HUG AND HOLD THOSE KIDS.** Most importantly, ***give yourself what you need.*** You will never be an effective parent or human being if you don't first take care of yourself. Some of you have loving and supportive partners/husbands, but many of you do not – so please learn how to better care for yourself. Care for yourself in a manner that is most suitable for you. Here are some suggestions that I use in my life ensuring that I am emotionally caring for myself.

- ➢ Hot Baths
- ➢ Regular Massages
- ➢ Pedicures/Manicures
- ➢ Plans with friends
- ➢ Walks
- ➢ Exercise
- ➢ Reading books
- ➢ Adult Coloring
- ➢ Small road trips or vacations
- ➢ Quiet Zen time/meditation
- ➢ Prayer time
- ➢ Watch a good movie
- ➢ Listen to music
- ➢ Go for a long car ride
- ➢ Take a class
- ➢ Pick up a new hobby

Personal Responsibility

The Healing Journey is all about personal responsibility. Own your healing. Want to be a better, more healed person. Want to transform. Take personal responsibility and make necessary changes in your life. ***Advocate hard for yourself.*** It is not your fault if you were neglected or abused, you did nothing wrong. Even if you were "bad" according to your parents or primary caregivers, you still didn't do anything wrong. You were simply being a kid. We can't change what happened to us, but we can change what happens for us. Start today, move forward, and don't look back. ***You're only as worthless /unlovable / not good enough / less than as you believe yourself to be based on earlier***

messages from childhood. Do better, be better, choose better. Start today.

Blessed

Blessed is the child abused and or emotionally neglected, for she is not of this world – just like an angel, she ascends straight into the heavens.

<u>A child never asks to be abused or emotionally neglected; she only asks to be loved.</u>

Review the Beatitudes listed below and note, "Blessed are those who mourn, for they will be comforted." **You will mourn as you heal, but you will be comforted.** Furthermore, "Blessed are the merciful, for they will be shown mercy." Those who abused you were not being merciful; therefore, they will not be shown mercy. **When you DON'T DO to your own child WHAT WAS DONE to you, you are showing mercy.** *<u>Please demonstrate mercy to your children so they might know mercy and demonstrate it to all others, and we ALL can begin to heal.</u>*

<u>Matthew 5:3-12</u>

"The Beatitudes"

He said:

[3] "Blessed are the poor in spirit,
*   for theirs is the kingdom of heaven.*
[4] Blessed are those who mourn,
*   for they will be comforted.*
[5] Blessed are the meek,
*   for they will inherit the earth.*
[6] Blessed are those who hunger and thirst for righteousness,
*   for they will be filled.*
[7] Blessed are the merciful,

for they will be shown mercy.
8 Blessed are the pure in heart,
   for they will see God.
9 Blessed are the peacemakers,
   for they will be called children of God.
10 Blessed are those who are persecuted because of
righteousness,
   for theirs is the kingdom of heaven."

If you are an abused and or neglected child, please know I am right here with you now, arm around your back, holding space for you. Holding you gently in my heart, dear sister.

Sister –You are a worthy human being.

Chapter 17 Takeaways

> You owe yourself the gift of healing.
> Healing is a personal journey.
> Childhood abuse and emotional neglect are more common than people realize.
> **Children are not bad- it is the adult who is unhealed.**
> Adults do to their children what was done to them – abuse and emotional neglect are modeled in childhood.
> **It is wise to heal before deciding to have children of your own.**
> Hold space for yourself.
> It is okay to forgive your parents if they take responsibility for what they did to you and apologize, understand, and acknowledge the pain they created.
> **_The best way to heal is to heal your parents._**
> Your parents are not mad at you; they are mad at their parents who abused them.

Share Your Story:

In the space provided, it is time to share your story. What kinds of abuse and emotional neglect have you suffered? How will you heal yourself moving forward?

Chapter 18
Endlessly Intriguing – The Everything Girl

"Stop hiding from the world."

Tell a Child She is Nothing, and Watch as She Becomes Everything

At the initial meetup with Jordan three months after he broke up with me, he told me something over dinner that I could not get out of my mind. Unsure exactly how it came up, he told me what kind of women he wanted and mentioned three distinct characteristics of his Dream Girl. 1) *I want someone I am proud to be with,* 2) *I want someone who will push me to be better for her, and the most interesting of all,* 3) *I want someone who is endlessly intriguing. Endlessly Intriguing.* Imagine that! It stuck with me, and I couldn't get this *endlessly intriguing* off my mind. I know I am *endlessly intriguing* because that is the girl I always strive to be. What does it mean to be *endlessly intriguing? Intriguing means arousing great interest.* Similar and related words are alluring / appealing / beguiling / captivating / curious / enthralling / fascinating / gripping / puzzling / interesting / stimulating / enchanting / attractive. Brian Nox in *Fuck Him, Nice Girls Always Finish Single* says, "although looks are important to most men, any great guy will always pick a less good-looking woman who's confident, content, and full of self-love over the needy but super attractive bombshell."

Be enigmatic. If you do not differentiate yourself then you will not stand out from the crowd, and therefore you will have the value of the crowd. *Nothing will be exciting or captivating about you.* No one will have the motivation to give to you, get to know you, respect you, want or desire you. *Do you want to feel this way?* Do you want to feel captivating, enthralling, interesting, and attractive? If the answer is yes, then you CAN feel this way. **You CAN be this way. It is a CHOICE.**

Do not Become Old Faithful

For most of my life, I felt like I was nothing. I felt the sting of being the second sex from the time I first entered this world. Boys are better than girls is the message I grew up with from family, society, the media, social circles etc. I felt like a disappointment for being born a female. But here I am, a female. I did not choose my assigned birth sex. There was a time in my life when I felt like nothing because I wasn't married or had kids yet. I wish I could have a conversation with my younger self when I felt that way. Society puts unnecessary pressure on women to marry and have babies as quickly as possible before they become an old maid, but in this process, they likely will become **Old Faithful. Never play the role of Old Faithful ever!** An **Old Faithful** woman is a doormat. Stop staying in abusive relationships because you think you can't get anyone else! Stop staying in abusive relationships because you think you are too old, don't want to upset the children, or have no money or independence!

Be endlessly intriguing! Become the Everything Girl. You have so much internal power bottled up inside just waiting to burst open. But you allow people, things, and situations to stop you. You allow it! **_You allow it because you are acting like Old Faithful. News flash: no man wants a woman who acts like Old Faithful._** He wants exciting, riveting, puzzling, questionable, powerful, confident, self-assured, take no bullshit ever woman – even if he says otherwise! Men like being challenged and put in their place. **_Deep down, they want you to destroy them with your fierce Femme Fatale attitude that is what keeps them on their toes and makes you endlessly intriguing._**

Alive

Do you feel alive? Growing up, we had a Doberman Pincher named Harley. He looked big and mean, but he was the sweetest, most loving dog. I used to put on the song *Born to Be Alive* by Patrick Hernandez, and Harley would just go crazy. The song would make him run as fast as a Cheetah all throughout the house, knocking things over in his path. He would run around and around in circles as fast as he could with the biggest, dumbest grin across his face. He embodied the song *Born to Be Alive*. **We all have this Harley energy inside, just waiting to be unleashed, just waiting to come ALIVE.**

Look around you, people look sad, depressed, miserable, and downcast. A bunch of Eeyore's going through the motions of life – these melancholy Eeyore-like people are not acting like they are Born to Be Alive. Now, imagine a 95-pound Doberman Pincher with a big dumb grin on his face charging through an 1800 square foot house full throttle, personality on fire, and the happiest he's ever been!

That Doberman Pincher is YOU, girl! You are **BORN TO BE ALIVE!** I have **created** my fairytale life out of nothing. Put down this book for a minute, go play *Born to Be Alive* and dance throughout your house. **Did it raise your vibration and enthusiasm?**

When Harley was alive, he lived, he truly lived; he was Born to Be Alive, and so are you, sweet sister.

Don't be an Eeyore!

Don't be an Eeyore. You don't have to coast through life in a downcast, pessimistic, and melancholic state of existence. You can be fervently happy and full of life, just like Harley running 100 miles an hour through the house, making his presence fully known. **You can make your presence fully known in this world.**

You allow everyone and everything around you to bring you down. Stop it! I went on a date once with an Eeyore. I did not want to, but he talked me into it. The second I saw him get out of his car, I wanted to leave and ditch the date, but I am not an asshole, so I went inside of the restaurant to meet him. I do not remember his name. Nothing about this man was even remotely memorable except for his disposition and personality, which was completely non-existent. He looked sad and miserable the entire date (not at me), just at his own unfortunate life. The next two hours were a bore for me as this man brought nothing to the table other than his obvious Depression and lack of enthusiasm.

He was a big blob of nothingness. I felt bad for him, but I cannot date him. I cannot work with a dull, pessimistic, downtrodden personality. Halfway through the date, I went to the bathroom and wanted to leave so badly, but being a nice person, I didn't. I decided to stick it out. I could not save this Eeyore man. He did pay for the date, and I hugged him, thanked him, and left. He was uninteresting and depleted, emotionless, and dead inside. The next day, he texted me, and I ghosted him. He was persistent and kept texting me, so I finally responded respectfully that I was not interested in moving forward, and he got upset and gaslit me, and that was the end of it.

If you are dating or married to an Eeyore, I am sorry. No one deserves to be with a person who doesn't even like themselves. *How we perceive ourselves is how others perceive us.* We perceive Eeyore as pessimistic, downtrodden, and melancholy because that is how he views himself, and he projects that perception into the world. If you project pessimism, Depression, and hopelessness into the world, then that is how people will perceive you. But if you are **Born to Be Alive,** then that is how people will perceive and remember you. **You determine how others perceive and understand you.**

This is the concept of enthusiasm. Notice how enthusiastic some people are, and others just aren't? Who would you rather be around? ***Emotions and energy are contagious, that is why it is called <u>emotional contagion</u>.*** People feel how you feel. If you are sad and miserable, then you make everyone around you sad and miserable, and people do not want to feel that way. If you are joyful and enthusiastic, then those around you will also be elevated in mood and disposition. ***Learn to become more enthusiastic if you have Eeyore tendencies.***

Harley was enthusiastic. All that running, that big dumb grin, that's enthusiasm. That is a magical zest for life. ***<u>Being sad and depressed is a waste of valuable time and energy.</u>*** If your circumstances suck, then you need to work on changing them. It won't happen overnight. There is no quick fix, but you can work little by little removing toxicity while inviting enthusiasm and purpose into your life. When you manifest all that is in store for you, you will want to run like Harley around the house with a big dumb grin across your face. ***Get out there and do all the things. All the things that give you purpose and passion.***

Gifts

Life wants to bless you abundantly. Life wants to give you wealth, health, opportunity, joy, love, romance, power, influence, and achievement. So now what? Now you exist. Welcome to life. Open yourself to receive these wonderful gifts of life. Open your heart and mind to receive all the blessings and gifts life offers you. Many of them will come as surprises, so embrace and cherish them fully in endless gratitude. Practice gratitude daily; always thank God, the Universe, or your lucky stars for everything you have been given. ***When you have a grateful heart, more will be given to you. Mark 4:25 KJV, <u>"For he that hath, to him shall be given and he that hath not, from him shall be taken even that which he hath."</u>***

You are Important!

Each human being has a desire to be important, to matter, and to make a meaningful impact. ***You matter; you are important.*** Do other people make you feel unimportant? ***We should treat others importantly, and we should also treat ourselves importantly. Each of us has an ordained purpose in this life. Each of us is here for a divine reason. You matter so much; more than you realize. Do not put ugly in the world because ugly was done to you. Heal.***

You had to beg for your parents' attention as a child. You just wanted to feel f*cking important to them. They couldn't be bothered by the trivial gripes of you. They were too wrapped up in their own lives to conceptualize that you even existed at all. Some of you may not be able to relate to this – that's okay. I'm not speaking to you right now. I am speaking directly to the heart of the rejected and dejected baby girl. The girl who would have killed just for her parents to acknowledge her…. *because children should be seen and not heard….*

Everything. You are everything. Say it with me now…
I am everything!
I am important!
I matter!
I can do anything!

If you want to be visible, then be visible, put yourself out there in the world. Say, "here I am, take me or leave me!" Act importantly. Dress importantly. Speak importantly. Become who TF you want to become. The world's most prominent powerhouses, celebrities, pioneers, trailblazers, all-star athletes, political influences, and thought leaders were not born famous; they became famous. They became important and influential. You are becoming too. You are constantly becoming exactly who you are meant to become. ***Believe that you are important and that you matter because you do.***

Little Girl Dreams

What did you want to be when you grew up? Whatever your answer, this is exactly who you truly are. Life easily gets in the way of what we really want, which is to be our unapologetic selves. Create the life you want for yourself. Become a powerful and magnetic woman. It starts in your mind permeating every aspect of your life and personhood. Embody the full package.

Buy a pack of GRE vocabulary flashcards and start learning and memorizing new words expanding your vocabulary. When you articulate words in speech, you appear intelligent. Build your vocabulary and your personal competency. Less movies, fewer TV shows, and more time for learning. **<u>When you speak, speak with confidence and authority.</u>** Your tone of voice should be grounded, calm, and assertive. It should not be a high-pitch or a low-pitch where no one can hear you, but rather *confident assuredness.* Master the way you speak. Speak calmly, slowly, and with *sincere intention. Speak diplomatically addressing people respectfully.* Most people lack confidence; you can hear it in their voice. Improve the way you speak. Study speech and body language. *Speak with liveliness and tenacity in your voice carrying yourself with regal authority. They will respect your level of intelligence.*

Dress to impress. Appearances matter. Wear form-fitting clothes complementing your body shape. Keep things classy and elegant with a natural allure of mystery. Wear colors. Do not wear all black or dark colors. Brighten up your life and those around you by showing different colors. Have a wardrobe full of designs, patterns, colors, styles, pants, slacks, blouses, blazers, skirts, dresses, and jackets. Wear accessories, including hats, scarves, jewelry, belts, shoes, headbands, bows, and gloves. *Be a woman of impeccable aesthetic taste.* When you dress to impress, you naturally feel better about yourself. It elevates your mood and confidence. Pay attention to the way you carry yourself. Walk with poise and high confidence. Head up, chest out. Speak, dress, walk, present, and relate diplomatically. Carry the ***I am important attitude*** and others will believe it. ***People treat you the way you treat yourself. Treat yourself like a queen.***

There will be many players in your life. All players play different roles and serve different purposes. Some of the common players are friends, family, colleagues, significant others, your kids, and acquaintances. The most valuable player or MVP in your life is you. Do not put someone else on a pedestal. ***Put yourself on a pedestal.*** You were born an individual, and you will die an individual. You have a unique Social Security Number that belongs only to you. Therefore, the person you are responsible for is you. ***Take ownership of your life. Own your life or it will own you. Treat yourself with high value and respect.*** Treat yourself as the MVP because you are the prize. Life is a journey with plenty of highs and lows. Every day is a gift, and every opportunity is a chance to build your empire. Yes, bad shit has happened to you, but what are you going to do roll over and die? No! ***You're going to get up, brush yourself off, and keep moving forward.***

Cheeseburgers

Always be a good and noble person. Seek to bless and serve others. ***We are commanded to love one another as love is the greatest gift to humanity.*** One time, I saw a homeless man, and instead of giving him money, I went and bought him five cheeseburgers and hand-delivered it to him. I felt compelled to do that for him. You can bless and serve others in a myriad of ways. Do not do anything that makes you uncomfortable. Do what makes you feel good and noble. This is the definition of love and kindness. ***What you put out into the world will come back to bless you.***

We are all Love Addicts

We are all love addicts because we need love to survive and thrive in this world, and without love, we cannot do either. Love is the foundation for all of life. An addiction is a need. Just as one is addicted to alcohol, drugs, gambling, shopping, or sex, for example, their addiction creates an unending need within them. An unending desire to partake in or consume the object of their addiction. We cannot deny our need for love. As discussed in Chapter 1 of **GIRL GRIT: SAVAGE NOT AVERAGE**, love is our **greatest emotional need**.

I am not writing this book or these words right now with a happy heart but rather a sad one. **Sadness and happiness are equal and necessary parts of the human experience here in life.** Why am I sad you ask? The two men I wrote about earlier in this book, both Jordan and Asher, I have loved very much. They were part of my human experience. They will both forever be imprinted on my heart, and I will smile whenever anyone says either of their names. **I do not regret meeting either of them or the experiences we shared.** They both played a role in my life, no matter how small or brief the time we spent together.

Those experiences were some of the greatest memories of my life. As the tears roll down my cheeks now as I write these very words, both men made me **feel alive** in every regard. They revitalized my soul and gave me a few hours or days of paradise. A few hours of paradise are better than none. As the tears turn into waterfalls, the adage goes, "it's better to have loved and lost than never to have loved at all" by Lord Alfred Tennyson. **What a blessing it is to cry! What a blessing it is to suffer hard! What a blessing it is to allow myself to be fully and completely human! These two men gave me the greatest gift of all... they made me FEEL again.**

I am crying right now as I am writing, and the pain I feel is insufferable. It is a blessing to share my humanity with you because it allows you also permission to be human. This is what makes both of us human, the fact that we can freely share our emotions with each other in a vulnerable and authentic way. Dr. Scott Peck calls this **constructive suffering,** as is discussed in his book *Further Along the Road Less Traveled.*

I cling to this suffering, *this constructive suffering*, as it is both transcending and revolutionizing my life. I am allowed to love. I am allowed to love Jordan and Asher even if neither one loves me back. *Be human and not perfect, always demonstrate humanness and authenticity. Demonstrating humanity makes you magnetic, and being magnetic helps you ascend ever higher. Ants do not ascend. Being an ant is a mindset. You, my dear, are a fierce dragon flying and soaring ever higher into the heavens among the angels.*

Jordan and Asher represent paradise to me *because of how both men made me feel.* The date with Asher was the best day of my entire life; everything about it almost dreamlike, as if I dreamed the entire experience. He was the best-looking man I have ever laid eyes on. An angelic figure electrocuting you with his passionate blue eyes. Looking at him can break your heart; that is how magnetically handsome he is, simply perfect, *simply unforgettable.*

Jordan, also extremely good-looking provided quite the experience. Life is a combination of *Heaven-States, Hell-States, and Purgatory-States.* Those moments I spent with Jordan and Asher are *Heaven-States*, as I felt like I was in heaven in those moments experiencing euphoria. *Hell-States* are what I am experiencing right now, the suffering and inexhaustible pain of not being with either of them anymore. *Purgatory-States* are neither hell-like nor heaven-like; they are neutral or in-between, neither painful nor euphoric. In fact, much of our existence can probably be categorized as a *Purgatory State* if we are on neither end of the *emotional spectrum.*

What is Love Then?

If you love someone, *you will let them go.* I have not yet let Jordan or Asher go; I was not ready to. Jordan and Asher are significant parts of this book because they represent all our long-lost loves. They both represent our past. Each of us has loved and lost. Each of us has gotten our hearts broken at least once, if not multiple times, and each of us has rejected at least once. You are familiar with the feeling of loving and letting go. ***I put these men in this book because I wanted to recognize and acknowledge the human in all of us.*** As a writer, I always want to first acknowledge our humanity. We are spiritual beings who are human.

Think about someone you love. Think about that person for a moment. Can we do something together right now, you and I? Can we together let go of this special someone? I am not talking about the man you are currently with, dating, or married to; I am speaking specifically about your long-lost love. ***The one you would do anything to see again.*** Anything. Just to see him one more time. Just to hear his voice once more (or hers if she is a woman). Just to have one more hug, one more kiss. Your one true love.

For me, it's the day on that beach hand-in-hand, twirling around, feeling the warm sand between my toes with Asher spinning me around, the laughter, the look, the lust, the passion, the embrace, the belonging, the acceptance, and the excitement of it all. The picture-perfect scene out of a romcom; a whole moment written in the sands of time. And as fleeting a good night's sleep. ***Are you hiding behind that pretty face?*** Where is that person hiding? Where is she? The little girl who couldn't acknowledge her humanity or womanhood because it was shameful? The little girl who wasn't wanted because her parents instead wanted a boy? ***The little girl taught to be quiet and obedient instead of having a voice that could inspire the*** *world.* The little girl raised to be a wife and mother, which would prohibit her from showing the world what she's really capable of? ***The little girl molested by her father or stepfather, whom no one believed, and she couldn't say or do anything to protect herself.*** The little girl raised in a homeless shelter with her mother because her father was an abuser. The little girl beaten, yelled at, neglected, and treated like nothing more than an ant? ***Are you hiding behind that pretty face?***

Come out now, sweet sister. It is okay, here, take my hand, it is okay. ***I am a safe person.*** You are allowed to be fully human. ***You do not need to hide from the world.*** You do not need to hide behind your pretty face. ***Wanted or not – you are a full human being. Loved or not – you are a full human being. <u>You exist because of the divine, and that is exactly and entirely what you are.</u>*** Now, it is time to let go. It is time to give up. You love your person, and I loved Jordan and Asher, and together, we must let go and move on. Ready? Let's do this together.

REPEAT:

I RELEASE YOU, THE LOVE OF MY LIFE, MY ONE TRUE LOVE, THE KEEPER OF MY HEART, INTO THE WILD OF THE UNKNOWN TO FIND YOUR TRUE SELF. I CANNOT HEAL YOU; I CAN ONLY HEAL ME. I DO PRAY, MY DEAREST LOVE, THAT YOU FIND AND FULLY HEAL YOURSELF. THAT YOU DISCOVER AND ACKNOWLEDGE YOUR OWN HUMANITY AND THAT YOU ALLOW YOURSELF TO BECOME FULLY HUMAN. GOODBYE, MY LOVES. GOODBYE (JORDAN), GOODBYE (ASHER). THANK YOU FOR ALL THAT YOU <u>WERE BUT NO LONGER ARE</u> TO ME. THE MEMORIES YOU GAVE ME WERE THE GREATEST MEMORIES OF MY LIFE, AND I WILL BE FOREVER GRATEFUL FOR THE BLESSING AND GIFT OF YOU.

(And release).

<u>Loving is the experience of letting go.</u>

The Worst Pain in the World

If you asked me what the worst pain in the world is, I would tell you without second-guessing that it is the pain of **rejection**. We accept people we love, so rejection is the opposite of love. **Rejection is the statement: I am not good enough; I am unworthy of (your love).** No human being wants to feel like they are not good enough or are unworthy of love. Rejection is the opposite of acceptance. Rejection is seeing someone else as an ant (they are not good enough for you, they are unworthy of your love).

Rejection happens as early as infancy. Many children are rejected in one way or another by their parents. **Usually, it is more subtle and almost unnoticeable.** For example, if your child is talking to you and you are not really listening or are uninterested in what they are telling you, you are rejecting your child. She is feeling rejected by you because she lacks your attention. Maybe your parent(s) are too busy to spend sufficient time with you. You have a parent who is always at home but never **emotionally present.** Your parents made promises to you that they didn't keep (rejecting). Maybe they are more consumed by their own problems and lives. They do not want to be bothered by you (all rejecting behaviors).

Rejection begins in childhood and is carried into adult romantic relationships and even friendships. Jordan and Asher both rejected me. Jordan broke up with me because, in his words, he lost the spark. After our magical day together, Asher disappeared. Asher did return a year later. I discuss that in my third book, **GIRL GLOW: TITAN OF TRANSFORMATON.** Both times rejected. You are worthy. You are good enough **independent** of how anybody else perceives you in their own world and perspective. **The pain of rejection is the pain of feeling like an ant.** Right now, acknowledge your own worthiness and ascend, sweet sister.

Compounded Success is Compounded Everything

In a world of scarcity, we desire to have MORE of everything. Yet so few of us have what we need, much less what we want. ***Everything is compounded.*** Once you gain some success, it is easy to gain more success. Once you make some friends, it is easy to establish and build new friendships. Everything gets easier with time and the work that you put in early on begins to compound itself. Remove scarcity from your mind. I didn't start this life with anything. I started from the bottom, but my knowledge, success, experience, learning, relationships, network, following etc. all grew with time and persistence. The key to success in anything is tenacity. ***<u>You only fail when you quit.</u>*** That doesn't mean the journey will be easy or pain-free. ***The journey is where the magic happens and not the finish line.***

Transform and ascend. Remove all bullshittery from your life. Learn and understand.

IT IS WRONG THAT THEY BEAT YOU.
IT IS WRONG THAT THEY RAPED YOU.
IT IS WRONG THAT THEY BROKE YOUR HEART.
IT IS WRONG THAT THEY REJECTED YOU.
IT IS WRONG THAT THEY DISMANTLED YOUR SELF-ESTEEM.
IT IS WRONG THAT THEY LIED TO YOU.
IT IS WRONG THAT THEY ROBBED YOU AND STOLE FROM YOU.
IT IS WRONG THAT THEY NEGLECTED YOU.
IT IS WRONG THAT THEY SAID YOU WEREN'T GOOD ENOUGH.
IT IS WRONG THAT THEY TREATED YOU LIKE YOU DIDN'T EVEN EXIST.
IT IS WRONG THAT THEY CHANGED ON YOU.
IT IS WRONG THAT THEY CHEATED ON YOU.
IT IS WRONG THAT THEY LEFT YOU FOR ANOTHER WOMAN.
IT IS WRONG THAT THEY ABANDONED YOU.
IT IS WRONG THAT THEY CALLED YOU FAT, UGLY, STUPID OR OTHER NAMES

NONE OF THIS CHANGES WHO YOU ARE! None of it! YOU ARE A PRECIOUS HUMAN BEING. Once a little baby who wanted nothing more than to be loved, held, seen, heard, and listened to.

Say this prayer now to yourself:

Dear love,

There there, it will all be all right. It is wrong what was done to you. You didn't deserve it. I promise you now that this is a return to yourself. This is a time of significant transformation and personal transcendence. No one will EVER hurt you again! I promise. Together – right here, right now, we will wise up, rise, and ASCEND EVERMORE INTO THE HEAVENS OF:

EXCELLENCY / LOVE / WISDOM / JOY / PEACE / CREATIVITY / RESOURCEFULNESS / ABUNDANCE / WORTHINESS / BEAUTY / MAGNIFICENCE / INFLUENCE / GENEROSITY

Although your pain has been insurmountable, your joy now is abiding. You are renewed and made new. The old self is washed away, and the new self is here today with a self-esteem ON FIRE.

All the injustices of childhood removed your self-esteem (your essential personhood), and like a little bird, you fly away far away from the pain and misery you once knew so well. Away from the unhealed parents and individuals who struggle with their own shattered self-esteem – may we all ascend. May we all heal. May we all start today and learn what it means to be fully and altruistically human. Therefore, may we NEVER EVER pass on those same tragedies to our own children or others in our lives.

Blessed are those who suffer so much, for they have the power within to ascend into the heavens.

ASCEND SISTER ASCEND! FLY – SOAR – EVER HIGHER – YES – EVER HIGHER!

Handle Yourself Diplomatically

Moving forward, always handle yourself diplomatically in all situations and circumstances. *Handle yourself as a person with supreme self-worth and confidence, an ever-calm presence with complete emotional mastery and self-awareness.* Be a beacon of light and hope, an effervescent, sprightly woman capable of achieving and acquiring anything. Love big, fill others with peace and inspiration, be a blessing and always act generously with attention, time, and resources. Exercise mindfulness in all you say and do. *Acting diplomatically means you are acting regally with power and authority.* A keen voice of reason and resounding presence of strength and healing so that everything you touch turns to gold (heals). You are the light, the warmth, the influence, and the positivity in a dark world.

The Best

Congrats! You have come to the end of this book; what an accomplishment! You should feel proud of yourself for reading an entire book! It is an accomplishment even if it doesn't feel like it. Think about all you have learned in this book. Learning is an accomplishment. Time to do one final activity as we close out this book. Play the Tina Turner song *The Best* and get up and start dancing in front of a mirror. Look yourself in the eye. Sing this song to yourself and dance. Dance like crazy. Dance like hell. Sing at the top of your voice. Sing with praise and gratitude for everything you have in your life. *Convince yourself that you are THE BEST.* Because, sister, **YOU ARE THE BEST.** And don't you ever forget it! Now dance like you are about to *TAKE ON THE WORLD – THE WORLD IS YOURS!*

Stop hiding behind that pretty face.

Sister – You are endlessly intriguing.

Chapter 18 Takeaways

> ➢ You are a magnetic *endlessly intriguing* woman.
> ➢ *Carry yourself with confidence, mystery, and regal authority.*
> ➢ Speak and dress with confidence and authority.
> ➢ Expand your vocabulary.
> ➢ *Always be a kind and noble person – live to bless and serve others but do not let them take advantage of you.*
> ➢ Truly loving is letting go.

Share Your Story:

In the space provided, it is time to share your story. What kind of woman do you want to be known as? What makes you *endlessly intriguing*?

To contact Dr. Alexandra Elinsky

Dr. Elinsky is an internationally recognized and multi-award-winning Bestselling Author, Entrepreneur, Empowerment and Ascension Coach. She is the CEO and Founder of Empower Human Potential LLC. Dr. Elinsky welcomes fan mail and connection requests.

Please feel free to contact her.

Phone – 440.812.1612

Email – team@empowerhp.org | www.empowerhp.org

Facebook – Author – Alexandra Elinsky, PhD

LinkedIn – https://www.linkedin.com/in/alexandraelinsky/

Instagram – https://www.instagram.com/bossdivalibra/

TikTok - https://www.tiktok.com/@alexandraelinsky

References

Argov, S. (2002). *Why men love bitches: From Doormat to Dreamgirl - A Woman's Guide to Holding Her Own in a Relationship.* Simon and Schuster.

Argov, S. (2006). *Why men marry bitches: A Woman's Guide to Winning Her Man's Heart.* Simon and Schuster.

Bernstein, G. (2019). *Super attractor: Methods for Manifesting a Life beyond Your Wildest Dreams.* Hay House, Inc.

Carter, S., & Sokol, J. (2000). *Men who can't love: How to recognize a commitment phobic man before he breaks your heart.* Berkley Books.

De Angelis, B. (2012). *Secrets about Men Every woman should know.* HarperCollins UK.

Forward, S., & Buck, C. (1990). *Toxic parents: Overcoming Their Hurtful Legacy and Reclaiming Your Life.* Bantam.

Harvey, S. (2014). *Act like a Lady, Think like a Man, Expanded Edition: What Men Really Think About Love, Relationships, Intimacy, and Commitment.* Harper Collins.

Jones, A. R. (1993). *When love goes wrong: What to Do When You Can't Do Anything Right.* Harper Collins.

Kinnison, Jeb. *Bad Boyfriends: Using Attachment Theory to Avoid Mr. (or Ms.) Wrong and Make You a Better Partner.* Jeb Kinnison, 2014.

Levine, A., & Heller, R. (2019). *Attached*. Bluebird.

Miller, A., Hannum, H., & Miller, A. (1990). *The untouched key tracing childhood trauma in creativity and destructiveness.* Virago.

Miller, A. (2002). *For your own good: Hidden Cruelty in Child-Rearing and the Roots of Violence.* Farrar, Straus, and Giroux.

Miller, A. (1990a). *Drama of the Gifted.* Basic Books.

Murphy, J. (2011). *The power of your subconscious mind: Deluxe Edition.* Penguin.

Naifeh, S., & Smith, G. W. (1984). *Why can't men open up? Overcoming Men's Fear of Intimacy.* Crown Publishing Group (NY).

Nox, B., & Keephimattached, B. (2016). *F*CK Him! - Nice Girls Always Finish Single - A guide for sassy women who want to get back in control of their love life.* Createspace Independent Publishing Platform.

Peck, M. S. (2012). *The road less traveled: A New Psychology of Love, Traditional Values and*

Spiritual Growth. Simon and Schuster.

Peck, M. S. (1993). *Further along the road less traveled: The Unending Journey Towards Spiritual Growth.* Simon and Schuster.

Russianoff, P. (n.d.). *Why do I think I am nothing without a man?* Bantam.

Russianoff, P. (1997). *When am I going to be happy?: How to Break the Emotional Bad Habits*

That Make You Miserable. Bantam.

Seuss. (1978). *I can read with my eyes shut!* Random House.

Seuss. (1990). *Oh, the Places You'll Go!* Random House.